To
Captain James J. Nance
and
Reverend Gerald A. Priest

Jim—cousin, fellow Airline Pilot, and award-winning World-Class Sculptor

Jerry—brother-in-law, World-Class Pastor, and the only Father Priest in all of Catholicism

. . . and both, truly, my brothers.

Pandora's Clock

JOHN J. NANCE

St. Martin's Paperbacks

Published by arrangement with Doubleday

PANDORA'S CLOCK

Library of Congress Catalog Card Number: 95-8409

ISBN: 0-312-96034-4

Printed in the United States of America

Doubleday hardcover edition/October 1995
St. Martin's Paperbacks edition/November 1996

St. Martin's Paperbacks are published by St. Martin's Press, 175 Fifth Avenue, New York, NY 10010.

10 9 8 7

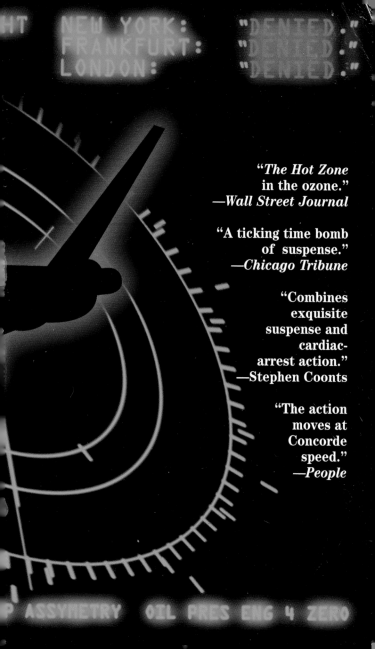

HT NEW YORK: "DENIED."
FRANKFURT: "DENIED."
LONDON: "DENIED."

"*The Hot Zone*
in the ozone."
—*Wall Street Journal*

"A ticking time bomb
of suspense."
—*Chicago Tribune*

"Combines
exquisite
suspense and
cardiac-
arrest action."
—Stephen Coonts

"The action
moves at
Concorde
speed."
—*People*

P ASSYMETRY   OIL PRES ENG 4 ZERO

FASTEN YOUR SEAT BELTS.
PANDORA'S CLOCK HAS TAKEN OFF!

"Nance combines exquisite suspense and cardiac-arrest action to create the ultimate flying adventure. If you read this on an airliner you're a lot braver than I am."
—Stephen Coonts, author of *Final Flight* and *The Minotaur*

"Nance is a wonderful storyteller, so go ahead—unlike Pandora's Box, you can open *Pandora's Clock* and expect the time of your life."
—*Chicago Tribune*

"*Pandora's Clock* will do for planes what the movie *Speed* did for buses. John Nance's riveting thriller is a fast, fun read that never lets up."
—Phillip M. Margolin, author of *Gone, But Not Forgotten* and *After Dark*

"Frightening and realistic . . . so well-written that it could have come from today's headlines."
—*Ocala Star-Banner*

"Exciting . . . This is suspense, dread and fear at its very best. You can't wait to read the next sentence."
—*Miami Herald*

"A nail-biting thriller . . . It's hard to put down, and more power to anyone who can read this on an airplane. Sniffling passengers will never be looked upon the same."
—Copley News Service

"First there was *The Stand*. Then came *The Hot Zone*. Now . . . virus fever is spiking for . . . *Pandora's Clock*."
—*Entertainment Weekly*

"Authentic . . . Horribly believable . . . *Pandora's Clock* is an unnerving flight."
—*St. Petersburg Times*

Other Books by John J. Nance

ACKNOWLEDGMENTS

With heartfelt appreciation to my agents, George Wieser and Olga Wieser, and to Editor-in-Chief David Gernert, Publisher Stephen Rubin, my editor Lori Lipsky, Jayne Schorn, Ellen Archer, and all of my new literary family at Doubleday.

And with special thanks to the following: the Center for Disease Control in Atlanta; the Boeing Company in Seattle; Captain Gary Rhodes, U.S. Air Force F-15 pilot; and Jay Molyneux, for his assistance with Ascension Island.

AUTHOR'S NOTE

As used in this book, and in the aviation world, "Z" time (or "Zulu" time) always refers to Universal Coordinated Time—formerly known as Greenwich Mean Time.

In the winter, when daylight saving time is not in use, Washington, D.C., is five hours earlier than Zulu time (in other words, 4 P.M. in D.C. is 2100Z, and 3 A.M. is 0800Z). The time in London in the winter is the same as Zulu, and Germany is an hour later (Zulu plus one hour).

PROLOGUE

Professor Ernest Helms had returned to the starting
point of the snowy forest trail just in time. Fifty yards
distant, someone was breaking into his car.

Security had been the last thing on his mind when
he'd parked amid the beauty of the snow-dusted Bavarian forest an hour before to tape some of the scenery
for his family. His had been the only car around.

But there was no mistaking the man's intent. The
thief was male, heavyset, wearing some sort of institutional coveralls, and frantically scraping away at the
door lock with some sort of tool—oblivious to Helms's
presence.

Helms hesitated and calculated the odds. He was not
in good physical shape, and the thief was probably
twenty years younger. Yet the man's effrontery triggered
a primal rage.

As he stood in shocked silence trying to decide what
to do, the sound of a helicopter reached his ears from
behind, faint at first but coming fast. For a moment
more his eyes remained on the thief. Then, without
thinking, he dropped his camera bag to the ground and
dashed out of the trees, yelling as he ran, trying to keep
his footing on the snow-covered ground.

"What the hell do you think you're doing? Get away
from that car!"

The thief jerked upright instantly, staring in Helms's

direction. Helms stopped in his tracks, uncertain what to expect, but the man just stood there acting confused, looking from Helms to the sky overhead and back again, his right hand pawing the car door ineffectually. His actions were more frantic than threatening.

The helicopter was closer now, and the man heard it too, his eyes darting away from Helms as he shielded his vision and strained to see the machine overhead. He stepped back and stumbled, then regained his balance and retreated a few more steps. Suddenly the chopper swooped in from behind Helms's position and slowed to a hover over the parking area, the occupants obviously spotting the thief as he turned and bolted into the forest on the opposite side as fast as he could go.

The pilot hesitated for a minute, as if inspecting the car amid the swirls of snow kicked up by the rotors' downwash. Helms could see someone in the left seat of the machine straining to look down. The helicopter accelerated then in the same direction the thief had taken, the noise of its rotor blades and jet engine receding slowly as it disappeared from view over the trees.

Ernest Helms had instinctively backed up a few steps and retreated into the edge of the forest when the helicopter appeared. He'd stumbled slightly over the edge of his camera bag, breaking a small strap that held an identification tag. Now he came forward and scooped up the bag, but the ID tag fell unnoticed to the forest floor.

The door handle bore deep scars from the metal tool the man had been using. Whoever he was, he was no professional car thief. In fact . . .

Helms turned and looked in the direction of the receding sounds of the helicopter, remembering the small crest on the side of the machine and the institutional clothes the man was wearing.

Suddenly it all made sense.

An escaped prisoner, I'll bet anything! And obviously trying to steal my rental car!

Helms realized his heart was pounding from the

adrenaline. He felt faint suddenly, and dizzy, and his chest hurt. He fumbled with the key and opened the car door, sitting down hard sideways in the driver's seat to catch his breath.

The helicopter was still less than a half mile away, apparently circling. He wondered if the pilot would end up herding the escapee back toward the parking area. Maybe it wasn't such a good idea to be sitting unarmed with the keys in the ignition.

Helms swung his legs into the car and closed the door. Just as his hand touched the ignition key, something slammed against the side of the vehicle.

Helms jerked his head to the left and found himself staring into the eyes of the wild-eyed man who'd dashed from the clearing minutes before.

With adrenaline pumping, Helms frantically twisted the key in the ignition, but nothing happened.

The man was pounding on the window now, his eyes wide with fear and panic. Somewhere in the background Helms heard the staccato sound of the helicopter, but the repeated impact of fists on window glass drowned it out.

Helms shook his head no again and again, as he tried to force his trembling hand to turn the ignition key, but something wasn't working. He was living the universal nightmare—running from an apparition but unable to move.

The man's face disappeared for a second and reappeared. This time a far louder report filled his ears, and Helms realized the man was striking the glass with a rock. The glass began to shatter as Helms turned the ignition key as far as it would go—and realized the engine had already started.

A gust of cold air on his left cheek told Helms the man was breaking through. He forced his hand to the gearshift and mashed the clutch, jamming the car into first.

Pieces of safety glass exploded into his face. Just as his left foot let up on the clutch and his right one shoved the accelerator to the floor, a hand came through the window and grabbed his collar.

Helms instinctively threw his arm up, knocking the man's grip free as the car lurched forward.

He gunned the engine and rocketed down the small road toward the main highway. At the same time, he looked in his rearview mirror and saw the man fall to his knees, making no move to give chase. He could see blood running down the man's arm.

Several miles away, when his heart rate had slowed, Professor Helms pulled to the side of the road to take inventory. His video camera was safe in the backseat along with the tape of the narration he had been doing for his son and daughter-in-law back in Maryland. During all six months of his sabbatical at the University of Heidelberg, he had intended to do some taping in Bavaria, but he had put it off until the last minute. He wished now he hadn't waited so long. In two more days he'd be back with them in the States anyway.

As Helms pressed the clutch again, preparing to enter the highway, he looked to his left through the shattered window. Something caught his eye on the lower jagged surface of the hole.

Blood.

The glass was drenched with blood, obviously from the crazed man in the woods.

But there was also an insistent burning on the side of his left hand.

With a cold chill climbing his back, Ernest Helms looked at his hand and found a deep cut.

ONE

———

Captain James Holland shifted the telephone receiver nervously to his other ear and glanced at the clock by the bed. There wasn't much time left. Irritation at being left on transatlantic hold was growing—almost as much as his anxiety at receiving the fax from Crew Scheduling.

In ten minutes ten flight attendants in a holiday mood would be waiting in the lobby for the short walk across the street to the train station for the brief rail trip to the Frankfurt airport. They knew the way on their own, of course, but protocol demanded the captain show up on time and lead the parade.

A series of clicks coursed through the line, but no voice. Where *was* the doctor anyway? The message had been urgent.

Holland unfolded the fax and read it again, looking for clues:

To: Capt. J. Holland, c/o **MAINZ HILTON.** Dr.
David Wilingham contacted us this morning requesting you call ASAP re: recent exam.#214-
361-1076/CrewSked/DFW.

A distant and disinterested voice finally drawled through the static. "Dr. Wilingham is not available right now. Do you wish to leave a message?"

Dammit! An answering service! "Tell him Captain

James Holland returned his call. Tell him I'm in Germany, and I'll call back within an hour. I'm . . . I really need to talk to him." He started to hang up, then pulled the phone back to his ear. "Uh, can you reach him by beeper?"

But the line was already dead.

Holland replaced the receiver, feeling his apprehension build. The exam three days ago was supposed to have been routine—a simple prostate sonogram—a checkup. He had no symptoms, no indication of cancer or any other problems, but if the doctor was calling like this . . .

He checked his watch again: 1:54 P.M. Six minutes left.

Holland folded and pocketed the note as he straightened his tie and closed the overnight bag. He pulled his uniform coat with its four gold command stripes over his white uniform shirt and placed the two bags on the folding handcart. There was a full-length mirror by the door, and he hesitated for a moment to check his appearance, all too aware of the dark circles under his eyes and how they telegraphed the weight of his forty-six years.

It had been Sandra who first noticed his face melting into bags and creases. Sandra, his wife—his former wife, he reminded himself—had wanted him to have plastic surgery. She didn't want to be married, she said, only half in jest, to a man who resembled Lyndon Johnson more each day.

But then she'd left him, for reasons that had nothing to do with appearance.

He opened the heavy door to the hallway, feeling old, tired, and defeated. Christmas was going to be a lonely agony. The flight attendants had been gift shopping all morning. They'd be excited and ebullient all the way to New York. The phrase "Bah, humbug!" replayed in his mind, but he was determined not to crush anyone else's mood.

Yet with the worry about the doctor's message, a six-hour flight over the Atlantic was going to be brutal—made even worse by the presence of Dick Robb as his copilot.

Holland glanced down the hall, relieved that Robb wasn't in sight. He would already be waiting in the lobby, of course, arrogant as ever, flirting with the younger flight attendants and monitoring his watch like a trainmaster. Robb, a young check captain from the training department assigned to give Senior Captain Holland an initial qualifying check ride in the Boeing 747-400, had spent the past two days energetically criticizing everything James Holland had done—and Holland had all but reached the breaking point.

Yet, as usual, he would say nothing.

He remembered trying to explain check captains once to Sandra. "They're training department pilots," he had told her, "some of whom are upgraded to captain years ahead of their seniority. They give check rides; they fly with and evaluate the competency of the rest of us who fly the daily schedules, the line pilots."

"And you don't like them?" she had asked.

"Most of them are gentlemen, but some of them become arrogant—little Caesars drunk with their own righteousness and power, more given to judging than instructing. An arrogant *young* check captain is the worst."

Robb fit the description perfectly.

Holland stepped on the elevator and checked his watch, noting with grim satisfaction that he'd be arriving with two minutes to spare.

As the captain left the elevator, Dick Robb moved toward him, pointedly looked at his watch, and asked if the flight was on time.

"As far as I know, Dick," Holland replied, realizing instantly he'd stepped into a trap.

"Wrong. It's delayed!" Robb said with barely disguised glee. "I called Operations a half hour ago to check on things. I figured you'd already called, but I was surprised when they said they hadn't heard from you."

A sticky fuel valve had to be replaced, Robb told him, and Flight 66 would now depart for New York thirty minutes late at 4:30 P.M. with a moderate load of two hundred forty-five passengers.

It was snowing very lightly in a beautiful wintry scene, but Robb was oblivious to it. He spent the train ride to Frankfurt importantly reminding Holland that his responsibilities as captain included staying in touch with Operations at overseas airports. Holland remained polite, nodding in all the right places, but his lips were white from the effort and Robb had noticed. As they neared the airport, Robb sighed to himself in resignation, regarding Holland as burned-out and lazy.

Holland, in turn, regarded Robb as a self-righteous jerk.

They parted at Operations, Holland leaving Robb to do the ground checks normally expected of first officers, while Holland himself headed for the departure gate, passing through the busy terminal without seeing it, oblivious to anything but the gnawing worry about the doctor's call. All his career he had envied those few pilots who could seem to put their troubles on a shelf in some mental closet when they went flying, but he could never achieve such detachment. When Sandra had stormed out, shattering what was left of a fragile marriage, she had left behind an aching hollowness that had become his constant companion. He'd flown with that emptiness for many months, and now this.

The immense image of the 747-400 loomed ahead outside the windows of Gate 34. There was a dusting of snow on the wings, but the deicing trucks were parked nearby. As he located an empty phone booth and slid inside, fumbling to find the number of AT&T Direct, he thought of the Air Florida crash in Washington back in 1982 and the effects of ice on an airplane. He made a mental note to double-check that Robb did the correct post-deicing inspection.

• • •

Standing near Gate 34, Rachael Sherwood brushed back her shoulder-length auburn hair and realized she was staring at the stranger just as hard as some men stared at her. *Poor manners for an ambassador's assistant,* she told herself. She adjusted her skirt self-consciously and glanced back down the concourse, slightly irritated that U.S. Ambassador-at-Large Lee Lancaster was so late. She'd already spent ten minutes standing in a pair of torturous pumps, scanning the onrushing Christmas crowd, when she'd noticed the big American pilot. He was leaning against an open phone booth near the gate, apparently in some distress, one arm draped along the top edge of the partition, his large hand beating a nervous tattoo on the smoked glass. She knew the four-stripe epaulets on his shoulders were the mark of a captain, but it was his deep-blue eyes that had captivated her. It was obvious he wasn't noticing her or anyone else at the moment. She quietly maneuvered in to get a closer look, slipping into another phone booth several yards away to watch. Rachael felt an odd rush of excitement, mixed with some embarrassment. She'd never done such a thing before.

I must be bored! she thought as she continued to stare openly at him.

He was at least six feet three, with thick eyebrows over heavy eyelids, a square-jawed, clean-shaven face framed by dark brown hair on its way to salt-and-pepper gray. She let her eyes linger on his broad shoulders and stray to his chest. Obviously a man who kept himself fit, she concluded. And obviously a man worried about something. The deep frown on his face was punctuated suddenly by a sigh she could almost hear across the concourse, and Rachael felt an illogical, empathetic urge to go comfort him—unaware that James Holland had been triggering such responses in women all his life.

Whatever was bothering him had apparently been resolved by the phone call. She could see that. She watched him square those magnificent shoulders as he replaced the receiver and stood up. He was even smiling slightly as he put on his hat with its gold-braided bill.

Rachael looked away at the moment he walked past, hoping he hadn't noticed her staring, then dared to turn and look again. A hint of cologne followed in his wake, a pleasant, woody fragrance she didn't recognize, but one that quietly urged her little fantasy along. She wondered which flight he was there to command—and hoped it was hers.

Where on earth is Lee? She reached for the cellular phone in her oversized handbag, then replaced it quickly as she saw Lancaster hurrying toward her down the long concourse.

Fifteen minutes later, alone in the cockpit of Flight 66, Captain James Holland began his preflight procedures with his mind on the phone call he'd just finished.

He'd finally reached the doctor back in New York.

"There was a shadow on your sonogram," the physician had said, "and at first I thought you should come in for another one, but I didn't mean to create a crisis."

"I . . . wasn't sure, Doctor. I'm in Germany, on a trip, and Crew Scheduling got hold of me over here saying you'd called. Frankly, it's scared me to death."

"I'm sorry, Captain."

"You say there's a shadow? As in tumor?"

He had been spring-loaded to the worst-case scenario: prostate cancer. He'd all but diagnosed himself out of fear, figuring he'd need surgery. But what happened after surgery? Would he be a sexual cripple? He'd heard terrible stories about the effects, and he couldn't imagine life without sex, without being able to satisfy a woman. The fact that he'd been all but celibate since Sandra had left was immaterial.

That was temporary.

This could be for life!

"Captain, I'm happy to report it was a mistake. You're perfectly okay!" the doctor was saying. "I went back in and looked at the sonogram tape again, and realized I'd misidentified it."

"I'm okay?" Holland asked.

"Completely. I'm truly sorry to have worried you."

"I don't need another one?"

"Not for at least a year. Stop worrying, and have a Merry Christmas!"

Holland had breathed a long sigh of relief and thanked the doctor. He smiled to himself now as he adjusted the rudder pedals and ran his hand down the center console, checking switch positions. With the exception of having to deal with Robb, he felt like a prisoner with a pardon—back from the dead.

I should grab the next pretty woman I see! he thought with a chuckle, feeling himself relax a bit.

As he put the radar into the test mode, he reached a long-postponed decision. He would start dating again. He was tired of being alone. For that matter, he was tired of sleeping alone.

One story below at door 2L, a small man with thinning hair and a battered briefcase left the line of passengers filtering in the door and leaned against the wall of the jetway, breathing hard. A tall redheaded flight attendant materialized at his side, holding his arm and inquiring urgently what was wrong.

Professor Ernest Helms looked up at Brenda Hopkins for a second before speaking.

"I'm . . . okay. Thank you. I . . . just felt very weak all of a sudden."

"What's your seat number, sir? I'll help you in."

". . . don't want to expose you to a . . . cold . . ."

She had taken his arm firmly, he realized, and his feet were obeying. He felt her take his briefcase as well.

Brenda winked at the senior flight attendant as she guided the man through the door and gently turned him to the right toward his seat. He was sweating profusely, though it was cool in the cabin and cold outside. She could feel a rapid pulse in his arm as well. Probably the flu. It would be a good idea, she told herself, to wash her hands as soon as she strapped him in.

At the same moment, on the snowy ramp some forty feet below, Dick Robb stuck his hands in the pockets of his overcoat and stood for a minute lost in the sight of the magnificent Boeing 747, its gleaming aluminum skin reflecting the filtered sunlight trying to break through the snow clouds above Frankfurt. Quantum had purchased four of the whales—as pilots called the 747s—for a total of over seven hundred million dollars, with interiors designed for three hundred sixty-five passengers in three classes. The big bird stood there like a mirage, he thought—an impossibly huge machine capable of lifting more than three quarters of a million pounds of metal and people and fuel with little more than a tug from his wrist at the appropriate moment.

And he was in charge! At age 32, with no military flying background, it was, nevertheless, *his* name that appeared on the dispatch release.

A baggage tug came roaring by, pushing a bow wave of slush. He stepped back quickly.

Holland would be nearly forty-five feet above the ramp in the cockpit by now. He was a competent pilot, Robb had decided grudgingly, but obviously from another generation and slowing down.

Of course, I'm hard to keep up with. I'm Dick Robb, hardass check captain.

Robb smiled to himself. He liked having a scary reputation. It brought respect, and being in the training department kept him from having to fly as a line captain, where there lurked the day-to-day danger that his lack of experience might lead to a serious mistake. He loved finding ways to one-up line captains, especially the older ones with thousands of hours of experience. Old pelicans like Holland were okay, but only marginally so when they relied too much on their experience, and he enjoyed cutting them down a notch. After all, he had *his* reputation to maintain. It pleased him no end to know

the line pilots called him the "Bustmaster." He'd earned
the name.

Technically, of course, he had to let Holland give the
commands and make the decisions on what was, after
all, a training ride—a passenger-carrying trip used to
complete a line captain's qualifications for a new type of
aircraft he hadn't commanded before. But until he
signed the last line in James Holland's training folder
and ended the check ride by declaring Holland fit to
serve as captain by himself on the 747-400, Captain
Richard Robb would remain legally the captain in
charge—the "master" of the aircraft.

Robb smiled to himself. It was confusing for the flight
attendants to have two captains aboard, but a necessary
evil. A captain had to be evaluated performing as a captain before he could be released to fly the public around
in a new airplane, and the only way to do that was actually to put him in the left seat under the watchful eye of
a check captain.

But who was *really* calling the shots was always a
problem.

Robb looked at his watch and realized he'd been day-
dreaming. There would be twenty minutes of cockpit
setups to go through before pushback, and five hours
ahead in which he could grill Holland and make him
sweat before signing him off as fully qualified. Such
power was a real turn-on, as was the act of controlling a
beast as huge as the 747.

The roaring whine of four powerful engines caught
his attention, and Dick Robb paused at the foot of the
stairway, entranced by the sight of another 747 rumbling
down the runway and lifting its mammoth bulk into the
air.

Better than sex! he thought.

The intricate choreography of a major airline departure
reached a crescendo just before 4:30 P.M., when the last
of the package-laden passengers were ushered aboard
by gate agents wearing Santa hats and large smiles. The

flight attendants were in the holiday mood as well.
Heading home on a wintry afternoon, most of them
were senior enough to have Christmas off. Husbands,
boyfriends, family, warm fires, and Christmas trees
beckoned across the Atlantic.

With the doors closed, and the deicing completed and
checked by the first officer–check captain, Flight 66
rumbled toward the end of Frankfurt's southern east–
west runway and lifted majestically into the darkening
sky.

TWO

As the English coastline passed beneath the nose of Quantum's westbound Flight 66, the flight attendant call chime began ringing in the cockpit—not once, but five times in rapid succession.

There was no procedure for such a signal.

James Holland toggled the interphone as he glanced at Dick Robb, who seemed equally alarmed.

"Flight deck," Holland said.

A tense feminine voice flooded his ear.

"Captain, this is Linda at door two B. I think we've got a heart attack back here!"

"Okay, how bad is it?"

"He's an older man. Brenda's started CPR. He got sick right after liftoff, but suddenly he just keeled over in his seat. We gave him oxygen, but he's almost stopped breathing."

"Have you checked to see if there's a doctor aboard?"

"We did, yes. A Swiss doctor responded, and he said we've got to get this man to a hospital fast or we'll lose him."

"Okay, Linda. Keep us informed."

Dick Robb had nodded and was already calling the air traffic controller, anticipating Holland's decision.

"London Center, Quantum Sixty-six. We have a medical emergency aboard and need immediate vectors for an emergency landing at . . ." Robb glanced at Holland and raised an eyebrow, aware he'd jumped the gun —and equally aware Holland wouldn't protest. What choice did they have?

"Let's go to London Heathrow," Holland shot back. "Ask for priority handling, and we need paramedics to meet us."

Robb repeated the request and took the new clearance as Captain Holland dialed in the course direct to London and began an autopilot descent out of thirty-three thousand feet. Holland reached forward at the same time to type "LON" into the flight management computer and hit the execute button. The big Boeing immediately began a turn to the left to follow the new course as Dick Robb folded his arms and sat back with a look of forced disgust.

"You're going to do this solo, then?" Robb asked.

Holland glanced at him, not comprehending. "What?"

"The book says that the pilot-not-flying programs the computer. You're the pilot-flying on this trip. I'm the pilot-*not*-flying."

Holland studied Robb's face. He was serious, and there wasn't time for a confrontation, even if he'd wanted one.

"Sorry, Dick," Holland said. "You were busy working the radios, and we've got an emergency here." He gestured toward the flight management computer, trying not to look disgusted. "Please give me direct London, and let's plan the ILS approach."

"That's more like it" was Robb's singular response.

One story below the cockpit, in the neutral zone between coach class and business class, a small group of flight attendants and several concerned passengers huddled around the figure of a small man lying prone on the floor. Brenda Hopkins, the redheaded flight attendant with supermodel features who had helped Ernest Helms to his seat, knelt by his head, trying to breathe life into his mouth between impassioned attempts to pump his chest and circulate enough blood to his brain. Her hair had gone wild and her uniform was stained, but with shoes off and stockings ripped, she was oblivious to anything but the battle to save her passenger.

Breathe into his mouth five times, listen, pump his chest fifteen times. Short, hard, downward strokes. Remember the training!

Over and over again.

She had been at it for fifteen minutes, but despite a routine of running and daily workouts, she was tiring.

The Swiss physician hovered over her, monitoring the rhythm of her efforts but making no attempt to take over until she was ready for relief. His frustration at having no medical tools to help the man was driving him to think frantically of other alternatives.

Another flight attendant had produced the airplane's emergency medical kit, but it was impossibly crude and there was no defibrillator, which was the one instrument he really needed.

As they felt the aircraft turning and descending, there was the spark of a response, a gasp of sorts, and the patient seemed to arch his back slightly as if taking a breath on his own. The doctor put his ear to the man's chest, verifying a weak, unstable heartbeat, which immediately faltered.

"We almost had him," he told Brenda.

She took a deep breath, wiped her forehead with the back of her hand, and started again. Her mouth closed around the patient's as she held his bald head and tried not to think about the fact he was sick—with what, she had no idea. She was terrified of AIDS, and bad cases of the flu, and any other malady she might get from direct contact.

But she had always wanted to be a doctor, and wasn't this where it began? Her passenger was desperate. She couldn't worry about the consequences.

AIR ROUTE TRAFFIC CONTROL CENTER, LONDON

Two hundred miles to the southwest, the radar target marked QUANTUM 66 had barely steadied on a course direct to London Heathrow when the controller handling that sector notified his supervisor of the emergency. The call triggered a carefully programmed series of steps designed to let airport authorities know that a medical emergency was in progress: Paramedics had to be summoned; customs, immigration, and health authorities had to be notified; and the airline itself had to be called.

The routine call to the British government's health service went to a sprawling complex within Heathrow's terminal buildings, where the deputy assistant inspector for British public health had immediately begun working on the problem. He verified the arrival time and location of the flight and secured the sick passenger's name from Quantum's Operations. Now he replaced the telephone receiver, checked the name he'd written on a yellow legal pad, and thought through the procedure. A U.S. airliner from Germany was unexpectedly arriving in the U.K. with a sick passenger. Just a suspected heart attack, of course, but precautions were always appropriate. His task was to guard against someone bringing in a communicable disease to Great Britain, though with the new Chunnel and the constant ferry services to the Continent, his attempts were akin to guarding the only remaining gate in a fence that had been largely removed. At least, he thought, it kept him employed.

He looked at the computer terminal and toyed with the idea of checking with his German counterparts by E-mail. Couldn't hurt, he decided, but should he use the computer? No, the phone would be more discreet.

He lifted the receiver and punched in the numbers for the Ministry of Health in Frankfurt, pleased that an English-speaking member of their staff answered. Just a routine check, he told the German. A suspected coronary case, and the man could easily be dead on arrival—no indication of anything viral or infectious—but as a precaution, did they by any chance have a medical case history on the man or any infectious health alerts?

"Did he originate in Germany, or is he German?" the man in Frankfurt asked.

"Ah, I think he boarded in Frankfurt. He's an American male. The name I have is Helms. Ernest Helms, age unknown."

The silence went on for so long that the British health officer suspected a disconnect. Suddenly, however, the German was back, his voice now tinged with tension. "You are certain the name is Helms? Ernest Helms?"

"Yes. I just checked with the airline. Why?"

The German ignored the question. "Please give me your number. I will call you back."

"Is there a difficulty?"

"I must check on something. Please give me your number."

The British health officer passed on the number and replaced the receiver, thoroughly puzzled.

BONN, GERMANY

Within ten minutes, in an obscure office deep within the federal government complex in Bonn, a middle-level official named Horst Zeitner hung up his phone and sat down hard in his desk chair. Feeling stunned, he stared blankly at the modest wall adorned with several diplomas. All his efforts to contain what had happened in Bavaria were coming apart.

No, he corrected himself, *had* come apart! Worst possible case! There was a fresh cup of coffee on the desk and a young brunette assistant sitting on the couch waiting for instructions, but he ignored both. For many hours he had pressed a dangerous and discreet search for a particularly dangerous individual within Germany.

At great risk to his job he had exceeded his authority by asking the national police to watch the highways leading to the major airports. The search had centered on Stuttgart after a computer reservation for the man had been found on an early evening flight to the States. He had told them all that it was an urgent matter of national security, and then—with all possible avenues of escape sealed at Stuttgart—Zeitner had sat back and waited, nervous but confident that the man named Professor Ernest Helms could not get away.

But he had! Ernest Helms had decided to catch an earlier flight and gone to Frankfurt instead! His rental car had just been found there, and the other airline had accepted his ticket.

Zeitner was furious with himself. He had never thought of another airport, and he should have done so. There was nothing left to do, he realized, but inform his minister—something he should have done many hours ago. There was no longer any chance of keeping his search quiet, but the U.K. must not be involved. If a major flu epidemic erupted there killing hundreds of people because the German government had failed to warn the British, there would be a diplomatic firestorm hot enough to incinerate his career. It was a German problem, and Germany would have to contain it by some sort of strict quarantine within their own borders.

Helms, in other words, could not be allowed to land in Great Britain dead or alive. He—and the other passengers—must be returned to Frankfurt.

Zeitner sighed and quickly reached for the phone, feeling a cold ball of fear in his stomach. Time was obviously running out, and he was losing control.

Zeitner dialed the number hurriedly with shaking hands. His minister would have to warn the Brits immediately.

At the same moment, in the forward coach section of Quantum 66, the exhausted flight attendant and the Swiss doctor decided there was renewed hope for Ernest Helms. A heartbeat—weak and unstable, but at least detectable—had returned. Maybe he'd make it after all!

But only, cautioned the doctor, if they delivered him to a properly equipped coronary care unit within the next few minutes.

The doctor had spelled Brenda Hopkins' CPR efforts several times, but Brenda had carried the brunt of the battle, and she now sat in a disheveled mess on the floor. With Helms's head in her lap, she gently placed her left hand on his bare chest as she closed her eyes for a second and tried to will his heart to keep beating.

The entire episode seemed unreal and was profoundly frightening. The enormity of a medical emergency seemed so much more threatening than she had imagined. Maybe she wasn't cut out to be a physician after all. Thank God there had been a real doctor on board to guide her.

She opened her eyes and looked at the unconscious face.

"Please, God," she muttered, "let him live!"

Barb Rollins, the lead flight attendant, picked up the interphone and reported the latest facts to the cockpit, surprised that both pilots answered. She could hear tension in their voices. James Holland thanked her and clicked off as he turned toward Robb to continue an interrupted argument. London now lay thirty miles to the south, and Dick Robb wanted to go off somewhere over the English Channel and dump fuel to lighten the aircraft.

"We don't have time," Holland told him. "We've got a man dying back there."

Robb shook his head angrily. "You're planning an overweight landing in a hundred-sixty-million-dollar airplane on the assumption that you can save one passenger? We have to get our landing weight down. We have to dump fuel like the book says."

Holland looked at him, trying to read the depth of Robb's resolve in the redness of his face and the angle of his head. Overweight landings were prohibited, except in emergencies. But this was an emergency, and if the touchdown was gentle enough, it didn't matter from a structural point of view.

Yet, Robb was in charge.

"You can overrule me, Dick, but that's my decision. I'll touch down way below the three-hundred-feet-per-minute descent rate limit. The aircraft won't be over-stressed."

Robb's voice, shrill and tense, shot back. "We'll have to pull an overweight landing inspection, and that'll take hours!"

Holland sat back and shook his head. "Okay, fine! Then what do *you* propose?" The thought of circling around offshore for thirty minutes to dump tens of thousands of dollars of jet fuel while a passenger died seemed idiotic.

Robb reacted as if hit with a cattle prod. Holland was dumping the decision in his lap, and he turned immediately and held up the palms of both hands.

"Oh no you don't, *Captain* Holland. I'm evaluating *your* decisions. You want to crunch the airplane on overweight instead of dumping fuel? Go ahead!"

"You're the one who signed for the airplane," Holland reminded him, keeping his voice deliberately laconic.

Robb's reply was instantaneous. "But you're the acting captain, and I'm *not* making this decision for you!"

Holland turned again toward Robb, leaning over the center console and looking the younger pilot squarely in the eyes. "Then kindly shut up and stop trying to bully me!"

The senior director of the London Approach Control facility had arrived unnoticed behind the left shoulder of the controller taking the handoff of Quantum 66 from London Center. The controller issued instructions for further descent to five thousand feet and a turn to a heading of one hundred eighty degrees. The 747 would be the next aircraft landing at Heathrow. All other traffic was being routed out of the way, and the controller knew that a contingent of medical personnel and fire equipment was already in position by the runway. Precautionary emergency landings were not wholly unusual, but a medical emergency knitted everyone together with a common purpose. His entire concentration was focused now on bringing the American jumbo in as fast as possible, and an unexpected tap on his shoulder caused him to jump.

The controller turned to snap at whoever it was, and found himself staring at his boss.

"Where is Quantum?" the senior director asked.

"I've turned him on base leg," the controller replied, wishing the chief would have the courtesy to watch in silence.

"Put him in a holding pattern and tell the captain to call us on the frequency his airline uses for Operations in Miami, Florida." He handed the controller a slip of paper with "124.35" written on it. "Don't state this frequency on the air," he added.

The controller shook his head slightly, frowned at his screen, then glanced back at his boss before focusing again on the screen. He must have misunderstood.

"Terribly sorry, sir . . . you said . . . *what?*"

The senior director took a deep breath and let it out before replying. This was not going to be easy. He leaned over to repeat the instructions directly into the controller's ear, mindful that several others were listening from their consoles.

"Please just do as I say. Immediately."

The controller's head snapped around, his eyes searching those of the senior director, who stared back at him with his jaw clenched.

The voice of the Quantum pilot crackled through an overhead speaker at his console as well as through his headset.

"Approach, Quantum Sixty-six. We have the airport. Request a visual approach."

Seconds of silence passed before the controller keyed his microphone. "Quantum, London Approach. I'm going to need to put you in holding. You are now cleared to hold on the London two-zero-zero-degree radial at ten miles, right-hand turns, ten-mile legs, at five thousand feet. And we'd like you to come up on the same radio frequency your company uses for . . ."

He glanced back at the senior director, who responded in a low voice. "Their Miami Operations frequency."

". . . your Operations frequency for Miami. We need to speak with you on that channel privately."

There was silence at first when he released the transmit button, then the sound of a deeply perplexed American voice.

"London . . . you want us to enter *holding*? Don't you realize we've got a probable heart attack victim aboard who's barely hanging on?"

The controller sat transfixed, unsure what to say. How could he answer that? The captain had declared an emergency!

The senior director had already donned a headset and plugged in. He keyed his microphone.

"Captain, this is London Approach. Did you understand the holding instructions?"

The voice was different, authoritative, and a distinct change from the controller's. In the cockpit of Quantum 66, James Holland watched London Heathrow sliding by his left window as his mind raced through various possibilities and came up with no feasible explanation. There was no traffic in their way. What on earth could be wrong?

Holland keyed the transmitter. "Yes, London, we copied your holding instructions . . . but, dammit, we *can't hold*. You're going to be responsible for a passenger's death!"

"Captain, I beg you to do as instructed. The sooner you come up on the appropriate frequency, the sooner I can explain."

James Holland looked to the right, finding the same puzzlement on Robb's face.

"You've got the airplane, Dick. Put her in a hold as instructed while I look up the goddam frequency."

For once, he noted, Robb responded without protest.

The frequency was buried on a page deep within Holland's flight kit, and it took a minute to wrestle it to the surface and dial it in.

The same authoritative voice responded immediately, identifying his rank and name before cutting to the heart of the matter.

"Captain, aside from your medical emergency, the British Ministry of Health has been informed by the German Health Bureau that one of your passengers has been exposed to a particularly nasty and dangerous strain of influenza. I have no other information, but because of this exposure, you must return to Frankfurt for appropriate processing and quarantine. Your company has been informed that the British government cannot permit you to land in the U.K."

Holland shook his head. "Because of a *flu* bug? I've been flying twenty-five years and I've never heard of such a thing! You quarantine individuals, not entire flights! Look, just let us get the heart attack victim off the airplane. I'll take the rest of us back, if that's what my company wants."

The sound of a transmitter being keyed was followed by a sigh.

"I'm sorry, Captain, this decision has been taken at the highest levels of the British government. It is not subject to negotiation."

"Why can't we at least get help for our heart attack, dammit?"

The senior director's voice was somber and slow.

"Captain, have you considered the possibility that your heart attack victim and the exposed passenger might be the same person?"

"Are you sure of that? Do you have the name of the exposed passenger?" Holland demanded.

"I will tell you they are one and the same, Captain, but I'm not at liberty to pass the name over the radio on a clear channel. Now, since you were a transatlantic flight, I assume you have more than enough fuel to return to Frankfurt?"

"Yes, but our passenger will be dead by the time we get there, flu or no flu!"

"That can't be helped, I'm afraid. If you'll return now to the previous frequency, we'll hand you back to London Center and clear you back east."

"What if I land at Heathrow anyway?" Holland snapped. "You planning to shoot us on short final?"

There was a telling hesitation, and he wondered if that was a key the man was hoping Holland would find. But the voice came back with even more authority.

"That would be quite foolish, Captain. You would create an international incident; your aircraft, crew, and passengers would be kept on the runway for many hours before you were still forced to depart for Germany; and you would ultimately have to answer to your government for violating a foreign government's domestic air rules. I would expect you to lose your pilot's license as well. Your sick passenger will get help in Frankfurt. He will get none here."

"I hope your tape recorders are running!" Holland shot back.

"Indeed they are, sir. And for the record, I regret being forced to do this as much as you do."

Several seconds of silence filled the frequency before Holland replied, the angry tone now absent.

"So we're to be quarantined? Two hundred and forty-five passengers and twelve crew members? For a stupid flu?"

"In Frankfurt, yes. I have no details, but you must hurry. I was told that everyone aboard would need immediate treatment to prevent an outbreak."

"Okay" was all Holland could manage. The whole thing was bizarre. Unreal. But what choice did they have?

He dialed in the previous frequency of London Approach and gestured to Dick Robb to make the call as he tried to focus on what the control chief had said.

So the heart attack victim had been exposed to a flu bug. So what? The man was still in the throes of a coronary, which couldn't possibly be connected.

Or could it?

Holland yanked the interphone from its cradle and punched in the code for door 2L. Barb Rollins answered immediately.

"Barb, our heart attack? Was he ill when he came aboard?"

There was a brief hesitation before she answered. The memory of Brenda helping the same man through the door played in Barb's mind.

"Yes, he was. How bad I don't know. Why?"

"Nothing. Just niggling questions from the ground. I'll explain in a few minutes," Holland told her. He replaced the handset, with a flurry of conflicting worries cascading through his head. The Germans wanted them back for quarantine and treatment to prevent an outbreak. That was good to hear.

Holland mulled it over as Robb read back the return clearance to Frankfurt and began programming the flight management computer—the FMC.

Isn't influenza a virus? How do you provide treatment for a virus?

He thought about the control chief's words.

Something wasn't right.

THREE

At precisely 4:48 P.M. London time—as Quantum 66 climbed away from the indignity of official British rejection to return to Frankfurt—the resident of a small flat in an unremarkable brick high-rise four miles from Heathrow Airport began punching in the number of CNN's London bureau eighteen miles distant.

The young man virtually quivered with excitement as he waited. He had most of the BBC's and CNN's private numbers now—the result of several years of reliable tips and the occasional sale of a tape recording of air-to-ground communications. No one monitored radio communications around Heathrow more thoroughly than he!

The young paraplegic adjusted the brake on his wheelchair and shifted the phone in his hand, proud of himself for snatching the frequency for Quantum's Miami Operations faster than the captain of Flight 66 could get it. A quick look into his *World Aviation Guide* and a call to Quantum's Operations office in Dallas had done the trick. He'd already been tuned to the right frequency, with his tape recorders rolling, when Flight 66's captain called the air traffic control chief.

The young man glanced again at the audiocassette in his hand and smiled. The entire conversation was there, ready for the highest bidder, and this emergency was something unique: a planeload of people exposed to

some nasty flu, as the controller had put it, being forced
into quarantine. It was a smashing newsbreak. CNN
would love it, and already he was feeling the rush as he
anticipated watching the anchor back in Atlanta break
the story—*his* story—to the world.

ABOARD FLIGHT 66

Ambassador Lee Lancaster drummed his fingers on the
leather-padded armrest of seat 2A as his mind assembled bits of evidence. The captain's announcement that
they were diverting to London for a critically ill passenger was understandable. But the latest announcement
from the captain about returning to Frankfurt for better
coronary medical aid made no sense.

He'd been watching the lifesaving efforts a dozen
yards behind him and knew that the poor fellow was
barely hanging on. Time was obviously critical. So, what
pilot in his right mind would fly an extra hour back to
Germany when he was minutes away from Heathrow?

No, something was definitely wrong, and the bizarre
and serious thought flickered across his mind that it
might have something to do with *him*. After all, half the
Arab world wanted him dead. Could the captain's return to Frankfurt be a smokescreen to hide a hijacking?

He was aware of Rachael Sherwood's eyes watching
him. She could almost always read him, and for some
reason the thought was pleasing. Rachael was as bright
as they came: a Rhodes scholar and a brilliant speech-
writer who should have been on the President's staff
instead of his.

But Rachael had had little experience in dealing with
the focused fury of the Shiite Islamic world, or gauging
the determined nature of those who hated him. This
time she wouldn't have guessed what he was thinking.

Hijacking's a ridiculous idea! he told himself. Yet . . .

As it often did, a lurid scene of a shattered car in
Madrid replayed itself in his mind. He'd decided to walk

that spring day a year ago, leaving an embassy employee
to ferry his rental car back to the American compound.
He'd been warned to be especially careful in Madrid,
but the beauty of the spring day and sheer bravado got
in the way. After all, he had survived a decade of threats
without a scratch. He had begun to believe that his own
sheer force of will made him invulnerable.

The explosion had reached his ears from a half mile
away. A powerful bomb under the dashboard fragmented the driver and the vehicle. An unrelated protest
against the Spanish government, the public had been
told. Lancaster's name had been kept out of it, but there
was no question who the target had been.

He winced at the memory. The funeral had been
gruesome. In a hysterical scene he would never, ever
forget, the widow had blamed him personally.

Lancaster shook his head and rubbed his temple to
expunge the memory, then glanced at Rachael. She was
such a beauty, he thought, and it was something even
her conservative way of dressing couldn't hide. He liked
the company of beautiful women on a sheer physical
level, and even with his eyes and ears closed, her physical presence a few inches away triggered a pleasant
glow.

The 747 changed course again slightly, diverting his
attention back to the problem at hand. As the roving
American ambassador primarily responsible for engi-
neering workable truces and economic relationships between Israel and the Arab states, he had long since been
branded a blood enemy of Islam. The fact that he was
an acknowledged Islamic scholar was immaterial to the
Shiites, and even he had lost track of the full list of
terrorist organizations, outlaw Islamic nations, splinter
groups, and others who had sworn to kill him over the
years. He had refused to become a prisoner of security
precautions, though the price was high. He found himself walking a knife edge of terror, always watching his
back, always aware that the balance could tip the wrong
way at any moment.

His wife and family had learned to live with the danger, if not fully accept it. But Jill Lancaster was never comfortable with the stereotype of the perpetually smiling, never complaining diplomat's wife. She hated not being able to talk about her fears, the constant wondering when her husband might come home in a flag-draped body bag.

He sighed and glanced around the first class cabin.

So, have they cornered me at last, or am I finally a certifiable paranoid?

No, he decided. Terrorists didn't bank on unpredictable opportunities like heart attacks.

But if not, then what was going on? Could another threat be waiting for him back in Frankfurt?

He turned and raised an index finger. "Rachael, I need you to do something for me."

"Sure, Lee."

He leaned close, talking barely above a whisper, ignoring the scent of her perfume.

"Something's very wrong here. I need to know exactly what's happening, just in case . . . in case it involves *me* somehow."

Her eyebrows fluttered up in alarm, her dark brown eyes boring into his. He raised the palm of his hand.

"It's not likely," he reassured her, "but this return to Frankfurt is very strange."

"You want me to go talk to the pilots?" she asked.

"Find the lead flight attendant first. Make sure she knows who we are, and try to find out what's really going on."

She was suddenly nervous, he could tell, but she smiled and unsnapped her seat belt without hesitation. She unfolded her long legs, stood up, and smoothed her skirt.

Twelve feet above the first class cabin in the cockpit of Flight 66, James Holland put a hand over the mouthpiece of the satellite phone receiver and turned to his copilot.

"We're apparently in the middle of a diplomatic firefight, Dick. Do you want to take over talking with the company?"

A look of momentary panic crossed Robb's face like the shadow of a passing cloud, and just as soon it was gone. He shook his head.

"Just tell me what they want us to do," he replied, acutely aware of how stupid that sounded. Of course Holland would relay any word from Dallas.

The satellite conversation resumed, then ended, and Holland replaced the receiver while shaking his head.

"Our people don't have a clue, Dick. That was the director of Flight Ops confirming that the German government has demanded that we return, but the Germans are claiming they didn't put the British up to denying us landing clearance. Our State Department is involved too, and they're also clueless. They claim we misunderstood."

"*Who* misunderstood?" Robb asked. "Misunderstood *what*?"

"That it was just a recommendation, rather than a British refusal to let us land."

"The hell it was!"

Holland nodded and frowned deeply. "So I told them. Problem is, they aren't providing us any reliable information." He began ticking off a list on his fingers: "No one knows what arrangements they're planning back in Frankfurt for us; no one knows anything about Mr. Helms down there; no one knows what kind of treatment they're planning for anyone else who may have already been exposed to Helms; no one's telling us how bad this strain of flu is; and the man who *should* be dealing with this—our Flight Operations vice president —is on his ranch near Texarkana with his phone turned off! The director of Flight Ops said he'll call us back when they know anything."

The flight attendant call chime rang, and Dick Robb reached to answer in nervous reaction.

There was a female voice in his ear, the worry apparent in her tone. "Is this the captain?"

"Sort of," Robb replied. "This is the check captain."

Robb could sense her confusion. He glanced at Holland, who was looking the other way and pretending not to hear. The distinction was silly, Robb decided. He adjusted the phone against his ear.

"This is the first officer. What's up?"

"This is Dee in first class. Ah, we have a U.S. ambassador aboard, and his assistant is here with me asking some questions I can't answer about what's . . . ah . . . what's happening with us. May I bring her up?"

"Sure. Door's unlocked," Robb replied, his left index finger finding the electronic unlock button on the center pedestal by feel. He was well aware that cockpit entry should be the captain's decision. Since the captain's interphone button was on, Holland had heard the exchange in his headset, and Robb glanced at him to see his reaction. There was none.

Holland had been deep in thought, but he stirred now and looked at Robb with a neutral expression.

They were back at thirty-three thousand feet headed east over the Channel, with the Netherlands just ahead. They were talking to Maastricht Control near Amsterdam, and had been recleared to Frankfurt. There was nothing else to do for the moment.

The silence was awkward, and Robb decided to fill it. "So where do we go?"

Holland hesitated, then pointed ahead without speaking, well aware that Robb was trying to fill a void. Frankfurt was the only reasonable solution, and they both knew it.

BONN

In fifteen minutes word had filtered up from the middle ministerial level that a major infectious disease emergency was taking place—and no one in the senior leadership of the German government had been informed. A man named Zeitner, deep within the Ministerium Gezunntheits, the German Health Ministry, had asked his minister to lean on the British to refuse landing permission for Flight 66 after he had illicitly involved the national police in a fruitless search for a man suspected of carrying a dreaded form of human influenza. The fact that the minister had done so without consulting anyone else, the Chancellor included, had created something of a political and diplomatic crisis. The thought of the potential embarrassment to the government if the press found out had propelled the Chancellor himself to assemble an emergency meeting and summon Zeitner along with his shell-shocked boss.

Zeitner straightened his striped blue tie and got to his feet as if he were facing an inquisition. Arrayed within the dark walls of the richly paneled conference room were the principal cabinet members of the Chancellor's staff, along with the Chancellor himself. Zeitner could see the head of state glowering at him from his seat at the head of the table, chin in hand, eyes boring in on the man who'd created the latest crisis for a government that seemed in perpetual turmoil.

"Proceed, Herr Zeitner," the Chancellor said, tight-lipped. Zeitner could hear the acid dripping from his words.

"An American professor, a Professor Helms, teaching at Heidelberg, was exposed two days ago in Bavaria to what we are told is an extremely bad strain of the flu. This professor came into contact with an employee of Hauptmann Research Laboratories who was suffering from the virus. It was Hauptmann's Bavarian director who informed us of the exposure." Horst Zeitner hesitated as he studied the stern faces before continuing. "We thought we could catch this professor and fully quarantine him before he reached an airport or populated area. We thought the problem was fully contained. But the effort failed, and an entire airliner full of people has been exposed as a result."

"Is this professor already showing signs of illness?" the Chancellor asked.

"Extremely ill aboard the aircraft with symptoms we think come from this flu, and which must have brought on a heart attack."

"The flu can cause a *heart attack*? You did call it an influenza?" The Chancellor's eyes were boring into his, making him even more nervous, but Zeitner continued.

"With this type of flu, as I understand it, if a person were already prone to heart disease, the stress could trigger a heart attack. It puts a terrible strain on the body."

"How was he exposed, this professor?"

"He . . . had contact with the blood of an exposed lab researcher. The researcher tried to break into Helms's rental car and cut himself on the glass in the process. He broke through the window, you see. I don't have all the details, but apparently the Hauptmann employee was delirious from fever. Hauptmann's helicopter pilot got the professor's license number as he left. We assume that Helms was directly exposed to this man's blood, which would have been teeming with the virus."

The Chancellor stirred in his chair and waved off an aide offering a cup of coffee.

"Is the lab worker still sick?"

Zeitner hesitated, recalling the conversation with the Hauptmann director in Bavaria.

"He . . . died, sir. Complications."

The Chancellor frowned even more deeply, the furrows on his brow becoming deep chasms.

"Zeitner, let me understand this fully. Hauptmann is a pharmaceutical firm engaged in far-reaching biological research, as I recall."

Zeitner nodded.

"This firm informs you that a citizen needs to be quarantined because he was exposed to an ill Hauptmann employee who later died, but that all we're dealing with here is a bad strain of influenza?"

"That's correct, Chancellor."

"Doesn't that sound suspicious to you, Zeitner? It sounds suspicious to me. How panicked were they?"

Horst Zeitner shook his head vigorously. "Not panicked at all, sir. They were simply concerned. I'm sure they're giving us the whole story."

The Chancellor tapped his fingers on the table and stared silently at Zeitner for an uncomfortable eternity before continuing.

"Has anyone else been exposed, Zeitner?"

"We . . . well, several, but we think we have them all. We've secured the people Helms stayed with at a nearby *Gasthaus* and those he contacted at Frankfurt's airport. But we don't know if we found everyone he touched or talked to in the airport before boarding the flight. We think so, but there's no guarantee."

"Where do you have them?"

"In an Army biological containment facility near Bitberg. They're safely out of the way, and so far, no one is ill."

Two of the men were conferring urgently. One of them—an aide to the Interior Minister, Zeitner decided —spoke up. "Herr Zeitner, my God, most people don't die from the flu. If this one is bad enough to kill, haven't you already lost control? What happens if you don't quarantine his contacts in time, or if you missed someone? This could explode!"

Horst Zeitner raised his hand. "I really, *truly* believe we've quarantined everyone who had any contact with Helms, but of course I can't guarantee it. Professor Helms could have stopped somewhere we don't know about."

"You've retraced his route?" the Chancellor asked.

Zeitner nodded. "And we're continuing to do it. The police, I mean. Every store, every *Gasthaus,* every restaurant along the routes he could have taken, using a picture received from Heidelberg University."

"And if someone has slipped past you," the Chancellor asked, "and then they are sick for several days and spreading it before we find out, what then?"

The question Zeitner dreaded the most was in his face. How could he tell them he didn't really know?

He swallowed hard and forced himself to answer.

"Any influenza can spread like wildfire based on a number of variables. Unfortunately, we don't know much of anything about this strain. I have asked for more information, but so far . . ."

The Interior Minister leaned forward with a panicked expression.

"You don't really know what this is, do you?"

"Well, sir, I was told . . ."

"Have Hauptmann's people given you exact details?"

Zeitner shook his head no with a sinking feeling.

"Then this could be anything. It might even be something far worse than a flu, and they don't want to admit it."

Horst Zeitner shook his head vigorously. "No, sir, I was assured—"

The Interior Minister cut him off.

"We have to do better than this! My God, Zeitner, what if this is that horrible virus from Africa?"

Zeitner shook his head. "This is a flu, sir. The African pathogen is called a filovirus, completely different from an influenza. Either a Marburg virus or an Ebola strain. Those are called hemorrhagic pathogens, and they're horribly dangerous. The walls of the body's organs slowly collapse and the victim bleeds to death internally and from every orifice. This is simply an influenza strain. A simple influenza, they assured me. The concern is that this strain is particularly dangerous because it has mutated to a form against which most of us have developed no immunity."

The Chancellor sighed and leaned forward. "What he's trying to get across to you, Zeitner, is that if this virus *was* something more terrible than a bad flu, we would already have lost control."

"Yes, sir."

"Zeitner, what are we facing here if the worst occurs and this spreads through the country?"

Horst Zeitner looked at the table, then back at the Chancellor. It was time to ad-lib again, Zeitner decided, hoping no one would question him more deeply. He had worried about not asking more questions of Hauptmann's director. He had trusted him too readily, but they were a huge, trustworthy firm.

"From the description I received, this, at worst, is an influenza that could kill thousands of weaker and elderly people around the world if it got a foothold in an open population," Zeitner said. "In terms of lost productivity alone, German industries could face staggering costs."

He finished the description and surveyed the faces in front of him. The assembled members of the German government wore various expressions of shock.

"Germany can't chance spreading this to other nations and other large populations," Zeitner continued, "especially since it might be transmitted by airborne moisture. That's why I acted immediately, and without waiting for proper authority, sir. There was no time to lose, and when I discovered, quite by accident, that Mr. Helms was on an earlier flight, I knew we couldn't let them land in London without telling the British government. *They* made the decision—the British—to refuse landing permission."

"But you suggested it."

Zeitner hesitated too long and swallowed hard. "Yes, sir."

The Chancellor glanced at several of his ministers, his eyebrows raised. His eyes locked on Zeitner again.

"You propose we impound nearly three hundred people, Herr Zeitner, based on the possibility that one single passenger has been exposed to the flu?"

"Sir, that passenger is ill with this flu, and the airplane he is on, a Boeing seven-forty-seven, recirculates its cabin air and can spread any virus throughout the aircraft in a matter of minutes. We have to assume that everyone on board has been exposed."

"For how long do you need to quarantine?"

Zeitner calculated frantically. "We don't know. Perhaps up to five days. Perhaps more. Anyone who doesn't get ill is no threat."

"And one last question, Herr Zeitner," the Chancellor began, letting a long silence follow. "Since you were so determined to bring this plane full of dangerously exposed people back to German soil—and it appears you have succeeded—surely you must already have arranged quarantine facilities for nearly three hundred people, facilities that are at least as secure as those used in cases of biological warfare contamination. And surely you have already fielded a team to set up communications, command and control facilities, press, radio, and television liaison teams to deal with the worldwide firestorm of reaction and with the families of those quarantined, as well as notified all elements of our government that will have to deal with the diplomatic, legal, financial, logistic, military, and domestic consequences? You must have already done all these things, eh, Herr Zeitner?" He forced a false laugh and waved his right hand in a gesture of dismissal. "Otherwise, why would you bring them back here, *ja*? That would not be a rational act."

The Chancellor cocked his head and stared at Horst Zeitner, who was dying inside.

"Well, Herr Zeitner? These precautions are ready?"

Zeitner tried to speak with some dignity, but his voice emerged as little more than a constrained croak.

"No, sir, not yet. There has not been time."

The Chancellor nodded slowly like a professor who's heard the same answer from the same unprepared students several thousand times. He took a deep breath and loudly let it out as he rose to his feet looking at the table, then raised his eyes and focused them on Zeitner in a look of monumental disapproval.

"I see," he said. "Then it appears we have much work

to do in the few minutes remaining before this winged
version of Pandora's box arrives back in our laps." He
turned to his Foreign Minister, pointing to the phone.
"Karl, please accompany me back to my office. We must
get the American ambassador on the speakerphone."

The Chancellor looked down at the table and made a
small show of gathering some briefing papers, purposefully letting the silence impress everyone in the room. It
was a practiced gesture, and chillingly effective. Suddenly his head snapped back up, his eyes once again
dismembering Zeitner as he finished speaking to the
Foreign Minister.

"We're going to owe the Americans a substantial
apology."

The Foreign Minister nodded as the Chancellor
turned and left, and Zeitner realized he'd been holding
his breath.

He exhaled at last, feeling dizzy and utterly over his
head.

BAVARIA

In the windowless control room of the Hauptmann Research Laboratories, the facility's director sat before a
bank of flickering television monitors transmitting images of empty rooms. He didn't need to look. In the
adjacent isolation chambers two of his employees—his
colleagues—had died a frightening death, and he had
lied about the cause.

The agonizing telephone conversation with the senior
director in Berlin almost twenty-four hours ago
wouldn't stop replaying in his head. It was time to tell
the government what they were facing, he had said.

Yet his company had decided to lie as well. Officially,
it was to be a flu.

"A *flu*?" he had almost screamed. This virus caused
accelerated heart rate, high temperature, incredible
pain, nausea, then rapid onset of disorientation, hyste-

ria, and panic, similar to paranoid delusions, possibly coupled with hallucinations. Rolf Bronchmann, the second researcher to become infected, had given them detailed reports. "This becomes psychoactive and affects the mind—changes the personality," the director had told them. "No flu does that!"

But the word from Berlin was stern and certain. No one outside Hauptmann's inner circle was to know as long as there was a chance it could still be contained.

The director placed his hand on the telephone one more time. He knew the number of the government's man in Bonn, and he knew his career would end with such a call.

The dilemma was driving him mad.

FOUR

Brenda Hopkins adjusted the oxygen mask on Ernest Helms's face and looked up at the Swiss physician, who was patting her arm. There was nothing else they could do now, he had told her several times. The heartbeat was as stable as possible.

"How long until we land, do you suppose?" the doctor asked.

"I . . . think within thirty minutes." Brenda gestured with her head to Helms. "Can he hold out?"

The physician looked down the aisle into the distance before answering, his eyes not meeting hers.

"Perhaps," he said, not wanting to discourage her.

At the same moment, Rachael Sherwood was following the flight attendant named Dee up a staircase and forward through the upper-deck section to a small door leading to the cockpit of the 747-400. Dee knocked twice, then pulled it open and introduced Rachael. James Holland motioned her to sit on the raised jump seat positioned right behind the center pedestal, which sat between the two pilots.

Dick Robb introduced himself as co-captain and shook her hand, letting his eyes openly wander down to her chest for a second or two before resuming eye contact. She had already turned her head back toward Holland and hadn't noticed Robb's interest, so he turned back to the instruments. Holland motored his electrically positioned seat back so he could partially turn and see her as he talked.

"James Holland, Ms. Sherwood. Good to meet you."

It was the handsome pilot she'd noticed in the airport. She extended her hand and he took it gently, his huge warm palm completely enfolding hers as those deep blue eyes looked up at her, triggering a flutter of visceral feelings that surprised her. There was something about him—something very disturbingly sensual, she thought, though he carried an air of sadness.

The same vibrations that had shuddered through her back in Frankfurt erupted again now with seismic force, and she cleared her throat, worried that the professional ambassadorial assistant was going to sound like a giddy young girl.

Looking directly at Holland, unable to even glance away, she explained the ambassador's worries.

"No. No hijackers here," he assured her, "but since you folks are from the State Department, let me ask *you* a question. Isn't there a major diplomatic problem when a foreign country effectively orders an American airliner full of American citizens back for quarantine?"

Rachael stopped dead for a second. What was the word "quarantine" doing in that sentence? On the PA, Holland had said only that they were returning to Frankfurt for better medical aid for the heart attack victim in coach.

"There's more, I'm afraid," Holland began, understanding her puzzled expression. "I forgot you didn't know." He relayed what had happened, and the fact that the heart attack victim had come aboard ill with a serious strain of the flu, and that everyone aboard could be exposed.

Alarm flared in Rachael's eyes. "*All* of us?"

He shrugged. "Apparently."

She stared into space a few seconds, saying nothing before he pointed to the floor. "Your boss, Ambassador, ah . . ."

"Lancaster. Lee Lancaster," she replied, jumping slightly as she jolted herself out of a shocked stupor.

"Right. Ambassador Lancaster. He might want to help us deal with this on a governmental level, since both of you are affected as much as we are."

"How long a quarantine is it to be?" she asked, her mind reeling at the thought. They had schedules. They had to be in Washington, and then there was the speech to the National Press Club . . .

He shook his head and glanced at Robb, who was pretending to pay no attention.

"I don't know, Ms. Sherwood," Holland said.

"Rachael," she replied, far too quickly.

He nodded. "Rachael. Of course." He paused and almost smiled, as if he saw her differently all of a sudden. He could see the quarantine information had upset her even more than the possibility of exposure to a bad flu.

"We don't have any idea, Rachael, how long they mean to keep us, or what kind of treatment they're talking about. I mean, how do you stop a virus? How do you impound foreigners legally? This is uncharted territory and I could sure use some diplomatic guidance."

Rachael stood and, almost without realizing it, touched his shoulder with her left hand in a gesture of reassurance.

"Please," he continued, "say nothing about this to anyone else. I haven't even briefed my crew."

Her voice was soft and distracted. "No problem. I'll ask the ambassador to come up."

Rachael returned to the first class cabin, oblivious of the tall, familiar, silver-haired occupant of seat 3B, who was hunched over and urgently discussing changed schedules with someone half a world away. Now he slammed the satellite telephone handset back in its cradle and mashed the flight attendant call button in anger. The Reverend Garson W. Wilson, a household name in American evangelism, turned to his startled secretary—

a young man named Roger—and gestured toward the ceiling with undisguised disgust.

"We can't reschedule the NBC interview! That was their producer, Casey somebody, and the . . . the . . . *sumbitch* . . ." He almost whispered the word conspiratorily, but Roger sat forward with a wide-eyed expression and put his finger to his lips as his boss frowned and rolled his eyes.

". . . the misguided young miscreant, how's that?" Wilson continued, his voice still a whisper.

"Better," Roger replied. "There are ears everywhere."

"Okay, the *misguided young cretin*." Wilson mouthed the words with exaggerated theatrics, his famous Tennessee accent a slow, precise drawl that tinged the words with special sarcasm, as if he were tasting each one and finding it acidic. "He says he's got some movie star booked for Thursday's show. We either get there this evening, in time, or we lose it."

"It's okay, sir. We can rebook later. I'll call them."

Wilson shook his head in disgust. "We can't afford to sit around Frankfurt, Roger! As soon as we get on the ground, I want you to find whoever's in charge, tell him who I am, and get us the heck out of there. Rebook us to London and get us on the Concorde. I'm not going to miss that show! The audience is too big, and we need the kickoff momentum for the new book."

Roger rubbed his fingers together frantically and stared at the seat back. He hated these confrontations, but he had no choice. He took a deep breath and turned to Wilson at last.

"You know I'm worried about that interview, don't you? You remember I told you they could be setting you up on the income tax questions regarding the Kansas City hospital, right?"

"Yes, yes, yes. I remember, but I can handle it. I've been handling it for forty years, haven't I, praise the Lord."

Roger shifted in his seat. "Sir, have you considered

that perhaps God arranged for us to be on *this* flight just to keep you off that show?"

It was a good argument, Roger knew, and it had worked in the past.

Wilson snorted and shook his head. He hated it when an aide was right. *He* was supposed to be the omnipotent one, not the little college snot to his left. But maybe he *was* being too eager for publicity, and the TV newsmagazine was smelling blood. A national spotlight on the deductibility issue of the Wilson hospital chain was not the best idea for the business right now. The business of saving lives and souls, he reminded himself. *Never forget your image!*

He straightened himself in the plush first class seat and adopted a stern expression seen by no one. He imagined himself wearing the most righteous of expressions, clutching his Bible, and speaking into a phalanx of outstretched microphones. *My business, sir, is spreading the word of God through various testimonies.* The unspoken phrase sounded as good as it always had. He was a man of the cloth, not an accountant. He was trying to serve God, not the IRS. He would look persecuted. The exposure wouldn't hurt.

He realized he wasn't interested in hearing an alternative point of view. He just wanted to get to New York.

Some thirty rows to the rear, Keith Erickson passed the telephone handset to his wife, Lisa, and bit his lip. The kids sounded fine, and his sister-in-law seemed okay with the news that they'd be delayed. The connection in New York to their homebound flight would be too tight to accommodate a delay. They'd miss it for sure.

He glanced at Lisa as she spoke to two-year-old Jason, then five-year-old Tommy. The baby was too young to hold a conversation, but Keith knew that Lisa would insist on the phone's being held against her youngest child's ear so she could say reassuring things. He could imagine even his sister-in-law rolling her eyes.

He looked down the aisle and wondered how the

heart attack victim was doing, and how fast they could
get him to a hospital and get under way again. It had
taken a year of almost constant cajoling to get Lisa to
come on a vacation without the kids.

"Of course they need a mother, but I need a lover
too," he had told her.

"Why Europe?" she'd countered.

He remembered his response all too well. "Because
you can't call the kids every day."

But she had, with a manic vengeance that had become obsessive. The whole trip had been a tense disaster. It had started with an embarrassing goodbye scene
at the Des Moines airport, where she'd held up the
plane with repeated tearful hugs that had reduced the
boys to tears as well. She had fretted and worried all
the way to Frankfurt, and refused to leave a pay phone
at the airport for nearly two hours until her mother had
returned with the kids from a simple evening excursion.
And now the tearful response when Lisa discovered
they'd be delayed. It was becoming typical, and frightening, as was her dark, furious resentment at him for taking her away.

She had looked at little for two weeks other than pay
phones that might reconnect her with her children.
There was no interest in history, no interest in sex, no
interest in him, and no room for anything else in her
mind but the hysterical reaction to being separated from
her children. She hated him for it, she had screamed in
the Paris hotel. No. No, she'd said, without meaning,
prowling the bed with a wild-eyed expression. He was
plotting, wasn't he, to take her children away from her.
It was all a scheme!

He had known deep down, even in Des Moines, that
her reactions were not right, that she needed professional help. But at home the eccentricities could be tol-
erated.

In Frankfurt he'd slipped out of the hotel to call a
psychiatrist back in Des Moines, scheduling an appointment for her the following week. The doctor had lis-

tened intently. Hospitalization, he had warned, was not an outlandish possibility.

Lisa finished cooing at the baby, wiped her tears away, and asked to talk to Jason again. Keith Erickson cupped his chin in his hand and waited, knowing the dollars were flowing at a heavy clip on the satellite call.

But he knew better than to interrupt her again.

DUTCH AIR ROUTE TRAFFIC CONTROL CENTER, AMSTERDAM

The word arrived in Amsterdam Center in the form of a simple teletype message, followed by a phone call from Frankfurt Center. When it was handed to the puzzled Dutch controller handling Flight 66, he read it and shook his head in puzzlement—but keyed his microphone immediately. The aircraft was passing thirty-three thousand feet above the Dutch town of Tilburg, around fifty miles from the German border. He had no time to think about it.

"Quantum Sixty-six, Maastricht Control. Be advised, sir, that Frankfurt Center has just canceled your clearance into German airspace. We must reclear you now to another destination. What are your intentions?"

In the cockpit of Flight 66, the words fell like a hand grenade. "How could they cancel the clearance?" Robb asked. "First the British and now the Germans? The Germans *started* it all!"

Dick Robb squeezed the transmit button on the back of the control yoke immediately.

"Maastricht Control, Quantum Sixty-six is returning to Frankfurt at the specific direction of the German government, and we've got a medical emergency on board."

The reply was unsettlingly swift.

"Quantum Sixty-six, according to the communication we have just received, you are prohibited from entering German airspace. I will be forced to put you in a hold-

ing pattern before you reach the border if you fail to
request something else."

James Holland raised his hand, signaling Robb to
wait. His mind was racing over the possibilities. Had
Quantum headquarters changed the game plan and forgotten to tell him? Maybe the dispatcher had refiled
them for another destination, informed Frankfurt Center, and simply neglected a small detail like telling the
crew.

Possibly. But the word "prohibited" kept ringing in
his ears. They wouldn't have used "prohibited" if it were
just a simple change.

Holland felt the hair standing up on the back of his
neck. Suddenly he wanted to get on the ground somewhere as fast as possible—as much for himself as for the
sick passenger in the back. There was a mindless rush of
apprehension that time was running out, and he had to
act fast.

He triggered the transmit button.

"Maastricht Control, we're requesting vectors for a
landing at Schiphol in Amsterdam immediately."

The controller sounded relieved. "Understand, sir.
Turn left now to a heading of two-nine-zero degrees,
and descend to and maintain six thousand feet. Amsterdam's altimeter is two-nine-eight-eight, and set transponder code three-four-five-seven."

Robb repeated the clearance as Holland disconnected
the autopilot and autothrottles and banked the huge
747 gently to the left, beginning a descent with the
power back to idle. He could trust the Dutch to help.

I should have diverted to Amsterdam to begin with!
Holland chided himself. *The Dutch would never refuse a
civil aircraft in distress.*

FIVE

With a freshly brewed cup of coffee sitting before him and his office door closed, the director of airports for the Transport Ministry of the Government of the Netherlands leaned back slightly in his swivel chair and relaxed as he punched up the sound on his television with the handheld remote. All day he'd looked forward to this, especially the coffee. The small grinder and French press in the credenza were prized possessions that he kept stocked with an ample supply of imported beans from Starbucks in the United States. It was a European indulgence American-style that he usually allowed himself in the late afternoon, but his addiction to world news was entirely American—and CNN was his connection.

It was a small extravagance—a perk of office—but having a cable-connected color TV on his office wall made him feel plugged into world events, and something on the screen had just snagged his attention: the picture of an airliner that had flashed on and off while he had been on the phone.

A crash somewhere, perhaps? Curiosity seized him, but so far nothing more had aired. Now the anchor in Atlanta cleared his throat as a small picture of a Boeing 747 appeared in the upper-right-hand corner of the screen, and the director leaned forward to listen.

"There are reports out of the U.K. this afternoon that an

American airliner headed for London has been refused landing permission and forced to leave British airspace. In a radioed exchange between the pilot and an air traffic control supervisor monitored in London, the captain of the Quantum Airlines flight reported that he had a heart attack victim aboard who needed immediate help, but he was reportedly told that the British government would not permit the aircraft to land. Apparently, according to the same radio conversation, a passenger aboard the flight is reputed to have been exposed to an especially dangerous strain of the flu, and authorities are worried that . . ."

His phone rang and the director frowned. His secretary knew better than that. No, wait a minute. His secretary was gone for the day.

It rang again, and he picked it up angrily as the CNN report continued.

"Yes?"

". . . now said to be en route to an airport in Germany where the passengers and crew are to be quarantined in what may be an unprecedented incident in international civil aviation involving biological . . ."

"Say that again, please." His attention was divided, but the aide's voice sounded concerned about something. There was an emergency of some sort at Schiphol, the man reported.

". . . reported to be Quantum Flight Sixty-six, which was headed originally for New York. We emphasize that the aircraft and passengers are safe, but at present their new destination is not known. CNN will continue to monitor this breaking story as it develops."

"What kind of emergency?" The director glanced at the screen, irritated at the interruption. He picked up a pen and scribbled down the information coming across the phone line, including the call sign of the inbound airliner.

"He'll be down in fifteen minutes and needs a medical crew," the aide reported. The director nodded an invisible response and laid the pen down, then picked it up again and added the name of Quantum Airlines Flight 66.

He thanked the aide and ended the call, trying to focus on the screen once again. But the story was over.

What had he missed? There was something about a contaminated plane in London? Oh yes, it was refused landing and sent to be quarantined. They'd probably declared an emergency by now. Strange, he thought, that there would be two emergencies in the same area at the same time . . .

He stared at the notepad in front of him. All at once the number 66 on the pad coalesced with the words of the CNN anchor. It had to be the same flight the British had turned away. A 747, he had been told, but the aide had said nothing about potentially contagious passengers.

And it was diverting into Amsterdam! No one at Schiphol was ready to handle such a problem!

The director fairly dove for the phone.

ABOARD FLIGHT 66

Captain James Holland eased the big Boeing into a course correction to the right and waited for approach clearance. Amsterdam was a carpet of twinkling lights in the distance.

The controller's voice came back as expected. "Quantum Sixty-six, you're cleared for the ILS approach to runway three-five. Turn right now to a heading of three-two-zero degrees and join the localizer. Call Schiphol tower at the outer marker."

"Quantum Sixty-six, cleared approach, tower at the marker," Dick Robb replied, reaching down to touch the small toggle switch separating the current radio channel from the one for Schiphol's control tower. He hesitated the usual few seconds before switching, in case the controller had anything more to say on the old frequency.

This time the controller's voice returned almost instantly with an urgent tone.

"Quantum, are you still there?"

"Roger," Robb replied.

"We have a change to your clearance, sir."

The controller's voice trailed off for a few seconds, and another male voice could be heard in the background through the open transmitter. The controller had left his finger on the transmit button, but the background conversation was in Dutch—an exchange ending with *"ja"* as the controller noisily adjusted his microphone.

". . . Ah, Sixty-six, how many hours of fuel do you have on board, sir?"

An odd question, Holland thought. He looked at the fuel gauges again and ran a routine calculation. Eighty-two thousand pounds against an average fuel burn of twelve thousand per hour meant just under seven hours. Holland relayed the figure and Robb transmitted it.

The controller's voice came back within a minute.

"I am sorry, sir, but you will please turn left now to a heading of two-seven-zero degrees, and climb to flight level two-four-zero. Landing clearance for Schiphol Airport has been temporarily suspended, and we must put you in a holding pattern over water."

Holland and Robb looked at each other in alarm.

Holland triggered the radio first.

"Amsterdam Control, Sixty-six. We have a critically ill heart attack victim on board. We don't have any more time to waste. We have to get medical help instantly."

The reply was slow, apologetic, and very reluctant.

"I understand this, Sixty-six, but I am now directed to inform you that until we have permission to bring you in, you may not remain in Dutch airspace and you may not land at Schiphol. I am very sorry. We are working on it, I assure you."

Dick Robb came forward in his seat, his eyes flaring in alarm. He triggered the transmitter and fairly yelled into his headset microphone.

"Amsterdam Control, *WHY*? Why are we being treated like this?" Robb was almost sputtering. "Don't you understand the meaning of an emergency declaration? We're declaring an . . . an . . . emergency right now, and you have no choice but to let us land!"

Holland shook his head aggressively, but Robb continued.

"Amsterdam Control, Quantum Sixty-six is landing at Schiphol whether you like it or not!"

"Dick, good grief!" Holland said. "That won't work. I already tried it with London." He tried unsuccessfully to catch Robb's eye, but Robb wouldn't meet his gaze. He didn't want to be told no. He was scared, and James Holland knew the feeling well.

There was silence from Center for almost half a minute before the Dutch controller responded. It was a different voice this time, with no hint of sympathy. Obviously a supervisor or manager, his English impeccable but the Dutch accent pronounced.

"Quantum Sixty-six, any attempt to land on Dutch soil, or to stay in Dutch airspace without approval, will subject you to severe penalties, and may even be met with armed intervention. Because of your statement just now, we are asking for Dutch military assistance. Unless your aircraft cannot remain aloft mechanically, you must honor our instructions. We will make necessary arrangements as soon as possible."

Robb slumped in his seat as Holland took over the radio, his voice calm and authoritative.

"Amsterdam Control, Quantum Sixty-six is complying and turning left to a heading of two-seven-zero and beginning a climb to two-four-zero, awaiting holding instructions. The military will not be necessary. Would you please check to see if we could divert to either Brussels or Copenhagen, and if not, would Oslo or Stockholm take us?"

"We will check, Sixty-six. Please . . . believe us, we understand your emergency, but we are told there is a

. . . a possibility of sickness aboard your aircraft, and our authorities are not prepared to deal with that."

"Well, we need your help, Amsterdam Control, that's all I can say."

Holland pushed the power up and reconnected the autoflight systems before turning to Robb, who was staring straight ahead.

"Get the company on the satellite phone, Dick. Find out what they've got in mind. There's got to be a plan. We have to bring this ship down somewhere! Even if our patient in the back recovers, we don't have enough fuel now to make New York with legal reserves."

The interphone call chime rang at the same instant and Robb answered it. He mumbled a few words and disconnected, then stared out the windscreen again for a while. When he spoke at last, his eyes were straight ahead on the horizon.

"That was the head mama downstairs," he said in a matter-of-fact tone. "She says to tell you the emergency's over. Your passenger is dead."

SIX

By the time James Holland reached Dallas Operations
on the satellite phone, Quantum 66 had stabilized at
thirty-one thousand feet in a holding pattern over the
blackness of the nighttime North Sea. With a confused
cadre of executives and dispatchers on the other end,
Holland begged for assistance and instructions as the
747 bored circular holes in the sky, flying fifteen miles to
the north, turning left a hundred eighty degrees, then
flying fifteen miles to the south before turning left again
to fly north along the same track. The holding pattern
path was programmed in the flight management computer, and the computer, in turn, could keep the big
Boeing on the same racetrack until the fuel tanks ran
dry. At least, Holland thought, it was a safe place in the
sky to park the seven-hundred-thousand-pound aircraft
until the Dutch made up their minds to let them land in
Amsterdam.

Dick Robb was fuming at the delay, and fuming at
Holland's low-key negotiations with the company, but
he refused to take control. His eyes darted minute by
minute from the instruments to the captain to the fading, post-sunset visage of stratus clouds over the North
Sea ahead of them, but he said nothing.

Back in Texas, Quantum's vice president of Operations had been snatched from his ranch in a helicopter,
but he sounded as confused as the dispatchers at Dal-

las–Fort Worth airport, who had been unwilling to make any decisions without him.

"Captain, you say the Dutch controllers have you in holding?" the Operations chief asked.

Holland recited the facts for the third time. *Yes,* they were in holding. *Yes,* the Dutch had held out hope they might be allowed to land. *Yes,* their heart attack victim was dead, and was supposed to be carrying a terrible strain of the flu. And *yes,* they were in need of a place to land. With a few more hours at low altitude, Holland told him, that need could become critical.

"Well," began the highly paid decision maker from the left seat of a Jet Ranger hurtling toward the airline's Dallas headquarters, "have we contacted our State Department?"

There was another confused burble of voices from Dallas as the director of Flight Control confessed he didn't know whom to call.

"We've called the FAA. We've reported this to their headquarters," the DFC offered.

"What'd they say?" the Operations VP asked.

"They said to stand by. I got the impression they were assembling a team in their command post in Washington."

"Did they *say* that? *Are* they calling the Dutch authorities?" the VP asked.

There was a telling hesitation from the director of Flight Control as Holland listened, the voices crisp on the satellite connection.

The director sighed. "Sir, I don't think they have any better idea than we do who to dial. There are no procedures for this. We have telephone numbers for our Operations at Schiphol Airport and we've called the Dutch Aviation Authority—that's their version of the FAA—but they told us to stand by, and that the order not to let Sixty-six land came from somewhere in the Dutch government."

The Operations VP knew everyone was waiting for his pronouncement. He'd built an organization that knew better than to function without his instant involvement and approval. Now they were all waiting for him to be brilliant. He cleared his throat and tried to sound confident. "Okay, get the FAA command post up on the telephone net here, maintain an open line, and have them contact the State Department duty officer."

"What," Holland interrupted, "do you want us to do in the meantime?"

"Who's that?" the VP asked.

"This is Flight Sixty-six."

"Oh. Sorry, Captain. Stay in holding and keep the line open for a callback. We'll have an answer shortly. You have enough fuel?"

"Enough for five hours at altitude and perhaps three down low, but we're already too low on fuel to make New York with legal reserves."

"Okay . . . okay. Hang in there. We'll call you back."

"Sir," Holland continued, "we have no information on exactly what kind of flu our passenger, and we, have been exposed to. It's a strange coincidence, to say the least. I mean, the very passenger who brings aboard a bad strain of the flu drops dead from a heart attack? That's hard to buy. Whatever type of flu this is we supposedly have aboard, it's obviously scaring the Germans, and I need to know why. What are we facing up here?"

He heard the vice president sigh. "As I say, Captain, just stand by. We'll work on getting you some answers, and we'll call you back."

Holland terminated the connection and briefed Robb on the call, shaking his head. "Their instructions were to keep holding, and don't call us, we'll call you."

Robb's jaw clenched even tighter as Holland unstrapped and moved out of the seat.

"You've got her," Holland told him. "I'll be back in a few minutes."

It was interesting, Holland thought, that Robb hadn't even questioned where he was going. He was obviously on the verge of exploding.

Holland left the cockpit and entered the small rest-room just outside the cockpit, locking the door behind him. The mirror framed the image of an unhappy man, and he looked at himself in resignation. He looked tired. Hell, he *was* tired. The lines and creases in what passed for a face were becoming alarming, and the past six months as a bachelor had done nothing to help.

Thoughts of the present interceded. Getting away from Robb for even a few seconds had seemed even more important than dealing with this curious crisis, which hadn't begun to frighten him until now. Barb, of course, was already panicked, as was Brenda, whose heroic efforts to save Helms had directly exposed her to whatever he was carrying. Could it be bad enough and dangerous enough to justify treating them as pariahs, or was a thundering herd of cowardly bureaucrats simply overreacting to something they didn't understand?

Holland shuddered at both thoughts. What flu could be so bad that Great Britain wouldn't even admit a heart patient who'd allegedly been exposed?

But the passenger was already sick! Holland reminded himself. *We are exposed!*

The idea of quarantining an entire 747 full of passengers was unheard of. The fact that the German authorities were frightened by whatever Helms had been exposed to was beginning to frighten Holland. That and the simple fact that they still weren't sure where to land —or who was going to make that decision.

He finished in the restroom and walked back through the sixty-foot length of the upper-deck section, then descended the stairway to the main cabin below, feeling disgusted. The satellite conversation had done nothing to calm the gnawing worry that the crew of Flight 66 was all but on its own in solving this crisis.

Holland stopped at the foot of the stairway and chided himself. That attitude was unacceptable. It was Quantum's aircraft, Quantum's crew, and Quantum's liability, and the same Operations chief he had just talked to had crushed the careers of pilots who had tried to get innovative without company direction. There was only one way to handle it, Holland concluded as he stepped off the last step.

Wait for instructions.

The stairway descended into the side of the business class cabin. With several dozen eyes tracking him, Captain Holland turned toward the rear of the aircraft. Helms's body had been moved forward from coach into the rear of business class, and a blanket now covered the deceased man. Brenda Hopkins stood nearby, exhausted. He'd been briefed on her heroics, and she moved toward him now. He put his arm around her and held her for a few minutes, walking her forward of the dividing curtain for a bit of privacy as she lowered her head and sobbed quietly on his shoulder, the emotional dam breaking at last. He was aware of her exposure, but she needed the support.

"I tried my best," she began, but he shushed her.

"I know. I know you did. I'm proud of you. He might have made it, too, if London had let us land."

Barb Rollins, the lead flight attendant, materialized beside them, waiting until Brenda had raised her head before asking for an update.

He motioned them forward into the first class galley and pulled the curtains, filling them in on the situation and the holding pattern and the reluctance of three separate nations to let them land.

Barb's eyes were suddenly huge. "What are you saying? You mean someone's exposed us to some superflu? A swine flu type of thing?" Her New York accent had sharpened to a cutting edge, and Holland raised his hand to calm her.

"It's probably precautionary and everyone's overreacting," he said. "We'll get it sorted out. In the meantime, I . . . can't tell the passengers what I don't know."

"They're all asking for explanations!" Barb said, pushing. "All you've said on the PA is that we're awaiting clearance to land. Most everyone aboard knows it

doesn't take this long. They know Frankfurt isn't surrounded by water. They know something's wrong, and
they know the heart attack patient didn't make it. And
many of them, James, know he came on ill."

Holland rubbed his forehead and closed his eyes before replying. "Barb, if I even suggest what's really going
on, at least a dozen people will get sick out of fear
alone."

"You want to lie to them?" she asked, much too
loudly.

He motioned for her to quiet down and looked
around, making certain no feet could be seen beneath
the curtains on either side of the galley.

"No, I don't want to lie to them. But I can hardly tell
them that at the moment we have no place to go and
our company's too confused to figure out what we
should do, and that . . . that they may have been exposed to some dreadful flu for which no one's been vac-
cinated—a badass flu scary enough to force three
governments into turning away a civil aircraft in distress."

"You're going to have to tell them something, Captain. And quickly."

The curtain to their right parted and a tall, distin-
guished-looking black man with silver hair stuck his face
inside, his eyes locking on Holland.

"Captain, excuse me for interrupting. I'm Lee Lancaster. My aide said you wanted to speak with me."

Barb quietly gathered Brenda and left the galley as
Holland motioned him in and extended his hand.

"Yes, Ambassador, I do."

"Rachael explained what's happening. Any change?"

They leaned against the serving counter as Holland
described the confusion back in Texas.

"Bottom line, Ambassador? They don't know who to
call."

"Well"—Lancaster looked Holland squarely in the
eye—"so happens, I do."

"I was hoping you'd say that."

"You have a satellite phone in your cockpit I could use?"

Holland nodded.

"Then let's go. There are civilized ways to handle these things."

AMSTERDAM

The director of airports for the Netherlands replaced the receiver gently and stared at the wall for a few seconds, hoping no one would ask why his face had turned ashen. He could imagine the cross section of humanity aboard Flight 66: businessmen, children, husbands, wives, lovers, saints, and sinners. All together in an aluminum tube.

An aluminum tube no one wanted.

He looked down at the telephone again as if a better answer might appear on the liquid crystal readout. It was shameful! The Dutch were a caring people. *He* was a caring person. How could they refuse safe haven to two hundred fifty or more people in need of a little medical observation?

"What is the verdict?" The chief of Amsterdam Approach had walked up quietly. Flight 66 was becoming a fixture in the holding pattern over the water fifty miles west, and every controller in the building ached to bring them in.

The director of airports shook his head sadly without looking up.

"Our government says no. Until we know how dangerous this influenza strain is to which they've been exposed, we cannot allow them in."

"What, then?"

The director looked the chief in the eye. "We've tried Belgium, Denmark, Sweden"—he lofted a frustrated gesture of dismissal at the ceiling—"all of our dear EC members . . . everyone. They're all pressing the Germans for answers and getting only dark cautions. No one wants a major flu outbreak."

"These people have to go somewhere!"

He nodded. "I know it, Hans. My God, I know it, but apparently not on this continent." He looked at the distant window, roughly facing west. The sun had long since disappeared, and only a galaxy of twinkling lights was visible, punctuated by an occasional jetliner on final approach. "The American government will have to find them a destination."

"Can't we at least refuel them?"

The director shook his head again. "Political decision. The orders are clear and certain. This aircraft is not allowed in Dutch airspace. They're so afraid of this particular flu virus, they're even worried it could contaminate the area through the cabin air expelled out of the airplane's pressurization outflow valves. That is completely odd! I'm told"—he shook his head again disgustedly—"I'm told we've even launched a couple of fighters to make sure they don't come back. So much for humanitarian concern, eh?"

The chief nodded slowly as he furiously scratched his head in a nervous gesture the director understood.

"Don't worry, Hans, I'll tell them. That's my job."

"No, I was calculating their flying range. I suppose they could still reach Canada with their remaining fuel, and certainly Iceland or Greenland. Those are the only airports within range to the west, I think."

"They'd better do it secretly, then," the director said.

The chief looked alarmed as he examined the director's eyes and realized he was dead serious.

"Why?"

"Because Canada, Greenland, and Iceland have also said no."

SEVEN

Deputy Director Jonathan Roth entered the small, secure conference room as he usually did: peering suspiciously over the top of his half-frame glasses and clutching an overstuffed folder covered with classified markings. With his bow tie and his slightly gaunt, six-foot-two-inch frame, he looked—one long-departed underling had once written—like an expatriate Oxford don reduced to the role of intimidating prep school freshmen in the colonies.

Roth laid the folder at the head of the mahogany table and surveyed the room with no hint of a smile. He hated being rousted out of a productive afternoon by a crisis in which the Company wasn't even on center stage. Yet he had no choice. The order to involve the CIA had come from the Situation Room at the White House as a direct result of the State Department's hitting the panic button.

Roth motioned wordlessly toward the chairs, and the three men and one woman—including two analysts pressed into service during the previous hour—sat down as the door was shut and the CONFERENCE IN PROGRESS sign illuminated. His prime area was terrorism and the Middle East, but with the Director in the hospital in a coma and not expected to recover, the watch was his.

"I've been told," Roth began, removing his glasses,

"that you have all been briefed about this airliner, Quantum Sixty-six. Is that correct?"

They all nodded, and several exchanged small glances. Roth was known as difficult to please—everyone at Langley had his or her own favorite story about hapless employees drawing the fury of his imperious contempt for small shortcomings.

"Very well," he said. "What we need to find out within the next sixty minutes is the following. One, exactly what type of influenza, or viral agent, are we dealing with? And two, precisely how hot, or dangerous, is it? And three, what are the technical parameters of this flu—if it is a flu—in terms of incubation period, pathology, symptomatology, infectious potential, et cetera."

They all scribbled notes as Roth raised a finger.

"In addition, I want to know who the ranking expert is in the country on such a strain, and I want to know whether we have anyone here at Langley who knows whether an influenza virus like this can be spread by the air-conditioning system of a jetliner."

A dark-haired man with the square-jawed features of an NFL linebacker raised an index finger and Roth nodded in his direction.

"You're speaking for the group, I take it, Mark?" Roth said.

"Yes, sir," Mark Hastings replied.

On his left side, an analyst significantly junior to Hastings smiled inwardly but commanded himself to keep a poker face. *Showtime again,* he thought. Everyone knew Hastings was a trusted clandestine operative for Roth when it came to internal projects. So why the charade?

"Here's what we have so far," Hastings was saying. "The person believed to have been exposed *is* the same passenger who died aboard the flight nearly two hours ago, supposedly from a heart attack; an American professor named Helms. The German Health Ministry was informed early this morning, their time, that two days ago this man Helms unwittingly came into contact with a quarantined German citizen in the contagious stages of a dangerous strain of what they're calling a human influenza virus. According to what they'll tell us, it was an employee of a biological testing lab belonging to Hauptmann Pharmaceutical who had been isolated with a bad case of flu. He became delirious and left the building, and exposed this man Helms when he tried to break into the professor's rental car. Helms is an American college professor. Or was. When Professor Helms left the scene, Hauptmann triggered a nationwide government-backed search for him. Helms slipped through their net, however, and turned up ill on Flight Sixty-six —and then had a heart attack."

Roth leaned forward. "That's not believable! They're going berserk over a *flu*? They isolated a worker with flu, and he *got away*?"

Hastings was shaking his head and smiling. "We don't believe a word of it either, sir, but that's still the official line."

"What about the heart attack? Was it really that, or did this professor die from this so-called flu?"

Hastings shook his head. "We don't know. The professor's body is still on the plane, but the Germans insist that this flu may be able to bring on a heart attack. We won't know until we can run an autopsy."

Jon Roth leaned back in his chair and scratched his chin before looking back at the members of the group, one by one.

"What if something lethal got away from that lab? What do they do there? Do we know?"

One of the analysts explained that the facility was just coming on-line to do research in antibiotics and vaccines.

"Which means they would be fooling around with live cultures and live viruses," Roth said.

"Yes, sir"—Mark nodded—"but they were just starting up. The facility really hasn't formally opened, but when it does, they'll be equipped, we're told, for up to full Level Four pathogen research."

Roth nodded silently and leveled a finger at the others.

"You are all aware of what a Level Four pathogen is?"

All except one nodded.

"A highly infectious human disease, usually viral, which has a high mortality rate and virtually no cure, vaccine, or treatment," Roth added.

"Like the Ebola Zaire, or the Marburg viruses," Mark said.

Jon Roth nodded again. "If they were gearing up for such research, it's possible that something frightening could have gotten away from them." Roth looked at Hastings. "Could this be a military bug, Mark? Did it get loose from some lab that they want to hide from us?"

Hastings hesitated, this time looking Roth squarely in the eye.

"There's no way to know yet. We're querying all the sources we can think of. They could be holding back, but then, Hauptmann could be lying to the German officials as well."

"Your best guess?" Roth asked.

Hastings looked at the others. They had held a quick caucus before Jon Roth's arrival. Hastings was de facto spokesman now as he turned back to the deputy director.

"We do indeed think something got away from them, and I think the German government suspects it but doesn't really know. Was it the German military doing prohibited research?" Mark shook his head and raised his hands palms up. "I can tell you the German health officials are scared out of their minds. Their reactions indicate they really *do* believe it's far more serious than a simple flu."

He pushed a small stack of papers across the table marked SECRET. "In terms of major epidemics—or worldwide *pan*demics—this was prepared last year, based on the Ebola Reston scare, and in anticipation of some breakout of a Level Four pathogen someday in the future. This was prepared by *our* Army specialists. It's scary as hell!"

"Do we have a name for this so-called new flu strain?" Roth asked quietly as he leafed through the report.

"Not a clue, sir. We need to twist their arms for the straight story, and get some idea what this really is and where it came from. So far, they've just tried to contain it. No one over there's had time to think about what to do if they can't contain it. It's time to confront them with that."

Roth nodded. "But they turned around and refused to let the aircraft come back into Germany. Why?"

Hastings nodded. "We think"—he glanced around, visually polling the rest of the group—"we think that's evidence of how scared they are. That was undoubtedly a political decision made in Bonn by someone high up, and now, by refusing reentry, they've managed to scare all the other European member nations as well."

"Which is why," Roth finished, "that plane is still circling over the North Sea with nowhere to go."

"Sir," Hastings added, "let me reemphasize that the German Health Ministry over there—a man named Zeitner to be precise—is telling us they believe the incubation period of this so-called flu bug is between forty-eight and sixty hours. That's bizarre. That's almost unheard of speed for a virus! If Professor Helms is any example—if it was this virus that killed him and not a heart attack—then it's important to remember that only fifty-one hours elapsed from time of exposure to his death aboard Flight Sixty-six."

Roth put down the report, removed his glasses again, and rubbed his eyes. "All right. How about the question of the aircraft cabin? Even if this professor was contaminated and infectious, does that necessarily mean those not touching him would get it?" Roth dropped his hand to the table and looked back at Hastings.

"We can't answer that yet, sir, but we do have an

expert right here on staff, and we're trying to locate
him. He's an ex-FAA doc by the name of Sanders, uh"
—Hastings consulted his notes—"Rusty Sanders. Got
himself booted out of the FAA a few years ago by going
public with worries about jetliner air-conditioning systems recirculating airborne viruses."

"The FAA fires him for insubordination, so, of
course, *we* hire him." Roth smirked and shook his head
in mock wonder.

"He knows his stuff, Mr. Roth," Hastings said.

"He'd better," Roth replied. "He damn well better."

ABOARD FLIGHT 66—8:45 P.M. (1945Z)

James Holland picked up the interphone handset and
hesitated over the button that would tie him into the
public address system. His mind raced through the possibilities of what to tell them now. An hour before, as
Ambassador Lancaster had huddled over the satellite
phone and held a hot poker to the backside of the State
Department in Washington, Holland had tried to be
truthful—to a point. It was true, he had told them, that
the passenger with the heart attack had not made it. No,
they were not now planning to return to Frankfurt. And
yes, they were in a holding pattern over the North Sea.
The reason, he had told them, was an international diplomatic brouhaha involving what to do about a death
from unknown causes over international waters. Holland could hear the expressions of anger from the passengers on the upper deck through the cockpit door as
he spoke. Bureaucratic nonsense was keeping them in
limbo while the diplomats tried to sort out where to go.
They had burned too much fuel to continue to Kennedy,
he told them.

But he had said nothing of the flu virus or quaran-
tines.

Now, it was unavoidable. Two hundred forty-four passengers were beginning to demand action.

Holland pressed the PA button and raised the handset to his mouth.

"Folks, this is Captain Holland."

He glanced at Dick Robb. He'd told Robb what he was going to do, and Robb hadn't objected. In fact, he'd hardly reacted. Holland pressed the PA button:

"I apologize for keeping you in suspense, and I again deeply apologize for this unprecedented delay. I . . . . our situation here needs some straight-talk explanation. Please listen carefully and bear with me. I didn't tell you the whole story a while ago because, frankly, I wasn't sure I believed it myself. There *is* a diplomatic brouhaha in progress, as I told you before, but it's not because of someone's dying over international waters.

"After we left Frankfurt, the German government notified us, and all other European nations, that one passenger who boarded this aircraft with us in Frankfurt had been exposed to a new strain of the flu, but did not know it. So, what that means, I'm sorry to have to tell you, is that we're facing a potential quarantine. All of us. For how long—whether days or hours—I do not know.

"Please understand that this is not my choice. Your pilots have been trying unsuccessfully for the last hour to get landing clearance first in London, then Frankfurt, and then Amsterdam. Now our State Department is involved and searching for the best place to bring us down. We've already burned too much gas flying around at low altitude to continue on to New York without refueling, so we *will* be landing somewhere fairly shortly.

"Personally, I suspect this is a monstrous over-reaction. But the inescapable fact is that just about every government down there believes that all of us may now be exposed to this mystery strain, and as long as they believe that, we're essentially at the mercy of their decisions."

Holland paused and organized his thoughts while he kept the PA button depressed. In the cabin below, virtually no one was speaking as they all strained to hear the next words. Wide eyes and worried looks painted every face, and in the corner of the 2L door alcove, Brenda Hopkins felt for the fold-out flight attendant seat and slid into it, her heart pounding. The memory of Ernest Helms's mouth surrounded by hers became a mockery now. Was he the sick passenger? Whatever he had, she would get it for certain.

Holland's voice rang through the cabin again:

"Here's the point, folks. Exactly how the health authorities below are going to want to proceed with this—whether we're looking at a three- or four-day quarantine or some such—I do not know. I'm well aware that many of you have critical schedules, and none of you wants to be delayed over Christmas by something like this, but until we can sort this out, I'm afraid we're just going to have to be patient.

"I'm also well aware that all of us are vitally interested in staying healthy, and that you'll want to know a lot more—as I do—about this mystery malady, and whether it's really a threat or not. As of this moment, I can't answer those questions, but I promise to keep you informed. In the meantime, in return for my being completely frank with you about this, I hope, and in fact I expect, that all of you will refrain from panic or overreaction or groundless speculation."

The interphone chimes began ringing almost immediately as the cabin exploded with worried voices, with people getting to their feet in various stages of shock and upset. The flight attendants were checking in from all over the aircraft to relay the passengers' many anxious questions. The roar from below was audible in the cockpit.

Holland punched on the PA again:

"This is Captain Holland again. Folks, please don't batter my flight attendants with questions they can't answer. Since I haven't had time to brief *them,* they don't know anything more than you know. And flight attendants, I want all of you to please check in on interphone for a quick briefing."

He held the handset to his ear and waited for all the flight attendant stations, the upper deck, and the crew rest loft above the rear galley to check in.

"Okay, everyone," he said. "I've told the passengers everything, except this: It was Helms who was exposed to the flu, but no one knows if the heart attack was related. Someone else may get sick while we're up here. If you see anyone showing signs of illness, *quietly* let me know. I'll want to get them apart from the rest of the passengers as quickly as possible."

"Where to, Captain?" The question came from three flight attendants at once.

"The crew rest loft. That would isolate them completely. Enlist the help of that Swiss doctor. First, of course, make sure they're really ill with valid symptoms."

"Captain, this . . . this is Brenda at two-left. I've been horribly exposed. So has Dr. Turnheir, the Swiss physician. We both gave Professor Helms mouth-to-mouth . . ."

James Holland heard her frightened voice trail off.

"Brenda, we don't even know if it's really dangerous," he said. "But . . . perhaps we'd better get the professor's body to the crew rest loft and confine those who've, ah, handled him there too."

"With him, in the loft?" Brenda asked.

Barb Rollins chimed in. "James, the loft's okay for

the body, but let's just isolate Brenda and the doctor on the upper deck."

Holland was nodding, unseen. "Absolutely, Barb. Good suggestion. Brenda, I'll be back to talk to you as soon as I know anything about this bug, but keep in mind that it's probably all a false alarm."

The satellite phone rang in the cockpit at the same moment that Dick Robb spotted airborne lights approaching from the west.

Holland pulled the handset to his ear.

"Sixty-six? Dallas Operations."

"This is Sixty-six," Holland said.

"Okay, we've got a solution, I think, Captain. The diplomats have gotten the Air Force involved, and they're sending a couple of fighters out to escort you to Mildenhall Air Base."

Holland hesitated. What appeared to be a pair of fighters were off his left wing, and he reached up to flip on the wing illumination lights. They were F-15 Eagles, and unlike the Dutch F-16s, which had flown with them for a while, he could see the U.S. Air Force markings.

"Mildenhall is in the U.K., right?" Holland asked, knowing very well the base sat less than a hundred miles north of London.

"I think so," Operations confirmed. "Anyway, you're supposed to contact them on one-twenty-four-point-five-five. The fighters, I mean."

"They're already here. But have the British relented about our landing on their soil?"

There was a pause on the line from Dallas.

"Apparently, Captain. Just follow their instructions. The Air Force will take care of you and the passengers at Mildenhall."

"Are we looking at a quarantine or what?"

Holland could hear voices at the other end of the connection before the dispatcher returned the handset to his face. "Ah, we don't know what they're planning.

We just want to get you on the ground. Contact us as soon as you're there."

Holland thanked him and replaced the receiver, glad that Robb had been listening in through the interphone panel.

Robb nodded and dialed in the frequency. "Sixty-six is up one-twenty-four-point-five-five," Robb transmitted.

"Roger, Sixty-six, this is Fox One, off your left wing on a handheld radio. Turn off your transponder now, please, and follow us. You are now to answer only to the call Fox Three. Understand, sir?"

"Roger," Robb replied. "I take it our hosts are not in agreement with this visit?"

There was silence from the fighters and Robb regretted saying it. These fellows were flyers acting on orders, just like himself.

"Ah . . . our commander is ready for you, sir. Now, please stay on this frequency and do not talk to any air traffic control facility. We're going to start a left turn and begin descending. We'll keep it slow and smooth for you, so just stay on my wing."

The two Eagles began a left bank and Holland clicked off the autopilot to follow them. They began descending, keeping their speed back as promised in deference to the huge 747.

"You understand what's happening here?" Holland asked Robb, who seemed excited all of a sudden.

"They're sneaking us in, of course," Robb replied.

Holland nodded. "And unless the Brits have approved it, there's going to be hell to pay."

In the first class cabin Lee Lancaster had noticed the lights to the left, but couldn't make them out at first. Finally a light came on illuminating the jets, and Old Glory came into view—as did the Air Force symbol on the fuselage.

Why Eagles? he wondered. There were no U.S. bases left in the Netherlands, and only a few in the U.K. with joint British and American tenants. The Eagles couldn't make it to Iceland or Canada without a tanker escort, and with no one shooting at them, why was a fighter escort necessary to begin with?

Unless some people had lost their minds at the Pentagon and decided to pull an end run on the British.

Lancaster was nibbling a fingernail and watching the formation as they began banking left. When Flight 66 followed, he knew.

The ambassador covered the distance to the stairway and the cockpit door inside a minute and knocked with as restrained a beat as he could manage.

The door lock was released and he pushed it open and stuck his head inside.

"Captain, Lee Lancaster. Are those fighters taking us into the U.K.?"

Holland turned in his seat slightly and nodded before turning back to the task of holding formation.

Lancaster closed the door behind him and sat on the elevated jump seat behind the center pedestal.

"Did the British approve this?"

Holland began shaking his head in the negative before replying.

Robb beat him to it.

"Doesn't matter, Mr. Ambassador," Robb said. "We're sneaking into Mildenhall cleverly disguised as their wingman, although a bit overfed."

Lancaster missed the attempt at humor and shook his head, addressing only Holland.

"Do you realize that if we touch down without their permission, we'll create a major diplomatic incident?"

Holland glanced around at the ambassador again briefly. "What choice do I have? My company ordered us to comply. Why would it be a problem if the Air Force arranged it?"

"Because Mildenhall is a Royal Air Force base, with the U.S. Air Force there as a tenant unit. We don't own that real estate, and it sounds to me like someone back at the Pentagon is trying to be a hero. You can't handle

diplomatic problems like this without creating fifty
more. May I use your satellite phone again?"

"Anytime, sir."

Lancaster picked up the receiver and began punching
in numbers.

"Lee, please," he said.

Holland had been distracted. He glanced around
again. "What? Sir?"

"You call me Lee, I'll call you James. Okay?"

"Sure, uh, Lee. Thanks."

"Might as well be less formal. We're going to be together for quite a while—especially if we land somewhere without permission."

MILDENHALL AIR BASE, U.K.

The brigadier general running the U.S. Air Force wing
at Mildenhall Air Base had been firing off orders for the
past twenty minutes with growing concern. He had
heard of the crisis two hours before on CNN, but the
thought that it could engulf his operation had been un-
thinkable—until his emergency communications network had corked off. An overly excited three-star
general in a command post at the Pentagon had had a
single question: Did they have enough chemical warfare
gear to handle a 747 and its passengers?

He'd done a quick mental calculation and answered
yes. Within ten minutes the chief master sergeant who
handled such things delivered an agonized no, but it was
too late to back out. While two Eagles were dispatched
with special instructions, a huge hangar was being
cleared of all aircraft while no fewer than a hundred
officers and airmen were told to suit up in chemical
warfare gear they'd hardly touched since Desert Storm.
The plan, the general had briefed everyone, was to get
the 747's nose as far into the hangar as possible, try to
rig a plastic-sealed stairway to the forward door, and use
the airplane itself for a holding area until the disease

control specialists could give them more guidance. The flight doctor in charge of the base clinic, a full colonel, had been summoned, and had confirmed that all but a special class of viral pathogens could be handled safely.

"Under no circumstances," the general had warned everyone, "is anyone across the field in the Royal Air Force to be told. This is a U.S. operation only."

AIR ROUTE TRAFFIC CONTROL CENTER, LONDON

With his supervisor at his elbow, the air traffic controller monitoring the North Sea sector between Amsterdam and Great Britain now hunched over his scope, watching a flight of American F-15 Eagles approach the east coast.

"You're sure?" the supervisor asked.

"Quite certain. Normally they would have been on the fringe of my radar sector, but I saw the data block drop out—I'd been watching Sixty-six in his holding pattern—then the two Eagles who'd been cleared over to Maastricht Control suddenly changed their clearance back to Mildenhall and I spotted a faint return from Sixty-six in an apparent left turn with the Eagles."

"You've cleared them in?"

"Right, but they're not alone. The buggers are trying to ferret him in."

The supervisor stood up with his jaw open. "Unbelievable!"

"What do I do?" the controller asked.

"Well . . . play along, by all means, while I get someone on the phone."

The supervisor disappeared into the background muttering the same word over and over again: "Incredible!"

EIGHT

Jonathan Roth sat pensively behind his ornate mahogany desk and rubbed his temple with one hand while holding a telephone receiver with the other. He had waved in Mark Hastings minutes before, but Hastings refused to sit. He stood now like a dutiful soldier on the other side of the desk as Roth waited for the White House aide to return to the phone.

"Yes, I'm still here. Who the hell are we reporting to over there? You? The President? The Pentagon? State? Who, for Chrissakes?"

Roth nodded a few times as he picked up a sheet of paper and handed it to Hastings, who could hear the echo of a voice coming from the receiver.

"So State's handling it, right?" Roth cupped his hand over the mouthpiece and looked at Hastings. "For God's sake, sit down, Mark! You're making me nervous."

He turned back to the phone.

"What fight?" he asked. He nodded a few times as the reply came, then scribbled a note before ending the call and turning back to Hastings.

"Well, here is the latest installment. It seems the Pentagon is trying to sneak the aircraft into a base north of London without British permission. The State Department, which claims it knew nothing of this plan, says it was tipped off by one of our ambassadors who happens to be on board. Now, while the assistant secretary of state is tearing up the phone lines trying to reach the President to convince him to order the Air Force to stop their infiltration attempt before they start a small war, all of them are turning to us and demanding we tell them *right now* how big a threat this virus really is."

"Good grief," Hastings said.

"That . . . would be as appropriate a comment as any, I suppose," Roth replied. "But the bottom line is, they're still waiting for us. They want to know how scared everyone should be. So. Given that latest flash, how scared are we, Mark?" Roth leaned forward in his desk chair with an artificial air of expectancy.

"Ah . . ." Hastings began.

A new voice washed over Mark Hastings from behind.

"Scared as hell, I'm afraid, if it's anything like a Biosafety Level Four virus!"

Mark turned to see a man of medium build wearing a wrinkled suit with a red tie loosely hanging around an open collar. The voice was tinged with friendliness.

"Sorry for the intrusion, Director Roth, but I was told you needed to see me instantly, if not sooner, and I kinda ran all the way here."

Jonathan Roth peered at the man's clothes with obvious disapproval. "So it would appear. And you are . . . ?"

The newcomer entered the room with his hand outstretched. "Oh, sorry, sir. I'm Dr. Rusty Sanders, from downstairs."

Roth met his handshake reluctantly, then introduced Mark Hastings.

"You've been briefed, then?" Hastings asked pleasantly, shaking Sanders' hand in turn.

Sanders inclined his head toward the door. "Sherry Ellis, I believe her name was, from your department. She filled me in on a secure line." He looked around at the ornate paneling replete with certificates and plaques.

"Impressive office, sir. Never been in this section before."

Roth leaned forward testily. "We didn't ask you here to approve the decor, Doctor. We need answers immediately, and we need answers with impeccable authority."

Sanders was still looking around as he replied. "Understood, sir. I understand the Germans are telling us this is a flu, but we're worried that their panicked conduct indicates something worse, maybe even a Level Four. If we have even the slightest reason to suspect something that bad, the highest level of caution and concern is fully justified, which is why I don't think I'd even want that aircraft back in the U.S."

Roth sat back hard. "Really?"

Sanders placed both hands on the edge of the desk, still standing, and leaned over slightly. "Yep. But there's a major problem here."

"Which is?" Roth asked.

"We don't know exactly *what* this virus is, whether it is an influenza, and whether it belongs to any known class. I need to know precisely what the sick research worker went through in terms of symptoms, and whether he has recovered. We need to know how bad a strain it is so we can predict how less healthy people will react. The elderly, for instance. If it's really bad, what's the mortality rate? How does it transfer? What properties does this strain have? The Germans probably don't know, so they're playing it safe, which is smart. But if I have the correct information, all we know about this is that it seems to have started in a new biological research lab in Bavaria, and the Germans are insisting it's just a bad strain of the flu while acting like it's much worse."

Mark Hastings handed over the single sheet of paper to Rusty Sanders and watched his face for a response.

Sanders whistled faintly as he read. "So the lab worker who exposed the American professor has died, and *he's the second one*?"

Roth nodded. "We just received that from Bonn. They claim to have just found out."

Sanders nodded and handed the page back.

"Okay. We've got two dead patients, and a little idea of how fast this flu can progress. We have no electron microscope examinations or samples of the virus itself, we have no classifications, we're totally in the dark! Then we have one passenger who died on the aircraft who was admittedly exposed to this agent, but whose overt symptoms leading to death could also be those of a simple heart attack. The Germans are talking two-day incubation periods, which is almost unprecedented for a virus. Even the hottest virus needs time to get into the host at the cellular level and replicate itself, and two days isn't much! But if their statements are correct, this one could rewrite the texts. Bottom line? We don't know what the Germans encountered, we have no confirmed knowledge that it killed—or infected—the deceased passenger, and until we know *what* it is, we'll have no idea what it *does* . . . that is, the symptomatology." Sanders folded his arms as he resumed admiring the walls and began moving toward a large painting of the Old West.

Roth sighed. "Mark, you recommended we treat this like a Level Four until we know otherwise, correct?"

Sanders answered before Hastings could reply. "Mark, if you said that, you're right." Sanders turned to Roth. "I've been briefed, Director, that this might even be the result of clandestine military research in Germany. But the most frightening potential to me is if we have a combination of a short incubation period and high mortality rate. If these two are present—if this kills within three days, for instance, with a seventy or eighty percent death rate—we're in terrible danger if it spreads to the general population anywhere in the world."

"Well? What are the possibilities, Dr. Sanders, what's the danger level, and what should we do?" Roth asked, irritated at the doctor's continuing survey of his office.

"The worst case is that this is some sort of mutated

viral pathogen and not a flu at all—something that can
be transmitted by an airborne medium, survive in that
medium for several hours, and produce illness and rapid
death within forty-eight hours. The airborne transmission aspect is the scariest, and that's probably why you
called for me. I know the recirculation systems on Boeing, Airbus, and Douglas aircraft."

"Could they spread it, if it were a worst-case bug?"

Sanders nodded. "If it can be transmitted by air at all,
theoretically a jetliner's recirculation system could
spread it if it got past the filters." He removed his hands
from his pockets and sat down in the chair.

"Okay, would everyone on a seven-forty-seven get it?
Probably not. Can the air filters on the recirc fans filter
out viral pathogens? Some, under certain circumstances, but perhaps not a virulent strain." He started to
get up, then thought better of it and sank back in the
chair. "Bottom line, sir? If there is a killer virus on
board that aircraft and it can spread by air, we have to
assume virtually everyone's exposed. If it's highly communicable by air, those not now exposed will soon be
exposed, and if it has a high mortality rate, we could
lose them all."

Roth sat back and swiveled his chair toward the window. "That's exactly what I was afraid of."

Sanders continued, ticking off a list on his fingers.

"We need an autopsy of the heart attack victim, we
need cultures, we need immediate lab animal exposure,
we need a biologically safe enclosure, bioisolation suits,
and a portable lab. The Army people at Fort Detrick
can make this happen. And, just in case—just in case
this really is something very, very contagious and deadly
along the lines of a true Biosafety Level Four—I'd recommend we do the autopsy somewhere offshore."

Roth and Hastings looked at each other before Roth
replied.

"Such as?"

Sanders spotted a world map on the wall by the window. He sprang to his feet and moved to it, his finger

tracing a path up the center of the Atlantic Ocean and stopping on Iceland.

"We have a base here called Keflavík, I believe. Either bring them there or somewhere in Greenland. Somewhere cold and isolated." Sanders turned to Roth. "Can we do that?"

Roth sighed and shook his head. Mark Hastings filled in the details of the planned landing at Mildenhall, noting the shock on Sanders' face.

"You're kidding!" Sanders said. "In Britain? Can you stop them?"

"Why?" Roth asked.

Rusty Sanders gestured to the map. "If there is a lethal pathogen on that aircraft and it can travel by air, we don't want it anywhere near the damp air of England. Epidemics begin with the exposure of lots of people. There are lots of people in that part of Great Britain, and they all breathe air."

MILDENHALL AIR BASE, U.K.—8:15 P.M. (2015Z)

The sound of screeching tires of a British staff car reverberated inside the American Air Force Command Post as a curious sergeant stepped to the window and peered over the ledge—amazed to see the British commander in the garish sodium vapor lights as he popped out of the backseat like a jack-in-the-box and dashed from view toward the main entrance below. The sound of heavy boots on metal stair treads could be heard reverberating in the hall.

The sergeant moved to the general's side and quietly filled him in, just before the clearly upset British commander entered the room and came nose-to-nose with the Air Force brigadier general.

"What the bloody hell do you think you're doing, General?" was the only greeting. "And don't try to feed me a line of bullshit!"

"Wing Commander Crandall! How nice to see you. Is there a problem?"

"As if you weren't aware! You've got half your bloody base suiting up in chemical gear, you've kicked a half-dozen airplanes out of the hangar and off the ramp, and people are being rearranged at the hospital. Having a soiree, are we, General?"

"Now, look—"

"This is still British soil, and my orders are that the seven-forty-seven you're trying to help will not land here. Is that clear, General?"

"David, *my* orders are to get it on the ground safely, keep it sealed, and wait for more instructions. We have a humanitarian crisis here. I can't believe you'd turn them away!"

"I'm not making the decision. Her Majesty's properly elected government is, and I carry out the orders the military branch is given. It's as simple as that. I'm sorry the decision seems harsh, but we've a few score Britons to see after on this island as well."

"Lord, David, all they've got is a possible exposure to some new strain of flu."

"You know this personally, do you?"

"Of course not, but—"

"Neither do I, and certainly not well enough to second-guess my orders. I would have thought your knowledge of biological warfare would trigger greater caution, but if this hasn't worried you, it sure as the devil should have! Now I strongly suggest that you call your Eagles and wave him off."

The general shook his head. "I can't do that, David."

"Unless you want to create a major crisis between our two countries, you jolly well can. After all, the cheek of you people to send a couple of Eagles out to adopt a seven-forty-seven as a pretend wingman is unbelievable. London Center spotted this farce the second it started!"

"We own this airfield jointly, David. We're under treaties here. If they're American, we can land whomever we choose."

A British aide who had been standing quietly behind and to the side of the British wing commander was now motioned over. The aide plopped a handheld radio in his hand, and without taking his eyes off the American general, the RAF commander brought the radio to his lips and keyed it.

"This is Crandall. Block it. Now!"

"What's that all about?" the general asked, suspicious.

Wing Commander Crandall carefully handed the radio back to his aide before turning to the general and answering. "It's about sovereignty, sir," he said before turning on his heel. "Ours."

As the general watched him go, the sergeant stepped forward with a red handset.

"Sir? It's the command post at the Pentagon again. He needs to speak with you immediately."

The spectacle of a huge airplane of some sort flying in a low formation with two smaller planes and passing over the normally tranquil nighttime countryside caused the few residents still out to look up as the aircraft passed over a village eight miles from the air base. Holland and Robb had already spotted the runway lights ahead and run the landing checklist when the lead F-15 pilot keyed the radio.

"Uh, Fox Three, or Sixty-six, I'm being instructed by my commander, sir, to tell you there's a change in plans."

Holland looked over at the F-15 pilot in disbelief as Dick Robb pressed the transmit button.

"Say again?"

"I'm now instructed to escort you out of British airspace. I'm to tell you that this word comes directly from Washington, and your company will follow up with a satellite call in a few minutes telling you exactly where they want you to go."

"Jesus Christ, not *again*!" Robb exploded.

Holland looked ahead. They were less than fifteen

hundred feet above the surface now, with the runway lights coming more clearly into view. Normally at night he would be able to see nothing of the runway surface, but now in the darkness there were extra lights and markings confusing the issue, and slowly they emerged as something else. Between the runway lights, stretching from the approach end to the departure end, was a solid line of red and white flashing lights, blue flashing lights, and what appeared to be . . . *vehicles*!

"Good Lord," Holland said quietly, "they've completely blocked the runway."

Robb had changed to Mildenhall tower frequency. An American voice came through immediately.

"Sixty-six, Mildenhall tower. Go around, sir! Go around! You are *not* cleared to land. The runway is blocked and closed. Men and equipment on all parts of the runway. Please acknowledge!"

Holland nodded. "Tell him we see it. We're going missed approach."

"I don't believe this!" Robb muttered.

Holland shook his head as his hands eased the throttles forward.

"Max power. Flaps fifteen."

The veins were showing in Robb's neck as his voice reached a new frantic timbre. "Dammit, we can't stay up here all day!"

The tower controller's voice came back again. "Sixty-six, I say again, go around. Runway is blocked and closed!"

Holland looked at Robb. "Flaps fifteen, please."

Dick Robb hesitated, his lips pressed tightly together, fighting himself to calm down. Mildenhall had been a solution. To have it snatched away left him stunned.

Holland reached around the throttle quadrant with his right hand and snapped the flap lever up to the fifteen-degree gate, then returned his hand to the throttles. Robb looked over, chagrined that he hadn't responded.

"I'm sorry . . . flaps fifteen," Robb apologized.

"Already got it. Positive rate, gear up," Holland said. Robb reached for the gear handle and brought it up. The countryside began to drop away as Holland climbed after the lead F-15 and wondered in an almost detached fashion where and when the nightmare was going to end.

Logically, the fuel situation was not critical, he thought. They had enough for at least four more hours of flight and there were hundreds of runways within reach and plenty of options, and if everything else failed, he could always just pop up at some unsuspecting airport with a long enough runway and land. But the realization that they had become instant international pariahs unable to secure landing permission on anyone's soil scared him profoundly. It was one thing to assume a bureaucratic overreaction, but the reality was that the world was increasingly scared of them.

What if, Holland thought, *what if we all come down with something that can kill? How long will we have? How long will I have to get this ship safely parked before I'm too sick to fly?*

Holland glanced over, making sure the gear was up and locked, and adjusted the throttles. Robb, he noticed, was still sitting in stunned silence.

He had to rely on other people's decisions now, Holland reminded himself. The company, the State Department, the government, whoever. It wasn't his airplane; he just had to keep it safe while they figured things out down below.

He remembered the early days when he'd just left the Air Force and been hired as a flight engineer. Airline captains were different then. They were expected to make their own decisions.

But those days were gone.

James Holland engaged the autothrottles and adjusted his climb rate slightly as he settled back in his seat, feeling all but helpless. The company would call on the satellite phone with instructions, he'd been told.

He glanced at the phone at the same moment it rang.

NINE

Horst Zeitner of the German Ministry of Health looked up from the corner of the conference room to see an aide motioning to him frantically. He quickly ended the phone call and crossed the room, too exhausted and numb to be irritated.

"What is it?"

"Sir, there is someone here I believe you need to talk to immediately."

"Who? And why?"

The aide took his boss by the elbow and began guiding him out of the conference room to a high-ceilinged government hallway, but Zeitner pulled away in irritation. "Stop that! Answer my questions!"

The aide looked around nervously before half-whispering to Zeitner. "The chief officer of Hauptmann Pharmaceutical has just arrived. He flew here. He has information you need to hear immediately."

Zeitner straightened up, with a dozen thoughts of caution zinging through his mind. Such a visit could not be routine. Something new was wrong. Zeitner motioned down the hall and the aide led the way.

Andrew Hauptmann was an impeccably groomed Berliner in a thousand-dollar suit who owned several companies and was worth several fortunes. In his seventies now, gaunt and frail, he had a reputation for arrogance, but he met Horst Zeitner with a mixture of concern and panic in his eyes.

"Where can we talk privately?" he asked. Zeitner was sure he heard a quiver in his voice, and it shocked him. He motioned Hauptmann to his office and closed the door behind them. Hauptmann took a chair across from the desk and shook his head.

"Herr Zeitner, my people in Bavaria have misled you. All that you're doing here—the searching for people, the government's refusal to let that airliner land—is based on incorrect statements."

Zeitner sat back in his chair with his heart rate climbing, dreading whatever was coming. If this was a false alarm, his career was over.

"What . . . exactly do you mean, sir?"

"My people in Bavaria told you this was a virus . . . an influenza of some sort, is that correct?"

Zeitner nodded.

"My people were scared, Herr Zeitner, and they guessed. You see, this is most likely not an influenza at all."

Zeitner's heart stopped.

"What, then?" Zeitner asked.

Hauptmann riveted Zeitner with his small, intense eyes. Seconds elapsed before he answered—seconds that seemed like minutes.

"Permit me tell you what we do know . . . *all* that we know," he said at last. "First, we have two men dead. A lab technician, thoroughly qualified, and a medical doctor, a researcher. Both were good men. The technician made a mistake five days ago. He was stacking a shipment of research samples we had obtained—potentially dangerous samples of various viral and bacteriological research, which we knew to treat with great care —when he fell, hitting his head and knocking himself out. In the process, one of the boxes dropped and cracked open. The biologically dangerous samples were in heavy, sealed glass vials, but several dislodged and broke. He was alone in the isolation chamber, and it was several hours, we think, before the other man—the doctor—walked in, also without protection, and found him. Fortunately, the chamber had an operating air lock and all the precautions for Level Three safeguards against airborne disease transmission, including negative air pressure. The doctor did all the right things: He sounded the alarm, cleaned up and sterilized the room, and then impounded both of them for observation."

"Neither of them had protective suits?"

"No. Just white company coveralls. Two days later the technician became very ill. High fever, he told us, hot and cold flashes, skin malaise. The doctor fell ill within a few hours afterward, and tried to take care of the first man as he died. Without warning, the doctor suddenly became delirious and hysterical, as if claustrophobic. He broke the seal, operated the emergency door locks, and raced away."

Andrew Hauptmann reached for a pitcher of water on the table and poured himself a glass. Zeitner watched his shaking hands negotiate the task, but he was too stunned to think about assisting. Hauptmann drank carefully and replaced the glass on the table, his eyes boring once again into Zeitner's.

"My people took our helicopter and gave chase," he went on, "but they didn't locate him before he apparently had broken a window in the car of this American professor for whom you were searching. They spotted the car in the clearing about the time our doctor ran off into the forest. They didn't see him double back to the clearing. When the doctor was spotted there a few minutes later, he was alone and the car was gone."

Hauptmann sat back slightly and took a deep breath, followed by another. His face had reddened from the efforts of talking so rapidly, but then he leaned forward again and continued, his bony hands gesturing constantly.

"My facility director knew that whatever the doctor had caught from the spilled contents of that vial was very bad and very contagious, and when his team found bits of broken window glass on the ground, he tried to find whoever had been in that car. Our people searched the area and found this American's luggage tag. They were very frightened because they believed he had been exposed and did not know it. That is when they called your office for help. I was out of the country at the time. I found out only around midday from my facility director in Bavaria that we were still reporting this to you as an influenza."

"And . . . it's not," Zeitner said quietly.

Hauptmann shook his head. "No, it is not. It is far, far more serious, and frightening . . . and deadly."

Zeitner had been leaning forward too. He straightened up now with a puzzled expression and raised the palms of his hands toward the ceiling. "What, exactly, was in that vial?"

Hauptmann looked at the floor, then back at Zeitner. "We're not certain," he said.

"What? How could . . ."

Hauptmann nodded and sighed.

"In the former Soviet Union, as you know, there were numerous biological research centers operating. Last year we were quietly contacted by the managers of two such facilities. They were trying to raise hard cash in exchange for their many years of research. We agreed in secret to purchase much of it, hoping that somewhere in that body of work there would be marketable advances in drugs and vaccines. From the first, however, the deal presented substantial problems. Many research samples *were* properly documented and maintained, but too many shipments were in terrible disarray, with live virus cultures in tubes adjacent to bacilli cultures in mixed-up sequences, and some research vials were simply shipped unlabeled. We never knew what we were receiving from them until we unpacked it, and then, if it wasn't properly documented, we had to destroy it. We'd been screening such samples in our Hamburg facility before shipment to our new facility in Bavaria. *This* collection, however, was misdirected. It was sent to Bavaria directly from Russia. My facility director thought it had been screened. It had not."

"You mean you have no idea what the name, or the type . . ."

Hauptmann shook his head slowly. "None. What killed our two men could be viral, bacteriological, or even chemical, though we very much doubt that. It is most likely viral."

"My God, that means we have no background data!" Zeitner said.

Hauptmann nodded and continued, his words coming more carefully and slowly.

"We contacted today one of the doctors who used to work in the Russian lab. We had never talked to him before. He was a chief research scientist in the facility involved and lives now in the Ukraine. Fortunately, he kept excellent lab journals from his years in that facility. He told us several important things we did not know. Perhaps Western intelligence services knew these things, or suspected, but we did not in the private sector."

"I'm not understanding you," Zeitner replied.

"Herr Zeitner, this facility was a Soviet military biological warfare research center. For decades they had been searching for efficient ways of killing human beings in great numbers by developing viral and bacteriological agents against which the Russian Army and the Russian people could be inoculated, but agents that would devastate any other human population. They made significant progress and pushed the frontier of that deadly science, but there was a certain rare class of pathogens discovered over the years that scared even the generals—ones that could spread through a primate population within days, killing with great certainty, and ones against which no vaccine seemed possible. The Soviet authorities were afraid of this class, because if such a virus were ever to be unleashed against a human enemy anywhere, it could just as easily double back and devastate the Russian population too. These are horrible human diseases—viruses mostly, including an early

form of the filoviruses identified recently in Africa—all
of them incurable and unstoppable. Some kill by destroying all the internal tissues of the body. Some by
destroying specific organs. One, I am told, causes incredible temperatures, almost burning up the body from
within, and still others cause circulatory collapse, beginning with the brain. To be in this rare class, the pathogen had to infect and kill within days, with no hope of
an effective cure, and it had to be easily transferred by
air and by touch. When such a pathogen was discovered
to be in this class, all samples would be locked away in a
special underground storage bunker beneath this facility. In Russian, it was called *chortnee* class, which,
roughly translated, means the 'omega stock.' "

Horst Zeitner had almost come out of his chair.

"My God, are you saying that the vials in Bavaria . . ."

Hauptmann nodded.

"That, Herr Zeitner, is exactly what I'm saying. What
my researcher unpacked in Bavaria—and dropped—was
from the omega stock."

ABOARD FLIGHT 66

The banging on the cockpit door had become irritating,
interrupting the detailed clearance being relayed by
Shannon Control as Flight 66 climbed through thirty-
three thousand feet on the way to thirty-five thousand.

Now, what? James Holland looked around in exasper-
ation and pushed the electronic door release while Dick
Robb read back the oceanic route. He expected to see
one of the flight attendants. Instead, the doorway was
filled with a vaguely familiar face whose owner stormed
in and stood for a moment, his eyes evaluating the cockpit and which of the two men was in charge.

He settled on Holland.

"Captain? Reverend Garson Wilson." A large, beefy

hand was offered over the center console, and Holland shook it with his left hand without enthusiasm.

Wilson noted the lack of recognition.

"I'm Wilson, the evangelist," he added.

Holland nodded. "Of course. Ah, Mr. Wilson, I'm afraid we're in violation of FAA regulations for unlocking that door and letting you in. My mistake. I thought with all the knocking one of my crew had an emergency. I'm going to have to ask you to return to the cabin."

Wilson rested his right hand on the top edge of the copilot's seat, wiggling it slightly.

"Your name, Captain, is . . ." He turned a hand palm-up in search of a name.

"Holland, James Holland."

"Good. Well, James, I don't think the FAA will give you any guff for having ole Pastor Wilson with you for a few minutes. I'm a private pilot myself, and I've known the administrator since he was a pup."

He moved back and closed the cockpit door before returning to the center jumpseat and continuing.

Holland turned to look at him. "Reverend, *please*! Honor my wishes here. I need you to return to the cabin."

"In a minute, James. I needed to speak to you personally because we're in a time crisis here. We need to be in New York in just a few more hours for a major, ah, appearance. I know you've got other problems to consider up here, but I'm not the one exposed to this virus you mentioned. I've gotta get off and get to New York as soon as possible—unless we're headed there now. I figured you could arrange that for me. I'm sure whatever quarantine they're planning will be a necessary inconvenience for the others, but I don't have time for it."

Holland swiveled around slightly to look the man in the eyes, remembering his face from countless paid television broadcasts and "Garson for God" rallies. He'd never been to one, never wanted to go to one. Religion was far too personal to him. Making a religious service into a circus was a curious Southern pastime he'd never had a desire to watch.

"Reverend Wilson," the captain said, "I'm in no position to negotiate with you about any quarantine plans, and again, sir, I'm going to have to ask you to leave. Every word you say up here digs us all a bigger hole because it's on the cockpit voice recorder." He pointed to a small microphone in the ceiling.

Wilson nodded and smiled. "Okay, I'm going, I'm going, but won't you just tell the ole preacher where he's being taken against his will?"

Holland took a deep breath and glanced at Robb, who returned the glance with a raised eyebrow. He turned to Wilson again. "Reverend, all I can tell you is we're not going to New York. I'll explain everything over the PA in a few minutes. Now, please, sir, I must ask you to leave the cockpit."

Wilson stood in thought for a few seconds and decided not to protest. His smile reminded Holland of a crocodile as he cocked his head toward the door. "I'll get out of your hair, James. No offense, but just for the record, whenever and wherever we land, I'm getting off this aircraft."

The Reverend Wilson waved goodbye and closed the cockpit door carefully, making sure no one but his secretary heard the obscene string of epithets he was muttering as he stalked angrily through the upper cabin back to the head of the stairway.

Holland stabilized the 747 at flight level three-five-zero and double-checked the flight computer. The course wound its way through a series of points in midair, each defined by a latitude and longitude, the path ending in Gander, Newfoundland—but both of them knew that wasn't the true destination. The satellite call ten minutes before from Dallas Operations had brought a long-awaited solution, and some of the rising tension had drained from both Holland and Robb.

"Okay, Sixty-six," the Operations vice president had

said, "we're going to send you up to Keflavík, Iceland, to the Air Force base there, but we can't advertise it. File a flight plan for Gander. Somewhere south of Iceland, you'll be intercepted by Air Force fighters and escorted in."

"We tried that at Mildenhall," Holland reminded him. "And we're still airborne."

"I know. I know. They blew it, and I don't have the details, but that won't happen here, they assure me."

"Sir, who is 'they' in all of this?"

"We're literally talking now to the White House Situation Room," the Operations vice president told him, "and they, in turn, are coordinating a bunch of agencies including the Air Force, the State Department, the FAA, and the CIA."

CIA? Holland thought. *Why CIA?* The question of Icelandic consent loomed before him. He'd had enough glib assurances.

"Sir, Iceland has its own government. Are they in agreement with our coming in?"

"I honestly don't know, Captain," the vice president said, "and I don't think we should care. I can tell you this. Iceland doesn't have a military force to block the runway, and our Air Force is already preparing for you. They'll get you refueled and serviced, and you can refile for whatever U.S. destination we decide on back here. I think, in other words, we've about got it solved."

"But are we supposed to be quarantined back in the U.S.? And if so, how long? What should I tell the people? Christmas Eve is two days away."

There was a small chuckle on the other end that sounded suspiciously forced. "We may bring you on to Edwards Air Force Base in California, or maybe Holloman Air Force Base in New Mexico. The Air Force and Red Cross and the Center for Disease Control in Atlanta are all figuring out where to set up safe facilities for everyone. They'll need two days of observation, and anyone not ill by then can go home. Tell them we'll be paying the bill and flying them to final destinations first class. I know that means many of them will have a late Christmas, but we'll do the best we can."

"Anyone who doesn't get sick will be released? What if someone *does* get sick? What if several do? They won't release us until the disease has completely run its course. This so-called two-day quarantine could end up being two weeks, or longer, and I'm supposed to tell these people it'll be over in two days?"

"What else can we do, Captain? It might be no more than that."

There was a silence on the line for a few seconds while Holland thought through the implications.

"So they really think we're exposed."

"Captain, this could be a false alarm. Even if your passenger died from this virus, it might not spread."

"What?" Holland almost snarled the word. "What do you mean, sir, if our passenger died from this virus?"

"It's a far-out possibility, okay? You said he was sick when he came on board. We're told the heart attack could have been a symptom, but that's the worst case."

Holland shook his head and tried to restrain his own growing anger. His flight attendants had worked with the victim, given mouth-to-mouth CPR, moved him to the back! If he was *that* contagious, they were sure now to get sick!

"James, we're gonna get you home, and take care of anyone, including your crew, who might fall ill."

"Sir? I've got to have some substantive information, okay? Exactly how bad is this stuff?"

"We've been asking that constantly of Washington. Here's exactly what they told me from the Situation Room. They said, quote, that 'the refusals to land in Europe were purely precautionary reactions to the fact that the Germans hadn't clearly described the nature of this infectious disease.' They said the Germans have officially called this a new mutation of influenza virus. That's all they're telling us."

"That's not good enough. I need to know the symptoms. I need to know what to expect. For that matter, I need to know how long *I* have to get this plane parked safely somewhere in case *I* come down with it."

"That's all I can tell you, James, but we'll try to get more as quickly as possible."

Holland ended the call and replaced the handset, then glanced at Dick Robb, who was looking a little less grim.

"We'll make it, Dick," he said. Robb rolled his eyes and nodded.

The weather ahead in Iceland had been reported gray and stormy, with fifteen-knot winds from the west and blowing snow, the temperature in the twenties. It was the visibility, however, that determined whether they could land, and the visibility was holding steady at more than three miles. Holland calculated the fuel state. They could hold for more than an hour after arriving at Keflavík, but one way or another, they would have to land there.

"You going to tell them?" Robb asked suddenly.

"Sorry?"

"The passengers. About the plan, and everything? Are you going to do another PA?"

Holland sighed and nodded. "Unless you'd like to take over that duty, Dick."

Dick Robb looked at him with a bemused expression. "Hey, it's your line check. I'm just a dumb copilot."

Holland was surprised to find himself laughing easily. "Right! With a sharp eye, a biting tongue, and a red pen."

Holland expected Robb to smile. Instead, Robb turned away and stared out the window as Holland punched the PA button and tried to organize his thoughts.

He'll come around and revert to his normal, obnoxious self, Holland thought. *Especially now that the worst is over.*

TEN

The nearest conference room to Jonathan Roth's office had become a working command post by 4 P.M. Washington time, with papers strewn everywhere and members of the analysis team coming and going. With the White House Situation Room now essentially managing the crisis, the CIA was being looked to more and more for guidance—and it was all Deputy Director Jonathan Roth's show. With the polished ease of a master bureaucrat he had pushed and pulled and bullied his people in the background at Langley while presenting a calm, unruffled face to 1600 Pennsylvania Avenue—along with a constant flow of analysis and interpretations. By 6 P.M. the central remaining question being asked in the Situation Room was the same one Rusty Sanders had to answer: How dangerous is the bug aboard Quantum 66?

"Look, we're not sure there *is* a bug aboard Sixty-six!" Sanders had cautioned Roth earlier, sensing a stampede. "We need an autopsy of this man Helms first to be sure."

Roth had ripped off his half-frame glasses, risen to his feet, and angrily motioned Sanders into the corridor, speaking through clenched teeth.

"The question, Doctor, is not whether it's there, but how do we deal with it if it is? *I* make the decision on whether to consider it there, do you understand that? That's *my* decision, based on *my* analysis."

"Sir," Sanders had begun, "I'm sorry to upset you, but I just wanted to make sure you understand that so far we have nothing to go on to make that decision."

"We have a dead man on an airplane nobody wants around, Sanders. A dead man known to have been exposed to this bug. We have the German government admitting this virus, whatever it is, has killed two people, not counting the professor. Isn't that enough for you?"

Sanders could see Roth getting even angrier.

"I just want us to be sure, Director. It could have been an ordinary heart attack. We don't know that it killed him."

"Again, Sanders, I make that decision. We can't take chances here. Now, find out for me, dammit, how bad this is and how we should respond based on the assumption that there *is* a bug running rampant on Flight Sixty-six. And do it now!"

Twenty minutes had passed and Sanders was back, ashen-faced, with an answer. Roth closed the door, and the others found chairs.

"Okay. I've got new information, and as we suspected, the Germans haven't been getting—or giving—all the facts. Basically we're in deep trouble," Sanders began, pacing down one side of the room along the wall, his tie now hanging even lower than before. He described the visit of Andrew Hauptmann and relayed the conversation he'd just completed with Zeitner in Bonn, and his own call to the Russian doctor in the Ukraine.

"Fortunately, I speak reasonably passable Russian," Sanders continued, "so I didn't use a translator, and I'm pretty sure I understand it. Russian, you know, can lead some translators to—"

"Sanders! Get to the point!" Roth snarled.

"Sorry, sir." He moved around to the far end of the table, opposite Roth's seat at the head. "Here's the bottom line. Assuming, as Director Roth says I must, that Helms was not only exposed but suffering from an actual case of this pathogen on departure from Frankfurt, and applying known standards from the Russian scientist's findings to the worst of the agents mistakenly shipped to Bavaria, we have to assume an almost ninety percent certainty that every person on that aircraft has now been exposed to an active—for want of a better word—*particle* of the same virus. And, it's *not* a flu!"

"Everyone?" Roth asked.

Sanders nodded. "Yes, sir. That exposure would have occurred within two hours of departure. Now, since we really don't know much about this particular virus, other than what it did to the two men in the Bavarian lab, I'm extrapolating based on what the Russian researcher told me about omega-class pathogens. One of their basic qualifications for declaring a pathogen an omega, it seems, was extreme communicability. In other words, if you were exposed, you contracted it. The methods of exposure differed, but omega-class viruses, he said, had to hold the very real threat of being essentially unstoppable in a civilian population. That would usually mean airborne transmission through exhaled breath, and the ability of the virus to live on and penetrate unlacerated human skin, which meant that if you simply touched a drop of infected bodily fluid from someone who'd fallen ill, you would be exposed. In addition, the mortality rate had to exceed eighty-five percent, and the last requirement was a rapid incubation period—and this Bavarian pathogen apparently incubates in as little as forty-eight hours, which is incredible."

Roth shifted in his chair. "How did they know this, Sanders?"

"The Russian told me they arrived at such conclusions by primate testing, but he's just guessing at precisely which bug we have. There were . . . tests on humans as well. Political prisoners, he said. Especially back in the fifties. Our Bavarian bug has to have at least those characteristics. *And,* one of their more contemporary fears was that even if it was a lesser human threat than an omega class, by the seventies any pathogen taking hold anywhere in the world could be spread anywhere around the world within forty-eight hours by the modern jet airliner! It starts today in Frankfurt, and before we know it's there, we've got carriers getting sick and spreading it in New York, Los Angeles, Chicago, and Tokyo, and in two more days each infected person is spreading it in dozens of other locales. It's like a pyramid plan for Armageddon. The Russian scientist said— and I've long agreed with this—that the world's airline system has become the potential instrument of a viral holocaust, which is what I tried to tell the FAA for years with these cabin recirculation—"

Roth held his hand up to stop. "Stick to the point, Doctor! I'm aware of your crusade back at the FAA."

Rusty Sanders fell silent for a few seconds as he studied Jon Roth's face and decided not to push. He cleared his throat and gestured at the papers in his hand.

"At any rate, sir, we've got a winged messenger of death if this omega-class pathogen from Bavaria is actually aboard that seven-forty-seven."

Several of the research team exhaled loudly, and Mark Hastings sat forward. "What . . . kind of death are we talking about here? Quick, or something more . . . ah . . ."

"You mean are we talking gruesome?" Sanders asked.

"Yeah. Gruesome. I mean, we've got two hundred forty-four people on that jet, plus a crew of twelve!"

Sanders looked down the table at Roth before continuing. Roth's chin was resting in the palm of his hand, his eyes following Sanders, and there was no reaction.

"Well," Sanders began again, "death can take numerous forms, depending on exactly which pathogen this is, but we've got the two victims in the Bavarian lab. I'm told autopsies are in progress by a highly trained German team, and I've been promised the results instantly on completion. That should help with comparisons when we get an autopsy on the professor. By the way, respiratory collapse, internal bleeding, coronary involvement imitating a heart attack, and thermal collapse are all possible, but the only two known victims demonstrated different symptoms, including dementia and bizarre psychological episodes. Now, since the period from onset to death could take several hours, there could be substantial suffering involved, especially if everyone on that aircraft—including the flight crew—goes crazy at once."

Jon Roth did not move, but Mark Hastings sat forward with a wide-eyed expression.

"Jesus, the flight crew! I hadn't considered them!"

Sanders motioned for calm. "Their exposure began just a few hours ago, Mark. If we get them on the ground somewhere within, say, forty hours, there's probably zero chance of the flight crew being affected in the meantime."

"Yeah, but we'd need to take the keys to the airplane from them after that, so to speak. Disable the airplane."

Sanders shook his head and took a deep breath as he examined his feet and then locked eyes with Roth. "I'd . . . hate like hell to see those people facing the end still locked up in that jumbo. I'd hate to see them go through that without some human assistance, even if the care is futile and provided by people in protective moon suits."

Sanders hadn't realized he'd begun pacing again as he talked. He saw he was now on the opposite end of the room, beside the deputy director's chair. Roth had followed his movements by swiveling the chair, but Sanders stopped and surveyed the room, noting that everyone was in shock.

He wondered at his own detachment. Here he was talking in routine tones about a horrible scourge that might be ready to kill nearly three hundred people on a jumbo jet in an agonizing and bizarre sequence of human misery. He was detached, he realized, because he didn't believe it. Not yet, at least. There was still nothing to confirm the presence of the malady aboard Flight 66, even if he accepted the idea that the American professor had indeed been exposed.

"Okay, as to the external dangers." Sanders walked over to an easel with blank paper and picked up a felt marker, drawing as he talked.

"Again, I'm extrapolating and basically guessing from what the Russian researcher told me about omega-class pathogens in general. But, we'd better err on the conservative side and worry that the Bavarian strain might be able to stay active in above-freezing airborne environments for up to, say, an hour, depending on humidity. That's enough time to circulate around the inside of a seven-forty-seven and infect everyone, *if* the particles are small enough to slip through the rather ineffective biofilters in those airborne air-conditioning systems. The warmer and wetter the conditions, the longer an airborne-transmittable virus can live and be deadly. Viruses like this ride tiny aerosols—airborne droplets of moisture. In temperate climates they can even linger for several hours. Think of how easy it is to transmit a common cold by sneezing or touching. That's the level of communicability we have to assume, with a virus that doesn't just give people a runny nose and fever but kills them within three to four days." Sanders replaced the marker and crossed his arms.

"So, Doctor," Roth began, "your assessment of the danger to any exposed population is . . . ?"

"Danger to population centers. Okay. Considering the fact that I'm told it comes from a class whose mortality rate is at or above eighty-five percent fatal, I'd have to say that we could hardly find anything biologically more dangerous to human life on a broad scale—other than some other Biosafety Level Four horror like the Ebola Zaire filovirus. The horror of Ebola is that you basically disintegrate, die, and putrefy from the inside out, but the Bavarian strain may provide a less gruesome death while being even more dangerous to human life. In other words, this is absolutely nothing to take chances with. Quarantine in the strictest sense is vital."

Roth cleared his throat. "Doctor, the plan was to refuel them in Iceland and then bring them back home, as you know. Is that still a reasonable plan? Finding a place to quarantine them in the Southwest?"

Rusty Sanders looked at the floor for a second to organize his response. He knew Roth would use the same words in talking with the White House. They needed to be right.

"Okay." He looked Roth in the eye. "The risks of bringing that aircraft back to the mainland of North America, let alone to any warmer climate, are enormous and, in my view, unwarranted. In theory, the absolute worst-case scenario with a pathogen as bad and infectious and contagious as we think this one could be is that it could lead to an uncontrollable epidemic. Even a worldwide *pan*demic. I do *not* want to engage in scare tactics, but truthfully, sir, if such a wave of infection ever got started, it could *theoretically* depopulate the entire continent of· human life! At the very least, it would kill tens of millions. I know science fiction writers have been playing with this theme for years, but this is not fiction! This type of pandemic threat is very real—thanks, to a great extent, to modern aviation."

There was silence again, until Mark Hastings spoke up in a constrained voice.

"There's no hope for those aboard Sixty-six? They're doomed, no matter what?"

Sanders looked at him and raised an index finger.

"Well, maybe, but let's qualify that. They *are* probably doomed to die, at least eighty-five percent or more of them, *if . . . IF . . .*"—he waited until he had everyone's undivided attention, knowing the answer would once again anger Roth—"*IF* this deceased passenger had in fact been suffering from the precise same malady that killed the two lab researchers in Bavaria. Remember, there has to have been an active case aboard to infect any of the other passengers. If the professor didn't have an active case, he couldn't have been throwing viral particles in the air."

Roth sat forward suddenly. "Thank you, Dr. Sanders. Anyone have anything to add?"

No one volunteered.

"Very well. This is, of course, open to discussion and dissent, but I'm ready to recommend to the White House that we . . . deny this aircraft reentry into the United States, and impound them—or quarantine them —in Iceland when they land."

Rusty Sanders had been leaning against the wall. Now he rocked forward on his feet and raised the palm of his right hand.

"Sir? There's one more very important priority."

"Go ahead." Roth folded his hands to listen.

"We need an autopsy on Helms as fast as possible. I'd recommend we get an Army pathology team from Fort Detrick—one skilled in chemical and biological warfare, with full biosafe space suits—on the way by the fastest aircraft, and I'd like to brief them first. You can't detect a virus like this directly, but even a field autopsy can reveal whether the man died from something more than a simple coronary." Sanders stood and watched Roth's face as it alternated between interest and anger for his having brought up the same subject again.

Interest won out.

"See to the arrangements, Dr. Sanders," Roth said.

There was a small knock at the door as Sherry Ellis, the attractive analyst who had briefed him earlier, moved into the room.

"Sorry to interrupt, but you need to hear this," she said.

"What now?" Roth asked, shaking his head slightly.

"Our Russian scientist called Zeitner fifteen minutes ago. He wanted to make sure Zeitner understood that the eighty-five percent mortality rate for omega-class pathogens was just a threshold qualification."

"We understood that," Rusty Sanders answered.

Sherry nodded and raised an index finger. Her face

was ashen. "Yes, but he wanted to let Zeitner know that they had never classified a pathogen as an omega which had less than a one hundred percent kill rate."

The reaction was stunned silence.

ABOARD FLIGHT 66

In her twenty-three years with the airline, Barb Rollins had never faced a truly serious emergency. "Oh, sure," she'd tell nonairline friends, "I've been scared a few times—mainly when we run out of coffee on a breakfast flight full of suits."

She closed the cockpit door behind her now and stood in the darkened alcove for a second, her mind racing. The lead flight attendant was expected to be the mother hen of the cabin crew, but she didn't feel much like a leader. She felt like a scared little girl. There was an unseen predator stalking them, a predator too small and too clever to be fought directly. The thought that it might already be racing around inside her bloodstream was terrifying.

Passengers in the upper-deck area were looking, she noticed, and she smiled at them as she negotiated the stairway to the main deck, standing on the bottom step for a few more seconds.

You're overreacting, Barb! she told herself. *At worst it's just the flu!* But the small, cold center of worry churning her stomach refused to go away. Why would governments react so violently to just a flu bug? What had her passenger really had? What were its symptoms? How fast would it hit them?

James Holland had done a beautiful job with the PA, explaining in smooth, reassuring tones about the fuel stop in Iceland and the uncertain quarantine destination in the United States and the gross overreaction of foreign governments. But it wasn't enough to stem the feeling of deep alarm and fright that had gripped everyone in the passenger cabin. If they had to wait more than four days, they'd miss Christmas at home, wherever home might be, but the questions fired at her with the staccato pace of a machine gun were almost all about the nature of the disease that had left Frankfurt with them.

Back in Frankfurt the toys and presents and the holiday atmosphere had spilled onto the airplane as if the big Boeing were a giant sleigh, and she'd teased Holland that he should have been flying in a Santa suit. There were students coming home to their families for Christmas, GIs and military families doing the same thing, and a large tour group on their return leg. There was also a scattering of serious-minded businesspeople, plus a few lonely individuals who seemed oblivious to the season, but they were in the minority.

Barb headed toward the back, strolling carefully down the aisle through the coach cabin, letting her eyes make contact with as many people as possible, the way she routinely did. She loved people, though her New York manners got in the way sometimes. More than anything else, she knew, she needed normalcy just now —routine. She needed to think of this as a routine flight.

She flashed her patented flight attendant smile at everyone, while another part of her consciousness stood aside and assessed each of her passengers as if she were narrating a taped memo:

There's the young man in the bulkhead seat with his leg in a cast. I helped him on. Very courteous. Crutches are stowed in the first class closet. Skiing accident, where? Oh yeah, Switzerland. Handsome young boy, and handling the pain well. Probably shy. He's spotted that stunning young German girl in the aisle seat, but he doesn't want his parents to know he's aching for her. Raging hormones! Probably nineteen, and dangerous. There! He's stealing another glance at her. He doesn't see me watching, uh-oh, he sees me. Now he's mortified. And she's glancing at him! Interesting.

Hormones . . . yeah, and there's that couple that can't

keep their hands off each other, and now she's snuggled in close and they've got a blanket. The old blanket trick! She's smiling at me. She thinks I can't tell where their hands are! Barb laughed to herself. She'd done the same thing herself a few times. The trick lay in not wearing too big a smile.

An overweight gentleman was sitting with a very elderly lady. She guessed a mother and son, but guesses were often wrong. The man was looking to his left at a couple across the aisle, and Barb followed his gaze to a young woman in silent hysterics, her husband in the seat next to her trying to calm her. One of the telephone handsets was clutched to her chest, her fist in her mouth. She was sobbing with wide-eyed grief.

Barb leaned over the man, quietly, and gestured to his wife with a tilt of her head. "Excuse me. Is something wrong? Can I do anything for you?"

Keith Erickson looked up, his eyes filled with concern.

"I . . . I can't reason with her. When the captain said we might be several days getting home . . . she's been distraught over being away from our children. When he said we might miss Christmas . . ."

Lisa Erickson looked up at Barb and took her fist out of her mouth. A tiny, agonized voice followed.

"He doesn't mean it, does he? We can't miss Christmas! My babies need me! I can't be away!"

Barb leaned farther in toward the window, toward the wife.

"Mrs. . . . ah . . ."

"Erickson," her husband said. "Lisa."

"Lisa, now listen. We're all going to be just fine, and you're probably going to get home by Christmas Eve. The captain was just giving you the worst-case scenario, you know? Everything will be fine. You need to use the phone?"

Lisa Erickson nodded like a frightened child, in staccato motion, then turned to the window and reinserted her fist.

Keith Erickson motioned Barb closer and spoke in her ear.

"I'm sorry. We'll be okay. She's already been using the phone. She's just . . . very upset."

Barb found Brenda in the rear galley sitting alone by door 5L while the rest of the cabin crew worked on an accelerated dinner service. Barb put her hand on Brenda's shoulder and got a tired smile in return.

"How're you doing, kid?"

"Fine," Brenda lied. Barb could see the turmoil inside. She didn't want to contribute to it, but there was an additional duty the captain had saddled her with and it had to be done.

Barb kept her voice low. "You heard the captain's PA, didn't you?"

"Yeah. This is the weirdest flight of my life."

Brenda looked up and Barb could see tears filling her eyes. Her voice was small and shaky when she spoke at last.

"I'm scared, Barb. I'm . . . going to get sick. I . . . had direct contact with him! Whatever he had, I'll get for certain, and I . . . I don't know what it was he had, but it killed him, and I . . . ."

Barb sat down beside her and put her arm around Brenda. The younger woman was shaking.

"Brenda, it'll be okay! It *will*! There's no guarantee that you'll catch whatever he had, and Mr. Helms was decades older than you and probably in bad health. We don't know."

Brenda's head was down, cradled by her hands. She shook it side to side slowly.

"Countries don't refuse landing clearance to big airliners at Christmas because someone has the flu. If Europe and England are scared of us, we're in real trouble. *I'm* in real trouble!" she corrected herself. She looked up at Barb. "That's why I'm not helping in the galley. I'm probably . . . dangerous!"

Barb shook her head no, but she was right. "Brenda,

did you forget? The captain wanted you and Dee and anyone else who touched him to be reseated upstairs in the upper deck. We've got a number of rows of empty seats up there."

Brenda's hand went to her mouth. "Oh my!"

"It's *okay*," Barb said.

Brenda nodded. "Yeah, I know. I'm fine. But that just . . . just . . ." Her right hand was flailing the air.

"Confirms?" Barb said, regretting it instantly.

Brenda sobbed openly once and nodded.

. "Right."

"Go on, now. Pull yourself together," Barb told her gently. "Find Dee and get upstairs. This is a paid break, by the way."

The image of the deceased passenger burning up with fever when she had helped him on board tumbled through Brenda's head with chilling clarity. He had been sweating, and he'd complained of feeling strange. She remembered the feel of his mouth as she tried to breathe him back to life, and she remembered the panic in his eyes before he lost consciousness. *How long,* she wondered, *do I have?*

KEFLAVÍK AIR FORCE BASE, ICELAND

From the control tower the persistent snow flurries carried sideways on a twenty-knot wind from the east obscured much of the runway, but for the past hour the frantic movement of Air Force vehicles in the Arctic night had escalated. The acting tower chief, a senior master sergeant, had already been snapped at once for calling base operations and asking what it was all about, but curiosity was about to kill him. Something was up, and no one wanted to tell him what it was.

"Eddie, look at that! They're moving the jumbo-sized airstairs down to the west end." He handed the field glasses to the staff sergeant working ground control.

"Earlier they sent a couple of power carts, some light carts, the large tow tractor, and now the big airstairs."

"Aren't those for seven-forty-sevens and other jumbos?" the staff sergeant asked.

"Yep. Which has to mean . . ." The chief made a sweeping motion toward his partner, waiting for him to finish the thought.

The staff sergeant looked puzzled for a second.

"What? Oh. Well, either a commercial jet is diverting in here, which we've heard nothing about, or, you must be thinking, Air Force One."

The chief nodded. "Air Force One is a seven-forty-seven, right? What else could it be?"

The staff sergeant put down the glasses.

"Hate to burst your bubble, but the President's in D.C. He gave a speech this evening. CNN carried it."

The chief grabbed the glasses again. The field was awash in vehicles scurrying back and forth to the west end of the field, and two F-15s from Keflavík were flying in the vicinity—a highly unusual occurrence.

"You don't suppose . . ." the staff sergeant began.

"What?"

"That story that's all over CNN about a U.S. airliner being refused landing permission all over Europe because someone's sick aboard?"

The chief lowered the field glasses and looked at the sergeant.

"Yeah?"

"Could they be coming in here?"

The chief turned to look at the radar scope just as a target crawled onto the display from the west.

ABOARD FLIGHT 66

In the cockpit of Quantum 66, James Holland double-checked the instrument landing system frequency and called for gear down and the final checklist. The pair of F-15 Eagles on either side pulled away slightly as they made the radio calls to Keflavík tower and received landing clearance. At four miles Holland reached up and flicked on the landing lights, expecting a surprised response from the tower controllers. The lights of a 747 couldn't possibly be mistaken for a flight of Eagles, but there was no response. Holland eased the power back in the flare as Robb called out the last fifty feet in ten-foot increments, and the huge Boeing touched down gently and rolled out adjacent to the tower.

Immediately two small trucks with the lighted sign FOLLOW ME appeared to the right of the runway as a voice came over the tower frequency.

"Sixty-six, follow the 'Follow Me's.' Do not open any doors or hatches, and do not shut down your engines until instructed. Do not open your cockpit windows either."

"Sixty-six, roger," Robb replied.

Holland worked the nosewheel steering tiller and the throttles to pivot the 747 around to the taxiway and trundle slowly back to the west. There was a contingent of vehicles waiting, he saw. No fuel trucks, but 747-sized mobile airstairs and a small retinue of other vehicles—including a large articulated fire truck. He expected to see the firemen in bulky, protective garb, but neither pilot expected to have one of the firemen in a big space suit, complete with the full face mask and headgear, holding two lighted wands to guide them to a stop.

Holland followed the man's signals and turned the 747 back to the east and into the stiff wind, then cut off the taxi lights and brought the ship to a halt. There were several figures moving around in front of the aircraft, and he squinted at them for a closer look. They, too, seemed to be firemen, all of them in the same full-body protective suits. That was very odd. He looked to the left at the airstairs, but no one was moving them into position. Instead, more firemen were now moving around on both sides, each of them carrying something.

"What's going on out there?" Robb asked.

Holland moved his head to the left, trying to confirm

what he was seeing. The snow and the subdued light
from several portable light stands made it difficult to tell
for certain.

"I've got a squadron of firemen on this side," Robb
said, "and more coming. What in hell? Do we have hot
brakes or something?"

"Turn on the landing lights!" Holland commanded,
his face still turned to the left side of the aircraft. His
voice carried a note of urgency, and Robb complied,
flooding the scene ahead of them with lights and causing the men outside to raise their arms against the sudden brightness.

Dick Robb strained forward in his seat, looking at the
strange suits ahead of the airplane. They weren't the
normal silver protective outfits worn by firemen. In fact,
they weren't firemen's suits at all.

"What the hell are those? What on earth are they
wearing?" Robb asked. "And are those *guns* they're carrying?"

Holland turned back toward Robb after confirming
that virtually everyone outside was encased in the same
sort of outfit. A cold feeling of fear began to gnaw away
at his stomach.

"Oh shit!" he said.

"What?" Robb asked again.

"Those *are* protective suits . . . chem-warfare suits.
I'm all too familiar with them from the Air Force."

"Protective suits? Protecting against what?"

Holland looked him in the eye.

"Us."

ELEVEN

A small buzzer sounded in the cockpit as James Holland shut down the 747's four engines. Someone forty feet below had opened the ground communications panel and pressed the call button.

Robb and Holland simultaneously punched on their flight interphones and a voice filled their headsets immediately.

"Anyone hear me up there?"

Holland pressed the transmit rocker switch on the control yoke.

"This is the captain. Who's this? And what's going on down there?"

"I'm one of the ground crew, sir. Stand by. We're running a line out to the command vehicle. The colonel . . . the base commander . . . wants to talk to you."

That feeling again in the pit of the stomach. It was becoming too familiar. Why didn't they just call on ground control frequency?

Because someone of greater authority wants to talk to you privately, James. Someone wants to tell you something you don't want to hear: that you've got virtually no control over this situation!

Holland looked at Dick Robb, who was checking the fuel gauges and shaking his head.

"They're not fueling us yet," Robb announced in a puzzled tone.

Holland shook his head. "I didn't see a single fuel truck, and I'm sure this isn't a regular parking spot with a fuel outlet. We're on a taxiway, as close to the down-wind edge of the field as they could get us."

A chime sounded, confusing them for a moment, until Holland punched on the cabin interphone and recognized Barb Rollins' voice instantly.

"James?"

"Go ahead, Barb."

"So what now? Should we keep everyone seated, or serve drinks, or what?"

A new voice coursed through their headsets from outside.

"Captain? Colonel Nasher."

Holland checked to make sure he still had the cabin interphone selected. "Barb, go ahead and run a drink service. I'll call you back."

Then he punched on the ground interphone.

"Yes, Colonel, we can hear you. Captain James Holland here. Are you ready to refuel us?"

Holland could see the interphone cord snaking away in front of them to what looked like a heavy truck. Obviously the portable command post. He could almost make out the details of a face at the window. The face, he presumed, of the colonel who'd just called.

There was a worrisome pause.

"Uh, Captain, you understand I'm the base commander here, but I'm acting on orders from my leaders at the Pentagon, and they're apparently coordinating with a lot of other U.S. government agencies."

Holland could hear voices in the background, along with the howl of the frigid wind sweeping down from the northeast.

"I understand, Colonel. But we need fuel, and it wouldn't hurt to check our engine oil levels as well."

"Okay," Holland heard the man sigh, "okay, now please listen, Captain. My orders are to keep you in place here, make certain no one opens any hatch or door, make absolutely certain no one leaves the aircraft, and keep the situation completely static. We've closed the base entirely for the interim."

Holland cocked his head in puzzlement. "Well, that's acceptable to us. We'll keep the doors closed, and we weren't planning on taxiing anywhere else other than to the end of the runway when we're ready to go."

Another pause from outside.

"Ah . . . I don't think you're understanding me, Captain Holland. I can't allow you to depart from this airfield unless I get orders to that effect."

Holland moved back in the seat slightly, as if stung. He took a deep breath and turned to Robb. "Quick, call Dallas on the satellite phone. Fill them in. Find out what the hell's going on."

He punched the transmit button again.

"Colonel, the plan was to get refueled and then proceed on to Edwards Air Force Base, or possibly Holloman in New Mexico. I don't mean to be rude, but I don't particularly give a damn what your orders are. I'm not going to keep two hundred forty-four passengers sitting here two days before Christmas. Now, we need quite a bit of fuel."

The reply came swiftly.

"Captain, I'm very sorry about this, I really am. But unless my orders change, we are *not* going to refuel you, and we *will* physically prevent you from leaving, if necessary. You have a major biological emergency on board, and your aircraft is now impounded under emergency military authority."

Holland was shaking his head in growing irritation. He jabbed the transmit button again. "I don't *believe* this! Unless you've got a place to isolate over two hundred and fifty people, you're telling us we have to live on this aircraft for the next however many days? Colonel, the toilets will be overflowing in six hours, and on that note, whether we leave or stay, can you at least refill our water, provide more food, and service the restrooms?"

Again a pause. A long one. *They haven't thought this*

through, Holland decided. *They're making this up as they go along and leaving us completely out of it.*

The base commander's voice came back all business, the solicitous tone of the first few exchanges now completely gone. "Okay, here's the deal, Captain. The only thing I'm authorized to allow off your airplane is a body . . . the body of one of your passengers, who apparently died en route. When we get the word—and it could be twelve hours or more—we'll have the airstairs brought up to one of the doors, and when our people are safely clear, we'll let you push the body out on the airstairs. An autopsy is of great urgency, I'm told, to find out what this man died of, and a forensic team's on the way up right now from stateside. As to servicing your toilets, we can't allow any potentially contaminated matter off the airplane, so the answer is 'Sorry but no.' We've got your tail hanging over the seawall to keep the cabin air coming out of your outflow valve heading out to sea, I've got all my people wrapped up in these godawful Rube Goldberg chemical suits, and my ass is on the line if one molecule of a virus gets off your airplane and infects anyone or anything! Now, *you've* got to explain all this to your passengers, and you also need to make sure they understand that absolutely no one else is allowed off *for any reason.*"

"I'm not a jailer, Colonel. If someone jumps ship, I can't control it."

"Captain, listen up. This is dead serious, man. I've got security police all around your aircraft, understand? My orders are to absolutely prevent—not *try* to prevent, but absolutely prevent—any human being from leaving your airplane. That's a deadly force authorized order. Do I make myself crystal clear?"

Holland sat back hard in the seat. "Jesus!" he said to no one in particular.

The cabin call chime rang again, and Dick Robb answered on his headset, then unlocked the door. Holland was vaguely aware of Lee Lancaster and Rachael Sherwood's entering and closing the door behind them.

Holland punched the interphone button again. "Are you trying to tell me, Colonel, that if someone tries to leave this airplane, you'll *shoot* them?"

"Precisely. Man, woman, or child. I have no choice."

Robb turned to the ambassador with a wild look in his eye. "They've trapped us here! They suckered us in here and now they're not going to let us leave!"

Lancaster calmly motioned Rachael to the jump seat directly behind the captain's seat, while he sat in the middle jump seat. Robb was holding the satellite phone to his ear and waiting for an answer from Dallas.

Holland punched the transmit button again. "How about food, Colonel? Anyone thought about that?"

"Yes, we have." The voice was slightly less forceful. "I'm going to get creative with my orders. They didn't say I couldn't pass anything in to you. I'm going to have the airstairs stacked high with flight lunches when we retrieve the body. We have about three hundred. How much food do you have on board now?"

Holland shrugged. "Hell, I don't know. We had a dinner service and breakfast service for this flight. I'm sure the breakfast service is still loaded and ready."

"Okay. We won't let you starve, but you'd better ration the heads . . . the toilets. As for water, we *can* fill your tanks . . . we just can't let you dump anything."

Holland could see Robb had connected with Dallas Operations. He had huddled over to fill them in on the situation. Suddenly he was staring at Holland with the color draining away from his face.

"The Operations veep wants to talk to you. You'd better hear this from him." Robb handed the phone over solemnly, and Holland brought the handset to his ear for a brief exchange that ended with the phone held loosely in his lap. Holland turned to the ambassador and swallowed hard.

"What is it, James?" Lancaster asked.

Holland took a long, ragged breath. "I don't understand why, but a half hour before we landed, Dallas got a call from the White House Situation Room people."

"And?" Lancaster prompted.

Holland shook his head and swallowed hard. "Even our own country's scared of us now." He gestured to the windscreen, his mind obviously drifting away in search of options.

"What are they telling you, James?" Lancaster asked, a bit more forcefully. Holland's eyes returned to his. The captain was tired; the ambassador had noticed it before. But the depth of fatigue in those eyes was worrisome.

"Dallas says," Holland replied evenly, "the government's convinced we're carrying something far worse than a simple flu. They consider us a major threat to population centers."

"What does that mean?" Robb asked.

"We've been refused reentry to the United States."

THE WHITE HOUSE, WASHINGTON, D.C.

The President of the United States had made it a point since taking office to stay the hell away from the Situation Room in a crisis—unless absolutely necessary.

"It starts a vicious feedback loop," he'd explained to his exasperated National Security Advisor late one evening when it appeared Panama City was on the brink of civil war. "Nixon refused to use it, and Reagan felt the same way—perhaps for a different reason. They'd go to the Pentagon and hang around the War Room."

"It's a lot more discreet to take the elevator two floors down, sir."

"Look, if I walk in down there, everyone thinks, Jeez, if the President's here, it's more serious than we thought! Pretty soon there's so much tension in that room I can't trust the advice to be cool-headed. I'll stay in the Oval Office or in my damn bed, and they can use the phone or come up two floors and talk to me. Besides," he added, "it's too close to the Press Room, and Sam Donaldson never sleeps."

At 6:30 P.M. Eastern standard time on the evening of December 22, after an endless stream of phone calls from the Situation Room to the living quarters regarding Flight 66, the President junked the rule and took the elevator downstairs.

A dozen men and women looked up in surprise as the President blew into the room looking weary and considerably older than his forty-nine years.

"Okay, *now* what?" He stopped and leaned forward, supporting his weight with both hands on one of the communications consoles.

The assistant to the National Security Advisor waved toward one of the display screens where a map of the North Atlantic now glowed with an orange circle around Keflavík.

"The Icelandic ambassador is tearing up State's phone lines to speak with you, sir. Someone was watching all this on television when they heard a seven-forty-seven had landed with Quantum's logo on the tail. It's a small community. That person picked up his phone and called the government, and now the Icelandic government is aware of our quarterback sneak and they're madder than hell. They've even rousted the UN Secretary General out of bed. They want that airplane gone."

The President merely nodded.

"The next move will be press conferences and treaty problems with our base there."

"Wonderful! It took nearly two hours on the phone to calm down the British PM after the Air Force tried that trick at Mildenhall. I should bust a three-star general back to lieutenant for that one!"

"Sir, I . . . thought you authorized the Icelandic landing?"

The President looked at the floor and shook his head. "Yeah, yeah, yeah. I did. Like an idiot. I really thought they could sneak him in there."

"And, sir, Jonathan Roth, CIA deputy director, is here, if you want a briefing."

The President spotted Roth in the doorway of the

small, adjoining conference room. He stood up and waved Roth over.

"Anything new, Jon?"

Roth shook his head. "The Germans have a team of specialists at that Bavarian lab now to try to discover as quickly as possible the profile, or characteristics, of this bug we're dealing with, but we won't get results for several days at best." Roth shifted around and dropped his voice slightly as the President sat sideways on the console and folded his arms.

"Give me your best guess, Jon, based on what you know now. If they all come down with this stuff, how long does it take to recover, and what's the mortality rate?"

Jonathan Roth cleared his throat and looked away before fielding the question. He hadn't realized the President didn't know. It would make things more difficult, since the assistant to the National Security Advisor had been asked to pass that on—and hadn't.

"Mr. President, I apologize," he began. "I thought you'd been informed."

The President looked at him quizzically.

"Spit it out, Jon."

"Sir, the communicability rate is considered one hundred percent on that aircraft, and the mortality rate we had at first was above eighty-five percent, but just before I came over here, we talked with one of the Russian scientists again. He's telling us we should expect a one hundred percent kill rate."

The President looked at Roth with an incredulous expression, his mouth half open in a contemplative habit familiar to American TV audiences.

"You're telling me that . . . everyone on board who comes down with this bug will die?"

"Yes, sir. Most likely all."

"Oh my God in heaven! I . . . I was dealing with this as a containable panic. I figured we'd hold on to them for a few days and no one would get sick, and if they did, no big deal."

As the President looked at the wall and exhaled loudly, Roth shook his head sadly.

"Mr. President, looking ahead beyond the two-day minimum incubation period, we have to prepare for two hundred fifty-six passengers and crew members dying on that aircraft. At least while they're in Iceland we can get to them with some completely safe biochemical protection suits and send volunteers on board to help. I mean, we can't euthanize anyone, but they could administer morphine, or whatever, to make the end a little easier. What we can't do is take them off the airplane."

"What're you saying, Jon? There's a recommendation in there somewhere."

Roth took a deep breath, staring at the floor for a second as he bit his lower lip. His eyes returned suddenly to lock on the President's.

"I guess what I'm saying, Mr. President, is that we've got one horrible human tragedy about to occur which will go down in history as a dark chapter in human experience. What's about to occur on that seven-forty-seven is going to wrench the hearts of even the most cynical. I . . . just wanted to make sure you know that, because however we handle this, it'll be microanalyzed for decades."

"And you're sure there's no hope?" The President uncrossed his arms and slid off the console, standing with his hands on his hips. "Have we had any autopsy reports on the dead passenger? That professor?"

The President paced slowly toward the corner of the room, one hand pulling at his chin.

Jonathan Roth shook his head and followed, ticking off points on the fingers of his left hand.

"The autopsy team's on the way. But, Mr. President, the chain of exposure is already very clear. First, we know this biological agent is deadly beyond previous experience because it comes from a small stock of doomsday viruses discovered by the Soviets over the years—a stock that even they were afraid to exploit. We know it was shipped accidentally to that Bavarian lab. We know two researchers there were exposed, fell ill within two days, and died a demented death. We know that while fully in the throes of the disease, one of the researchers panicked and fled, and ended up in direct contact with Professor Helms. The Germans think blood was probably transferred between them in a struggle through a broken car window. And, sir, we know that Professor Helms, *also two days later,* suddenly fell ill and died aboard a seven-forty-seven full of people. The fact that he was ill with the disease means he was communicable, and the chances of exposure for everyone on board through the air-conditioning system, my experts tell me, is one hundred percent."

The President turned toward him, standing inches away, his voice also subdued.

"Wait a minute. You said it was a heart attack! That was in your initial briefing four hours ago, Jon."

"Yes, sir. But we're told this could easily be another effect of the same virus. We don't yet know *how* this virus kills. We simply know that it does. It could be a kinder, gentler set of symptoms than some . . ."

Roth saw the President wince and scowl at him.

"Sorry for the Bushism. What I'm saying is, whether it kills in a horrible way, or causes coronary or respiratory failure, the result is still the same. One hundred percent fatal."

"You said the Bavarian researcher died a demented death. Well, did this professor also go berserk like the scientist in Bavaria?"

Roth shook his head again. "Not that I'm aware, but a psychoactive reaction isn't necessarily required. Some may have it, some may not, and the reaction of the lab tech could have been panic or hysteria with regard to his illness."

The President was shaking his head vigorously. "Jon, this doesn't sound like an airtight connection to me. There could still be hope. Maybe Helms wasn't infected. Maybe we *will* have a few survivors. Maybe we'll have a *lot* of survivors!"

Roth waited a few seconds before answering. "And if so, maybe even the survivors will be permanently infectious and can't ever come home. An infected person never gets rid of the HIV virus, for instance."

Once again the President turned and stared in stunned silence.

Roth decided to continue.

"Sir, I'm trying to hold on to some hope too, but all my instincts tell me it isn't justified. And if my instincts are right, we need to prepare rapidly. Where do we want this to occur?"

"You mean for public relations purposes?" the President almost sneered. He could see the searing investigative stories in his mind's eye: *President Schemes for Political Advantage While Hundreds Die in Agony.*

Roth's hands were up instantly. "No, no, no! I mean in terms of further exposure of the population. The airplane will have to be burned, as will all the bodies. It may even be necessary to fly the airplane to a remote desert location and use a very small, low-yield nuclear warhead to make sure no biological component could survive. My God, Mr. President, if we mishandle this and it enters the general population, it could kill half the humans on Earth! I'm not kidding, sir. This is the biological equivalent of a thermonuclear war if we don't contain it! There is no cure for it, and it kills within three days. The implications are staggering!"

The President stared silently at his acting CIA director for so long Jonathan Roth worried that he'd dropped into some sort of trance.

"Nuclear . . . ?"

Finally the President turned away, shaking his head, and looked at the map for a few seconds before speaking, his voice coming in careful meter with a different tone—a command tone.

"Okay, Jon. You mentioned a desert. That's a good idea. Find me a spot in an overseas desert somewhere with a long-enough runway. Find me some place we can send in emergency aid, tents, and other facilities to get these people off that airplane and give them a little dignity if . . . if they're really doomed." He turned suddenly, looking Roth in the eye. "Find me a place where we can do as much for them as is humanly possible, without endangering any other population center. Get with State and Defense—get the secretaries out of bed —use the room here and work with your people at Langley by phone. Get me an answer in an hour if you possibly can. Meanwhile, I'm going to talk to the Icelandic ambassador and buy some time."

Roth nodded as the President swept out the door toward the elevator, then returned, holding on to the doorjamb and leaning into the room at a precarious angle.

"Jon? Find me the most humane way to help these people that preserves all our options."

CIA HEADQUARTERS, LANGLEY, VIRGINIA—
6:45 P.M. (2345Z)

Mark Hastings stood in the doorway of the conference room Jonathan Roth had turned into a command post, surprised to find Dr. Rusty Sanders still working away at a rapidly connected computer terminal. Hastings moved quietly behind Sanders, looking at the monitor over his shoulder. A long list of medical terminology was scrolling across the screen—lists of infectious human viruses with detailed descriptions of their symptoms.

"I thought you'd be gone by now," Hastings said.

Sanders jumped slightly and turned around.

"What? Oh, Mark." He turned back to the screen and gestured at the data. "This is getting too interesting, and frustrating." He gestured again. "I'm trying to find a viral pathogen similar to the one our Russian friend described, the one Director Roth is so sure we're dealing with on Flight Sixty-six. This is without precedent."

Hastings pulled up a chair next to Sanders and sat

down, letting his eyes follow Sanders' finger on the screen.

"See, this one here, for instance. High fever, delirium, respiratory complications, and numerous chemical imbalances as the body tries to respond—but no coronary involvement."

Hastings looked from the screen to Sanders. The lopsided tie was gone, which was just as well.

Totally disorganized, but likable . . . and sharp, Hastings thought.

There was a yellow legal pad in Sanders' lap covered with notations, and a full cup of coffee, grown cold, sitting next to the computer.

Dedicated and intense too.

Sanders detected the silence and looked at Hastings, who pointed to the screen himself.

"Why are you digging so far into this? We don't even know which of the Russian doomsday bugs we're dealing with yet."

"True," Sanders said, nodding hastily and moving his chair back slightly. "But, Mark, I . . . I'm getting the wrong vibrations. I mean, I can't find any evidence to support the theory that a guy can suddenly keel over and go into coronary arrest or fibrillation and attribute it to a virus—unless this attacks the heart muscle first."

"You're talking about the professor, right?"

"Yeah. Exactly." Sanders sprang to his feet suddenly, startling Hastings. He gestured to the screen again broadly with his left hand.

"I mean, Mark . . . *Mark* . . . the only connection that virus has with Flight Sixty-six is Professor Helms. Without that, we don't have an infected airplane. If the guy really had a heart attack, it greatly reduces the chances that he was in the contagious stages of a lethal virus."

Hastings nodded. "Granted, but I'm bothered by one aspect of what you say. Now, I'm not a physician like you, but isn't it possible for someone like this professor to be suffering from such a virus in an infectious stage,

yet have a heart attack that's purely coincidental . . .
in other words, wholly unconnected with the virus?"

Sanders paced a few feet away and drummed his fingers on the table in thought, then returned and plopped down in the chair again, leaning forward with a questioning expression.

"You trained as a lawyer, Mark? I feel like an expert witness under cross-examination. That's a good question."

Hastings laughed. "It's that obvious?"

Sanders rotated his hands, palms up. "I wouldn't say, *obvious* . . ."

"Yes, you would, Doctor. Yeah, I'm another attorney who hated practicing. But let's get back to the point. If he had a heart attack, does that logically mean he couldn't be infected with this . . . what'd you call it . . . pathogen?"

"Pathogen is correct. Webster's defines 'pathogen' as the specific cause of a disease. And you're right. One conclusion does not logically flow from the other. Also, I have to admit that the stress alone of physically dealing with a virus even in early stages could have brought on an attack, provided he already had a heart problem. To that end, I'm trying to get his medical records." Sanders tilted his head and raised an eyebrow. "Did you know I talked to one of the flight attendants on the phone a few minutes ago?"

Hastings shook his head. He was impressed Sanders had figured out the communications.

"The pilots called the head flight attendant up to the cockpit to talk to me. She said the professor was ill when he came on board. One of her crew had to help him to his seat. Yet the initial onset of a heart attack can produce the symptoms she described: high fever, excessive weakness, respiratory difficulties, and nausea—even delirium if the circulatory impairment gets sufficiently severe before the main onset."

Sanders looked at Hastings and shrugged. "But the Director seems to believe it's a closed issue."

Hastings smiled and looked away a second, gauging how much to say. He could tell Sanders was a fireball of energy and curiosity, and obviously the Company trusted him enough to give him a paycheck and a security clearance, but the subtle shades of nuance needed to survive life at Langley seemed to be missing.

"Can I call you Rusty?"

"Sure. I've been calling you Mark."

Mark Hastings nodded and held up an index finger.

"Rusty, a word of advice. Be very, very careful around Jonathan Roth. He's powerful, connected, and capable, and can and has gotten rid of anyone who rubs him the wrong way. You'd do well to consider him dangerous, but I'm not going to explain that. He's been in the intelligence business most of his life. He was a field agent for years in Covert Ops, station chief in more places than I can count, and he's the ranking expert on tracking and interdicting Middle East terrorism. His reputation for sniffing out terrorist organizations before they can strike American interests is legendary around here."

Sanders nodded. "I know. I've read his history. I was astounded when you guys and gals called me up here to brief him. Usually I just write esoteric analytical reports in the basement. Interesting stuff to research, but low level."

"You're no slouch yourself, Rusty. You come highly recommended. Just . . . just be as diplomatic with him as you can."

"Mark, I appreciate that, but I'm not pulling my punches. He's rushing to judgment on this, and others could make some pretty serious decisions based on what could be a wrong assumption. I mean, my God, he's over there briefing the *President*."

Hastings cocked his head. "I'm not asking you to pull punches, but you've got to have proof, Rusty, to convince this man."

Sanders nodded and chewed his lip. "I know that, but I've also learned to trust my intuition, and it's screaming at me that we're rushing to an unsupported conclusion which could lead to other, more frightening conclusions about what to do."

One of the other analysts in the room, Sherry Ellis, had been talking earnestly on the phone for the previous minute. She replaced the receiver and appeared at Mark Hastings' side as she smiled at Rusty Sanders.

"Mr. Roth just called from the White House," she said with a pronounced Southern drawl. "We're to drop everything else and check out three possible desert landing fields."

"Can I help?" Sanders asked, getting out of his chair.

"The way you dance around that computer keyboard, Doctor? I wouldn't let you out of here if you tried. Mark, we've got thirty minutes."

Hastings got to his feet as well, a suspicious look on his face.

"What's he planning?"

Sherry shook her head and sighed.

"You're not going to like this, Mark. He needs to find some place in the desert where the President can send them to die. Some place too far from civilization to spread this bug."

Hastings turned to Sanders. "Didn't you say we shouldn't send them to a warm area?"

Rusty Sanders nodded slowly but held up a finger. "A damp, warm area is the worst. A dry, hot desert climate would not be a particular problem, but you see what I mean, Mark? One conclusion leading to another?"

Sherry continued.

"And, fellows, the location's got to be within ten hours' flight time of the East Coast, yet remote enough to contain a small nuclear blast."

The words hit Hastings and Sanders like a physical blow.

"What?!" both men exclaimed simultaneously.

Sherry nodded sternly. "That's exactly what he said. After they're all dead, the seven-forty-seven and the bodies will have to be incinerated. A nuclear fireball would be foolproof."

Sanders turned and paced toward the window. "I don't believe this! No one's even got a cold up there and he's already vaporizing the bodies!" He turned back toward Sherry, glancing at Hastings, who was still standing slack-jawed and stunned.

"My God," Hastings said, working hard to recover his professional balance. "What . . . what are the candidate sites, Sherry?"

"The first is a remote airstrip in the Sahara built by the Soviets. Twenty degrees north latitude, eight degrees west longitude. Technically in Mauritania, though I doubt there's a governmental presence for five hundred miles. There's another in southern Egypt, and one in southern Algeria. All airfields, all essentially abandoned and in the middle of nowhere. State's checking on receptivity of the respective nations, the UN is involved, DOD is handling the facilities report and suitability for receiving a large transport as well as airlift from the U.S., and we're tasked with checking the rest of it. In the meantime, I'm told there are C-15 and C-17 transports being loaded at Dover as we speak, to launch ASAP. They'll be given their destination in the air."

Mark Hastings nodded. "We'll need the latest intelligence on the political situations, governmental stability, insurgency, nomadic threats, military threats, et cetera, for each spot, plus the National Security Agency's latest satellite shots, and current orbital tracks of available satellites, and which ones we can seize and how soon."

"That's all?" Sherry asked sarcastically.

"I suppose," Hastings replied.

"Wrong!" Sherry said, her index finger raised to eye level. "There's one other directive. Director Roth was adamant, as you know Director Roth can be. The thundering herd at the Defense Intelligence Agency, he says, is going to try to upstage us on this and present their report to the President before we do. So, we either beat the DIA with the analysis, or you and I, Mark, will share station chief duties in Tierra del Fuego!"

Rusty Sanders looked from Sherry to Mark and back

again with an incredulous expression, ignoring their exchange. "The DIA thing. Is . . . is that what it always comes down to around here? People's lives are hanging in the balance, and Roth's worried about interagency competition?"

Mark smiled thinly and patted Rusty on the shoulder as he turned toward the door.

"We could answer that, Doctor, but then we'd have to kill you," he said, tongue in cheek.

At the door he turned and smiled again.

"Before the DIA did, of course."

TWELVE

———

Frigid winds were now howling from the east in icy gusts up to thirty knots and snow showers were blowing sideways, rocking the giant Boeing back and forth every few minutes. The auxiliary power unit was running steadily and the cabin was warm and comfortable, but all Holland could think about was the phone conversation he'd just completed with Dallas.

Earlier, thirty-eight passengers seated in the upper-deck section had been quietly asked to relocate to the main cabin below. All had complied without argument. With Brenda Hopkins—and the four others who'd come into direct contact with Ernest Helms—seated in the forward rows, James Holland had then asked the rest of his crew upstairs for a face-to-face briefing, leaving the cockpit empty for the first time in nine hours.

Holland looked at the now anxious faces of his crew as he leaned against a railing at the front of the cabin. They had taken the first two rows of seats, except for Dick Robb, who was standing to one side of him with his arms folded, saying nothing.

Ambassador Lancaster and Rachael Sherwood had also been asked to come upstairs and were seated in the third row. The increasingly difficult evangelist, Garson Wilson, had jumped up and headed for the stairs to the upper deck too, until an exasperated Barb Rollins, the lead flight attendant, barred his way and ordered him to go back and stay in his seat. He complied, more out of shock at her strong determination than out of any willingness to obey. Sitting heavily in his seat, Wilson glared in her direction, snarling ugly names under his breath as his secretary winced and looked around quickly to see if anyone else had heard.

Holland cleared his throat, stared at the carpet, then tried to look his crew in the eye. He didn't want to lie to them, but how much to tell was an agony. His emotions were screaming to tell it all, but his instincts held him back.

"Okay, folks, we're in a strange, unprecedented situation here, but we're going to get through it just fine. Now, we're going to need all the strength of character and professionalism we've got to keep our passengers encouraged and steady, and having said that, let me tell you the latest word I have from the vice president of Operations."

Holland paused and forced a smile.

"Folks, the powers that be are telling our company that our passenger was exposed to a particularly serious virus. What we know about this virus is that it can make you pretty sick for a while, but as long as you've got enough fluids and rest, you know, most viruses go away in a week or so."

Holland looked each of the flight attendants in the eye, one by one, then let his eyes wander to Rachael Sherwood, who was watching him closely. She smiled a little flicker of a smile and gave a tiny nod of encouragement.

The vice president's voice played again in his head. *This could be a false alarm. Even if your passenger died from this virus, it might not spread.*

Holland looked at Barb Rollins and continued.

"Now, our company is *convinced* that this is a false alarm and a bureaucratic overreaction, at least to the extent that the reactions from all these countries have been way out of proportion to reality. Our passenger may well have died of a simple heart attack and nothing more. Instead of this virus that has everyone worried, he may have had a simple case of the flu. The doctor who helped Brenda with her heroic CPR efforts confirmed that it seemed like nothing more than a coronary, with a few precursor symptoms, such as the nausea and complaints of dizziness."

Holland looked around the group once more before continuing. He tried to smile, and hoped the result looked sincere.

"Now, all that nonsense back in London and our abortive attempt to return to Frankfurt, and then our inability to get clearance to land at either Amsterdam or Mildenhall Air Base in Great Britain—all that was merely the by-product of governments scaring each other into hysteria with half-truths and misinformation. There are some really wild rumors, and some have even been broadcast by the media, so even governmental agencies that should know better are reacting by slamming the door in our faces. I'm sorry I couldn't keep you better informed, but things were happening awfully fast, and a two-person cockpit gets really busy."

James, since we last talked, well . . . you need to know that the European nations are convinced you're all contaminated with a virus so lethal, they're scared to death of you. I think they're nuts, of course, but we have to work with that. Our government knows it isn't that bad, but they've got diplomatic problems too, and the bottom line is, the White House wants to keep you away from North America until we get this figured out. Political concerns, you understand. If Europe panicked, North America would panic. We'll just keep you there until everyone's well, or no one's gotten sick; then there's no problem.

Holland looked to the side, through one of the windows, noting the snowflakes streaming by horizontally, almost as if the plane were in flight.

"I know it's Christmas," he began. "I know the effect this is having—and going to have—on all of us, even if not a single person gets as much as a cold and we all get home by Christmas Day. We're going to have some deeply upset passengers, and we're going to be fighting our own emotions, and to that end, the company wants you to know that we're going to provide satellite phone calls home for everyone free of charge. You're included in that. You need to let your loved ones know you're okay, because the press coverage out there may be frightening to them."

James, we're not in control of this. Our government is, and we're told that the President of the United States is personally calling the shots. We're still trying to break through the nonsense and get you clearance to fly back here, somewhere.

"Our company is working hand in glove with the U.S. government to take care of us, folks, and break through the Public Health Service regulations we'd run afoul of if we flew directly to New York right now. Our best bet may be to stay right here."

He told them the refueling was being postponed until they had agreed on a new destination. And he told them that absolutely no one was allowed outside the aircraft, omitting the part about armed guards and intent to kill.

"I'm going to make a critical PA," he told them. "I'm going to tell them pretty much what I've told you, and I'm going to sound even more optimistic and upbeat and confident. Please smile and support me, and let me know if we have any bad reactions. I'll come down myself in a bit."

Then he took questions, and sent those not quarantined back to their crew positions to watch the passengers closely.

When most of the crew had left the upper deck, Holland turned to Dick Robb and gestured toward the stairway.

"Dick, anything you can suggest, any observations, anything, for heaven's sake jump in and tell me, okay? I'm . . . sorry I snapped at you back there in the London area. I do want your advice and counsel."

Robb flicked his right hand to the side to dismiss the incident and concentrated on his shoes.

"It's okay," Robb said.

"You okay with my briefing?"

Robb turned and met his gaze. "Yeah. Sure."

"I mean, you are still in charge."

"You're the acting captain." The younger man looked up at Holland with a sudden movement of his head.

"James, you ever been through anything like this before?"

Holland shook his head no. "I'm not sure *anyone's* ever been through anything exactly like this."

Robb sighed and looked away again, then back at his shoes. "I've got a really bad feeling about this. I'm kind of glad we're staying here, y'know?" He looked up again. "At least this is an American base. Even if they won't let us come home for Christmas, this is safe."

Silence filled the space between them for several lengthy seconds before Holland gestured to the cockpit. "I'd, ah, better make that PA."

Robb nodded without looking and turned away.

In the rear of the coach cabin, Lisa Erickson listened with focused intensity to every word James Holland was speaking on the PA. Clutching a small airline pillow tightly to her chest, her eyes locked on the speaker above her head, she pursed her lips and waited for word that it was over and they would be home in a few hours.

Her children were waiting.

"We would love nothing better than to get all of us home for Christmas," the captain was saying. She smiled a little at that and nodded silently. She would like nothing better as well. There could be nothing better. There *would* be nothing else. She had to get home!

". . . but I'm afraid, folks, that we've got to face a reality. It will be at least Christmas Eve by the time they release us from this miniature quarantine, so we probably won't make it in time."

Keith Erickson thought at first a siren had gone off. The piercing, high-pitched scream was too sustained to come from a human being. But very quickly, as every head in coach turned in his direction, he realized the ungodly noise was coming from his wife.

It was a monstrous wail of agony that knew no modulation or limits. It came from the depth of a tortured mind and continued for an eternity until the lungs propelling it demanded more air, and then it began anew as two alarmed flight attendants converged on the scene with their nerves frazzled and eardrums in shock.

Keith grabbed Lisa and held her. He rocked her, talked to her, shook her, and finally got through. The pitch declined to a whimper, and then died out to nothing but a strange expression as she sat with her lips slack, looking at but not seeing the seat back in front of her. She pulled her knees up and encircled them with her arms, rocking back and forth slowly.

"Are you okay? Honey, can you hear me?" Keith was saying in her ear, over and over again.

At first there was no response. Then she turned toward her husband and smiled a vacant smile as she looked through him.

"I'm perfectly fine, Keith," she said with the deliberate meter of a Stepford wife. Her words came with excessive slowness, as if nothing had happened. "I am fine."

As Barb Rollins backed slowly away from the couple, Lisa resumed her rocking, her eyes returning to the seat back, the same strange expression on her face.

After the crew briefing, Lee Lancaster had excused himself to return to the first class cabin below, leaving word with Rachael for the captain to call him up if there was anything more he could do. Rachael had remained behind in a front-row seat in the upper cabin within view of the cockpit. She saw Dick Robb stroll to the back, and watched through the open cockpit door as James Holland sat heavily on the center jump seat and organized what he was going to say to the passengers.

When he had finished the PA, she was waiting at the cockpit door.

Holland looked up and smiled, slightly startled.

"Rachael. Come on in."

"Thanks. Should I close the door or anything?"

James Holland looked beyond her to the door and then to the cabin. Dick Robb was nowhere in sight, and the passageway was deserted. But he nodded to her anyway, and she felt behind her for the doorknob, and quietly pulled the door closed.

"This cockpit's a little cramped, but not too bad," he said by way of apology. He leaned over and motored the copilot's seat back toward the right, motioning for her to sit sideways facing him. She slid in carefully around the center console before looking up and getting momentarily lost in his eyes again.

Holland held her gaze for a few seconds and looked away, feeling suddenly embarrassed and not knowing why. The snowfall outside had increased in intensity, and though the winds had decreased, a gust gently rocked the aircraft as Holland's eyes followed the runway lights to the east.

"I, ah . . . appreciate you and the ambassador helping with all this," he finally said.

"Not a problem," she replied, smiling. "I'm glad we were here."

He looked at her again with a puzzled expression, and she blushed.

"Oh well, I mean, I'm not glad we're in the middle of . . . of this situation, but . . ."

"I understand." He chuckled.

"I mean . . . if someone had to be here, I guess I'm . . ."

"Glad it's you?"

She laughed easily, he noticed. Her smile was captivating, and it felt good to be talking to her.

"Stupid statement, right?" she said. "I'm just happy we could help, since we're certainly in this together."

They fell silent for a few seconds, listening to the gusts of wind and to the hum of electronics coursing like a pulse through the cockpit.

Holland gestured toward the floor, toward the first class cabin below.

"I've got a question for you. Are you familiar with this fellow Wilson, Garson Wilson?"

"God's registered agent?" She laughed. "Yeah, I've been watching him. He wants off this airplane badly, and his poor little secretary is trying to shut him up half the time. It's almost funny, but I'm more intrigued by some of the other passengers."

"Oh?"

"You've got the sweetest little couple down there. Honeymooners, in their eighties if they're a day, wearing natty clothes and returning from three weeks around the Continent on their own. The Palmers. Betty and Bill. They're taking all this in stride, and I really enjoyed talking with them. They're so cute with each other. They've been holding hands since we took off."

She noticed his attention drifting and stopped talking. He was looking at the door.

He brought his eyes back to her and smiled. "I'm being selfish. I need to go down there and walk through and talk to everyone. They need to see and talk to the person behind the voice."

She cocked her head. "Selfish?"

James Holland got to his feet and held out his hand to help her up. Rachael took it and let him gently pull her to her feet.

"Yeah, selfish," he said. "I'd much rather be up here with you than dealing with the realities of all this."

"Why, *thank* you, sir." Rachael tried to keep an even smile on her face and hide the blush that had suddenly begun very deep inside and was working its way out, a tiny wave of delight that was at once inappropriate for where they were and yet in a strange way compensatory.

Holland started to turn but she held on to his right hand, and he looked back at her.

"James, you are telling me . . . I mean us . . . everything, aren't you? You don't really think we're all going to get sick?"

He looked away for a second and the gesture caused her stomach to tighten, but just as quickly his eyes returned to hers and he nodded.

"I think we're in more danger from panicked bureaucrats than from any virus, Rachael. No, I don't think we're going to get sick."

He let her hand go slowly—reluctantly, she thought—and turned to open the door. He paused then and turned back to her with the same hollow, haunted expression she had seen in Frankfurt.

"I just hope they're telling *me* everything."

THIRTEEN

THE WHITE HOUSE, WASHINGTON, D.C.—
FRIDAY, DECEMBER 22—9 P.M. (0200Z)

Jonathan Roth shot from the front portico of the White House and climbed into his black Mercedes where he'd left it on the front drive. It was 9 P.M. and the streets of the capital were mostly deserted on what had become a cold, overcast night. He was a mile down Pennsylvania Avenue heading toward Georgetown before his thoughts returned to the Saharan airfield that would be the final resting place for Flight 66.

What a tragedy, he thought. Two hundred forty-four men, women, and children, and twelve airline crew members, doomed to die what would probably be an agonizing death.

It had taken the President only a few minutes to accept his recommendation of the Mauritanian site. It was the field closest to the Atlantic Ocean, and five hundred miles in all directions from the nearest outpost—which was why the Soviets had once invested money for a secret airfield there before the collapse of the U.S.S.R.

The image of all those people getting sick one by one came swimming back, pulling at his emotions and surprising him. He thought he was case-hardened against such things. He'd seen more than a little death and carnage before, and had been responsible for the demise of several people during his years in Covert Ops. He'd also been the Company's first man on the scene in Jonestown. The sight of those bloated bodies had been even more horrifying than the stench, which he could remember with nauseating clarity.

His thoughts snapped back to the present.

All those people, and a brand-new Boeing 747-400 to boot! What a waste!

He thought about the airline's Operations staff in Dallas. They had sounded so hopeful on the phone. The President had ordered him not to tell them the truth about the suspected nature of the virus, or the mortality rate. The political protests and personal pleas might cloud the cooler heads that were trying to do what had to be done. Quantum had no idea they were about to lose most, if not all, of their passengers and crew—as well as the airplane—in a historic tragedy.

Too bad the airplane doesn't just roll over and dive into the Atlantic. It'd be a coup de grâce. Over in a second. No pain, no suffering, and no spectacle of having to incinerate hundreds of contaminated bodies with the media trying to televise it live.

Roth automatically maneuvered onto a deserted Conrail Road west of Georgetown, heading for the Chain Bridge—his course back to Langley little more than an automatic program in the back of his busy mind.

The President was already distraught about the impending loss of Ambassador Lee Lancaster, and was fretting about when to call him and whether to tell him what the others certainly didn't know: that everyone aboard would be dead within the next seventy-two hours.

Roth sighed, and then snorted. What irony! He had met Ambassador Lancaster many times. Brilliant diplomat, but a pain in the butt to the intelligence community. Every time Lancaster traveled, the CIA had to work overtime to ferret out the latest terrorist plot to kill him. Roth had lost count of the number of airliners the ambassador had boarded that had been the unfulfilled targets of terrorist bombs.

He shook his head.

The one time in recent memory there's no active plot against Lancaster is exactly when we need one!

He thought of Al Aqbah, the newest, most lethal member of the Iranian-backed suicidal terrorist groups. Aqbah was doubly frightening because of a technical expertise never seen before in such circles. Roth remembered the American-trained Iranian pilot caught months before preparing to fly a MIG-29 fighter on a low-level suicide mission into Rome. His target had been the Vatican—and the Pope. No longer, it seemed, did terrorists need to hijack airliners and ships to reach out and touch their targets. They had fighters and missiles and probably more than a few nuclear warheads, most of them purchased from cash-hungry military units in the former Soviet Union. He knew only too well how easy it was to buy sophisticated military hardware from the former Eastern Bloc.

Is there any possibility, however remote, that Aqbah could be involved with exposing those people to this virus? They're ruthless enough.

He had sworn to wipe out Aqbah just as he'd helped destroy Black September and cripple Fatah. His reputation as a spymaster rested on those "brilliant" achievements. The whole intelligence community considered him a genius at knowing what such groups were thinking even before *they* knew.

But now they were waiting for Roth to move against Aqbah, and so far he'd been impotent where their operations were concerned. Electronic assets weren't his strong suit. Human assets were. He could guess what Aqbah was up to sooner than he could prove it with satellites.

The sight of a late-model Cadillac on the side of the road snagged his conscious attention. The hood was up and someone was shining a flashlight at the engine. Roth's instincts from too many years in the field kicked in, and he realized he had automatically sized up the car and driver as potentially hostile and had formulated an escape plan.

He chuckled and let his attention snap back to Aqbah as he passed the stranded car.

According to the first intelligence reports from Beirut in 1994, Aqbah had formed in the wake of the Gulf War, using Saddam Hussein's money to build a sophisticated arsenal, then double-crossing Hussein and defecting to Iran. With a string of bombings and assassinations to its "credit," when Aqbah issued a threat, the world took notice. But much to the disgust of the CIA and others, there was a twisted sort of admiration growing in the intelligence community for Aqbah's extremely sophisticated abilities. With an incredibly close-knit directorate, mindlessly fanatical Shiite Muslim operatives, and world-class experts in digital satellite technology and weaponry, Aqbah was building a superhuman reputation—at Roth's and the rest of the free world's expense.

Roth shook his head and smiled. Only he knew his vaunted reputation was all chance and circumstance. He'd blundered into the correct solutions time after time, like a real-life Inspector Clouseau. His successes were largely a function of luck.

He wondered if Aqbah's leaders were even aware that Lee Lancaster was aboard Flight 66. It was a strange truth, he thought, that blowing Flight 66 out of the sky would be an act of charity, though the world would never see it that way.

Aqbah wouldn't waste their time, but if they tried, we'd have to stop them.

Lancaster was a particularly important target for Aqbah. They had promised the Iranian clergy they would execute him for crimes against Islam—crimes so obscure he could never recall the details.

The Chain Bridge loomed before him and he negotiated the ON ramp and crossed the Potomac into Arlington County as his mind worked the problem.

Suddenly everything coalesced.

Roth yanked the steering wheel to the right and slammed on the brakes, stopping the Mercedes on the shoulder of the Georgetown Pike with a nerve-shattering squeal of tires. He sat there a second, his mind racing, before reaching over the backseat and pulling out his briefcase.

Roth laid the briefcase in the passenger seat and snapped it open. He pulled out his small notebook computer and toggled the slider switch, listening as the hard drive began spinning up on battery power. He waited impatiently for the shell menu, then selected a personnel database and called up a search menu. At last a blank line and blinking cursor dominated the screen, and he typed in a few key words and hit the ENTER button, pleased when the information appeared on the screen.

He scanned the information carefully, then turned off the computer and closed the lid.

Roth sat in deep thought behind the wheel of his idling car. He would have only a few hours to act to checkmate the enemy. If Aqbah was moving, he had to move faster, but he could do it using his personal network. Knowing the enemy's next move conferred immense power, and there was no question what Aqbah would do if they had the information and the opportunity: bring down Flight 66 on their own.

It was the opportunity he had been looking for since 1992!

Roth put the Mercedes in gear and accelerated back onto the road toward Langley.

ABOARD FLIGHT 66, KEFLAVÍK AIR FORCE BASE, ICELAND

With Holland in the main cabin below, Dick Robb had returned to the cockpit and plugged in his headset when the sound of turbine engines rose to a substantial pitch on the left and an Air Force Lockheed C-141B transport flashed by as it landed on the western end of the runway adjacent to their position, its lights slicing in otherworldly fashion through the driving snow flurries.

Robb keyed the interphone, wondering if the command truck was still manned.

"Anyone out there?"

The response was almost instantaneous. "Yes, sir."

"I thought the airport was closed. Who landed?"

"That's the team from Dover, sir. The autopsy team."

Various lights were moving on the airfield now. An Air Force staff car raced up to the command truck as the lights of the taxiing C-141 could be seen in the distance. Another moving shape caught his eye to the right, but he had looked too late and it had already disappeared behind the right wing.

"When are they going to want the body off?" Robb asked.

"In maybe an hour, sir. They'll need to set up. We'll call you."

The appearance of the six-foot-three-inch captain on the main deck of Flight 66 created an instant stir. Several passengers leapt to their feet to come ask questions, others stood but hung back, forming small groups that ebbed and flowed around him like a human current as James Holland began working his way down the right-hand aisle toward the rear of the 747.

"Captain, if New York won't let us in, why not some other state?"

"We're working on that."

"Captain, we had a flu shot before leaving on this trip. Doesn't that exclude us?"

"It's possible, but the problem is, no one has yet told us whether this even resembles a flu, and you know how even the flu changes into new strains all the time."

"Captain, my daughter's only eight, and she's scared to death. Would you talk to her?"

"Sure. Where is she?"

"Captain, you're not telling us the truth, are you?"

Holland stopped moving and looked in the face of a woman in her seventies who was watching his reaction with an unflinchingly stern expression. She looked like

an angry schoolteacher, he thought, or maybe the stereotype of an offended librarian, her half-glasses on a
cord, a light sweater tied around her neck.

He looked at her and shook his head. "Ma'am, I'm
telling you what I know."

"This is a doomsday illness," she shot back, "and if
it's really on board and that heart attack victim was a
carrier, we're dead, aren't we? You're just trying to keep
us calm."

"That's not true, ma'am, I . . ."

"I can read it in your voice and I can see it in your
eyes, young man. And you *are* young compared to me."

He smiled at that. "Thanks."

"Fact, not compliment, Captain. We're in mortal danger of dying together, aren't we?"

Holland glanced around. Several passengers were
pressing closer to listen to the exchange, and the woman
was relentlessly boring into him with her eyes, waiting
for a straightforward answer.

"Ma'am, do I looked panicked to you?" Holland
asked. "If what you're implying is true, I'd be doomed
as well, and I'm not exactly eager to . . . to . . ."

" 'Die' is the word you're choking on, Captain," she
said, "and I'm not ready either. No, you're not panicked, but I don't trust you. You know why?"

He sighed and shook his head. "No, ma'am. Why?"

"Because you're letting the so-called 'authorities' run
this show."

"Ma'am, this isn't my personal airplane. I represent a
large company, and we're all citizens of a very large
country with laws and procedures . . ."

"And coldhearted officials who don't give a tinker's
damn when it comes to us. We're a problem, Captain.
Just a problem. I don't trust you because you're not
thinking for yourself."

She turned and walked away down the aisle before he
could say anything more.

There were more children on board than he'd expected. To the right there was a family with three young

boys, the oldest maybe eight. Behind them was a young mother breast-feeding an infant. Her husband sat next to her watching the process. He looked all of sixteen but was probably in his twenties. And there was a group in the center section. High school seniors or young college students, he figured, all wearing some sort of logo on their sweatshirts and pullovers, some wearing baseball caps, and all obviously traveling together on an organized trip. There would be a legion of panicked parents back home glued to their television screens, worrying about their sons and daughters. The thought caused a small stream of adrenaline to flow into his bloodstream.

Holland looked around and tried to smile evenly at the anxious faces before him. Flying was what he did, not public relations. He felt silly and amateurish, as if forced to play the role of the sage captain when he was just a pilot.

An elderly man approached, his back hunched over with the weight of years, but his eyes bright as he fastened them on Holland. He stuck out a surprisingly large hand and Holland took it.

"Captain? I'm Homer Knutsen, former captain with Pan Am for thirty-four years, flying boats through seven-forty-sevens." Knutsen squeezed his hand, and Holland could feel a slight palsy in the older man's hand. "I'm aware of what you're doing down here. I just wanted to tell you to hang in there. I've been in some real tough situations myself; and somehow things all seem to work out. You've done good by coming downstairs."

"Thanks, Captain." Holland patted Knutsen's hand with his left palm and moved on, the old woman's words still stinging in his mind:

". . . *because you're not thinking for yourself*"!

The comments and questions began again in earnest.

"Captain, we've got a real problem if we can't get home by Christmas."

"Captain, your flight attendant was rude as hell to me when I asked her, but I need to know exactly what this virus is. I'm a microbiologist and might be able to help explain things."

"Captain, we're starving to death and your crew is refusing to serve anything."

"Captain, do you realize how bad those toilets stink?"

"Captain, my husband's medicine is in our bag which is checked. He'll run out in several hours. What do we do?"

Holland passed the woman with the checked medication to one of the crew and found Barb in the back. He asked about the food situation.

"We're ready to go with the breakfast service, but I was going to wait until at least six A.M. If you want, we can go ahead with it now, or I could serve all the crackers and peanuts we have with a drink service, then turn down the lights and try to get them to sleep," she told him.

He nodded. "Hold the breakfast and do the snacks now. What can I do to help?"

"Heat up the cabin a bit when we're ready. That'll help put 'em to sleep."

She gestured to the crew rest loft in the back of the plane. "How long before we put the professor's body outside?"

He shook his head and shrugged. "They'll let us know. Why?"

Barb looked forward, checking something, then back at Holland.

"We've got a young man in coach, in a bulkhead seat, with a cast on a broken leg. The leg is swelling and that Swiss doctor says he needs it elevated. We thought we'd put him in one of the other beds up in the loft when . . . you know. But I don't want to expose him to . . . you know, Mr. Helms."

"Make sure Helms's body is curtained off in one of the bunks, and—I hate to say this, but maybe Brenda and the doctor, since they've already been exposed, could use some of the large plastic sacks from the galley to seal him up. As long as no one touches the body, I wouldn't worry about the other beds up there."

"Okay. And James . . ." Barb reached up and took his chin in her hand, rotating his head to one side and then the other as she inspected his face.

"Yes?"

"If this goes on much longer, we're going to have to start sleeping the crew in shifts, and that includes you. You're exhausted. Can I get you anything?"

She dropped her hand and Holland patted her on the shoulder.

"About a quart of adrenaline," he said, "and a hundred fifty thousand pounds of jet fuel."

"You settle for two Excedrin and a Diet Coke?"

He chuckled and nodded. "I'll need it. I've got to run the gauntlet back to the cockpit."

Barb promptly supplied him with both. He tossed the pills in his mouth and washed them down with the Coke, polishing off the contents of the can in several quick gulps.

The flight attendant call chime rang and Barb answered it, handing the handset immediately to Holland.

"It's your costar, calling from the bridge," she said.

"Oh yeah?" He took the handset. "Yeah, Dick?"

Barb could see his features change, first to puzzlement, then to a broad smile. He replaced the phone and turned to her, saying nothing at first.

"What is it? *What?*" she asked in her nasal Brooklyn twang.

"They're fueling us," he said. "They haven't said why. That probably means they're going to change their minds and release us."

He turned to leave.

Barb's hands shot out and caught him by the shoulders, turning him back toward her as her eyes sought his. Her expression was deadly serious. "What do you mean, 'release,' James? I thought sitting here was optional. You're telling me we were being forced to stay?"

"Well . . ."

"James, please don't fib to your crew."

"I'm not, Barb. It's just that they weren't going to refuel us until they received new orders, which was going to happen when the company decided where in the U.S. to send us. Obviously that's now been decided."

"Okay," she said, unconvinced, as Holland twisted free and headed forward at an energetic clip.

Robb looked off-balance when Holland reentered the cockpit.

"I was looking at the damned fuel gauges, James, and they just started rising without warning. The sergeant down there says they just received orders to fill the tanks. No other explanation."

Holland slipped into the left seat. "You try Dallas on the satellite line?"

"Not yet," Robb replied.

Holland reestablished contact with the Operations vice president, who wasn't surprised.

"There's been a decision, James, to get you out of there to a safer place."

"Safer? I don't understand. Safer for whom? We're perfectly safe here."

There was a telling pause. "Ah, James, remember I told you everyone was overreacting to this threat? Well, the Icelandic government found out you were there, and they want you the hell out of there, preferably yesterday."

"Afraid we'll contaminate them, huh?"

"Yeah, you know, based on the doomsday assessment."

That word again! Holland thought. Where had he heard it in the last thirty minutes? Oh, yeah. The angry lady downstairs. A "doomsday illness," she'd called it.

"What, exactly, is the 'doomsday assessment'?" Holland asked him.

Another pause. Much too long this time.

"Okay, ah, probably the wrong word," the vice president began, "but the German government has spooked everyone now by telling the media that this bug they're convinced you're carrying around on our airplane could kill off half the human population of Earth. That's asinine, of course! They're trying to justify their actions in refusing to take you back in Frankfurt. But I warned you that if Europe panicked, North America would too—and now Iceland."

"So who's panicked in the U.S., and where are we going?"

"We're . . . not going to be able to get you back where we'd like to just yet. The White House and the Defense Department have worked out an airfield you can fly to safely, though. It's one that's away from any protesting civilian populations or politicians, okay? Over an hour ago they launched a pretty good-sized fleet of Air Force cargo planes loaded with doctors, tents, food, and everything else you'd need if the worst possible case occurred—which it won't."

"And they're all wearing moon suits, right?"

"I . . . would imagine they are, James, until they're sure this is a false alarm."

"So where are we going for Christmas? Arizona? Nevada? New Mexico?" He knew his voice had taken on an unfriendly edge, but he really didn't care. This was getting stupid.

"Africa," the veep replied. "There's an airfield there with a perfectly adequate runway built originally by the Soviets."

"*WHAT!*" Holland vaguely realized he had yelled into the receiver.

Robb, an alarmed look on his face, reached down and punched on the satellite phone monitor button so he could hear both sides of the call on his headset.

"What do you mean, Africa?" Holland asked. "That's the opposite direction!"

"I know this sounds crazy, James, but it's for the best. Dispatch will transmit the flight plan on the satellite link to your ACARS printer in a few minutes, but you're going to fly to twenty degrees north latitude, eight degrees west longitude, in the western Sahara. You might want to write that down."

Robb's eyes were growing large as Holland lowered his voice and tried to reply evenly.

"Sir, I don't think that's wise. These passengers are upset enough. If we go the wrong way, they're going to think we're being written off. They won't believe a thing I say from now on. Why don't you just tell whoever's coming up with this idea that the captain refused? After all, we don't know how long it might be before we get sick."

Robb was nodding vigorously and giving Holland a sweeping thumbs-up sign.

The Operations vice president was talking again.

"James, listen up. This is not optional, okay? There's a major diplomatic problem here. I'm told the Icelandic government is threatening to abrogate the treaty and close that base if you don't leave. I need you to cooperate. Unless you've got a valid safety problem that they can independently verify, you have to do it. And by the way, they assure me there's no way you could get sick inside the next forty hours, okay? But we don't have time to keep arguing."

Holland was rubbing his temple with his right hand.

"I really don't believe this."

"James, look, I'm sorry. The pressure on us from Washington is enormous. The President himself is involved in these decisions."

James Holland sighed deeply and sat back in the seat with his eyes closed and the phone pressed tightly to his ear. He heard his voice, or a subdued version of his voice, say what neither his heart nor his copilot wanted to hear.

"Okay, sir, okay. If that's what you want us to do, we'll take the bird to Africa."

There was a rising rumble of sound and fury from the right seat.

"LIKE HELL YOU WILL!" Robb roared.

Holland's head snapped to the right. Dick Robb's jaw was set, his eyes flaring.

"Tell him we're not moving this friggin' airplane!" Robb snarled.

Holland shook his head and raised the palm of his free hand.

"Dick, that's . . ."

"TELL HIM, dammit!"

Holland could hear the Operations vice president's voice on the other end.

"What's going on there, James? Who's that?"

"Just a momentary command disagreement, sir. Disregard. Go ahead and send the flight plan. I'm going to disconnect now."

Holland replaced the receiver, aware that Robb had panicked, and that the panic was triggering extreme anger.

"You *gave in* to him, just like that! Who the hell's in charge, anyway? Jesus Christ, James! There's no way— NO WAY—we should leave here until this thing is over."

Both Holland's large hands were engaged in furiously rubbing his temples, his eyes closed tight. He almost mumbled the reply.

"Why?"

"What?" Robb seemed stunned. "Did you ask why? Why what?"

Holland dropped his hands and turned to him, his voice low and steady.

"Why shouldn't we leave? They're giving us no help here at all, and it's freezing out there. Maybe the desert will be more comfortable, and we can get out of the airplane."

"You'd do any damn thing they tell you, wouldn't you?"

Robb was careening dangerously into personal abuse, his voice shaking at times. Rage was masking panic.

Holland sighed. "That doesn't deserve an answer, Dick."

"Goddammit, Holland! I give you complete latitude to exercise a captain's authority, and when the crunch comes, the best you can do is follow orders? We expect to see command authority in our captains, not Caspar Milquetoast and his amazing toady act. I've never seen such a pussy!"

"I asked for your advice, Dick, not your personal abuse. I'm asking again. Since you obviously think I'm failing command one-oh-one, please tell me what *you'd* do?"

There was a short silence as the explosion built.

"Show some fucking backbone for starters!"

Holland nodded slowly, deliberately.

"Do you want to assume command?"

Robb shook his head. "Hell no, I want *you* to!"

"In other words, you want me to tell them no?"

"Hell yes, tell them no! We're not going to fly this tub anywhere but back home! If you'd just say no, that vice president of stupidity back in Dallas would call the White House and say, sorry, the captain's exercised his emergency authority and you're overruled."

Holland looked down at the floor between his feet and shook his head.

"Dick, I'm a lot older than you . . ."

Robb sneered out loud. "Yeah! Not that it shows in your fucking attitude, or anything!"

Holland chose to ignore that. ". . . and I think I've got a little more experience in trying to fight the system than you. Since leaving Frankfurt, we've tried to push the emergency authority button at least twice. Hasn't worked, has it?"

"You're . . . talking about governments. I'm talking about our fucking airline."

"*And* our government," Holland replied. "But since you mention our airline, has it occurred to you that the man I was just talking to could fire us both in an instant?"

"That's all you're fucking concerned with, isn't it? Keeping your job!"

Holland straightened up in the seat and glowered over at Robb, leveling a finger at his face.

"Stop using that word to me! Do you understand? I expect a little professionalism out of you, Check Captain Robb, and I'm not going to put up with you spouting the *f* word in my cockpit."

Robb looked startled. His mouth flapped open and shut a few times before he found his voice. "I . . . okay. But the point still stands! You're in charge, and you're letting yourself be led around by the nose."

"And you'd tell him no?"

"You bet I would."

"And this from the company man who's been beating me bloody on the subject of strict compliance with all procedures?"

Robb's right hand flew up in a gesture of disgust. "A good captain knows when to tell the company to shove it and make his own decisions!"

"So making my own decisions constitutes command decisiveness?"

"Damn right!"

"You've got it, mister. I'm exercising my command authority to make my own decision, and I decide that the best course of action is to follow the company's orders and go to Africa! That's what we're doing. Forceful enough for you?"

"You don't get it, do you, James?"

"Guess not."

"Command forcefulness means saying no!"

Holland shook his head.

"I've had enough of this. I'm tired of your bullying, Dick. Get off my back!"

Holland leaned to his left suddenly and began rummaging around in his flight bag, then straightened up and slapped a manila training folder in Robb's lap with surprising force.

"What's this for?" Robb asked in surprise.

Holland leaned over the center console with genuine menace until his face seemed to Robb to be inches away, his physical size becoming intimidating. His voice was a guttural roar at low volume, but the anger welling up inside him from everything Robb had said was barely controlled.

"Okay, here's the deal. You either sign me off this minute, you snot-nosed little son of a bitch, or have the backbone to take over!"

Robb looked him in the eye for the longest time, then finally dropped his eyes to the training folder.

Taking over—making all the decisions himself—was the last thing he wanted.

Slowly, without a word, Robb's right hand went to his shirt pocket to retrieve his pen.

FOURTEEN

How long the telephone had been ringing in the frigid predawn darkness Yuri Steblinko couldn't tell, but it had finally invaded his dream. He had been in space, a cosmonaut at last, on his way to . . . somewhere. It didn't matter now. The images were fading fast.

He opened his eyes to total darkness. He was on his back and aware of the soft female body draped over him, her hair cascading down the side of his face, her scent in his nostrils. She was snoring softly, almost in counterpoint to the telephone's insistent, harsh rings. He tried to move out from under her but realized with an involuntary smile that they were still coupled beneath the warmth of the blankets. There was no way but to roll her over, and he did so gently, pulling away and sliding out of bed into the icy cold of the room, making sure she was still snug beneath the covers.

He stood and listened, expecting the ringing to stop, but it continued in arrogant insistence. Sometimes the terrible Russian phone system rang for no reason. Sometimes the right party was actually on the other end.

But who would be calling him at such an hour?

Anya had not awakened, and he was glad of that. He thought of ignoring the call and returning to the warmth of her arms, but his curiosity was too strong.

By memory he moved from the bedroom across the

small living room of the old apartment and found the receiver.

"Da?" he said, keeping his voice low.

The words on the other end were Russian spoken with a pronounced accent he recognized.

"Yes, this is Yuri. Who is calling?"

"A friend and potential employer," the voice said.

"Very well. Am I to guess?"

"Yes. No names, though."

Yuri shook his head to clear the cobwebs. He was naked and freezing. "Please wait a minute."

There was a small lamp on the telephone table and he turned it on, spotting Anya's robe on a chair. It was a shapeless affair, but warm, and he wrapped it around himself as he picked up the receiver again.

"Very well, we shall play games, then. What clues can you give me?"

"Remember Vladivostok, my friend?" the man on the other end asked. "Remember the individual you met at the Metropole Hotel, the one who could perhaps give you some assignments and perhaps help you make the career move you desired?"

All his instincts from twenty years with the KGB came on-line. The man didn't want his name used. This wasn't a game. He thought furiously, but sleep was still clouding his mind. He had last been east . . . when? Oh yes, two, maybe three years ago, on an Air Force matter. One of his last acts as a Russian Air Force colonel.

Wait a minute. The man had said Vladivostok, and there was only one trip he'd made to the eastern port city, and for a very personal reason.

"This person was you?" he asked.

"Correct. You sought me out. Two years ago in Vladivostok."

The image of the man coalesced in Yuri's head. With the U.S.S.R. in shambles around him along with his Air Force career, Yuri had indeed been looking for escape.

He was merely interested then. Now, with jobs and money waning, he was bordering on desperation.

"I had almost given up hope. Yes! I remember Vladivostok, and you! I thought you had forgotten."

"Not for a minute, Yuri. Are you still flying? Do you have access to the same equipment you discussed?"

"I am test-flying now, various airplanes. The new Sukoi supersonic business jet project, for instance. I am sometimes their chief test pilot."

"Good. I may have an assignment for you, but we must not discuss it here."

"Where, then? Should I come to you?"

"No. There's no time."

Yuri sat on the chair. The robe was hanging open, but he was oblivious to the cold now.

"If you're still interested in the arrangement we discussed, my organization would be willing to cut such a deal, provided you can accomplish something very, very important for us immediately. It will involve securing the right equipment within hours."

"Tell me where to come."

"I'm going to give you an address in Kiev. I want you to be there at exactly nine A.M. your time. A Russian who will call himself Alexander will explain what we need. If you agree, you are to relay through him what *you* need in the way of funds, and they will be provided within, say, three hours. Can you move immediately?"

"Yes! Yes, of course!"

"Good. We have only a matter of hours before you will need to have everything in place and depart."

In the old days, he thought, this conversation would have been impossible. No operative would have spoken such things in the clear, and on a commercial telephone.

He took down the address quickly, and the line went dead without the old familiar sound of a secondary click from some monitoring post.

Anya!

He crossed into the bedroom in an instant, his freezing hands reaching beneath the covers to startle her, and she came awake with a small shriek.

Her head emerged in a cascade of blond hair, her eyes wide, as if he'd lost his mind.

"What are you doing, Yuri?"

He put his finger to his lips to quiet her, then leaned forward and kissed her.

"I have had a wonderful call, and I've got to go. I may be back today, or it may be in several weeks. But when I come back, Anya, if we are lucky, we'll be leaving here."

"And going where?"

He kissed her again, then drew the covers down and kissed her substantial breasts one at a time before he looked into her eyes and stroked her hair.

"To a place we must not speak about right now. A place we have both discussed. A place where we can really live, Anya. Live, get married, and make babies."

Her eyes were wide, and a smile began to spread across her face.

Yuri smiled too, then brought his index finger to his lips.

"Just like the old days, my love, you know nothing of this, or where I have gone."

ABOARD FLIGHT 66

Brenda Hopkins had been sleeping in her upper-deck seat when she awoke to find the captain leaning over her.

"Brenda? Sorry to wake you, but we need your help in the back."

"I'm sorry, what?" She rubbed her eyes and refocused, recognizing Captain Holland.

"We've got to move Mr. Helms's body from the crew rest loft. We need to use the same people who handled him before."

She nodded. No need to expose anyone else who hadn't touched him.

• • •

In the crew rest loft Brenda completed the unsettling task of sealing Professor Helms's body in plastic bags as the mobile airstairs nudged the side of the aircraft by the left rear door. At the same moment, the seat belt sign was illuminated and James Holland's voice boomed through the cabin:

> "Folks, this is Captain Holland on the flight deck. I'd like everyone to be seated, please. While we're not ready to depart just yet, we've got to open one of the doors and bring more food on board. We'll also be delivering the body of our deceased passenger to the authorities outside."

Murmurs of dissent rumbled lightly through the cabin, startling Brenda, who was standing in the rear galley. She peered around the corner. Halfway up the coach cabin several men stood in the aisle, refusing to sit down, and one of them had turned angrily to snarl at a seated passenger who'd shouted at him to comply. She'd seen some of them earlier demanding more liquor.

"Screw you, buddy!" the individual on his feet said with a predictably obscene gesture. *"You* be a sheep if you want to! I'm tired of being bossed around by some overpaid throttle jockey!"

Two other passengers raised their voices at the protester, who yelled back. Then two more leapt to their feet to argue with him, and another stood up to support him.

Holland's voice returned:

> "I'm going to give you an update now on where we are in this strange saga, folks. We're going to be departing Iceland hopefully within a few hours . . ."

Applause broke out in the cabin along with hoots and supportive yells, almost drowning Holland's voice as he continued:

". . . but we're not headed home yet. Our airline, in conjunction with the U.S. government, has decided to launch a couple of Air Force transports carrying medical people and precautionary equipment for a field hospital in the remote event that anyone on board, uh, comes down with this specific strain of virus. I can't tell you just yet where we'll be meeting them, but it'll be a lot warmer and more comfortable than Iceland, and when we reach that quarantine destination, we'll be able to get everyone off the aircraft."

More cheers, but subdued this time. The men on their feet were shaking their heads.

"I've been asked repeatedly whether we're going to make it home for Christmas. Folks, the answer, sadly, is no."

There were moans through the cabin, and more words from the protesters.

"We'll be together for a couple of days total, and it *is* possible it could be a bit longer. But we'll get you back home as soon as they'll let us."

The four men on their feet had begun moving into the aisle, arguing loudly with Barb and two other flight attendants, who were rapidly losing control.

Brenda grabbed the interphone to alert the cockpit.

James Holland appeared on the main deck within forty seconds. The malcontents had backed Barb and the other two crew members forward. Brenda could hear Barb's voice, angry and loud, countered by the men, and she could see Holland moving in the background as he fished in an overhead compartment for something.

The megaphone! He came forward suddenly, triggering the instrument. "Everybody freeze right there! You men, shut up and return to your seats instantly. This is the captain."

Two of them quieted down and retreated, but the instigator and his friend advanced on the captain with raised voices. Holland let them come, saying nothing as they babbled their way toward him complaining bitterly about their treatment. He lowered the megaphone and prepared to answer them as Barb unwittingly stepped out of the forward coach galley in front of the two. In an instant the passenger in the lead stiff-armed her, knocking her backward in the galley, where she landed with a thud, her head slamming against the metal side of a serving cart.

The man hesitated in confusion, surprised by what he'd done, but Holland's reaction was instantaneous. His right hand shot out and grabbed the shorter man by his shirt collar, yanking him forward into the galley and shoving him roughly against the wall. Holland could see Barb getting to her feet, stunned and furious, and he looked at her now.

"Barb, do you want to press federal charges against this man?"

Barb rubbed the back of her head and moved within inches of the frightened passenger.

"It depends," she said.

Holland brought his face inches from the passenger's face.

"What's your name? NOW! What's your name?"

"Uh . . . ah . . . I'm . . . Chet Walters. I'm sorry . . . I . . ."

Holland could smell the liquor on the man's breath. "Okay, listen up, Mr. Walters. For the rest of this odyssey you're going to be mute, do you understand me? You've just committed a felony. You assaulted an airline crew member and interfered with other crew members in the performance of their duties. When we return home, if you've even breathed too loudly on the remainder of this trip, you're going to be bound over to the FBI for jailing, arraignment, and prosecution. As it is, the lead flight attendant here, Ms. Rollins, may well sue you separately, and I'll be a willing witness. You understand this?"

"Yes, sir!" the man said, his eyes wide with fear.

Holland noticed the other man had beaten a hasty retreat and was nowhere to be seen.

"Ms. Rollins will make the final decision on whether the FBI gets you, or we let you go. Now you get back to your seat and keep your mouth welded shut. Is that clear?"

"Yes, sir."

Holland let him go, and in confusion and embarrassment, the man backed down the aisle to regain his seat.

"Thanks, James. We had four of them screaming at us, but he was the ringleader."

"You okay?" He turned to her and they moved together into the galley.

She nodded, still rubbing her head. "It may get worse, you know. There were boos and rowdy reactions to your words a few minutes ago. They're upset and restless, James, and the world's no longer a gentlemanly place."

He patted her shoulder and picked up the megaphone.

"Never was, Barb."

Holland moved to the front of the forward coach cabin by door 3L and pulled out an interphone handset, activating the PA:

"Folks, we're in this together, but I'm legally in command and I will not tolerate a riot. If there's anyone in here who doesn't understand that, come forward right this second and I'll explain it to you. I'm sorry to be harsh—most everyone here is an exemplary citizen doing nothing but helping us all wait out this unfortunate turn of events. But for anyone who thinks he wants to interfere with me or one of my crew, rest assured you'll end up standing trial for a federal felony. For the vast majority of you who are trying to help, thank you sincerely. Please stay in your seats now."

Holland replaced the handset as a woman in her early thirties got to her feet from one of the window seats and moved into the aisle.

Oh Lord, what now? he thought.

The man next to her was obviously trying to restrain her, but she broke free and began half-running up the aisle with a wild look in her eye.

Holland stepped forward to meet her. "Ma'am, I need you to . . ."

She flashed past without even acknowledging him.

Holland turned to follow her as she headed toward first class. There were footsteps behind him, and he turned around to see a worried man hard on his heels, obviously trying to catch up with her.

"That's my wife, Captain. She's not well."

Holland nodded as they continued the chase.

As Lisa Erickson entered the first class cabin, Garson Wilson spotted the captain and got to his feet, ignoring the frantic woman.

"Ma'am! Please stop!" Holland shouted.

Lisa passed Wilson just before he stepped into the aisle, blocking Holland.

"James? I need to talk to you. Right now!" Wilson boomed.

Lisa had reached the forward bulkhead and found a door. She yanked it open, surprised to find nothing but a closet. She turned, moving back toward Wilson, who heard her approach. He turned, assessing the situation, and put his arm around the woman.

"Little lady, what's the matter?" he said.

"My children! I've got to get off. I've got to . . ." She gestured weakly toward the outside as Keith Erickson passed Holland and approached her. She cowered and moved closer to Wilson as she saw her husband approach.

"NO!" she shrieked, melting into Wilson's side.

Garson Wilson turned to Keith Erickson and raised his free hand.

"Now, leave her alone, sir. She's afraid of you."

"That's . . . she's my wife. She's very upset." Keith Erickson was fumbling for words. "She's trying to leave."

"Well," said Wilson with a snort, "so happens I am too."

"No-o-o-o!" she wailed. "He wants to take my kids!" She leaned in toward Wilson's ear, her voice dropping to a stage whisper as he leaned down to listen. "He's trying to get me! He's trying to get rid of me! He wants my kids!"

A sudden fluctuation in the cabin pressure announced the opening of the left rear door some three hundred feet back at the end of the main deck. Lisa Erickson had felt it too. She looked around wildly and spotted the opposite aisle leading from first class toward the back. She pushed away from Wilson and dashed erratically in that direction.

Keith Erickson lunged for his wife, but Wilson blocked his way momentarily. Then Wilson, moving surprisingly fast for a man of his bulk, rushed toward the back himself as Holland and Erickson cut through a row of seats and went after Lisa.

Lisa had a head start, but she was stumbling as she ran. Wilson kept up with her, paralleling her down the other aisle, as they raced past forty rows of startled passengers, who shrank back from the aisle as they approached. Holland and Erickson, however, were hampered and slowed by people leaning in the aisle to see where Lisa was going.

The rear door had been unsealed and pushed out. A figure in a white protective suit was standing just outside, handing in small boxed lunches two at a time to Brenda and two other flight attendants. Lisa Erickson arrived in the rear passageway and instantly spotted the door standing ajar. No one expected the small figure that came bursting upon them, followed immediately by the large bulk of Garson Wilson from the other aisle. Lisa hesitated and Wilson yelled, "Go, little lady! Now's your chance, and I'm right behind you!" Lisa pushed past the crew members and the suited figure on the top of the stairs outside and thrust herself down the stairs and into the night.

Wilson followed her to the head of the stairs and began to descend, but stopped in his tracks at the sight of security police in the same protective suits running toward them with their M-16s raised.

Wilson backed up to the doorway, thoroughly startled, as the man in the protective suit grabbed his shoulders and shoved him back inside.

Holland and Erickson arrived at the back of the aircraft in time to see Lisa disappearing through the doorway, followed by Wilson, who reappeared within seconds.

Holland pushed past Wilson and squeezed through the door, yelling back at Erickson, who was trying to follow.

"Stay there! No one's allowed outside." The startled man in the protective suit was already halfway down the stairs, yelling in a muffled voice for Lisa to come back. He noticed more movement behind him and turned to see Holland flash by as well.

There were shouts in the distance as James Holland reached the foot of the boarding stairs. The wind was vicious, and instantly, it seemed, he was shivering.

Lisa Erickson had slowed to a stumbling walk only a dozen yards from a red rope on the ground, her arms crossed, her body trembling.

Several figures were converging from the right and left on the far side of a roped-off security zone. Holland looked both ways and realized the red rope ran completely around the 747 at a distance of maybe a hundred yards. Lisa was at least a hundred feet away from him and still headed toward the rope.

Holland knew security police mentality. They would threaten anyone approaching that zone, but if anyone tried to cross the rope . . .

As Holland stepped off the stairway, the sound of gunfire erupted, several tracers passing just in front of him. The advancing force waved him back and tried to get Lisa's attention.

Each of the security men was in a protective suit, and each of them had raised his weapon and moved to either side of the advancing Mrs. Erickson. It was a classic formation. They were trained to position for a clean shot without hitting the airplane behind.

Their voices were unintelligible because of the protective gear and the howling wind, but Holland could make out their gestures to go back.

He cupped his hands and yelled. "She's disturbed! Leave her alone!"

The wind took his words.

He took another step forward and more bullets chewed the tarmac just in front of him, causing him to jump back.

Two of the men on the left had dropped to a shooter's stance, both of them aiming at him. Another on the right was aiming at Lisa. And another guard well upwind had ripped off his mask to use a bullhorn.

"Go back or we'll shoot! You by the stairs, do not take another step. We will drop you if you take another step. Ma'am! You near the rope. Freeze this instant or we'll be forced to shoot!"

He yelled the warnings over and over again.

But like a sleepwalker, Lisa kept right on going toward the rope.

Holland raised his arms and waved to hold them off, yelling again that the woman was disturbed. It wasn't working. Two more guards had approached from the right and drawn a bead on her. Holland moved sideways and saw the guns move *with* him, the gloved hands holding the M-16s fumbling for the triggers.

He yelled as loudly as he could to the woman.

"Lisa, please stop! We have your children in the airplane!"

She was still walking, moving slowly, steadily, now less than fifteen feet from the rope. Any single guard could have held her back, but Holland knew that none of them would risk it. Holland was sure the guards had been warned that the people on the 747 were contaminated. *Touch them without adequate protection and you'll die.*

The voice on the bullhorn grew more frantic. Another burst of automatic gunfire rang out as one of the guards tried shooting over her head.

Nothing seemed to faze her.

Holland could hear her husband's voice behind him from the top of the stairs, pleading with her.

More gunfire, still high, and more warnings followed in close succession.

Holland could see the man in charge drop the bullhorn from his mouth reluctantly and issue an order he couldn't hear. In response, the security policeman next to him raised his M-16 and pointed it at Lisa's legs, while Holland yelled once more, as loudly as he could.

"No! Don't shoot! Just restrain her! She's out of her mind!"

Lisa stopped suddenly less than eight feet from the rope and turned. He could see her shaking violently, wearing nothing but a thin dress, which the wind was whipping around her. Her hair was standing out horizontally from her head.

She looked vacantly back at the airplane, her back to the guards, who began dropping their muzzles toward the concrete. Holland waved her forward, gently, calling to her, encouraging her, unsure if she was even looking at him. Keith Erickson's voice called plaintively from behind as he, too, approached the bottom of the stairs.

"Honey! Please! I love you, Lisa. Come back to me and the kids, honey!"

But Lisa remained stock still and merely stared at him. He stepped to the ground and started to bolt for his wife, but Holland grabbed him by the shoulders as several more bursts of gunfire hit right in front of them.

"She's my wife! Don't shoot!" Erickson yelled, scared, distraught, and shaking from the cold.

There was an odd toss of Lisa Erickson's head. Her arms came up to encircle her head, then slowly she held them out to each side perfectly parallel to the ground and stood for many seconds. Holland could see several security policemen standing just on the other side of the rope, within fifteen feet of her, their guns aimed. They had just turned to their sergeant and asked what to do when Lisa caught them off-guard by suddenly pivoting and bolting toward them, her arms still outstretched, her voice screaming incoherently.

The young airmen with the M-16s were taken by surprise. She was from inside the plane. To touch her meant to die. Female or not, if anyone crossed the line, that person was to be shot. All those thoughts ran through their collective heads as they watched a wild-eyed, screaming woman coming at them with outstretched arms.

Keith Erickson tried to bolt toward his wife, but Holland dragged him to the ground as a brief burst of automatic gunfire reached their ears.

Lisa Erickson's shattered body hit the frozen concrete and skidded into the rope, then lay motionless, a rapidly growing pond of crimson encircling her as the two shooters staggered back, horrified at the result of their reactions. One of them approached slowly then and knelt to prod the lifeless form with his gun, while the other turned his gun toward Holland and Keith Erickson. The man with the bullhorn ordered them back in the aircraft. Four of the guards were advancing on them. A few more rounds were squeezed off, hitting right in front of their feet.

Erickson seemed transfixed. "Oh God, *NO!*" he sobbed, trying to break away, testing Holland's strength.

"They'll shoot you too! Don't do it! Your kids need you! Do you hear me? Your kids need you!"

With guns following their every move, Holland dragged the grief-stricken man back up the stairs, into the aircraft, and into Barb's care. He began to explain what had happened.

"I know," Barb interrupted, "everyone on board knows."

"Take him to the upper deck," Holland said quietly.

"Where's the goddam captain?" One of the guards had arrived at the top of the stairway. His muffled voice was clear enough to understand at close quarters.

Holland pushed the door open a bit more and stuck his head out, his face mere inches from the man's protective visor.

"You bastards! Couldn't you figure out what was happening? Did she look like a damn terrorist to you? You just murdered a young mother. And for *what?*"

"Goddammit, Captain, you were told no one could leave!" Holland could hear that the man was almost as upset as he was. "Our orders are to prevent anyone from crossing that line out there, and to do so with deadly force. We gave her, and you, more latitude than we should have. If I'd followed my orders, I would've shot you too!"

Holland shook his head in disgust and despair. "I was trying to tell you she was mentally unbalanced, couldn't you tell?"

The man in the suit was obviously in charge of the others. A sergeant, probably. He held his M-16 down to his side and shook his head. "We couldn't let her run, sir. Our orders are crystal clear. We warned her and you!"

Holland shook his head sadly. There was no point to the argument. "What about her body?" he asked at last.

The sergeant turned and looked at the small, crumpled form on the concrete a hundred yards away as several of his men began to cover it. He shook his head.

He turned back to Holland. "Not my decision, sir. They'll let you know. Now, we have to finish loading these boxes, secure the dead man's body, and get this door closed. And this time, tell your people if anyone's foot hits the bottom of those stairs, we'll blow them away where they stand."

Holland could feel his temper give way like an overloaded dam. With both hands he grabbed what passed for the lapel of the man's suit and pulled him closer, expecting a fight. Surprisingly, the sergeant didn't resist.

"You pathetic little automaton!" Holland snarled. "And what *would* you do if we just all came marching out at once? Your orders say to kill us all?"

The man hesitated, then nodded slowly, deliberately. Holland could almost make out his eyes through the thick visor. He released his grip.

"In that case, Captain, there would be a massacre. My men and I would probably spend the rest of our lives grieving in a personal hell. Our orders are clear, Captain. We tried to warn you."

Barb Rollins forced herself to resume functioning after the killing, but it took great effort. She supervised the removal of Professor Helms's body and made sure all the food boxes had been brought in before securing the door. Then she roped off the bed the professor's body had occupied in the crew rest loft, pulled the curtain, and had the young man with the broken leg moved from the coach cabin to an unused bed in the loft.

She returned to the main cabin level to find Brenda distraught and needing to talk.

"If they're willing to shoot us, Barb—if they're that scared of us—that has to mean we're really in trouble!"

"Calm down, honey, it's going to work out. It's a false alarm, remember?"

"I don't think it is!"

Barb took her by the shoulders.

"Look! They may be panicked out there, but we know that Helms had a heart attack, whether he was sick or not."

Brenda closed her eyes and began shaking her head.

"Brenda, listen to me. Everyone out there thinks we've got a doomsday virus that could kill the planet, but James says that can't be true."

"He doesn't really know! He's trying to protect us. He's doing his best, but he can't really know."

"And you do?" Barb said, more sharply than she'd intended.

Brenda looked up at her and nodded silently.

Barb dropped her arms from Brenda's shoulders as she tried to ignore the cold jolt of fear that was creeping up her back. She had resigned herself to not getting home for Christmas. Her husband could live with that. They'd celebrate a day or two later.

Now she felt herself beginning to wonder if she'd ever see him again.

Brenda's eyes were on the floor again, her voice little more than a ready whisper.

"I think maybe Mrs. Erickson was the lucky one."

FIFTEEN

Sherry Ellis had worked directly under Jonathan Roth for four years, she told Dr. Rusty Sanders in a quiet moment as they sat in the conference room–crisis command post.

"Director Roth has a professional veneer as thick as stainless steel," she added, "a practiced result of years in Covert Ops coupled with years as a master bureaucrat able to fuzz up simple issues with a single briefing. It's not easy to read him."

Rusty watched her bright green eyes narrow just a bit and a very slow, very slight smile spread over her face. He had been noticing her quite a bit as the hours passed, and he was enticed by what he saw: an attractive, diminutive, highly intelligent, and self-confident young woman who happened to be turning him on with her wry sense of humor and quiet energy—not to mention her looks. It was no time for such thoughts, he knew, but as the hours carrying the unfolding horror of Flight 66's dilemma dragged past, his busy mind was crying out for diversion.

"You like him?" Rusty asked.

"Why?" she shot back without defensiveness.

"Curiosity, that's all. I just work in the basement, remember? I don't get to know the superspies or the movers and shakers."

She nodded and smiled, cocking her head. "I've heard

the old self-effacing routine before, Doctor. It's been used by everyone from Andy Griffith and Columbo to Nikita Khrushchev and Yasir Arafat. I'm on to you."

"No, really, I'm just curious." He laughed, holding his hands out, palms up.

She looked at him without speaking for several long moments, then smiled.

"I take it you're not going home tonight."

Rusty nodded. "I'd rather stay and see this through. Besides, there's no one home but my psychotic cat, EPR." He pronounced it "eeper."

"EPR?" she asked.

"Stands for 'engine pressure ratio.' I'm a pilot with a few business jet ratings, and that's the scale you use to set power in turbojets. My cat takes off about as fast when he's startled. EPR seemed the natural name for him."

Rusty realized she was only half-listening. Sherry smiled then and rose from the chair in a fluid motion, moving toward the door like a feminine wave, with Rusty's eyes following her appreciatively. He was doubly glad he'd stayed, and wondered at the same time where she was going.

Sherry returned. She'd checked the hallway and closed the heavy, soundproof door rather surreptitiously, which puzzled Rusty. She sat down again, her eyes boring into his. For several long moments she said nothing. He guessed she was trying to gauge how much to tell him, since they'd never worked together before.

She inclined her head toward the hallway.

"You asked if I liked him. Rusty, I *work* for Jon Roth. He's incredibly talented. I'm not required to like him or dislike him."

Rusty nodded, feeling off-balance as she sat back and watched him. "I'm sorry. I didn't mean to pry."

"Yes, you did." She smiled. "You're carrying an ID from the CIA, right? You'd better pry. That's what you're paid to do."

• • •

When news of the killing of Lisa Erickson entered the warrens at Langley, Sherry disappeared to brief Roth in his office. She returned a short time later with a grim-faced Mark Hastings, who slid a box of doughnuts across the table.

"Coffee's coming," Mark said. "Looks like this is going to be a marathon."

"Something new?" Sanders had been searching databases again.

Mark nodded. "We're going to hold them on the ground in Iceland until the African site is staffed and ready. Could be half a day. They're going to try to hush up the shooting, but the media are swarming to Iceland right now and, we can assume, monitoring communications. The story's getting as big as the invasion of Kuwait."

Mark gestured to a bank of television monitors hastily set up along one wall. CNN's coverage was becoming constant, and the three major networks were planning live satellite feeds from Keflavík at first light—if they could get their portable earth stations there in time.

"By the way, Rusty, Roth said to thank you specifically for helping beat the deadline. We skunked Defense Intelligence by twenty minutes."

Rusty Sanders acknowledged the words with a slight wave of his hand as Mark briefed them on the latest assignments. With the political assessments of northwest Africa done and delivered to Roth and the White House, and the satellite surveillance of the desert airfield arranged, the deputy director wanted to monitor the international intelligence community's reactions. Specifically, he had told Mark, he wanted them to search for any hint that Ambassador Lee Lancaster's presence on Flight 66 had become a matter of operational interest to the Iranians or their pet terrorists.

"What's he asking?" Rusty wanted to know. "Does he think Hezbollah or Aqbah might *target* Flight Sixty-six? They couldn't do a better job than the Germans have already done."

Mark and Sherry agreed, as did three other analysts who had joined them.

Mark shook his head. "I think it borders on busywork, but Roth wants to make sure no one interferes with the President's plan. So let's get on it."

They fanned out again as Mark realized he had forgotten to leave a sheaf of briefing papers on Roth's desk.

"I'll take them," Rusty volunteered. "I wanted to talk to him anyway."

Mark Hastings turned and looked quizzically at Rusty Sanders. An underling in the Central Intelligence Agency did not just go chat with the people at Director level without invitation, and Sanders had already been typed by Roth as a loose cannon. But Sanders had also been invited before to Roth's office.

Mark held out the papers, and Sanders took them and headed out the door.

Jon Roth was on the phone when Rusty Sanders stuck his head in the inner office door. Roth waved him in and finished the call. Rusty forced himself to sit quietly until Roth looked up from his notebook computer.

"Yes, Doctor?"

Rusty pushed the papers across the desk. Roth thanked him and sat back, examining Rusty.

"Director, the autopsy team will be starting on Helms's body shortly," Rusty began. "I've asked them to call me immediately if they find symptomatic evidence of viral involvement or not, but the fact is, there's no way to rapidly determine whether a specific virus was carried in his body. In most cases of high communicability, it can take longer to culture a virus than it does to have other humans catch it. Even if we knew exactly what bug we're looking for, and even if we were prepared to search for growth of that precise virus, it could take days to weeks. This isn't like a bacteriological culture that grows in a petri dish in hours."

The phone rang and Roth motioned for Rusty to wait

as he picked it up, acknowledged some request, and replaced the receiver. Roth got to his feet. Rusty rose from the chair as well, but Roth waved him down.

"Stay put, Doctor. I'll be right back."

Rusty concentrated on staying in the chair, which was not easy. He needed to roam and move and think.

He sat back in the chair, taking in the open notebook computer on Roth's desk and the stapled sheets of paper with a familiar format he hadn't noticed before. He leaned forward and looked at the papers, recognizing them as an international flight plan starting in Keflavík, Iceland. Curious, Rusty thought, that a flight plan for Flight 66 would cross Roth's desk. That was a task for the Air Force and the airline. Why would CIA care?

Of course! We'd need to look for political threats along the way.

He rotated the flight plan around. The route was almost totally over water down the middle of the Atlantic Ocean for three thousand miles. He looked at the final fixes with the familiar eye of an experienced pilot. It crossed the African coast line about a hundred fifty miles east of the Canary Islands over the tiny Moroccan settlement of Tan-Tan, then over a corner of Morocco into Mauritania. The landing site was at least a hundred fifty miles in all directions from any significant vestige of civilization. Other than the Moroccans—who had a small air force—any threat to Flight 66 would have to travel a long distance in a short period of time to get there from some other part of the Arab world. And so far, he knew, the destination was not public knowledge.

There were footsteps in the hall and Rusty rotated the flight plan back to its original position before Roth reentered the room and sat down heavily in his chair.

"Sorry, Doctor. Message traffic." He noticed the illuminated computer screen and turned to the keyboard, entering a couple of keystrokes to save the message and return the screen to black.

"All right, Doctor, please continue." Roth had started drumming his fingers on the arm of his chair.

Rusty nodded. "Okay. The point is, what if the autopsy team finds zero evidence of infection in his lungs, his heart, his blood? That *would* prove that Professor Helms wasn't suffering the overt effects of a viral infection, but it *wouldn't* prove that he was free of the virus."

"And," Roth added, "it would *not* remove the possibility that he was able to spread the virus, now would it?"

Rusty sighed and shook his head. "No, sir. I couldn't tell you categorically that it would."

"So, Doctor, what's your point?"

"Well, if I come back to you and tell you there's no overt evidence, what do we do? I mean, I know we're not planning to shoot them. They'll either get sick or they won't."

Roth nodded. "I believe you just asked and answered your own question."

Rusty stared at him, trying to comprehend his thinking.

"In other words, Director, in regard to what we're going to do with Flight Sixty-six, am I correct that it doesn't matter what the autopsy shows, because we won't be able to get a rapid result that could conclusively rule out the virus?"

"That, I believe, sums it up, Doctor. Of course I want to know their conclusions immediately, but it will have no effect on the plan. If no one gets sick, they'll go home quickly. If anyone gets sick, then as you warned, they'll all die. In any event, whatever happens will happen in a safe place, with professionals there to care for them."

Rusty was halfway out the door when Roth called him back, pulling his half-glasses off and obviously searching for the right words.

"Doctor, a question if you please. Tell me honestly, considering the exposure of Helms in Bavaria, the confirmed infection and death of the researcher who apparently fought with him"—Roth was ticking off each point on his fingers—"the requisite forty-eight-hour incubation period corresponding with Helms's becoming ill on the aircraft, and Helms's demise, do you really have any substantive doubts? Or are you working from the position of hope and perhaps a bit of denial, considering how terrible this is?"

Rusty reentered the office in surprise. Roth wasn't posturing, he was genuinely asking—and listening for an answer. Rusty sat down in the same plush chair and clasped his hands as he leaned forward in thought, then met the deputy director's eyes.

"Well, being as absolutely honest and unemotional as I can be, I have to say I have one final reservation that's gnawing at me, sir."

"Which is?"

"Did Professor Helms have any symptoms when he walked on that airplane which are inconsistent with the onset of a coronary? If so, I'd have to agree with you that it's probably hopeless, though I always try to hope. If not—if each and every symptom could be explained by a coronary episode—then I'd say there's still reason to believe he might not have been infected, or contagious, and the other passengers might not be infected. I can find no history of any virus which produces only the classic symptoms of a coronary. Maybe this one can, but I'm still troubled that we're leaping too far in our conclusions."

Roth was nodding slowly and studying him.

"Doctor, call the airplane again. Question that lead flight attendant one more time, and anyone else who dealt with the professor. Can you do that quickly?"

"You bet!" Rusty replied, getting to his feet.

It took more than twenty minutes to reach Quantum 66's cockpit satellite line. All the passenger lines were busy with outgoing calls to relatives, but the one line held open for the crew had also been in rather constant use.

Finally the circuit transmitted a ringing sound.

Rusty explained what he needed, and held on while

Brenda was summoned to the phone to begin answering questions. She was in shock over what had happened to Lisa Erickson, but she struggled to focus. No, there were no new illnesses to report, except for some worrisome swelling in the broken leg of a young man in coach.

Rusty asked her about the condition of Ernest Helms when he came on board. Could she remember any more details? There was silence on the other end.

"Ah, Brenda? Are you still there?"

"Yes."

"Tell me again with great precision and in as much detail as you can each and every symptom the professor had when he came aboard, and when he had the attack."

She talked slowly and steadily for several minutes, not stopping to hear a reaction. When she had finished, there was silence on the Washington end.

Rusty Sanders took a deep breath. He'd felt his heart sink as she spoke.

"Brenda, you said he was coughing deeply?"

"Yes."

"And he apologized about it?"

"Yes. He said he'd been coughing for the last few hours and couldn't seem to stop. It was a deep, croupy cough."

"Okay. I see. Thanks very much."

"What does that mean, Doctor?"

"Oh, probably nothing. I was just trying to make sure of our facts."

He disconnected the call, feeling ill himself. A deep cough by itself was nothing, but it was unlikely to have any logical connection with a coronary event. Something besides heart disease was at work on Professor Helms as he came aboard in Frankfurt.

Roth had probably been right all along. Apparently, everyone aboard was infected, making Flight 66 a pariah—and a major threat to the rest of the world.

KIEV, UKRANIAN REPUBLIC—SATURDAY, DECEMBER 23

Yuri Steblinko left the meeting arranged by his early morning caller and walked briskly toward the heart of Kiev's downtown district, his mind rapidly working through the tasks ahead. He had recognized the Russian operative who showed up at the appointed place and time as "Alexander." He was a capable agent, and formerly one of the KGB's sharpest men in the Middle East. It was not surprising to find him here.

What his client wanted was possible, but it was going to take a rapid series of telephone calls and a lot of cash.

Alexander had given him a briefcase containing the equivalent of a hundred thousand American dollars in rubles. Alexander would have more for him by noon, he said, when a second bank opened—if Yuri needed it. Bribes were expected. They could access whatever funds he required to get the job done.

What Yuri wanted now was a telephone in a totally private place. His own apartment was out of the question. His normal instincts had always been to keep Anya ignorant of the details of his covert activities and never to use his own telephone line. It was safer for her—and for him—if she knew nothing. She understood this. She never asked questions.

Yuri allowed himself a brief smile at the thought of Anya, an expression that caused two people walking toward him to stare curiously.

I'm out of practice. I'm not supposed to wear my feelings on my face.

He headed for the office of a friend who ran a struggling export business. His friend did not act surprised when Yuri handed him twenty thousand rubles to take his employees and get lost for a few hours. A big aviation deal, he explained. The man knew Yuri's KGB past. He merely winked and cleared out with his four employees. Twenty thousand rubles was more than he used to make in a year.

After double-checking to make sure he was alone, Yuri began a marathon of calls.

First he enlisted the aid of two trusted friends to check the availability of operational MIG-25s or -29s or any other Air Force hardware that, for a price, could be made instantly available, explaining he was acting as broker for a rich Western businessman. He knew the source to call for brokering heavyweight military equipment, a man he detested named Yvchenko. But even Yvchenko couldn't produce an airplane that fast—and there was the problem of range.

What he really needed was something with a range of close to four thousand miles.

But there were no fighters in the former Soviet inventory with that sort of reach. Only big, lumbering bombers requiring many pilots and engineers.

There would be a solution, of course, Yuri assured himself. No matter what the odds, life had taught him that there was *always* a solution. But the odds against finding the right equipment in time were overwhelming.

He put down the phone and sat back in a creaky chair in the drafty second-floor office and tried to concentrate. Such a mission ordinarily required months of planning, even with the full cooperation of the Air Force. Without the official connection and with himself acting as a free agent, he could do it with money and time, but all he had was money.

Very well, what do we have, and what do we need? I need an airplane with a four-thousand-mile range. I need the right weapons and a carefully thought out flight plan. I need an escape plan, appropriate documents, and maps and charts. And I need it all immediately!

Yuri shook his head and smiled to himself. What was that American phrase he had liked so much? Oh, yes: "The improbable we do immediately, the impossible takes a few hours." He would adopt that as his credo if he pulled this off. *When* he pulled it off! There could be no question of succeeding. It meant a new life for Anya and him, and it would make him an instant legend in the intelligence community—if they ever found out.

Enough! he cautioned himself. *Focus on the aircraft first.*

Fighters were everywhere and easily "bought" with a bribe, but even if it had the range, he couldn't just roar out of town in a fully armed MIG-29 and casually drop into various international airfields to refuel without attracting a lot of attention. And there would be no time to paint over the military markings.

Appearance was important.

With an American airliner carrying a hated ambassador friendly to Israel, the world would come to a quick, logical conclusion that Aqbah was involved, and create a feeding frenzy for information about the shadowy but technically awesome organization. He must do nothing to diminish the impression that a full-time Aqbah team had executed the plan. He was like a ghost writer that way, his contact had explained. He did the work, someone else got the credit, giving his clients the ability to project themselves worldwide with minimal risk by using freelance operatives.

Yuri remembered a quiet briefing two years before in Tehran from an Iranian intelligence contact. Aqbah walked a delicate line, the Iranian had said. Unlike more hysterical terrorist organizations, which took credit for even the sloppiest acts, Aqbah cultivated the art of the *suspected* connection, greatly multiplying the fear factor.

"Let the evil West come to their own conclusion that a given murderous act was Aqbah's doing—perhaps with a little help from phoned-in tips to news organizations," the man had explained. "But *never* take open credit."

Okay, Yuri thought, other than MIG-29s, what was instantly available?

On one of his phone calls a longtime friend had laughed at the idea of finding the right plane the same afternoon.

"Yuri, Yuri, the only way you're going to get a plane that quickly is to steal one. This is Russia, after all!"

"It's the Ukraine, Pavel."

"Same difference. Nothing moves fast here."

Steal a plane indeed. Yuri Steblinko, a decorated colonel of the Soviet Air Force.

There is no Soviet Air Force anymore, idiot! he reminded himself.

He had laughed at Pavel's suggestion. Now he came forward in his chair, his mind racing through the rationale.

WAIT a minute!

That was consistent with Aqbah's style. They didn't have an air force of their own. Of course they would steal what they needed, and he didn't need to check with the client to make sure it was an acceptable solution. It was the only solution!

The excitement faded. All well and good to decide to steal the equipment, but there had to be something to steal, and so far he was drawing a blank.

Yuri almost chuckled at the idea of sneaking up on a Russian Air Force base and simply flying off by himself in a Bear or Bison bomber. He was a fighter pilot. He could handle a MIG-25 or -29, but he couldn't even start a Bear without help, let alone fly the beast.

What I need is a long-range business jet.

The image of the beautiful blue-and-white Gulfstream IV he had test-flown a month before danced across his mind, and a smile began to spread across his face.

Of course!

What a lovely aircraft that had been to fly! Two powerful turbofan engines, a custom-made wood-trimmed cabin, and an up-to-date glass cockpit of flat-panel electronic instruments crammed with satellite communications and navigation equipment, satellite television and radio links, and a defense system.

That had been his role—to test-fly the hidden defense systems. The Saudi prince who owned the Gulfstream had become a raving paranoid about being jumped by Iraqi or even Israeli fighters. He refused to be a sitting duck. He wanted protection, and the only protection he could imagine was a perpetual fighter escort, which King Khalid refused to let him have.

"Why not arm your Gulfstream?" an acquaintance had suggested. "There's a place in the Ukraine that can get air-to-air missiles and modify your airplane to carry them on retractable racks."

With the price no object, the prince had done just that, paying the equivalent of three million dollars in hard cash for the added tactical and threat radar, plus all the necessary modifications. What he would fly back to Saudi Arabia would have four air-to-air missiles, chaff dispensers, antimissile electronic countermeasures for confusing a missile's radar, as well as the ability to tell if a fighter was painting him with targeting radar.

Secrecy was paramount, Yuri had been told. The prince was very concerned that someone in Iran or Iraq would find out about the equipment.

Oh my God! When is the delivery date?

Yuri realized he was standing and his heart pounding. Where was the aircraft right this minute?

Let's see, it was to be delivered on . . . the twenty-sixth of December. He lunged at a calendar on the adjacent desk before realizing he already knew the date.

It was Saturday, December 23.

The Gulfstream IV would still be sitting on the tarmac at Kharkov, several hundred miles to the east. An airplane with a four-thousand-mile range. A nondescript business jet with the ability to launch four air-to-air missiles, and a communications system able to tune in any other aircraft and even eavesdrop on other satellite channels.

And an airplane he knew how to fly—and knew how to steal.

He shook his head.

It was almost too ironic. Aqbah steals the cherished airplane of what Tehran would consider an enemy of Islam, a hated Sunni Muslim and member of the Saudi royal family, and uses it to strike the West.

He sat at the battered desk and looked at the phone.

To this point it had all been planning, but once he began the calls necessary to trick the modification center into fueling and arming the plane, he would be lighting a fuse and committing to a mission that turned his stomach.

He thought of his investigation of the Sakhalin Island fighter unit that had brought down the Korean Airlines 747 in 1985. He had been a major then on special assignment as an accident investigator for the Soviet Air Force. He was part of the KGB's frantic attempt to help the General Secretary decide which Air Force commanders were to be executed for the worldwide embarrassment they had caused the U.S.S.R.

And he remembered the devastated pilot who had pulled the trigger.

A small wave of shame washed over him, just as it had in the meeting with Alexander. His price of admission to a new life for himself and Anya was the murder of several hundred Americans, as well as the destruction of a beautiful 747-400 in flight.

But they are all going to die a horrible death anyway— slowly, painfully. Remember? This is an act of mercy. You must remember that! You must concentrate on nothing else!

He had seen the effects of germ warfare in the infamous Russian Army tests of 1972. Political prisoners were the guinea pigs, and the image of their suffering still tormented him occasionally in nightmares.

The man called Alexander had said the sickness aboard the target 747 came from a Russian lab. If it was anything similar to what he had witnessed in those tests, what he was about to do would indeed be an act of mercy.

Yuri shook the thoughts from his head and pulled the receiver to his ear as he dialed the appropriate numbers.

SIXTEEN

The shooting of Lisa Erickson had instantly changed the mood of the passengers of Flight 66. Before, where there had been irritation and mild alarm, a deep, pervading fear now reigned.

"My God, if they're *that* afraid of us . . ." had become a whispered theme throughout the aircraft, and many had been shocked into tense silence.

James Holland's painful PA announcement about the shooting was heartfelt and moving—and desperately needed. Everyone could hear the agony in the captain's voice as he explained what had happened at the back door, the mindless methods used by the security police force, and why Lisa's sudden dash toward the red security line had triggered an instant and deadly response:

"Those young security troops out there, folks, have been told by their commander that all of us are extremely dangerous biologically because of the virus they think we're carrying. I have great faith that this is going to turn out to be a false alarm, but in the meantime—until enough hours have gone by with no one getting ill—the attitude of the outside world toward us isn't going to change. I know you're worried. But please, let's stay calm and cooperative. And please understand that we're being controlled for at least a while longer by outside forces trying to keep us separated from the rest of humanity."

Holland had tried to sound confident and optimistic. He'd tried to convince himself that optimism was justified. Yes, we'll get out of this. Yes, it's only a false alarm.

But the solid front of global rejection made such assurances seem ridiculous. Who was he to second-guess the rest of humanity?

At 3:20 A.M., Dick Robb recommended the crew be divided into an "A watch" and a "B watch," each with a four-hour duty period, until they could depart Keflavík. An exhausted James Holland agreed.

With the plan explained, cabin lights were turned out, the shades were pulled, and curtains were drawn between the cabins. The upper-deck cabin was left lighted. Holland directed the B-watch flight attendants to find seats and get some sleep, and promised to do the same himself—having assigned himself to B watch.

Lying in one of the two pilot bunks in a tiny cubicle just behind the cockpit, James Holland pulled a blanket over his legs and closed his eyes, feeling emotionally numb. He was exhausted, but sleep wouldn't come. In its place were the turbulent images of what had happened outside his aircraft, and the helplessness he'd felt watching his passenger run into a firing squad.

I should have tried to chase her! he told himself. *They wouldn't have shot me for trying.*

Intellectually he knew better. If he'd tried to reach her in those last few seconds when she'd bolted toward the rope, his body would be lying out there too.

Yet maybe he could have tried harder.

After they had brought Keith Erickson back on board, he'd been gently guided to an empty row in the upper-deck cabin, and the flight attendants had taken turns sitting with the distraught man. Holland, too, had stayed with him for a while before returning to the cockpit. Now, sitting below in the dark, the yawning chasm of Erickson's horror and grief was all Holland could think about.

He knew what it was like to lose a wife and lover—not to death, but to divorce. He remembered with cutting clarity the void Sandra had left behind when she'd reached the end of her patience with his solitary nature. It was a poor comparison, he chided himself. Sandra was still alive.

He thought of Sandra in the early days of their marriage, when they were so thunderously in love, and what it would have been like to have her snatched away in the middle of an Arctic night, her beautiful body mangled and ruined by a hail of gunfire—like Lisa Erickson's.

He shuddered at the thought. *What Erickson must be feeling is unfathomable!*

He was wide awake, and it was useless to stay in the dark. Holland quietly got to his feet and opened the door. He hesitated at the privacy curtain that separated the cockpit and pilot rest facility from the forward section of the upper-deck cabin, then opened it. There was a small group around Keith Erickson at the back of the cabin. The gloom of the scene was cut only by the beam of light from an overhead reading lamp. Holland felt a powerful responsibility to go talk to him, but at the same time, he felt fearful of coming too close to the power and depth of Erickson's grief. There was an aura of tragedy that surrounded the man now like the event horizon around a black hole.

In the role of captain, he could deal with Erickson's loss. But on a personal level, it was too much, too close, too real. He'd spent a lifetime trying to shield himself from pain and sorrow and the sort of emptiness he'd felt so often growing up.

James Holland held on to the railing and turned away toward the windows on the right side of the cabin. He wished there was some compartment—some place—he could go and just be alone.

Utterly and completely alone!

He needed to close his eyes and be scared and miserable and guilty and a thousand other terrible feelings he couldn't show. He probably even needed to cry.

But not as captain.

Holland took a deep breath and drew himself up to his full six-foot-three-inch height, turned, and walked toward Keith Erickson's seat.

Two hundred fifty feet to the rear in the crew rest loft of Quantum 66, where they had relocated him, twenty-year-old Gary Strauss was trying to control the smile on his face. It was exciting enough that Stefani Steigal, the beautiful German girl he'd met in Switzerland, had turned up on the same flight, but to have her seated next to him across the aisle was too good to be true. Now she was climbing the top step into the crew rest loft to check on him. Her tousled blond hair cascaded around her athletic shoulders and perfectly framed her breasts in a way that had nearly driven him crazy with desire when they'd met on the ski slopes a week before.

"Hello, Herr Strauss!" she said with a smile and the pronounced German accent that tinged her melodic, slightly breathy voice.

"Wie geht es Ihnen?"

He cocked his head and feigned puzzlement. "Huh?"

"How *are* you, I asked."

"I knew that! One helluva lot better now that you're here," he replied, grinning at her.

Stefani moved to his side and knelt down, knowing very well where his eyes had landed. She reached out and put her hand under his chin, raising his head up until his eyes met hers.

"You will stop looking at my breasts and look at me, *ja?*"

He smiled a bit sheepishly. "I have great admiration for your breasts."

She ignored the remark. "Really, Gary, how are you feeling? Is this lying down helping?"

He nodded. "A lot, I think. Dr. Turnheir thinks he may need to cut the cast off, though. He's worried about circulation. My leg has swollen so much, the cast is really tight."

"I'm so sorry. Is there something I can get you?"

"Just stay within view and I'll be fine."

"You're terrible! Keep your mind on serious things."

"Yes, ma'am."

Stefani looked back toward the ladder and sighed, her expression becoming serious.

"Gary, what do *you* think of all this?"

He thought about the question as he looked at her. She was athletic and tanned and a bit older than he at twenty-two, but there had been a serious mutual attraction from the first moment they'd met on the slopes. When she'd boarded and found him in pain with a broken leg, she was determined to mother him, but now her thoughts were turning inward, driven by apprehension.

Stefani turned back to him. "It frightens me, all of this. Those men out there, to kill a young woman like that just because she tried to cross a line . . ."

"As the captain said, Stefani, they're frightened of us."

"Are you?" she asked.

"What?"

"Are you afraid we're going to get sick? Could this end up like *The Andromeda Strain*? I saw that movie years ago when I was little. It scared me."

He shrugged his shoulders. "I don't know what to make of it. The crew here keeps saying it's a false alarm."

"I pray it is too, but I also think they're scared."

Gary reached out and took her hand, gently, delighted that she didn't resist. She was a student at Yale, a senior. He was a sophomore at Princeton. There were railroads. He'd been making plans even in Switzerland.

But to find her now on the same flight! He was almost glad he and his parents had been forced to cut short their vacation when he broke his leg.

He winced as the pain shot up his leg beneath the cast.

Almost glad.

"Aren't you going to spend Christmas with your family?" he asked.

She nodded. "Yes. My father works in the States. My mother died several years ago. I'll be with him for Christmas . . . I hope." She gestured toward the front of the aircraft. "If we get out of this."

"I appreciate you coming up here, Stefani. Look, the best medicine is just to put it out of our minds. I'm sure the captain's right. We're in the middle of a classic governmental, military, diplomatic overreaction. There's supposed to be a strange bug on board, so they go bonkers trying to keep us away from the rest of the world."

She gave him a blank look. "What is 'bonkers'? I'm not familiar with that."

"Idiomatic usage. Slang. Means, ah, going *crazy,* or going *nuts,* or going *bananas.*"

She shook her head. The smile was gone.

"English is such a strange language . . ." Her voice trailed off as she glanced back at the doorway again.

"We'll be okay, Stefani. Really."

She worked at turning on her smile again. A thousand-megawatt smile, he decided.

"You need sleep, Gary. So do I," she said.

He raised an eyebrow as he tried to gauge how much teasing he could get by with. "You, could . . . ah . . . sleep up here. I mean"—he gestured to his leg—"this bed's big enough and I'm quite harmless like this, and there's a privacy curtain."

She wasn't listening. The smile faded and she cocked her head.

"Why was your father so rude to me, Gary, when I asked if I could help you? Did I say something wrong?"

Endless paternal lectures on family history replayed all at once in his mind. His grandparents had been shipped to Auschwitz in the waning days of the war, and as a little boy his father had watched in agony from the other side of a fence as his parents were herded by in a long line of naked men, women, and children shuffling forward to be forced into a furnace—some without even the coup de grâce of a shot to the head. As a six-year-old male, little Abe Strauss had been saved for unspeakable purposes—but the Allies reached him first.

As a result, he hated all Germans, and all things German. He had been stunned and enraged that his family would have to change planes in Frankfurt instead of Paris for the unexpected early return home.

And he'd been none too pleased to find his son interested in a German girl.

"Stefani, we're Jewish. Dad lived through Auschwitz as a child," Gary said.

He heard her inhale suddenly and saw her eyes flicker away for a moment. She looked back at him and smiled weakly. "I understand, then. I'm sorry."

She pulled away, and he reached for her hand and pulled her back, gently but firmly. "Stefani, that's *their* generation. Not ours."

She nodded. "I don't want to cause trouble."

He smiled at her. "You're not. Unless you leave me alone up here, of course. Then all my wailing will keep everyone awake."

She shook her head again. "As I said, you're terrible. An oversexed baby. You're obviously too young for me!" She pulled away and stood up, unconsciously arching her back in a way that emphasized her considerable bustline. He made a fist of his right hand and bit the knuckle of his index finger with a slight moaning sound, and she swatted him.

"If you're in lust, I'm out of there," she teased.

"The phrase is 'out of *here*,' and I'm not in lust, I'm in love."

"*Schweinehund!* I'll be back in a while to see if you're dead."

He watched her descend the ladder and disappear. Then he smiled and lay back, calculating the average travel time between universities and the possible advantages of transferring to Yale.

All worries about deadly viruses and broken legs had been temporarily displaced.

As Stefani returned to the main cabin, a balding, slightly overweight man in his late fifties excused himself from a window seat and retrieved his briefcase from an overhead bin before heading for the upper deck. He found an unoccupied row on the right and settled in, pulling out a small notebook computer. Several passengers glanced over and he smiled at them, aware that he wouldn't be recognized. That was the advantage, he thought, of being both famous and invisible. As a Pulitzer Prize–winning journalist with twenty years at the *Washington Post,* he had a byline that was known and respected. But in person he could blend in like a chameleon, observing at will and getting to know the people behind a story without becoming a center of attention himself.

Don Moses opened his computer and snapped it on. For hours he had watched and taken notes on those around him, principally out of boredom. Before the shooting of Lisa Erickson, the entire emergency seemed rather trivial—the usual governmental overreaction to a misperceived threat, as the captain had indicated.

But it had all changed suddenly, and the atmosphere of irritation had turned to apprehension.

He fed a series of keystrokes into the computer and decided on a three-page submission. When he finished the story, he could hook up the computer's modem to the aircraft's satellite phone in the seat back and download it to the newspaper's computer back in Washington, ready to be edited.

He thought about his wife, Jaimie, waiting for him at the chalet they'd rented in Aspen. The kids should be there by now. Jill and Jake, together with their respective spouses and his grandkids, in their respective minivans. Thank God they'd taken well to his remarrying after their mother died, he thought, or Christmas together anywhere would end up a disaster. Jaimie, at thirty-four, was younger than his daughter, Jill, but everyone had embraced her as family.

Moses wrote a few lead lines setting the place and time, and let his mind roam back to the phone call he'd made to his family.

They'd been watching CNN's continuing coverage of the crisis and were terrified.

He had been blasé, had laughed and minimized the risk of any illness, let alone anything approaching a lethal virus. Yes, he told them, there *were* guards around the airplane as CNN had reported, but that was nothing but typical Air Force overreaction. No one close to the action *really* believed that a quarantine was anything but precautionary.

That was before the Air Force security police had provided deadly evidence that Flight 66's viral exposure was being taken with utter seriousness.

Suddenly they had become a genuine story, and his journalistic instincts had become impossible to ignore. But more than anything else, playing the journalist set him apart from the terror he felt. He could watch and comment and write—engaging in the calming illusion that when the story was composed, he could walk away unscathed.

SEVENTEEN

Rusty Sanders was not prepared for the alert he snagged from the CIA's station in Cairo. Having quietly become a consummate expert with the Company's computer systems in the previous two years, he'd loaded a special search program to look for any message traffic affecting Flight 66.

The Cairo communiqué had fallen into the net at 5:34 A.M.

Rusty caught Mark Hastings by phone in his office.

"I'll print it out for you," Rusty told him, "but the thrust of it is, Cairo has picked up information that Flight Sixty-six may be drawing the interest of a Shiite terrorist group. The report mentions rumors of terrorist efforts going on right now in Egypt and Libya to secure a military strike aircraft with a sufficient range to reach the western Sahara."

"Jesus Christ!" Mark exclaimed. "They already know the flight's *destination* field? Roth is going to have a coronary!"

"Can they move that fast? The Iranians, I mean?"

"Definitely, and they've got the money to back up whatever they decide to do, as well as the sophistication to do the job. Print a copy, I'll be right down. I'd better tell Roth."

When Mark had retrieved the message and left, Rusty

reentered the computer and called the message back to the screen. Sherry Ellis had entered the room and moved in behind his left shoulder as he read it again.

"Print a copy for me too, would you, Rusty?" she asked.

He nodded, enjoying the faint scent of her perfume while his fingers worked the keys. Sherry scanned it as Rusty examined the various numbers and routing codes.

"Finished?" he asked.

She nodded and stood up.

"What do you think?" Rusty asked her.

"Could be a credible report," Sherry said with a perplexed expression. "Any group with the right hardware could fly over the desert and reach that airfield for an attack, I suppose."

"Accomplishing what?" Rusty asked. "I mean, they've obviously got CNN and Reuters in the headquarters of every pipsqueak terrorist organization in the Middle East. If they've found out about the airfield, they know why Flight Sixty-six is headed there. Sure, Ambassador Lancaster's on board, but he's going to die along with the others as far as they know. Why risk your people and equipment to go kill a dead man in front of hundreds of witnesses? That doesn't make sense."

Sherry sat down and cupped her chin in her hand, elbow on the table, eyes on the wall.

"Doesn't, does it?"

Without changing position, she looked up at Rusty with a sideways glance. "But, you know, we've got so many of our people bored to tears out there, they think they've got to write up an alert whenever they wake up from a threatening dream."

"I've never worked in the field."

"I have, and it really can be a crashing bore." She stood up. "Main thing that bothers me, Rusty, is how they found the right location so fast. I mean, I'm sure the airline told their people by satellite phone, but the only organization with enough technical superiority to be listening to those channels is also the one with enough sophistication to pull off an attack."

"Which one is that?"

"I know you've read at least one briefing paper on them. It's Aqbah. They formed in the aftermath of the Gulf War, remember? Jon Roth is the expert on them, and I know for a fact they scare the deputy director half to death." She gave him a short recap of the emergence of Aqbah and their capabilities.

"One problem, Sherry," Rusty said when she'd finished.

"Which is?"

"If they're *that* sophisticated, they wouldn't be running all over the place openly trying to borrow a fighter squadron. We wouldn't be hearing a thing about it yet."

She cocked her head and smiled. "Good catch. You're right."

"Logic is my life." He chuckled.

"So what *do* we have here, Doctor? A bored fiction writer in the Cairo station, or what? You analyze these things all the time too."

"Yeah, but mainly medical and aviation-related messages."

They stared at each other for a few seconds in silence before Rusty turned back to the computer and began retrieving tracking numbers. He triggered a printout and tore it off as he got to his feet and turned to Sherry.

"Do you suppose Communications could get me a secure line to Cairo?"

"Worth a try," she said. "You know where the comm room is."

He stood up and started for the door, looking back over his shoulder. "I'll be back."

It took nearly twenty minutes of flashes, calls, and messages to the U.S. Embassy in Cairo and other secure locations in the Egyptian capital to confirm that there was no one formally on duty in Cairo. Whoever had sent the message had done so without coordination with the station chief, who had heard nothing of the reported rumor.

But someone had written the alert, and the more he thought about it, the more Rusty wanted to question him.

He turned his attention to the tracking numbers, following the trail deep into the computer room, where a friendly technician began digging for the computer tape that had brought the message into Langley in the first place. He waited while the man disappeared into the electronic labyrinth, returning a few minutes later with a puzzled expression.

"No record, Doctor. Those numbers don't match."

"I don't understand."

"Well, maybe there's a glitch or I looked in the wrong place, but if that message came in on any of the normal lines, the tracking codes got garbled. I also ran a search based on point of origin. The computer never logged it as a message from Cairo with that wording."

"But it obviously came in. You saw it too when you looked at the computer file."

The man nodded and looked around worriedly before turning back to Sanders and handing back the printout.

"Sorry, Doc. Dead end."

"But, how could . . . ?"

The technician put a hand on Sanders' shoulder and began walking him toward the door to the computer room.

"Two possibilities." His voice was barely above a whisper. "It's a glitch in the system, or the message didn't originate outside." He let that sink in for a moment, watching Rusty's reaction. "You didn't get that from me, okay?"

Rusty stopped and turned to him. "You mean, if someone here put this in the system with a bunch of bogus tracking numbers, you'd have no record?"

The man glanced around again, this time in both directions. Rusty followed his glance to a TV security camera hanging in a corner.

The man turned back. "We didn't talk, okay? You draw your own conclusions."

Rusty nodded, feeling more perplexed than ever.

Rusty returned to his office in deep thought. If the technician's implications were correct, the message hadn't come from Cairo at all. It had been typed into the computer within the complex at Langley.

But why? Did that mean the report itself was bogus and someone at Langley had simply fabricated the alert? Or was the message-sender simply trying to add believability to a verbal rumor from Cairo or somewhere else in the Middle East?

Rusty pulled out a yellow legal pad and began hastily scribbling out possibilities and motives. Someone could have phoned in the alert, he reasoned, but if so, whoever then transferred the message into the computer had gone to all the trouble of assigning it bogus tracking codes and reception times. For what possible purpose?

He looked at the message again, going over the language in detail. There was the usual cold, conservative, cryptic nature to the phrases, but there was also a difference he couldn't quite identify.

Okay, so someone's playing games at CIA headquarters. That's like carrying coals to Newcastle. Maybe the big guys do that on weekends to amuse themselves, watching schmucks like me trying to figure it out.

Rusty got up and wandered around his small office, wishing it had the floor space Roth enjoyed. He could really pace around with an office that size.

Why would someone want to plant a warning like that? To upset Roth? Mark said he'd go ballistic because the bad guys had discovered the identity of the West African landing site.

Rusty stopped suddenly in front of his desk as a connection coalesced.

Hold it. Suppose I wanted to implicate one of the terrorist groups like Aqbah even though I had no proof they were really planning an operation? What if I wanted to set them up for international condemnation? Would this be a first step?

He resumed pacing. To whip up international sentiment against a group like Aqbah, he thought, other governments would have to be involved, and possibly even the media. And in order to accomplish that—if the message was truly bogus—whoever planted it in the first place would be preparing to broadcast it as widely as possible.

Rusty returned to the conference room determined to keep his theory to himself for the time being. The room was empty, and he sat in front of the computer and began paging down the nonsecure outbound traffic, looking for any evidence that the warning was being sent to American allies.

He found nothing.

Sherry returned at the same moment Mark arrived from the quick meeting with Roth. The deputy director, Mark said, was massively upset, and was demanding to know how Aqbah could have intercepted the information about Flight 66's destination.

"He wants to make sure none of us, including you, Rusty, talked about it on nonsecure lines."

Rusty looked first at Mark, then at Sherry, then back to Mark.

"Sherry and I were discussing that earlier, Mark. We figured the airline would have discussed it with their crew by satellite phone. The airline already has the flight plan."

Mark tossed Sherry a questioning look. "Flight plan?" Mark hadn't known about that.

"Yeah," Rusty replied. "I noticed it on Roth's desk several hours ago. It was a Quantum Airlines computer flight plan, which means they probably transmitted it over their datalink satellite channels to their aircraft. Those channels are not scrambled, of course. They're digital, but anyone could have intercepted it with the right equipment."

As Mark nodded in deep thought, a red light flashed in the back of Rusty's consciousness.

"Wait a minute, Mark. Is Roth concluding that the message is referring to *Aqbah* when it talks about a Shiite terrorist group?"

"Yes, he is. Why?"

Rusty looked at Sherry, whose expression was neutral. Hadn't they concluded just an hour ago that Aqbah would gain nothing from attacking Flight 66? Hadn't she agreed with him? Why hadn't she mentioned it to Mark?

Caution, son! Rusty thought to himself. *You're out of your league here. They're not communicating for a reason, and you don't know what it is.*

"Rusty, why'd you ask?" Mark prompted again.

Rusty shook his head. "Ah, nothing. I'm confusing myself. I've been reading too many threat messages, I guess."

Mark Hastings was half-sitting on the edge of one of the tables, examining his shoes. Sherry was quietly watching him while Rusty waited.

Mark looked up at him suddenly.

"Rusty, you've talked with the flight crew several times during the night, correct?"

"Yes. I could find the times for you if . . ."

Mark raised his hand. "Not necessary. Just tell me this. At any time did you mention the Saharan destination on that hookup?"

"You mean with the pilots? I sure didn't say anything to the flight attendants."

"Anyone. Pilots, flight attendants, Ambassador Lancaster. Anyone."

Rusty took a deep breath and thought hard and fast. On the second call he had talked to the captain. They had just received the new flight plan. What had the captain asked? Oh, yeah. "Why Africa?" was the question. And he had answered him.

Rusty looked Mark in the eye. "In response to a question from the captain, I may have. They already had the destination. I can't remember who mentioned it, but the words were 'eastern Mauritania.' "

Mark looked away. "Oh Jesus Christ! Aqbah's monitors probably overheard your conversation."

"But they wouldn't have the exact coordinates. We didn't mention anything more specific."

Sherry Ellis had said nothing. Now she spoke up.

"Mark, the whole damn flight plan went chattering out on the same channels, as Rusty just told you, and he had nothing to do with that."

Mark turned to her. "Yeah, but Roth looks for easy targets and Rusty apparently fits the description."

"Wait a minute!" Sanders interjected, getting to his feet. "Are you trying to say that Roth is spending his time looking for who leaked a drop of water in a thunderstorm? The destination was declassified the moment Quantum Airlines was informed!"

Mark Hastings got to his feet and took a deep breath. "Rusty, I've got to run an errand for Roth that will take me about an hour. He's headed back over to the Situation Room at the White House. When he comes back, he'll want a report on who said what to whom, but if I haven't been able to talk to you, how can I know anything about your phone call? Otherwise, there's a pronounced risk."

"In other words, go home and lie low, pull the phone out of the wall, and speak to no one?" Rusty said.

Mark patted him on the shoulder and glanced at Sherry, who did not respond. "By tomorrow, this will be a tempest in a teapot. Get some sleep, and thanks for all the great help."

Mark walked swiftly from the room, leaving Rusty in confusion. The sudden focus on who might have found out about Flight 66's Saharan destination, the sudden implication that he was in trouble, didn't ring true.

Rusty looked around at the computers in the conference room. The message could have been planted by any of them.

He glanced at Sherry. She was busying herself with a
stack of messages, but she let him catch her eye.

"You agree with this, Sherry? Should I get the hell
out of Dodge?"

She inclined her head toward the door with a shadow
of a smile.

"See ya," she said simply.

Rusty picked up his notes and turned toward the
door, feeling somewhat betrayed.

Less than fifty yards from the conference room, Rusty
Sanders came to a halt as his mind forged a connection
he hadn't considered. He fumbled with the papers he
was carrying to see if he was right.

He was. The message held the same phrase, "pronounced risk."

Mark had just used the same words.

But I've seen or heard it somewhere else as well. Where?

Rusty began walking again until the hallway jogged to
the right. He stopped just around the corner and stood
with his back against the wall in thought.

*If the message was written on a standard personal com-
puter, it would have been saved as a specific file before
being transferred to the communications system by file
name. If I can find the right computer, I can probably find
the file.*

There were footsteps approaching down the corridor
to his left. Rusty glanced to the right and realized he
was near Jonathan Roth's office. He covered the twenty
feet to the entrance, surprised to find the outer office
door still ajar and half expecting Roth to be inside.

The outer office was empty, and Rusty stood for a
moment in thought before moving inside and quietly
closing the door behind him.

The footsteps were closer. Whoever it was would pass
harmlessly—unless he was headed to Roth's office.

Rusty looked around the waiting room. If the footsteps belonged to either Jonathan Roth or Mark and
one of them came swinging in the door, trying to physi-

cally hide in the office would be a monstrous risk. But if he was just waiting for the deputy director to return . . .

I'd look stupid to Mark or Roth if either walk in here and finds me sitting in an empty office, but at least I wouldn't look suspicious.

Rusty plunked himself down on the waiting room couch, a red leather affair opposite the secretary's vacant desk. He snuggled into the corner closest to the outer wall and waited as the footsteps slowed, then passed on by and disappeared down the corridor.

Rusty realized he was breathing hard.

I'd make a lousy agent! he thought. *The sound of chattering knees would give me away every time!*

He got up, prepared to leave, but the memory of the personal computer on Roth's desk resurfaced. It was an IBM-format machine. If Roth had left it on, it would take a simple series of keystrokes to get to the main hard-disk directory. If he could find it—if the message really had been written at Langley and there was no alert from Cairo—that fact alone would prove he hadn't compromised the operation by mentioning Mauritania on the satellite phone.

Rusty quietly moved to the inner office door and tried it. It was unlocked.

The office was lit by filtered light from an adjacent parking lot. He opened the door gingerly, realizing there could be no alibi for being caught inside.

Rusty studied the desk. The laptop computer was in the same place, still open and on, apparently connected to a power supply plugged into the wall.

He moved inside quickly and slid into Roth's chair and began working the keyboard. Getting to the main hard-disk directory was simple.

He studied the subdirectories, guessing which one to try and how to launch a search routine. He spotted a communications program and ordered the computer to bring up *its* subdirectory.

A message filled the screen instantly:

ENTER PASSWORD

Good Lord, for a directory? The whole directory is pass-word-protected?

He tried a few combinations, obvious pairings such as the office extension, Langley's zip code, and Roth's age. Predictably, none worked. He could assume it was a four-digit code, but Roth could have easily left a longer, more complicated one as well.

He was totally absorbed with the problem when a small noise reached his ears and he whirled toward the inner office door.

Sherry Ellis was standing in the open doorway.

Oh hell!

She said nothing, standing stock-still for a few seconds as her eyes ran from Rusty to the computer screen and back again. Her expression was stern and unyielding.

He stumbled for words. "Sherry, you startled me, I . . . ah . . ."

Without a flicker of a response to his words, she walked slowly toward him, moving around the back of the desk as he turned the chair to face her, wondering whether or not to get up.

"Sherry?"

She's Roth's assistant. There's no way to explain this!

Sherry stopped inches from him, her right arm reaching out suddenly to the computer keyboard as her eyes moved to the screen.

She entered a quick series of keystrokes and hit the ENTER button. She straightened up then and looked at Rusty.

"I believe that's the code you were looking for."

Rusty looked up at her in shock.

She looked back at him and inclined her head toward the computer.

"Come on! The Director could be back early. Move your fingers!"

"You . . . you're curious about the same thing?"

She leaned over him again, deciding not to wait, and entered a flurry of keystrokes to call up Roth's newly unlocked communications directory as she asked, "What, exactly, were you looking for?"

He held up the security alert message and she nodded knowingly.

"I wanted to see if this came from Roth," he said.

She shook her head. "No way. But you've already figured out that it didn't come from Cairo."

"You spotted that too?" he asked.

"Timing."

"Timing? What do you mean?"

"The message was supposedly transmitted Friday night, Saturday morning—about four A.M. Cairo time. No way! Even dedicated spooks drawing CIA paychecks don't like to work Friday nights. I know our macho men in Cairo. If there's liquor to be consumed or females to be serviced, they're not going to be slaving over a hot teletype around four A.M." She picked the message up from the desk where Rusty had laid it.

"This came from right here in the building, but"—she gestured to the computer—"Jon Roth isn't your suspect."

"Can you be sure?"

"Enter the damned search string, Bubba, before we both get arrested. Prove it to yourself."

Rusty keyed in a phrase from the message and launched a search routine. The computer began chattering to itself as it tried to find a file that had the exact same string of letters and spaces.

Rusty looked up at her.

"This started as curiosity, but when Mark implied I was to blame for leaking the location of the airfield, I had to find out. If that message came from this building —if it *is* bogus, as we both suspect—then I couldn't be guilty of leaking anything."

"Something's going on with Mark. I couldn't warn you, because I didn't see it in time."

Rusty knew he looked shocked. "But, you *know* Mark. You said you've worked with him for years."

She shook her head and frowned. "Rusty, you can never fully know anyone in this business. The bum's rush he gave you out of the building was very weird. It's possible he wants you out of here for his own reasons. Or maybe someone else here at Langley is worried about you, and Mark's responding to their worries."

"Worried about *me?*"

"You're too curious. You're not one of the good ole boys. For that matter, neither am I."

Rusty purposefully leered at her chest and cocked his head. "You definitely aren't one of the good ole boys."

"Stay focused, Rusty. This is serious."

"Sorry."

"I may not be a fully accepted insider, but I'm considered controllable and loyal. But you're a renegade. That's why someone at Langley wants you out of here, and I think, for your sake, we'd better comply." She looked back at him. "Mark thinks you're already gone. He may be checking with security any minute to make sure you cleared the gate."

"Sherry, how . . . how serious could this be? I mean, what's going on here?"

She shook her head. "You're in a puzzle palace in the middle of a crisis. It's possible someone's trying to seize an opportunity. It could get damn serious, especially if someone's going around Roth, outside channels, and launching their own operation."

"Is that possible here? With all the safeguards?"

She sighed and shook her head as if disappointed at the question.

"Is the Pope Catholic?"

The computer bleeped and they both looked at the screen:

STRING NOT FOUND

"Let me try one other possibility," Rusty said. He entered a lengthy flurry of commands and executed them in one fluid movement.

"What was that?"

"Just another idea, to see if he had any other locked directories."

The computer whirred and clicked for a half minute, then bleeped again, but the message flashed on and off the screen too fast for them to read.

"Dead end," Rusty said, biting his lip. "Damn!"

"You see what I mean?" she said.

Rusty nodded. "The message did not come from Roth's computer."

Sherry leaned over him and backed out of the secure directory, leaving the screen on the shell menu as Rusty had found it. She straightened up and took his hand roughly, pulling him out of Roth's chair.

"Let's get the flock out of here, double-oh-nothing. I told you my boss wasn't the bad guy."

"But who is?"

"You hit the road. I'll keep looking. None of this happened, okay?"

"You're scaring me," he said.

"Best defense is a good escape route. Go home."

Rusty returned to his tiny office and sat quickly at his desktop computer. He searched through several screens before keying in a series of commands and inserting a small floppy disk, then commanded a download. After two very long minutes he launched another short series of instructions into the computer, then turned it off and removed the floppy disk, which he stuffed into his coat pocket. Rusty gathered a few papers from his desk and retrieved his personal digital assistant—a small steno-pad-sized portable computer tied to the cellular network—from a desk drawer.

Sherry had the appropriate numbers. She could transmit directly to the small screen by phone or computer, and since she had an identical unit, he could reach her the same way without going through Langley's phone or computer systems.

The CIA's Langley complex was ten minutes behind him when the tiny personal digital assistant beeped at him and a terse message appeared on its screen:

Apparently too many questions asked downstairs of communications personnel. Internal security was around here a few minutes ago looking for a certain former FAA doc. Someone's upset. Watch this space. You stumbled into something.

EIGHTEEN

Yuri Steblinko turned the small twin-engine jet off the main runway and began taxiing slowly toward the ramp where the prince's Gulfstream sat armed, loaded, fueled, and ready. There had been a ruddy glow of twilight on the western horizon as they descended, but the ramp was now dark, with only a few overhead mercury-vapor lamps showing in the distance.

Fortunately, he had the airfield memorized.

Yuri glanced at the former Soviet Air Force major in the seat beside him, an old friend who was now fifty thousand dollars richer for securing the aging Hawker Siddeley business jet they were flying and for helping to file the outbound flight plan Yuri would need.

The prince's own pilot had relayed an order to the small company doing the missile installation. The prince's aircraft was to be made ready immediately. The royal pilot would arrive sometime during the night or early morning, they were told, to do an acceptance check flight. The prince would arrive a day later, and the money would be paid over at that time.

That part had been simple.

Making certain that the prince's real pilot was not coming to town early had taken several hours.

The taxi lights of the Hawker picked up several aircraft parked ahead on the tarmac. The upturned winglets of the Gulfstream IV loomed on the other side. He could see no one near the aircraft.

Yuri parked the Hawker and shut down the engines. They had gone over the plan numerous times. Yuri would depart with the Gulfstream under the Hawker's flight plan—unless something went wrong and he was seen. In that case, a separate departure plan for the Gulfstream had been prefiled under its real call sign, and the major would leave minutes later in the Hawker.

Yuri clapped his friend on the shoulder and slipped to the back cabin to put on the headdress of a Saudi royal pilot as well as a beard and mustache. After checking himself in a small mirror, he let down the steps and descended, carrying a small suitcase, and walked quickly to the Gulfstream.

The aircraft was dark, but a portable power cart was plugged in and sitting quietly by the nose. Yuri disconnected the wheeled unit and rolled it safely to one side before lowering the forward steps and placing his bag inside, his mind racing through the possibilities. What if they hadn't fueled it? What if they hadn't *armed* it?

He entered the cockpit and flipped on the battery switch. The fuel gauges showed full.

He searched for the new armaments panel and toggled it to STORES STATUS.

It, too, showed everything in readiness. There were four missiles installed and armed.

Yuri returned to the cabin to pull up the stairs and secure the door when the lights of a car caught his eye as it entered the ramp area a quarter mile distant. He watched, momentarily transfixed, as the car turned in his direction and headed directly toward the Gulfstream.

The decision in front of him was critical. He could still slam the door shut without detection and lie low inside the airplane, hoping no one tried to enter.

Or he could play the part he was dressed to play.

The car was accelerating. Its lights would fall on the

open door in less than ten seconds. He had to decide *now!*

Yuri grabbed his suitcase and a flashlight and climbed back down the steps just as the car came to a halt beside the aircraft. He waited to greet the man who was climbing from the backseat of the car.

"Sheik Farouk Akim?" the man asked.

"Ahmed Amani, his assistant and alternate captain," Yuri replied in Arabic-accented Russian.

"The control tower personnel alerted us someone was at the aircraft."

The man approached warily, his eyes darting to the aircraft's open door and back to Yuri. "We were not expecting you this evening!"

"Could you turn on and connect the power unit, please?" Yuri asked.

The man looked momentarily confused, then motioned to his driver, who moved toward the power unit, obviously familiar with its operation.

"We would have met you properly if we had been informed."

Yuri looked more closely at the man, keeping his expression level even as his mind raced. It was the owner of the company himself, a former member of the Soviet Aircraft Design Bureau named Nicolai Sakarov.

And Nicolai Sakarov knew Yuri Steblinko very well!

Yuri repressed the impulse to shake hands automatically. Inclining his head in more traditional Arab fashion, as if reluctant to stoop to a Western custom, he extended his hand.

Sakarov pumped it without enthusiasm while he examined Yuri's features in the dim light of the ramp, as if trying to place a slightly familiar face and voice.

"Have we met, Captain Amani?" Sakarov asked.

"I believe we have talked on the telephone. That is all," Yuri said.

Sakarov cocked his head slightly and decided that the features were sufficiently Arabian, but there was still something about the voice.

"I have come a little ahead of Sheik Farouk," Yuri said, being careful to keep his tone and accent under control, "because I was in Europe dealing with a small matter related to our Airbus purchases. I also have duties with Saudi Airlines. I am the one who decides to whom we should turn for maintenance and modification."

Sakarov's eyes lit up, and the pall of suspicion partly melted away. If the Arab before him had purchasing authority for Saudi Airlines, keeping him happy could mean additional modification contracts for his young company.

"Your early arrival is not a difficulty," Sakarov said broadly.

"The aircraft is ready as requested?" Yuri asked.

Sakarov nodded energetically. "Absolutely. All the requested items, including the armaments. As directed, they are installed and pins are pulled."

"I appreciate your efficiency. The sheik will arrive around ten tomorrow morning. I will be up about an hour tonight. There is a hotel arranged nearby, I trust?"

Sakarov looked alarmed. "You . . . will be flying tonight?"

Yuri turned to him with a stern expression. "This is a problem?"

"No . . . ah, no. We just weren't expecting a flight until tomorrow."

"My copilot will join me across the field shortly. We will do some ground checks, then a quick flight."

"As you wish," Sakarov said, nervously glancing at the aircraft again.

Yuri caught his look, understanding his nervousness.

"Mr. Sakarov. If there were any last-minute inspections you were planning on doing in the morning for quality control or cosmetic purposes, that is no problem —as long as the systems are ready tonight."

Sakarov nodded and looked relieved. "Last-minute quality checks, you understand, are all we have left to do. The sheik, as you know, was very specific."

Yuri nodded solemnly. "The sheik is always very specific when it comes to the prince's aircraft. On my return, the airplane is yours as planned until the sheik's arrival. I will be making no cosmetic evaluations tonight."

"Thank you!" Sakarov said.

"And on our return, would you have someone available to take us to a hotel?"

"Certainly," Sakarov said. "About an hour, then?"

"No earlier," Yuri replied.

Yuri could see there was still concern in Sakarov's mind. The man had been caught off-guard and was still off-balance. But the thought of the million and a half U.S. dollars that would be in his hands within twenty-four hours when the sheik arrived and formally accepted the job would keep his smile broad and sincere. After all, once expenses were paid, Sakarov stood to pocket personally a half-million dollars.

Sakarov seemed content to stay out of the way while Yuri did a thorough ground check, accepting his explanation that his copilot had gone to speak with tower personnel.

Sakarov made a show of waving goodbye and entering his car, but Yuri saw him drive to a remote corner of the ramp and shut off the lights.

He ran through the engine start procedures and taxied to the base of the control tower as stated, positioning the left side of the airplane, which contained the entrance door, away from Sakarov's position. He glanced back at the Hawker. The major would have seen Sakarov's arrival and would know to go to plan B. Yuri left the engines running and set the parking brake, then lowered the stairs and descended to the ramp for a few seconds before reversing the process and securing the door. Sakarov, watching through field glasses, would have only seen legs and feet, Yuri knew. He would assume the copilot had been standing in the dark and had now boarded.

As soon as the Gulfstream IV reached the end of the

runway, the sleepy tower controller issued the takeoff clearance. Within thirty seconds Yuri had lifted off and headed west, calculating Sakarov's reactions, which would come at predictable times. Having worked for his company, Yuri knew his excitable nature all too well. He was anything but a diplomat.

The prince's Gulfstream would not return in an hour, of course, in which case Sakarov would begin to worry about an hour and fifteen minutes after departure. Sakarov would make inquiries of the air traffic control officials around thirty minutes later, and be shocked to find that the prince's jet had left the country. He would suspect the prince of larceny. He would first seek help from the Air Force and the Russian Air Traffic System, but when that failed, he would call Riyadh, Saudi Arabia, and hurl an incautious accusation at Sheik Farouk Akim. The Saudis would inform him that there was no such person as Ahmed Amani in their employ, and hurl their own threats about finding the prince's aircraft. Sakarov would be convinced they had stolen their own aircraft to avoid paying. The Saudis would be convinced Sakarov had staged the theft for his own nefarious purposes.

And by that time Yuri would be in a different place under a different call sign over a thousand miles away over the Mediterranean.

Step two was successful! he thought to himself. *Now to send the departure message.*

As soon as he had reached cruising altitude, Yuri left the cockpit and opened the sophisticated communications panel located at the front of the passenger cabin. The panel had been engineered in a beautiful walnut console. He selected the appropriate satellite routing and turned on the communications computer, then entered the agreed-upon coded numbers and activated the transmit circuit.

Within one minute, he knew, the message would be seen by the intended recipient—a coldhearted professional monitoring that particular satellite transponder.

There would be a message in return sent back to the Gulfstream when the target was airborne, and one indicating the expected arrival time over the preplanned coordinates. A chime would ring in the cockpit when the message arrived. He'd checked out the communications system during the flight test phase several months before.

He found a bag of cookies and some pastries in the small galley and put them in a bag, then returned to the radio control panel and lowered the polished walnut cover.

Something clicked.

That's odd, he thought.

He raised the cover and spotted the source of the noise. The master power switch for the satellite link had been jarred to the OFF position when the lid closed. Yuri turned the computer on again, double-checked its operational status, and secured the lid in the UP position, just to be sure.

Yuri settled back into the left captain's seat of the Gulfstream and put on his seat belt, mentally running through the risky procedure just a half hour ahead of him. He had worked it out with surgical care. Some eighty miles before the Turkish border, he would begin a simulated landing approach to an uncontrolled airfield, but when low enough to be clear of radar, the Gulfstream would make a high-speed dash a hundred miles north. There he'd climb back up within radar coverage as if departing from a nearby airport, activate a new flight plan under a bogus call sign, and become a chartered American flight returning to the States by way of the Canary Islands.

In the old days, he knew, Soviet radar would have spotted the trick. Since the breakup of the U.S.S.R., however, the coverage had deteriorated. He had known about the Turkish coverage "hole" for eight months.

As soon as the Turkish border was behind him, there would be six hours of boredom ahead. With the flight plan carefully entered into the onboard flight management computer, he could relax and enjoy the prince's beautiful machine while it flew itself. Maybe he'd even nap in his seat for a while. He'd need to be sharp on the other end.

The act of taking a Gulfstream into combat would leave no margin for error.

ABOARD FLIGHT 66

At 2:50 P.M. word came from Dallas Operations to depart Iceland for the airfield in western Africa. Dick Robb sent for James Holland and passed the word to the flight attendants. The Air Force mobile command post just outside confirmed receiving the same message and promised to disconnect and move out of the way when the pilots were ready. The runway would be theirs.

Holland arrived on the flight deck with Barb in tow.

"You get any sleep?" Robb asked.

Holland leaned on the back of his seat and rubbed his eyes. "A little. Couple of hours."

Robb nodded. "Okay, here's the latest. They should be ready to load more than three hundred new box lunches through the rear door as we asked, we've got an updated flight plan, and they should have a pair of metal shears for us for the broken leg in the back."

"Shears?" Holland asked.

"The young man in the crew rest loft," Barb told him. "The Swiss doctor, who's been an incredible help, by the way, needs to cut the boy's cast off. His leg is badly swollen, and the doctor's worried about circulation."

Holland nodded. "Okay."

"And the meals are coming on," Barb added, pointing to the light on the overhead panel indicating door 5L had been opened.

Robb consulted his list and continued.

"I also demanded replacement medication for three passengers who'd left theirs in luggage. That's supposed to be coming on too."

Barb agreed.

"And we're completely fueled up to max takeoff weight, water tanks are filled, and they checked and topped the oil in all four engines. I've got the computer programmed, and the three inertial nav systems are aligned."

Holland slipped into the left seat and turned back to Barb.

"Are we ready from your perspective, Barb?"

She nodded. "The good news is, absolutely no one down there is sick as yet, or showing any symptoms. But, the way I understand it, we have another twenty-four hours to go before we would be seeing symptoms in at least a few."

He nodded, his eyes focused out the side window. "How's the morale?"

She shook her head and sighed.

"All I can tell you, James, is that we've got some deeply frightened people on this airplane, and it's showing. A lot of anxiety, scared kids, and scared crew members. Ambassador Lancaster has been wonderful. He's helped organize a bunch of volunteers to keep helping and checking on people. The man you had to throttle has been quiet as the Sphinx, and even holy Joe down there, Garson, has been helpful. Lancaster's keeping him in line. Most everyone, though, has been wonderful."

"And Mr. Erickson?"

"I got him to call home. He talked to his sister-in-law and his kids. Very wrenching, but they were very supportive. I think they've all realized his wife had been mentally deteriorating for several years. He's still in shock, but I feel sure he'll make it."

Holland patted her arm. "Get 'em ready, Barb. We'll roll as soon as you let me know you're ready. I'm . . . not sure that going anywhere is a solution of any sort, but . . ."

"Best medicine *I* can think of," Barb said. "We need to get in motion headed *anywhere*. These people need to see something happening. Just sitting here is killing everyone. All they've been able to do so far is worry who's going to be the first person to keel over with a high fever."

When the door had closed behind Barb, Robb looked over at Holland.

"James?"

"Yeah."

"I've been thinking, you know, about some stupid things I said last night . . ."

James Holland shook his head, stopping him.

"Forget it, Dick. We just need to get ourselves through this."

Robb bit his lip and looked away. "Yeah, well, I just want you to know I'm with you. Whatever you need, okay?"

"Okay, Dick. I appreciate it."

Quantum 66 had four engines running and the before-takeoff check completed by 3:45 P.M., when the satellite phone rang again with word from Dallas Operations to hold in position.

"For how long?" Holland asked. "We're ready to go with engines running."

"We think more than thirty minutes, Captain. We're waiting for final release from the Situation Room, and I guess they're waiting for the Defense Department to confirm the airfield is ready for you."

The snow showers had ended at midmorning. Holland could see patches of blue in the distance through the fast-moving clouds, but the wind was still blowing from the east and the weather was obviously still changeable. Earlier, the security police in their chemical gear had looked even more alien and frightening as they stood around the red-lined perimeter, freezing their tails off and wishing Quantum's airplane was anywhere else. Now they had all retreated into various vehicles and removed the barricades. There was no evidence of Lisa Erickson's death left on the ramp.

At 4:08 P.M. the word came from Dallas to depart, and within three minutes James Holland nudged the control yoke back at one hundred sixty miles per hour and lifted the seven hundred fifty thousand pounds of aircraft, people, and fuel into the Icelandic sky.

At five hundred feet above the surface, he began a turn to the right over the ocean and started climbing on course. Their destination, a string of numbers in the flight management computer reading simply "N2000 W00800," lay over three thousand miles ahead down the center of the Atlantic.

Robb reported the departure by open satellite telephone to Quantum Operations in Dallas, which reported it by nonsecure telephone lines to their Situation Room contact in the White House. At least a dozen television cameras recorded the departure from a ridge within two miles of Keflavík, the electronic images traveling instantly by as many portable satellite uplinks to geosynchronous communications satellites, which transmitted the signals back to all the major networks and then to a viewing audience that had grown to over two hundred eighty million worldwide.

From the right-side windows of a Learjet 25, another TV camera crew recorded the same scene as the business jet chased the 747 from a respectable distance, their video signal uplinked through a handheld dish antenna shakily positioned skyward from the copilot's seat.

One hundred miles south of Keflavík, the Lear—possessed of a much shorter range than the 747—peeled away and headed back to the United States.

Flight 66 was on its own again.

At 4:18 P.M. Icelandic time—8:18 P.M. in Moscow and Kiev—a small electronic chime sounded in the forward cabin of a solitary Gulfstream IV cruising steadily toward the border between the Ukranian Republic and Turkey.

The lone occupant, Yuri Steblinko, climbed out of the captain's seat long enough to examine the inbound message on the communications computer screen. The message was in Arabic, in which he was fluent.

He nodded to himself and triggered a printout. The target was airborne, and he had an initial ETA along with the coordinates.

Yuri returned to the left seat and began punching coordinates into the flight computer. If the anticipated low-altitude run north along the border took no longer than planned, he would arrive at the planned coordinates fifteen minutes ahead of his target.

Yuri sat back and pursed his lips. There wasn't much surplus time, and the winds over the Mediterranean worried him.

But the third phase of the mission should work.

He leaned forward and spread out the map again. The fourth phase was the problem. Once the missiles had been fired, there would be only so much time, airspace, and fuel left for a getaway.

Any mistake at all—or a single element of bad luck—and Anya would be waiting in vain for his return.

NINETEEN

WASHINGTON, D.C.—SATURDAY,
DECEMBER 23—12:45 P.M. (1745Z)

A shaken Dr. Rusty Sanders sat in the driver's seat of
his Chevy Blazer and wondered what to do next.

Three hours ago he had walked into his condo near
Herndon, Virginia, dead tired and ravenous. He remembered calmly walking through his dining room and
putting his briefcase and handheld computer on the table. The machine had beeped immediately with a message from Sherry Ellis:

Where are you?
Reply only to my PDA.

He had removed the stylus and handwritten the answer on the small screen, watching with the usual fascination as the tiny silicon brain deciphered his loops and
strokes and replaced his handwriting with the typed version—which he then transmitted with a few keystrokes:

I'm home.
In Herndon.
Why?

He'd set the PDA back on the table and gone to the
kitchen to find something to eat when it began beeping

again. Rusty put down the carton of eggs he'd removed from the refrigerator and walked back to the table.

The message was clear from five feet away:

GET OUT OF THERE!
GET OUT NOW!
CALL ME LATER ON PDA. DO NOT
TRANSMIT WHERE YOU ARE.

For almost three hours he had driven randomly, keeping his speed within the limit and trying in vain to communicate again with Sherry.

All transmissions went unanswered, as did the burning question in his mind: *What the hell is going on?*

Finally he'd pointed his Blazer toward the heart of the District and found the largest parking garage he could locate, a huge structure on M Street that went down several levels. He'd backed into the most remote stall available and hunkered down, wondering if Sherry's PDA had been confiscated by someone at Langley—and whether any messages he tried to send could be traced physically to the spot he occupied by tracing the geographic location of the cellular signal.

It would be safer now to be on foot, he decided.

Rusty popped the PDA computer in his briefcase, locked the Blazer, and walked up Connecticut to the Dupont Circle Metro station. In search of a pay phone, he joined a throng of people descending to track level on the escalator.

Wrong! If I'm traced making a call from here, they'll know I'm riding the Metro system.

He retraced his steps back up to street level and found a pay phone in the lobby of an office building. He punched in his own number for the condo.

It took three rings for the answering machine to pick up. Rusty hit the star button to end his recorded message, then entered a series of three digits—728—which activated the internal microphone. He'd used the fea-

ture several times to make sure the TV was off, or to
check to hear whether the cleaning lady was really
vacuuming the place.

This time the sounds of crashing and banging reached
his ears: furniture being moved and drawers being
pulled out. He could hear male voices in the background for a few seconds, then sudden silence.

He could hear footsteps then, getting louder as someone moved closer to the counter where the answering
machine sat. A voice suddenly spoke in the background:
"What are you . . ." But there was a loud "Shhh!"
from somewhere closer.

He could hear the handset being removed from its
cradle. There would be no dial tone, of course, and
whoever was holding the handset would know that the
caller had triggered the internal monitor.

If they were pros, he reasoned, they would also know
that the most likely caller to have the necessary code
would be the owner.

A strange voice suddenly coursed through the phone,
causing Rusty to jump. "I know that's you, Dr. Sanders.
Talk to me." The voice was soft and almost friendly, but
the menace behind the words was unmistakable.

The hair on the back of Rusty's neck stood up as an
involuntary chill shuddered through him. He wanted to
say nothing and hang up, but his home had been invaded!

"Who are you? What are you doing in my condo?"
Rusty asked as threateningly as he could.

"You have something that belongs to the Company.
You tell us where it is, we'll leave you something to
come home to. Deal?"

We?

Rusty's stomach was quivering. He tried to keep control of his voice. This wasn't happening!

"What something? Who the hell *are* you?"

"Your employer, Doctor. The Company."

"Bullshit! My employer doesn't break into my home."

"Who do you imagine yourself to be working for, Doctor? Some rural police force? Wake up." The words were even and quiet, the voice almost amused. Rusty knew he'd lost control of the exchange from the first.

"We know you copied information onto your computer, Doctor, from the terminals in the upstairs conference room. You shouldn't have done that. Big mistake. We know you erased the file on your computer before you left, and we know you transferred it to a disk. Another big mistake. Makes us think maybe you're stealing information to sell to someone."

"That's ridiculous!"

"Is it? The files you copied are top secret. That's a very serious security violation, but you might be able to minimize the seriousness by telling us where the disk is immediately."

Rusty fought to gain control of his breathing. He knew he sounded panicked. Why wouldn't they have called on his cellular first? Why send a team to break into his home?

There was silence on both ends.

Is he telling the truth? Did I download something I didn't intend to see?

"Doctor? You still there?" the man said.

"I'm here, but you're wrong. I copied no sensitive files at all. Nothing outside my clearance, and the last thing in the world I'd do is sell information."

"There are several people spending their lives in federal prisons who said the same thing, Doctor."

Rusty's head was spinning. The quiet little program he'd planted in the nonsecure conference room computers had been found. The program—a trap to collect any newly created files whenever someone tried to erase them—had been only a precaution. If the Cairo message *had* been written in the conference room, the secret program might catch it as soon as the person who wrote it tried to erase the evidence.

But how could they have found it so fast?

And more important, what had it collected that was so vital?

"Either tell us, Doctor, or we'll have to take a crowbar to every corner of this place."

Wait a minute! Rusty thought. *There's no way they could know whether I dumped the files to a floppy disk or not. Personal computers don't keep track of such things. They're guessing!*

He thought of Sherry Ellis, wondering where she fit into the equation. He couldn't mention her name, of course. If they didn't already know she'd helped him . . .

"Doctor? Last chance. Where's the disk? Give it up right now, and maybe we can save your job."

Rusty felt the floppy disk in his coat pocket. Once again he'd run afoul of the system, but this time he'd *really* screwed up.

But the bastards are in my home!

There was another pay phone next to one he was using. Rusty grabbed the receiver and punched in 911, holding the second receiver to his right ear and keeping the first one to his left.

The dispatcher came on for Washington, D.C.

"This is an emergency! Please connect me with the Herndon Police!"

"Hold on," the dispatcher said.

The man in Rusty's apartment chuckled. "That's not going to do you any good, Doctor. Your job and your personal freedom hang in the balance here."

The Herndon dispatcher came on the line, and Rusty passed him the information on the burglary in progress. "Use lights and siren. I can hear them moving around in there right now."

Rusty could hear the man turn to his partner and say something. He heard the other man murmuring in the background.

Why? Rusty wondered.

The dispatcher was asking a question. "Sir, I asked

you, are you listening in on some kind of burglar alarm?"

"No. I've got the bastards talking to me on my own phone."

"Okay. What are they saying?"

"Not much," he lied. "They put the phone down and they're trashing my place. Throwing things around. Please hurry."

There was a voice in his left ear. "Not bad, Doctor, for someone with no time in the field. But those clowns will take twenty minutes to get here, so you've accomplished nothing."

The dispatcher put him on hold, and Rusty again heard the murmur of a voice in the background in his condo. He tried to envision one of the others hunched over a cellular phone, talking to someone.

Why would someone do that?

Because they're running a phone trace on this pay phone with the very police department I'm talking to!

"The disk is not there!" Rusty snapped. "Now get the hell out of my house. I'm coming back to Langley with virtually everything I had when I left."

He slammed both phones down and ran from the building, retracing his steps to the Metro station. He stuffed several bills in one of the ticket machines and took the fare card, using it to get past the turnstiles and onto a southbound train, feeling his stomach tighten even further.

He had to think! But there were people in every direction, and by the time the train rolled into Metro Center station, he was suspecting half the people around him to be CIA operatives tracking his every move.

Rusty bolted from the train and jumped on the next southbound Blue Line. He got off at L'Enfant Plaza station and rode the escalator to the surface. Less than a block away, the National Air and Space Museum sat open and full of tourists. Rusty walked directly there and lost himself in the crowd, then slipped into the IMAX theater, where he found a seat near the back.

The movie had just begun when he heard a faint beep from his briefcase.

It was a message from Sherry, the first in hours:

Could not communicate before. High risk.
Someone here thinks you found something in
files threatening current operation. Very strange.
Mark apparently involved. Several field
operatives I've never seen descended on the
conference room and locked the rest of us out.
Not sure what operation is involved, but suspect
QNFLT66. Can't discuss w/ boss until his return
from W/H. He knows nothing as yet. Renegade
action. Watching my tail too. Warning: Team
looking for you not mainstream Company! Don't
come in. Not sure who to trust. I'll be in touch if
poss. Sorry for melodrama, but this is serious.
Sending this from ladies' room.

Rusty saved the message to the computer's memory and sat in silence for a second before composing a response:

Understood. They were trashing my condo looking for a disk. Talked to one on the phone. I
don't know what they think I have. Thanks for
the help.

The disk. What on earth could be on it? The download he'd done should have been of routine communications. He'd intended to study the list at length at home. Now he had to find a place to read its contents.

He needed some time with a computer. The PDA in his briefcase didn't have a floppy drive.

Rusty left the museum and took a cab to George Washington University. The computers in the main reading room of the university's library were for researching the electronic card catalogue, but several had floppy drives. Rusty found the most remote unit and pulled the disk from his pocket, inserting it into the machine. He bypassed the normal blocks and directed the computer to read the files on the floppy one by one.

The program he'd embedded in the conference room computers was exceedingly simple: Anything the computer was told to erase would first be copied to a specific compressed file, the one he had triggered and downloaded remotely from his office before leaving.

The resulting file on the floppy disk consisted of page after page of discarded data, and Rusty began paging through it.

First he found most of the night's compiled message traffic concerning the desert location for Flight 66, and it was a familiar litany. Some pages he'd written himself.

Then a copy of the flight plan from Iceland to Mauritania appeared. Rusty hadn't been aware that anyone had pulled it into the conference room computers.

Suddenly the Cairo message appeared on the screen, the one he'd first reported.

Oh, okay. That's a copy, he thought.

He reread the message. Something was wrong. It seemed different. He called up the next page and found another version, and then another, before realizing he was looking at the remains of a file someone had used to compose the message in the first place.

So it was written in the same room I was using! Son of a bitch!

Just as he had suspected, the message warning of terrorist moves against Flight 66 had originated at Langley. This was the proof—the smoking gun.

But why?

Did someone just suspect terrorist activity, or had the CIA's agents in Cairo actually picked up solid intelligence regarding Flight 66? There still wasn't a clue.

There were more pages, and he kept running them across the screen. A benign memo regarding the Air Force task force headed for the desert, an analysis of political stability in North Africa, a weather report for Iceland, and . . .

Rusty stopped cold and stared at the screen. A message in fragments, and apparently in Arabic! There were numbers that appeared to be a range of times and dates, and several strings of numbers with no explanation.

With one exception.

In the middle of the alphabet soup of computer-generated Arabic symbols and slashes was the very same sequence of a letter and two numbers he had seen on his PDA screen within the past hour: QNFLT66.

He thought about the northern African area where they were sending the 747. The aircraft would pass over and near quite a few Islamic countries. If this was a message to one of them, the use of Arabic would be understandable.

But had someone sat right next to him during the night composing a message in Arabic on an adjacent CIA computer?

Rusty studied the time sequences within the Arabic message again. Whatever was being discussed concerned a range of time between 2220 and 2235 Zulu, a shortened reference to Universal Coordinated Time. And, in the very last line of the Arabic message, there was a digital reference only a pilot or controller would understand: 3A/3966. Probably the four-digit code that Flight 66 should be transmitting through mode 3A of its radar transponder, Rusty concluded. The small "black box" found on almost every modern aircraft enhanced the radar image of the aircraft on air traffic control radars along with transmitting altitude and identification information. But such information would be useful only to someone who had the equipment to read the code on a radar screen, such as a fighter aircraft.

That fifteen-minute window and Flight 66. What is that, an arrival time in Mauritania, maybe?

That was probably it.

He paged through to the last entry. More routine items. Nothing even remotely sensitive. Only the strange fragmented message in Arabic referring to Flight 66.

Rusty triggered a printout of the first two of the three

Arabic pages and stuffed the resulting copies in his briefcase. He retrieved the disk, then began walking toward the exit.

Suddenly he felt a burning desire to see a world atlas. He retraced his steps and found the reference section.

The northwest coast of Africa loomed before him in a depiction that also showed Iceland to the north. He ran a rough approximation of the course Flight 66 would follow, then pulled out the handheld computer and composed a quick question for Sherry, hoping she was in a position to answer.

What was actual departure time and new ETA for FLT66?

The reply came back within five minutes:

Departed 1711Z. ETA 2356Z.

Rusty leaned forward and did some impassioned scribbling on a piece of paper. For 2220 Zulu to be an original ETA for Flight 66, it would have been scheduled to leave Keflavík at 1530 Zulu, or 10:30 A.M. in Washington.

But the earliest planned departure time from Iceland Rusty had seen had been 12 noon in Washington, or 1700 Zulu!

He sat back, thoroughly confused. With the departure time of 1711Z, a 2220Z arrival time would put Flight 66 where?

He toyed with the math a few minutes based on the normal cruise speed for a 747-400.

At 2220Z they would be approximately two hundred miles north-northwest of the African coast and over the Atlantic Ocean.

He looked closely at the latitude and longitude lines on the map and wrote down the approximate spot: thirty-one degrees, thirty minutes north latitude, thirteen degrees, zero minutes west longitude. Or, if entered in a navigation computer, N3130W013.

"Oh Lord!" Rusty said out loud as he pulled the printout from his briefcase and hastily ran his finger down the page looking for the two strings of numbers buried within the Arabic characters, and finding them at last: "313324" and "0132410."

Quantum's flight plan was on the disk!

He ran back to the computer and reloaded the disk, ignoring the increasingly curious stare of a librarian. It took several minutes to find the flight plan and page through its details. There were various latitude and longitude fixes at various points as the flight progressed southward, but five navigational points from the destination, he found what he was looking for:

N3133.24 W01324.10

Rusty realized his heart was pounding. A CIA source had informed someone in Arabic exactly when Flight 66 would be over a certain point several hundred miles short of land.

Why? Air defense notification of the inbound flight so a nearby nation wouldn't get excited?

There were more formal ways to accomplish that, however, such as direct teletypes between air traffic control facilities. That's what international flight clearances were for.

He looked again at the flight plan. There was always an indication when a navigational fix served as an entry point for some nation's airspace.

There was nothing listed. As far as he could tell, it was an arbitrary point in space.

Why? Why would it be of interest to anyone?

Rusty terminated the computer program again and stowed the disk and the printout. The urge to send a flurry of speculation to Sherry on the PDA was strong, but he didn't want to push his luck. Someone could be looking over her shoulder too. For that matter, *she* could be playing him for a fool.

A sudden chill ran up his back as he considered the possibility that Sherry was the enemy.

He shook his head to expunge the thought. It was Sherry who had warned him to get out of the apartment just in time, and besides, without her he was completely adrift.

He picked up his briefcase and left the library, walking eastbound in deep thought. The Blazer was within walking distance, and he vaguely realized he'd set an automatic course in that direction: eastbound toward the White House on Pennsylvania, then north on 19th.

What have I got here? They're panicked because I have the Arabic message, right? That's the only strange thing on that disk. That means the message was either nefarious, or they think I'll misinterpret it. I know the Cairo warning message was written at Langley. And I know someone's sent, in Arabic, a location and time that could be used to locate Flight 66 over the Atlantic. What I don't know is WHY!

The words of the Cairo warning message ran through his mind again undoubtedly referring to Aqbah: "A Shiite terrorist organization may be attempting to secure a military strike aircraft and armament suitable for reaching eastern Mauritania in the western Sahara."

Rusty felt his face grow cold.

Could someone inside the CIA be *helping* Aqbah?

ABOARD FLIGHT 66, 7:45 P.M. (1845Z)

As Quantum 66 passed a point over the Atlantic some eight hundred miles south of Iceland, the Reverend Garson Wilson stood in the rear of the 747 surveying his fellow passengers and arrived at a profound conclusion:

I'm going to die!

Twenty minutes earlier, with darkness outside and many of the passengers sleeping, Wilson had reached the end of his tolerance with just sitting. He left his seat with a vague idea of heading for a restroom, but the stench of the overburdened toilets hit him with more nauseating effect than the old "two-holer" outhouses of his youth on a hot day. Holding his breath long enough to survive the experience, he exited as fast as humanly possible.

Wilson had wandered the cabin then, nodding at the occasional upturned eyes, especially if they seemed to recognize him and had any latent respect for him. Several people wanted to talk, but he put them off with "perhaps later."

I'm too preoccupied with my own worries, he'd told himself. *I wouldn't be a fitting counselor right now.*

But the guilt was piling up. He was a minister, after all. He was supposed to be selfless. He was supposed to be willing to spend his last efforts on earth comforting people spiritually. And what had he done so far? Helped get a young mother killed. Everyone on the airplane knew he had urged her to run through the door.

And he knew he'd been too much of a coward to follow her.

All Garson Wilson could feel inside was fear—a gnawing, cold, living thing squirming around, making the thought of helping anyone else seem ridiculous. Fear of the virus. Fear of losing respect.

And fear of dying.

The cabin was a mess and that, too, was depressing. The flight attendants had been trying to pick up trash, but with people sprawled in all directions trying to sleep, the debris of papers and cups and blankets on the floor was becoming alarming—and depressing.

"Appearance, sir," Roger, his secretary, had reminded him before Lisa Erickson's death. "You have an image that's very important to your ability to do God's work. That image lets people trust you. You must control your temper, and your fears."

"Fears?" he had sneered at Roger in a barely contained whisper. "Where do you get off, young man, accusing me of being fearful?"

Roger had sighed and looked him in the eye. "Sir, frankly, if you're not fearful, you're an idiot, and I could never believe that of you. It's okay to admit being normal to your aide, but you can't show emotional extremes to your flock. That's all I'm saying."

Garson Wilson had snorted and scowled.

"When I took this job," Roger had reminded him, "you told me that one of my key duties was to help you maintain your image in stressful times."

I have struggled to maintain "the image," Wilson thought. *I am struggling.*

But he was losing the battle. Garson Wilson the man —the terrified actor who played the role of Garson Wilson, America's premier evangelist—was losing it.

Wilson began walking forward toward the front of the aircraft, stepping carefully over the legs of sleeping passengers thrust into the aisle.

The radio interview had changed everything.

Roger had performed whatever electronic magic was required to forward calls to their seats on the airplane by satellite phone, and a California radio talk show host had called, wanting a live interview.

Broadcasting is my life, Wilson had thought. *Can't hurt!*

The host did a breathless introduction about Wilson's background and the incredible prowess of any radio talk show staff that could find such a great man in the middle of a great crisis.

"How are you feeling, Reverend?" the host asked at last.

"Well, I think we're all a little tired. It was a long, dismal wait in Iceland for the authorities to release us to fly to a safer location. But the Lord's looking after us."

"Reverend, you're known throughout the world for providing hope and preaching salvation. And I'm sure you've counseled many a dying person, right?"

"I have, yes. It's never easy to leave this world for the next. People need help to understand."

"I know. But now that you're in that position yourself, how are *you* handling it?"

Wilson paused and thought through the question again.

"I'm not sure I understand what you're asking, Bill," he said. He was pretty sure the host's name was Bill. He couldn't remember the name or location of the station.

"What I mean, Reverend, is that you and all those other people are sitting up there with less than, what, thirty hours to live. The world has rejected you. We're all in a state of shock back here, but the truth is, they're sending you to the largest desert on earth to die. So I, for one, want to provide you an opportunity to say whatever you want to say, but I also think our listeners would like to know how someone of your stature faces his own death."

Sheer panic gripped Wilson. Where was the host getting such twisted information?

Back in Southern California at the radio station, the talk show host pulled a folder of clippings across the desk and flipped it open with a frown. The latest wire copy he remembered scanning before the show wasn't there, but he was sure it had said the autopsy was positive for the virus. He nodded to his producer and tried to prompt the guest again.

"Reverend?"

Wilson sighed audibly. The question had shaken him, and he mustn't show it.

"I'm sorry, Bill," he began confidently, "but I don't think you're getting the right information. There are rumors out there, we know, that have implied that we're in great danger, but our crew has assured everyone that this is a false alarm."

"Reverend, I'm really sorry to be the bearer of bad tidings, but I've got to tell you that the wire services are now saying an autopsy's been completed, and there you are, still headed for Africa."

An *autopsy* had come out positive for the virus? No one had mentioned that from the cockpit.

The host's voice was in his ear again.

"Reverend? Is anyone sick up there yet?"

"No!" Wilson heard himself snap. He forced himself to calm down, and continued. "No, Bill, no one's sick, and until at least one person comes down with something, I think it's premature to go writing us off."

"Well, sir, let me ask you *this* way. If someone does get sick and it *is* confirmed, how will you handle that?"

"Handle . . . the fact that the virus is on board?" he asked.

"Yes. The fact that it's completely fatal."

Wilson felt his head spinning. They were dealing with just a virus, right?

"What do you mean, 'completely fatal,' Bill? This is just a particularly nasty influenza virus, or something similar."

"Ah . . . well, Reverend, the airline may have *told* you that, but the rest of the world is hearing that this is a dread killer germ. Some sort of doomsday virus, and there's some speculation that it's the work of an Arab terrorist organization."

"Well," Wilson said, "I, ah, think we have to regard all that as, ah, rumors, you know? But if for some reason the Lord decides that this is our time, then we'll simply have to accept the Lord's will."

Wilson struggled through the rest of the interview, trying to stay professional and calm, describing the passengers as stoic and religious and prayerful. Was he conducting prayer services? Certainly, he said, for those who were saved, or wanted to be. He was a preacher, after all. He would preach.

But throughout, the host's words kept ringing in his ears: "completely fatal . . . the airline may have *told* you . . . dread killer germ . . . Arab terrorist organization . . ."

Wilson had replaced the receiver with a shaking hand and sat for a second in shocked silence before bounding out of his seat in need of escape. He thought of thundering up to the flight deck to question the captain, but somehow it seemed futile. The captain was trapped too.

There was no escape, and now he was wandering the cabin in shock.

Wilson realized he had walked all the way back up to the first class cabin. There was a little girl of perhaps seven or eight curled up in the recliner seat that had been his. Her blanket had fallen to the floor, and he could see she was cold by the way she had her arms wrapped tightly around her chest.

Wilson thought about his own daughter, Melissa. Melissa the rebel, whom he hardly knew. Melissa, who had grown up without her father while he sallied back and forth to save souls and build an empire. What was she now, twenty-six? It was shameful that he had to struggle to remember. At the age of eight there had been such promise in her eyes. But he'd never had time. He'd lost those years.

And now there would be no more time to make it right.

The little girl reminded him of Melissa at that age.

Wilson knelt down with a tear forming in his eye and quietly replaced the blanket over the sleeping child, tucking it gently around her shoulders, struck by a sudden realization:

This little girl, too, was going to die.

TWENTY

Rusty was halfway back to Dupont Circle when he remembered the autopsy. The team he'd helped dispatch to Iceland should have sent a preliminary report by now. Everything that was happening looped back to the same question, but he seemed to be the only one interested: Was Professor Ernest Helms really killed by the dread virus accidentally uncorked in Bavaria, or not?

He stopped in the alcove of a doorway and queried Sherry on the handheld computer. Her answer shot back as rapidly as before:

Have heard nothing. Now locked out of operation.

He'd have to call direct, but how? He tried to remember what method the team was supposed to use to report back. They were to set up in a remote location of the airfield at Keflavík. There would be no regular phones, but the lead pathologist would be carrying at least a handheld of some sort.

And the base commander would know the number.

Rusty stopped in the middle of a block, realizing he was close to the pay telephones he'd used earlier to call his own condo. The goons on the other end had surely pinpointed that exact location by now. It was best to avoid the area.

Rusty diverted several blocks to the north before cutting across to the east and working his way back down 14th toward the parking garage to retrieve his Blazer. He was worrying about everyone who even glanced his way. There were pictures of him on file at Langley. He would be recognizable in an instant to anyone who'd studied his features.

One block north of the parking structure a sandy-haired young man reading a paper and sitting on a concrete bench got up as soon as Rusty had passed. To his left, across the street, a tall black man in a business suit stood watching the traffic, but Rusty thought he saw him signal someone behind him, possibly the man with the newspaper. Rusty glanced around. The young man was following. He was wearing an overcoat, which might conceal anything.

Rusty quickened his pace, trying to decide if the footsteps behind him had sped up as well.

They had.

The end of the block was coming up. He would need to turn right to get to the garage entrance. There would be an elevator to negotiate, hopefully alone.

The moment of truth would come when he turned the corner. If the man keeping pace behind turned too, he'd know.

Maybe.

Rusty swung around the corner and spotted a small alcove in the facade of the building. He backed into it immediately, trying to blend in with the wall.

As he feared, the young man with the newspaper had made the same turn. He would see nothing of Rusty until he passed the edge of the alcove. Rusty could hear the footsteps. Suddenly the man was near, passing inches away.

He can't miss seeing me! Rusty thought.

But the man continued on without a backward glance to the end of the block, past the entrance to the garage. Rusty saw him enter a drugstore and disappear.

Obviously well trained, Rusty concluded. And obviously a member of a larger team. He passes, the others take up the point. The ploys of surveillance had been explained years ago by a friend with the FBI.

Rusty scanned the opposite side of the street across traffic. There were people standing in various places waiting for a bus, but no one seemed interested in him.

Yet any one of them could be watching.

He peered out from the edge of the alcove toward the corner from which he'd come.

No one was waiting there either.

But there were cars passing, and scores of windows within view, and if there was a team of at least four people looking for him, they could blend into the scenery.

This is stupid. Pure paranoia. They were in my home, but I have no reason to think they're here.

Rusty shot back onto the sidewalk and turned into the garage entrance a half block down the street. The lobby was empty, as was the elevator when the doors opened. He walked into the open elevator car and punched the button for the third level down, and waited.

The elevator doors remained open.

He could hear the front door to the lobby opening. There was a polished brass plaque visible from the interior of the elevator and set at an angle to the front entrance. Rusty could see the reflection of anyone approaching. He again punched the button for the third level as he studied the reflection of an oncoming figure, who looked familiar. The image finally coalesced.

It was the man with the newspaper, his sandy hair clearly visible in the brass reflection!

Rusty punched the button with a vengeance now as the man's footsteps drew closer. In the brass plate, behind the oncoming figure, the front door opened again and another man entered, one Rusty didn't recognize. He could see two more men standing outside on the sidewalk.

Oh Jesus!

There were only two paths out: the elevator and the same front door.

Rusty tensed to run, calculating the odds, but the elevator doors finally began to close.

Caught off-guard, the man with the sandy hair tried to race the elevator. Rusty knew he was deciding whether to stick his hand between the closing doors. Instead, he stopped and pounded the DOWN button a few times, hoping to stop the process, as Rusty held the CLOSE DOOR button and prayed it would work.

The doors stayed closed, and with agonizing slowness the elevator began to descend.

So now I'm a sitting duck. Great move, Sanders!

They would be racing down the stairs, he figured, and at least one of them would be waiting when the doors opened. He was probably trapped, but maybe if he rushed at full speed out of the elevator, he could catch them off-guard.

Rusty planted himself in the back corner and tensed. As soon as the doors were half open, he sprang forward and rushed through, holding his briefcase in front of him and racing into the garage at top speed, heading toward his Blazer and expecting to hear footsteps behind him—or worse.

Twenty feet from the Blazer he ducked between two cars and turned.

The garage was silent.

There was no one behind him. No footsteps, no voices, nothing.

He stayed in a crouching position for nearly two minutes before hearing the sound of the elevator doors opening again.

The same sandy-haired man strode from the elevator, still carrying his newspaper, looked around briefly, then began walking in Rusty's direction. Less than seventy-five feet remained.

From where he is, there's no way he can see me! Rusty told himself, hunching down a bit farther. *But if he keeps coming—if he walks past these cars—he'll see me for sure.*

Rusty figured there was a gun in the newspaper.
Sherry had said these weren't mainstream CIA people.
Maybe they hadn't been sent to apprehend him.

Maybe they'd been sent to kill him.

The man stopped behind a BMW twenty feet short of
Rusty's position. He fumbled in his pocket for something. He moved to the driver's door then, and as Rusty
watched in amazement, he climbed in, started the car,
and casually drove off.

For several minutes Rusty stayed crouched between
the cars, breathing hard, listening to his heart pound,
and feeling foolish.

At last he stood up and walked the short distance to
the Blazer. He unlocked the rear door and took out the
PDA computer before putting his briefcase in. Then he
closed the hatch, and was in the process of moving to
the driver's door when a hand grabbed his shoulder
from behind.

Rusty yelped and whirled around, pulling away in
confusion as he tried to focus on who had found him.

It was Sherry Ellis.

"Sh . . . Sherry? Sherry!"

"Good grief! Does my hair look *that bad?*"

"What the hell—?"

"Am I doin' here? Offer the lady a ride and she'll tell
you. I'd prefer not to stand out here and be a target."

Rusty was holding his chest, aware his heart rate was
at aerobic levels.

They left the garage and drove toward Silver Springs
as Sherry started to explain how she'd found him. "I had
to find you before they did. Your car phone was broadcasting your location all over creation."

"What do you mean?" Rusty asked. "My *phone?*"

"I called your car phone after you sent me one of the
PDA messages," Sherry replied. "You didn't answer, but
it's real easy to tell when the phone itself is responding.
I knew they'd track it down."

"Responding?"

"Come on. You're an electronics buff. You know this

stuff. When the cellular system whistles for this phone, it transmits back, 'I'm right here, but the dolt that owns me isn't answering.' "

Rusty was shaking his head. "Oh Lord, how stupid. I forgot. It can be tracked whenever it's on." He reached down and turned the car phone off, then reached over and switched off the PDA's cellular circuit.

"So," she continued, "I got to the cellular company's techs before the other guys did. They do good work. They have so many cell sites in D.C., they had this sucker triangulated down to a two-block area. I had your license plate. The rest was a simple search based on the idea that you'd bury your car deep. You did. So here we are, on the lam."

"Sherry, who are the other guys? What on earth have we stumbled into?"

She reverted to dead seriousness.

"There's a renegade operation in progress, Rusty, concerning Flight Sixty-six. I can't prove it, but I'm sure of it. It's outside normal approvals and controls, and no matter who we might call, we'll simply look paranoid, because they're leaving no tracks."

"But they were sloppy enough to leave that supposed Cairo message."

"They didn't figure on you. You don't follow procedures. You're a maverick who wasn't supposed to be so effectively curious."

"Well, they've made another mistake. I think I may know what they're up to, but I haven't a clue why."

He told her about the Arabic communication buried on the disk.

"So you did sneak something out! Impressive work! Probably get you ten years in Leavenworth, but impressive, and that explains it."

"What?"

"I got questioned, gently but pointedly, on whether I, or anyone else on the team, had taken a disk out of the conference room. I was so insulted, I practically spit at them."

"Who's involved?"

"Mark, I think. But someone else is behind it. They've pulled an end run around Director Roth, and I've tried to get him on the phone, but he's still buried at the White House and not returning calls. I finally figured they were going to get suspicious of the number of trips I was making to the sandbox with my PDA stuffed under my skirt to write love notes to you. I figured I'd better get out of there and find you in person so we could figure out a plan."

"Which way?"

"What?" Sherry seemed disoriented. Rusty had stopped at the entrance ramp to the beltway.

"Which way should we go?" he asked.

"Heck, I don't know. Away from Langley, I suppose. Go east, young man."

Rusty nodded agreement and accelerated up the ON ramp. They rode a few miles in silence before Rusty spoke. "So what should we do? I've probably blown my career, but I don't want you involved."

She turned and smiled and patted his knee. "I *am* involved. Anyway, as I said, it's a renegade operation, and if we don't get hit first, we'll probably get medals for exposing it."

"How? How do we expose it?"

She cocked her head. "What? You mean I've come all this way and you *don't* have a plan?"

Rusty shook his head and grimaced. "Roth is the key. We've got to get to him. He can stop this, right?"

"Stop what? We don't even know what these turkeys are up to."

"Sherry, I think they're trying to help Aqbah shoot down that planeload of people!"

"Why? Why would anyone here do that?"

"To help Aqbah destroy themselves in a flourish of self-righteous stupidity. To position them to be condemned internationally for destroying an airliner full of innocent people, with the idea that maybe the limp-wristed UN could be forced to economically freeze out their renegade client states, Iran and Libya."

"Libya's irrelevant. An impotent pipsqueak."

"Well, Iran sure isn't."

"Granted," she said. "But would Aqbah actually be unable to see the consequences of their actions? Are they that stupid?"

Rusty sighed. "I've thought about that a lot the last few hours. I had to remind myself how fanatical and insane the Shiite view of the Western world has become. They would twist the rationale around and consider Western condemnation religiously desirable, a form of corporate martyrdom. At least the insane element of the Islamic clergy in Iran would, and they have Aqbah by the short hairs."

"So we help them destroy themselves by destroying our own countrymen?"

"Who"—Rusty leaned over and raised his index finger—"who, don't forget, we have all but declared dead. Sherry, someone in the Company has seized this as a great opportunity. Deliver a coup de grâce to a planeload of people to prevent them from dying in agony—and, with the very same operation, start the end game to eradicate the world's scariest terrorist threat. No one would ever know of the connection, of course, but if it resulted in Aqbah's demise, the deaths aboard Flight Sixty-six would not be in vain."

Sherry recoiled and stared at Rusty. "That's revolting! But I . . . I guess I understand it."

"There's only one problem," Rusty said, "and it's a doozy."

"What's that?"

"There's no hard evidence yet that Flight Sixty-six carries that virus, even though the professor was ill. Our renegades could be shooting down a planeload of perfectly healthy people two days before Christmas. Until I hear the autopsy results . . ."

"We need to get those results, then," she agreed.

Rusty recalled the discussion with Jonathan Roth.

The autopsy would prove nothing, but it would be an indicator.

"I'll need to find a phone," he said. "And we shouldn't chance using the cellulars."

Sherry nodded as Rusty continued.

"I just . . . can't think of any other plan they could be pursuing, given that Arabic communication."

"Have you translated it?" she asked.

He shook his head no.

"You could be misinterpreting it."

He nodded. "I could be. But that wasn't the CIA benevolent association that trashed my condo this morning."

She sat in silence for a while, thinking, then nodded, slowly at first, then more energetically.

"Okay. Rusty, if we can provide some proof of what's happening, maybe we can sell this to Roth in time to stop it. That disk you have may be proof." She paused. "But that also means it's a ticking bomb. The author will not want Roth or anyone else in real authority to see it. They'll be expecting you—and maybe me—to try to get to Roth. They'll be ready to stop us. Anyone who'd put together a renegade operation like this will be ready to eliminate problems with a gun or a bomb or whatever. Breaking into your place was just an overture."

"Good Lord, Sherry, these are our own people. They're capable of killing us?"

They fell silent for nearly a minute.

"Remember what I told you this morning, Rusty? You never really get to know someone in this business?"

"I always thought that was fiction hype."

"Sometimes it is. But sometimes it isn't. Remember Iran-Contra?"

"Who doesn't?"

"Most people don't," she said. "Most people will never even suspect the full extent of what really happened, or why. Keep in mind that Ollie North was running a renegade operation, not from Langley but from the *White House,* for Christ's sake!"

"While Reagan slept."

She nodded. "Just because you've got an ID card from the CIA doesn't mean you're not expendable. Remember, you're not one of the good ole boys, and neither am I. Now, back to business. What the hell do we do, Kemo Sabe?"

"The Director is still in a coma, I take it?" Rusty asked.

"Still in intensive care at Bethesda. Forget him."

"Well then, how about Roth himself?"

"I told you, he's holed up in the White House Situation Room."

"As a kid I was always told the White House belonged to We the People."

Sherry draped her left arm over the back of the seat and looked at him through squinted eyes. "What are you getting at?"

"Instead of circling the White House at a distance of fifteen miles on the Beltway, why don't we just go there, find Roth, tell him the inmates are taking over the asylum, and the ball's in his court?"

"We'd never get in. You can't just charge the gates. The Secret Service gets very testy when you try something like that."

Rusty nodded. "You're right, but I think I know a way."

Sherry had rested her right elbow on the window ledge and was cupping her chin in her hand as she looked outside.

"We'd better hurry, then," she said. "If there's an aerial ambush waiting for Flight Sixty-six at those coordinates you discovered, they'll blunder into it in less than two hours."

"Sherry, one thing I need to ask you."

"Yeah?"

"Are you absolutely certain Jon Roth couldn't be behind this?"

She looked at Rusty and smiled.

"Absolutely!"

ABOARD FLIGHT 66

The rumor had spread slowly at first, then flared like a brushfire, running in whispered conversations and tearful exchanges from one end of the cabin to the other.

A coach passenger with a tiny worldband radio held against a window had heard the broadcast. The autopsy in Iceland of Professor Helms, it reported, had confirmed the virus. All hope for the humans aboard Quantum 66 was now gone.

They were flying to the Sahara to die.

Shock had left some of the passengers searching for an outlet for the rage and frustration they felt, and suddenly there was a delegation at the cockpit door demanding to know why Captain James Holland had lied to them.

"Look, I don't know who anyone else is in contact with, but we're talking to the White House through our company," Holland said. "I've made sure they give us the straight information each time. They're telling us that the autopsy results are *not.*complete. I called them as soon as I heard this rumor was going around. I've told you everything we knew when we knew it."

"How the hell can we believe anything you say?" a portly man in his fifties demanded. "The world out there says we're dying."

"Are we?" Holland snapped.

"Are we what?"

"Are we dying? Is anyone sick?"

"Apparently it's just a matter of time," the man replied.

There were nearly twenty faces before him, anger masking fear.

Holland got on the PA and tried to quell the rumor, but the simmering feelings of distrust and betrayal continued beneath the surface, driven by the helplessness they all were feeling.

WASHINGTON, D.C.—4:10 P.M. (2110Z)

Rusty Sanders replaced the receiver of the pay phone
and returned to the parking lot of a fast food restaurant
just south of Capitol Hill where Sherry was waiting for
him in the Blazer. It had taken nearly twenty minutes to
reach the head of the pathology team from Fort Detrick
that was performing the field autopsy on Professor
Helms.

"I finally got to him. The news reports are false.
Someone in Public Affairs at Keflavík made the mistake
of guessing out loud to a reporter," he reported to
Sherry. "He said they hadn't officially released anything
to anyone before my call, and are under strict orders to
say nothing publicly. They've been rechecking their results."

"And?"

Rusty shook his head. "There is substantial evidence
of a coronary thrombosis, but there is virtually no evidence of an active viral infection."

"Really?"

"Really. But remember what Roth pointed out, and
he was right. That means that as far as our pathology
abilities go, we know for certain a virus didn't kill
Helms, but we have no way of proving as yet that Helms
wasn't infected by, or carrying, that virus."

"But if he wasn't showing any signs?"

Rusty sighed. "This is confusing as hell. Even if he
was exposed, and even if he actually had the virus in his
bloodstream, unless it was growing rapidly and shedding
through the lungs, he wouldn't have been especially
contagious, and he certainly couldn't have infected the
whole aircraft. But before I left this morning, I talked to
the flight attendant who helped him on board in Frankfurt, and she said he was coughing deeply. Yet that's not
consistent with the autopsy findings. There was no fluid
in the lungs, and nothing to explain the coughing. It
could still be just a heart attack, in other words. Maybe
he'd sat next to a smoker somewhere on his way to the

airport. The autopsy shows no inflammation in places a virus would normally affect, nothing! Bottom line is, we still have no solid proof of infection."

"So, even though this doesn't prove it, it could support the theory that he wasn't infected?"

Rusty nodded as he put the Blazer in gear and looked at his watch.

"We've got to get to Roth. Now. The aircraft will reach those intercept coordinates in little more than an hour!"

TWENTY-ONE

Yuri Steblinko rechecked the coordinates of the Gulfstream's inertial navigation system with those of the
global positioning satellite system. The target area was
dead ahead, as planned. The flight management computer had been programmed to follow a racetrack orbit
at right angles to the oncoming airliner's flight path, and
it began carrying out his instructions now, issuing a silent stream of digital orders to the obedient autopilot.
He had nearly reversed course a few minutes before to
check for contrails—the sudden condensation of impacted, supercooled water at high altitude, which
formed thick vapor trails that could hang in the strato-
sphere for a half hour.

But tonight the Gulfstream's contrails were nearly invisible. Like an airborne spider, he would be spinning an
invisible, ethereal web of transparent ice crystals in the
night sky as he waited to ensnare his unsuspecting victim.

The Gulfstream reduced its own engine power and
began whispering along in a holding pattern at forty-
three thousand feet.

He'd tracked the 747's position reports through the
air traffic control system's satellite radio link, and had
waited expectantly for the last one. It had brought good
news: The 747-400 would cruise beneath him at precisely 2223Z.

Yuri checked his watch. It was 2144Z.

A full moon hanging just above the western horizon bathed the cockpit in soft light, competing with the subdued glow of the instruments electronically painted on the liquid crystal displays before him. A solid cloud cover hovered miles below just over the surface of the Atlantic, but the air above was crystal clear. With the Gulfstream's position lights and strobes turned off, the business jet was a fleeting ghost floating through an endless starfield. The possibility of the airliner's crew spotting him was essentially nil.

They, however, would be clearly visible, the moonlight reflecting beautifully off the wings and fuselage of the 747 as it soared beneath him.

There would be no excuse, he reminded himself, for missing such a target.

Yuri turned down the volume of the satellite receiver. He would need no more position reports from the 747, since the rest of Quantum's flight plan to Mauritania was irrelevant. They would never arrive.

A sudden flash of hunger flared up in his consciousness. With the autopilot doing its job keeping the Gulfstream IV in the preprogrammed orbit, he could leave the cockpit for a few minutes to raid the small refrigerator.

He hadn't realized how thoroughly Nicolai Sakara had stocked the galley. Yuri opened cabinet after cabinet of an incredibly expensive larder, which included decades-old Cuban cigars, liquor, food, wine, and a special blend of the prince's favorite Arabica coffee. Yuri made a pot of the exquisite coffee, added real cream from the refrigerator, found a box of biscuits, and returned to the captain's seat, where he sipped the coffee slowly and appreciatively. Yuri opened the biscuits and began munching them absently. With little to do for the next forty minutes but wait, he let his thoughts drift to Anya and the reason he was occupying the cockpit of a stolen jet in the first place.

The thought of the two of them making love endlessly

on some distant beach was idyllic. He would find such a home, even if it was a shack on a tropical beach on some long-forgotten island in the Pacific. Anya loved the sun, and she wore it well. Her perfectly proportioned body glowed even more sensuously in the embrace of a light tan.

In the previous hours of monotonous flight he had worked hard to keep from focusing on the enormity of what he was about to do. But occasionally, as now, images of a 747 in flames almost broke through the professional barriers in his mind.

There was a time, not so long ago, when he would have thought of nothing but the technical aspects of the job at hand. He would have been devoid of emotion—the ends of being a good officer justifying the means.

But things were different now. With the end of the Soviet Union had come the end of blind purpose, the end of the blanket justification for any action, no matter how deadly or outrageous. What he was doing now, he realized, was for himself and Anya, not for country or party or any other cause. Pure selfishness.

Ah, but Anya is a good enough cause! he thought, the happy flash of realization instantly quenched by a darker truth: he didn't want to do such things anymore. This was his last mission, the last "action."

The image of a 747 in flames taking over two hundred fifty people to their deaths in a long, agonizing spiral toward the ocean crept back in his mind. Such had been the end of KAL 007, but this time it would be *his* atrocity—*his* responsibility. Even if these people were already condemned, he regretted the terrible anxiety and confusion those last few seconds would bring them.

Yuri Steblinko shook the image away, and instead forced himself to picture Anya in an outrageously tiny bikini in front of their beach-house-to-be. A lifetime of comfort, insulated from the shortages and sorrows of the former U.S.S.R., for one last mission.

This is an act of mercy! he reminded himself for the hundredth time.

He must stay focused on Anya. Not her sensuous body, but Anya his love, who had never left him, even in terrible times.

Anya deserved the best.

ABOARD FLIGHT 66

The sudden illness downstairs caught James Holland completely off-guard. The little girl, an unaccompanied minor, had been sleeping in the first class cabin when she suddenly awoke, nauseated, chilled, and burning with fever. Barb Rollins, the Swiss physician, and two passengers had taken charge immediately, and the captain had been summoned. Her temperature was 103.5. With the little girl wrapped in blankets and cared for by so many, Holland returned to the cockpit and dispatched Robb to get a few hours' rest before crossing over the coast of Africa.

Neither of them discussed what had just happened.

Quite obviously, it was beginning.

THE WHITE HOUSE, WASHINGTON, D.C.

Dr. Rusty Sanders had gambled that the President's physician, an old friend from medical school, would be reachable on Saturday, and willing to race from his home in Georgetown to escort him into the nation's best-known residence, particularly when he hinted at an urgent CIA purpose.

He was right.

Dr. Irwin Seward was waiting at the East Wing entrance to the White House when Rusty arrived. Sherry Ellis dropped him off one block away. She would wait by a prearranged pay phone for Rusty to either call or return. Rusty had insisted. She worked for Roth, and she should not be directly involved in what he had to do.

Rusty knew that Irwin Seward was relying on trust in

vouching for him to the Secret Service. After all, Rusty thought, we've already proven the CIA can generate renegades who shouldn't necessarily be near the first family.

"I really appreciate this, Irwin," Rusty told him as they followed one of the senior White House guards into the main structure. "I'll have to explain the details later."

"Just don't get me in trouble," Seward replied. "Once we get you handed off downstairs to the Situation Room, I'm out of here."

Rusty grinned. "Golf game?"

Irwin Seward smiled and shook his head. "No, a better pastime. Sailing. I've got a cute lady in a fantastic bikini waiting for me and I can't wait to get it off her."

"Irwin! You're married, and it's December!" Rusty chided.

Irwin Seward grinned. "Yup, but the female in question is my wife, and the boat's cabin is heated."

They said goodbye at the door to the basement nerve center, and Rusty entered to find that Jonathan Roth had been alerted and was waiting for him.

"Dr. Sanders." He acknowledged Rusty with a nod but no handshake. "Let's go in the conference room here and close the door, Doctor. I trust this is truly urgent? Normally we conduct our business through channels at Langley."

Rusty ignored the rebuke.

"The President is due back in thirty minutes," Roth continued, "so we have a little time."

"No, sir, I don't think we do," Rusty told him.

They sat at the conference table and Rusty pushed the computer diskette across the surface to Jonathan Roth.

"Sir, I took this out of Langley because I was afraid the information would be otherwise destroyed. I could be wrong, but I think there's an extremely dangerous renegade operation going on within the Company."

Roth's eyebrows raised. "Tell me, Doctor. What do you have? What's your proof?"

Rusty told of his suspicions about the Cairo warning message, which Roth had already seen, and outlined the computer trap he had set for any erasures in the Langley conference room that had served as their crisis command post.

"I must say, I wondered myself about the speed of the response from the Cairo station," Roth said, drumming his fingers on the table. "If the warning was, as you suspect, manufactured by one of our people at Langley, it would make more sense—and would, of course, be completely false—as far as a valid warning was concerned. But whoever might have inserted that warning in the system might have actually been passing on a truly valid report from the field in unorthodox fashion."

Rusty nodded, pleased Roth was following his reasoning.

"Yes, sir. I considered that. No matter how it originated, the substance could still be accurate. Aqbah could indeed be trying to bring down that seven-forty-seven, and in fact, I'm convinced they are."

Roth looked him squarely in the eye. "Why? What evidence do you have? We've picked up nothing in the way of supporting intelligence other than the warning message."

Rusty pointed to the computer diskette. "It's on the diskette, sir. There's a message in Arabic sent to an unknown addressee from Langley. The message pinpoints a location from Flight Sixty-six's flight plan out over the Atlantic and the time of expected passage. That time comes up less than an hour from now. If it's what I think it is, someone is waiting out there to destroy that seven-forty-seven."

"That's quite a theory, Doctor. And if you're wrong?"

Rusty shrugged. "Well, then we just look a bit silly asking the captain to divert, or sending fighters if we've got any close at hand. Actually, I don't think anyone can reach him in time."

"So you want us to alter the flight's course to stay away from that location?" Roth asked. "What's there to prevent the potential attacker from watching the course change on radar and pursuing the seven-forty-seven anyway?"

"Nothing, sir, except distance and time, and we're running out of both."

Roth looked at the table and drummed his fingers some more.

"Sir," Rusty continued, "the same renegades have already made a move on me, trying to get this diskette." He recounted the raid on his apartment, and the threats over the phone, as Roth pulled over a pad of paper and made notes.

"Bottom line, Director?" Rusty said. "I think our renegade group is helping Aqbah directly. I think they're going way the hell outside the rules to try to aid what could be a self-destructive act for Aqbah. And since the autopsy on the professor in Iceland has come back negative for active viral illness, if we don't stop Aqbah, our assistance makes us complicit to mass murder—murder aided and abetted by the CIA, and I'm sure never authorized by any finding signed by the President."

Roth bit his lip and exhaled sharply.

"About the autopsy. We agreed, did we not, Doctor, that a negative finding did *not* mean the virus wasn't present? I mean, the professor was definitely exposed. We agreed on that."

Rusty nodded. "Yes, sir, we did. But the autopsy results add credence to my strong feeling that these people are not necessarily doomed. Regardless of what the flight attendant saw in terms of the professor seeming to be ill when he came on in Frankfurt, he may still have died of a simple heart attack, and not a virus. And even if he was carrying the virus, he may not have been infectious. We just don't know."

Roth looked slightly taken aback. He picked up the diskette and tapped the table with it. "So the Arabic message with the coordinates and the time and the transponder code is all here? Did you make any other copies?"

Rusty shook his head no.

"Well then. I agree we have to move very fast, and I'll take care of it. I'll contact the aircraft immediately." He stood up. "Excellent work. Now, since we don't know who's gone into business for himself, you go tuck yourself away somewhere out of the area. Not a safe house —well, you wouldn't know about those anyway. That's not your section, Doctor. Find a hole to crawl into. A hotel, for instance. Then call this number." He leaned over and scribbled a telephone number, then straightened up and handed it to Rusty. "That's a direct line in here. Ask for me. Speak only to me—at least until we've gotten to the bottom of this. Do not leave a message for anyone else, is that clear?"

"Yes, sir," Rusty assured him.

Roth escorted him to the door and the hallway and asked a White House aide to take him back to the East Wing entrance.

Rusty found Sherry waiting in the Blazer beside the telephone booth. She had her face buried in a *Washington Post,* but her eyes had followed his approach from two blocks away. He slipped behind the wheel of the Blazer and pulled into traffic, driving for half a block before whipping the car to the curb and slamming on the brakes.

Sherry looked at him with raised eyebrows. "Rusty, what is it?"

"My God, Sherry! Oh my God!"

"What *is* it? Speak to me!"

Rusty was staring wide-eyed to the east as Sherry tried to get a response.

"Dr. Sanders, *hello-o?* Are you in there?"

He nodded, finally, as he took a deep breath and pointed back toward the White House, then looked at her with a horrified expression.

"Sherry, Jonathan Roth mentioned the transponder code for Flight Sixty-six as I left him."

"Okay. So?"

"When he was wrapping up a few minutes ago, he said, 'So this diskette contains the coordinates, the time of passage, and the transponder code, right?' And I nodded yes."

"And?"

"Sherry, he hadn't looked at the diskette's contents yet! I didn't give him the paper printout, and I know for an absolute certainty that I never mentioned transponder code being in that Arabic message."

"I'm not following this, Rusty," she said.

He turned to her, his eyes wide.

"The only people besides myself who knew that the diskette included the transponder code were the ones that *sent* the Arabic message to Aqbah! Sherry, Jonathan Roth could not have spoken those words without being in on it somehow!"

Sherry recoiled against the passenger door with an incredulous expression. "*WHAT?* I thought we'd gotten past that. You saw Roth's computer files. There was nothing there."

"That was before I found the Arabic message, which came from one of the computers in the conference room! But that helps prove my point. If it wasn't on Roth's computer, yet he knew of something on that Arabic message which I hadn't mentioned, then he *has* to be involved!"

Sherry looked stunned. She examined his eyes, her mouth slightly open. She licked her lips and looked away, and spoke at last.

"Oh, my Lord! I never thought . . ." her voice trailed off.

"Sherry, he was going to call the aircraft immediately and get the captain to divert."

She looked back at him with a snap of her head. "Rusty, if Jon Roth *is* involved, he won't call it off. He won't call the airplane and tell them to run. He'll let it happen! I know him. I know how he takes hold of an idea and won't let go. Once he puts an operation in motion, he's not about to cancel it."

Rusty was nodding. "I reemphasized the fact that the negative autopsy means less of a chance that the passengers of Flight Sixty-six are infected. He didn't seem terribly impressed."

"We've got to get to a phone," she said.

"Absolutely!" Rusty shot back into traffic, headed east, oblivious to a black sedan that took up a trailing position several cars behind.

"How do we do it, Rusty? Can we just call the airplane like you did earlier? Do you still have the numbers?"

"Maybe."

"Where do we go? We can't just stand at a phone booth. They could be tailing us right now."

There were fewer than thirty minutes left. With the Washington Grand Hyatt in view, Rusty swung into the front entrance, parked, and tossed the keys to an attendant as he and Sherry raced through the revolving doors and headed for the elevators.

"We'll be checking in," he lied to the doorman.

Rusty and Sherry disappeared into the lobby, oblivious to the two nondescript men who came piling out of a black car that had just parked across the street. The men raced across traffic toward the lobby entrance, their progress tracked quietly by the watchful eyes of the doorman.

Interesting! he thought. *Somebody's got a tail!*

Rusty considered using the phone banks near the third-floor meeting rooms, but they were too public.

"Come on. I know an old trick," Sherry told him. They were alone in the elevator and she punched several of the higher floors in succession, darting out and around the corner on each floor until she found what she wanted.

She rushed back to the open elevator.

"Come on, but hang back and follow my lead!"

Rusty followed her around the corner and watched as she dashed toward a housekeeping cart parked in front of a pair of open doors midway down the hall.

He saw her stop and look into a room on the right, and then one on the left.

Sherry turned and motioned for him to follow, pointing to the one on the left as she poked her head into the room on the right, obviously talking to the housekeeper.

"You're through with our room, fourteen-forty-three?"

Rusty heard the response from around the corner as he entered 1443.

"Yes, ma'am."

"Thanks!" Sherry said, crossing the hall and pulling the door shut behind her. She turned and latched the door.

There were bags and other personal effects in the room.

"What if they come back?"

"I'll deal with it when it happens," she said.

Rusty headed for the phone and called Quantum Airlines in Dallas, asking to speak with the vice president of Operations.

"Your name, please?"

"Dr. Sanders, calling from Langley. I'm with CIA. This is an emergency."

There was an extended silence before the same voice came back.

"Mr. Sanders, we've been warned you would try to make some sort of bogus call. The police are being informed of this attempt. Don't try to interfere again."

The line went dead.

Sherry had pressed her ear against his as Rusty made the call, and he'd kept the receiver at an angle so she could hear.

Sherry re-placed the call immediately, under an assumed female name.

"We don't know anybody by that name" was the response. "Who did you say you were with?"

"Federal Aviation Administration. You've heard of us, we're in all the phone books. I'm calling from the Administrator's office."

"Very well. We have the number of the Administrator's office. Give us your four-digit extension and we'll call you right back in the interests of authentication."

Sherry hung up on her. "This is hopeless. Jon has blocked us with typical effectiveness. How about the satellite number?"

"I found it!" Rusty told her. He had been rummaging frantically through his shirt pocket. "It's an old and bad habit, writing on scraps of paper, but sometimes it works."

He placed the call, using his telephone credit card. After a series of clicks and tones, a recording came on: "We're sorry, but the vessel or aircraft you have called is not receiving calls at this time. Please try again later."

With less than thirty minutes left, they were out of options. All official access would certainly have been blocked.

Rusty sat on the edge of the bed with his head in his hands, trying to think. "There is a way, Sherry. There is a way. I just can't dredge it up!"

She was pacing. "Well, how else can you talk to a seven-forty-seven? Could we reach them by aviation radio?"

Rusty shook his head no.

"Okay," she said, "all phones are blocked, and we can't get to the satellite connection they must still have with their Operations people. What other communications would they have on that plane? Radio? Anything? Is there *any way* we could convince the airline to call the captain and turn him?"

Rusty sighed. "By now Roth has us completely blocked. No one will pay any attention to us unless we're CIA, and if we identify ourselves as CIA, we then become those renegade impostors they've been warned not to listen to. Given time, we could cure it. We don't have time. They're flying into a trap, Sherry."

Rusty stood up, eyes flaring, pounding his fist into his other palm.

."Roth is helping those terrorist bastards assassinate two hundred fifty people. *He* probably thinks it's justified! He thinks they're already dead, and goddammit, I was the one who told him they could die an agonizing death from a viral pathogen that probably isn't even there!"

"Okay, calm down!" she commanded. "Keep thinking. Is there any way we could reach someone's cellular aboard?"

Rusty had started to shake his head no. Suddenly he straightened up.

"Iridium!" ·

"What?"

"Iridium. The new satellite-based cellular system! Suppose someone on board has one? It can receive messages even in passive mode."

"Great. But who? What's the number? Will they have it on? Will they answer?"

Rusty shook his head. "I don't know, but Roth wouldn't have thought to poison that company against us."

"Why not?"

"It's too new."

Sherry was already reaching for a telephone directory, but Rusty's hand was up to stop her as he grabbed the receiver.

"That's okay. I know where their operations center is located."

"Hurry, Rusty! We've got nineteen minutes."

ABOARD FLIGHT 66

Rachael Sherwood appeared in the cockpit door as soon as James Holland pressed the unlock button. ·

"Mind if I come in?" Her voice was a soothing and welcome purr.

"Please! It's lonely up here."

"Where's your copilot?" she asked, seating herself on the center jump seat. Holland could see her well-proportioned legs in his peripheral vision, and he could detect a hint of perfume he hadn't remembered her wearing before. He recognized the scent but couldn't name it. It reminded him of flowers and beauty and things decidedly female.

"We've been sleeping in shifts," Holland told her. "I sent him back." Holland turned sideways as far as he could in the seat and smiled at her. "It's hard to see you when you're behind me there. Why don't you take the copilot's seat?"

She nodded and relocated to the right seat.

"Rachael, how's the little girl doing down there?"

She sighed. "If we weren't under the shadow of this . . . bug, I'd say it was just a typical viral infection all kids get. She probably overdid it and got rundown and chilled. I mean, no one else down there is ill, and she wasn't sitting anywhere near the heart attack victim. But, well, you know."

Rachael paused and looked out the windscreen.

"But?" Holland prompted.

She looked at him and smiled thinly. "Well, under the circumstances, it looks pretty suspicious."

"How are *you* holding up?" he asked.

She smiled broadly at that and looked away again, then returned her eyes to his.

"That's what I came up here to ask *you.* I'm fine. Lee's a tower of strength, just like you, and I've been leaning on him."

James Holland felt a strange twang of something disturbingly close to envy. She had been relying on the ambassador. James Holland wished she could be relying on him.

But she had said "a tower of strength, just like you." He took comfort in that.

"So, James, how are you doing, really?"

He tried unsuccessfully to chuckle. "That's like asking, 'Aside from that, Mrs. Lincoln, how was the play?' "

She held his gaze, looking him deeply in the eyes, a disturbing look of intimacy that caused him to turn away suddenly, embarrassed. "I'm doing as well as can be expected, I suppose."

That's rather lame, he thought. *What's the matter with me?*

She nibbled on her lower lip for a second before responding. "I get the feeling that there's no one here the commander can really talk to, especially not your co-pilot. You can't let anyone see you being human, right?"

He smiled and looked back at her.

"You think I'm secretly coming apart, Rachael?"

She shook her head.

"Certainly not! But you're not a case-hardened type who chews nails and really doesn't care about anything except looking macho. I see someone else in that uniform."

He cocked his head. "Oh?"

She nodded. "Let's just say I think I do. I'm a pretty good judge of character, James, and a pretty good listener who won't go for the nearest megaphone when I get back downstairs."

He laughed at that, a little more easily, she thought.

"Well," he said, "my ex-wife would tell you I'm not a good talker."

"Your ex-wife isn't aboard, though, is she?"

Holland gave her a quizzical look. He felt off-balance all of a sudden.

"No, she's not," he said in a measured way.

Rachael swept aside a flurry of cautions that had fluttered through her mind with the mention of his ex-wife. Too many times in the past she had stayed in her shell and played the diplomatic, correct lady who wouldn't dream of being forward or overly familiar. After all, she hardly knew this man. In fact, she *didn't* know him.

But wasn't that the point?

"Well, James, I *am* here. And I . . . care about you. Call it enlightened self-interest."

Something stirred inside James Holland as well, and as he met her penetrating gaze again, he could see she was serious—and determined. His instincts were trying to raise the shields, protect his inner self, back off before revealing anything personal.

But why? He felt the question ricochet around his mind, and finding no answer worthy of consideration, he smiled at Rachael and relaxed a bit, feeling a kinship he couldn't remember experiencing before with a beautiful woman. At least, not for a very long time.

He took a deep breath and let it out slowly.

"There are no . . . bombshell doubts to tell you about, Rachael. I mean, I think we're both worried . . ."

"Try scared to death," she said, noticing his large hands and the prominent veins in his forearms.

"Okay, a little of that," Holland replied. "I just don't know what to believe, you know? One moment Dallas is assuring me that this is probably a gross overreaction to a not-so-terrible virus, then I'm told that the world's afraid of us, and then one of my passengers is blown away . . ." The words were choked off and he looked away, suddenly overwhelmed.

"You did all you could, James. I know the whole story."

"Do you?" he asked somewhat bitterly. "I could have gone after her, tackled her, something. I mean, good Lord, Rachael, a young mother! They nearly cut her in half!"

"James, if there's nothing else that demonstrates how ready they were to kill you too, it's the fact that they shot *her.* Your own announcement said it all. They were programmed to be mindless about defending their perimeter."

He shook his head and looked at the center console without speaking.

"We need a strong leader, James. You'd do us no good lying back there on the ramp."

She'd said "strong" again.

Holland started to smile. Instead, he laughed ruefully. "I'm no damn leader, Rachael. I'm just a pilot who loves to fly. All I've ever wanted to do is fly."

"Was your father a pilot?" she asked.

Rachael could see she'd struck a nerve. He looked shocked, and slowly began shaking his head with a distasteful expression.

"What prompted that question?" he asked.

"I don't know. Instinct, maybe. Fathers and sons and professions and such."

"You ever been to Greeley, Colorado?"

"No. Denver, yes. But I have a friend from college who was from Greeley. It's north of Denver, right?"

"About fifty miles."

"Did you grow up there?"

He nodded. "In a manner of speaking."

She brightened, missing the implications. "I understand it's a small town. Maybe my friend knew your family."

"I hope not, Rachael," he said. "I hope not, because the memory couldn't be a good one. My father was well known in Greeley as a major municipal embarrassment. He was a petty self-promoter who did everything from starting ridiculous businesses to running for public office just to promote himself. I spent my youth trying to disavow any connection."

"Was his name James too?"

Holland snorted. "Big Jim. That's what he called himself. Big Jim Holland. The blowhard even ran for public office under that name. That's why I never let people call me Jim."

"What did he do for a living?"

"He was the closest thing to a legal con artist, Rachael, you can imagine. He could sell anything. He could sell additional jail time to a convict, refrigerators to Eskimos, brimstone to the damned. Only problem

was, he didn't care whether anything he sold happened
to work or be of any value. I spent my youth listening to
my mother deflecting angry customers and partners, bill
collectors, and tax collectors. My father would buy anything on credit—and he seemed to get endless credit.
There are buildings still named for him in Greeley, because the first thing he'd do when he bought or built
something was to slap his name on it, usually in stone or
concrete. Even when the place was repossessed, they
couldn't erase him."

"And by contrast you wanted to be anonymous?" she
asked.

He snorted and shook his head disgustedly.

"I wanted to be *invisible!*"

Holland lifted his big right hand, palm up, and hesitated as he searched for the right words. His eyes had
drifted to the forward panel. They came back to her
now.

"To him I *was* invisible, unless he needed a little boy
to briefly play the role of Big Jim's son for some promo-
tional purpose. That was the only time I mattered to
him."

"I'm very sorry," she said.

"I'm not much of a people person. I'm very much a
loner. I know it's a reaction."

"I've watched you with these passengers, James.
You're more of a people person than you think."

"That's just the professional James Holland." He gestured toward the windscreen, his eyes following his gesture. "The real me used to daydream constantly of
going back in time to the early eighteen hundreds and
being a solitary mountain man. I guess it was the urge to
escape the constant public disapproval—the embarrassment of actually *being* Big Jim's son. I never wanted a
spotlight. I was even one of those captains who'd never
make a PA announcement if it wasn't required."

The two of them fell silent for a few seconds before
Rachael looked back at him and cleared her throat.

"Is your father still living?"

Holland shook his head. "No. He died fifteen years ago. I didn't even go to the funeral." He looked over at her again. "I'm sorry. I don't know why I got into all that. It's water under the bridge."

She waved it away. "How did you get into flying?"

"Chance, and love at first flight, as I call it."

He told her of winning a free flight in high school, and how he suddenly couldn't get enough. He told her of the appointment to the Air Force Academy and how his love of soaring was amply rewarded by a long list of badges and honors. He told her about being number one in pilot training, and of Vietnam and his sixty-three missions in F-4 Phantoms out of Da Nang.

And he told her about Sandra, his ex-wife.

"My fault," he said, summarizing the divorce. "I really am a solitary type. I don't communicate well. You've heard more about me in the past few minutes than Sandra did in ten years of marriage."

He turned back to her. "Really, I'm sorry to unload . . ."

"That's what I wanted you to do."

"Well, you were right. You *are* a good listener, Rachael. You make me feel like we've known each other for a long, long time."

She smiled. "We have. We met at the beginning of this crisis, remember? A lot has happened in a short period of time."

James nodded, looking deeply in her eyes by obvious invitation. He looked down and noticed she wasn't wearing a ring.

He cleared his throat, a small but slightly frightening decision made.

"Now, I'd like to ask *you* something," he said.

"Okay. What?"

"I'd like to know something about the background of a beautiful and fascinating female passenger I have named Rachael Sherwood."

TWENTY-TWO

Sherry Ellis paced while Rusty Sanders hunched over the telephone, acutely aware of the time.

Sixteen more minutes!

"What's the holdup?" Sherry asked.

He cupped his hand over the receiver. "I've got the chief duty technician for the Iridium system checking his computer. They don't normally cross-check for geographical location, but he says he can do it."

Rusty had called the Iridium headquarters and demanded to speak with an officer. He was with the CIA, he said, this was a national emergency, and there was no time to go through normal authentication procedures. Besides, the information he needed *right now* was not terribly private or sensitive.

"You want *what?*" a senior vice president had asked.

"The access numbers of any of your units that have made outbound or received inbound calls in the past seven hours from the following locations: Iceland, until 1711Z, and then anywhere along a five-hundred-mile-an-hour line extending south from Iceland toward the western coast of Africa."

"Good grief, Dr. Sanders, you don't want much. Wait a minute, does this involve that seven-forty-seven with the doomsday virus?"

"Yes, sir, and I'm calling on behalf of the President's team trying to deal with this."

There was a long silence, then a quick response. "Okay. Hold on."

He had been handed over to the technical branch, then to the operations center, and now the corporate officer came back on the line.

"Well, Dr. Sanders, we have eleven different customers calling from Iceland during that time, but nine of them also made calls from Iceland more than an hour after the departure time you gave me. Since we're dealing with an aircraft, I think the two numbers that are left would be your targets. There are no more calls from them, but obviously they are the only ones not accounted for in Iceland after the departure."

"Wonderful. I've got a pen."

The man passed the access numbers, along with familiar instructions on how to reach them from an ordinary phone, and how to access the pager function on each phone.

"I must warn you, the phones aren't meant to be used in flight. If someone has the antenna next to a window, it might work, but it's more likely it won't."

"Understood. I don't suppose you know who these numbers belong to, do you?" Rusty asked.

More silence.

"Well, given the circumstances, yes. One is registered to a Carl Wilhoit of NBC News, New York. The other one belongs to . . . I can't read this first name . . . somebody Lancaster, of Manassas, Virginia."

"Okay. Thanks a million!"

Rusty recycled the line and punched in the first number. A male voice responded almost immediately.

"Wilhoit."

"Uh, Carl Wilhoit?"

"Yeah. Is that you, Bill? Didn't you get my ETA?"

"Mr. Wilhoit, this is Dr. Rusty Sanders of the CIA. Are you aboard Quantum Flight Sixty-six?"

"*Aboard* it? Good Lord no! I'm *covering* it. We're in a private jet on the way back to New York. How'd you get this number?"

"Sorry to bother you." Rusty disconnected and redialed the alternate number.

It rang eight times before a recording came on the line:

"I'm sorry, the Iridium world telephone you've called is not responding to our worldwide signal. The person you are calling will receive a message that a calling attempt was made. Please enter your country code, city code, and telephone number for a response, and speak your name at the sound of the tone."

Rusty disconnected and punched in the numbers again as Sherry stood and tapped her foot.

"Fourteen minutes, Rusty! Fourteen minutes left."

He nodded. "I know. I know."

Again the circuit rang. Four, five, six times, then a seventh. The recording was going to come on again. Rusty prepared to deal with it, but the female voice on the other end was different this time.

"Hello?"

"Uh, this isn't a recording?"

"No. Who's calling please?"

"Is this, ah," he consulted the notepad, "Ms. Lancaster?"

The tone on the other end was one of puzzlement. "No, it isn't. Are you looking for Lee Lancaster?"

The ambassador! This is the ambassador's phone!

"Yes, yes I am. Who's this?"

In the cockpit of Quantum 66, James Holland had been distracted by some sort of warning beep he had never heard before. If Boeing made it, he wasn't familiar with it, and his experienced eyes had scanned nearly every instrument on the flight deck before the beeping stopped.

To Rachael, the sound was familiar, but in the midst of the dials and gauges and instruments, she assumed it was some aircraft function.

When it began again, she realized her purse was beeping.

Rachael retrieved the Iridium phone and punched the ON key.

"This is Rachael Sherwood," she said after Rusty's fumbling attempts to make sense, "the ambassador's administrative assistant. Who is this?"

"Dr. Rusty Sanders of the CIA in Washington. Listen very carefully, Ms. Sherwood. This is a major emergency. Can you take this telephone and proceed to the flight deck and get the captain on the line immediately, and if I lose the connection, have him hold it by the window and wait for me to call back?"

"Certainly. I'm already there, and he's right here. Hold on."

Thousands of miles away in the Washington Grand Hyatt, Rusty Sanders felt himself wobble a bit out of balance. What did she mean, 'He's right here'?

Rachael handed the phone to James Holland, who took it gingerly in his big hand. "This is Captain Holland."

"Captain? You're in command of Quantum Flight Sixty-six?"

"Yes. Who are you?"

"I'm with the CIA, Captain. Dr. Rusty Sanders. I need you to listen very carefully, Captain. What I'm going to say is going to sound very odd, but if you don't listen to me and act immediately, the consequences could be fatal."

"Our situation is already fatal, Doctor, or haven't you heard?"

"Captain, please listen. You're aware an autopsy was done in Iceland on the body of Professor Helms?"

"Yes. And I'm aware the world media are saying it came back positive."

"Wrong, Captain. I spoke with the head pathologist in Iceland. The professor apparently died of a heart attack. There is virtually no evidence of an active viral infection. I know he showed signs of fever in Frankfurt, but that had to be the beginning of the coronary."

"Is this true?"

"Yes, sir. Now, that doesn't *prove* he wasn't carrying the virus, but it does indicate very strongly that the virus didn't kill him. And, Captain, I'm personally convinced that the majority of you have more than an even chance of being free of that bug. This whole thing could be a false alarm. Even if the professor carried the virus, if he wasn't in an infectious stage, he couldn't pass it around the airplane."

"Doctor, I'm sorry to tell you, we've already got someone else sick on board. A little girl. High fever and flulike symptoms."

Rusty calculated rapidly and nodded. "Too soon, Captain. That can't be the German bug. There hasn't been enough incubation time. No one could possibly be sick yet."

"All right. What is it you're afraid I won't believe?"

"Captain, you've got to alter course. Less than thirteen minutes ahead of you, some sort of attack aircraft is waiting to shoot you down. I'm convinced the attack has been mounted by a very effective Iranian-backed terrorist organization called Aqbah. I don't know exactly what type of plane is waiting for you, but I do know they've gotten hold of the coordinates of your next way point. We . . . intercepted an Arabic message. By the way, kill your transponder immediately. They've got the code."

James Holland looked over at Rachael with an expression of broad alarm. He cupped his hand over the receiver. "Rachael, would you go back and get the copilot for me? He's in the bunk room just behind the cockpit door on the right as you exit. I need him up here."

She nodded and left immediately.

Holland took his hand off the receiver and reached down, turning off the transponder, just in case.

"Doctor, why would anyone have anything to gain by shooting us down?" he asked. "Everyone thinks we're already dead."

"Lee Lancaster is on board, right?"

"Yes, if you mean the ambassador."

"Captain, every terrorist organization in the Middle East has been trying to kill Ambassador Lancaster for years. They don't give a damn who else they kill, and now you're flying Lancaster right into their backyard. He's the target, but you are too—in ways I don't have time to explain."

Holland was silent for a few seconds. "So you want me to change course and fly around that next way point, then continue on for the destination?"

Rusty realized suddenly that he'd been so focused on the impending intercept, he'd forgotten about the destination. If Aqbah couldn't get them in midair, they'd find a way to get them landing, or on the ground. Quantum 66 would never survive a trip to eastern Mauritania. In a microsecond he could see Roth's plan clearly. And a 747 was a sitting duck.

What, then, should they do?

Rusty rubbed his forehead, eyes closed, and tried to call up an image of the Atlantic Ocean off Africa. There were islands to the south, none of which would want Flight 66 on their soil.

"Captain, you can't proceed to Mauritania. If they don't get you just ahead, they'll get you over the desert."

Holland's voice sounded incredulous. "What are you suggesting, Sanders? Are you suggesting I disregard my company's instructions, the White House Situation Room's instructions, ignore a major effort to airlift supplies for us in the desert, and just . . . fly off somewhere? I don't know you! Hell, *you* could be a terrorist!"

"But I'm not telling you *where* to go, am I, Captain? I'm telling you you're a dead man if you go where they're expecting you."

There was a long pause. Rusty looked at his watch. Less than ten minutes remained.

"Captain, at *least* change course. Fast! Do you have enough fuel to make, say, the Canary Islands?"

More silence.

"Why should I believe you, Sanders? Are you the CIA Director, or something? Why aren't these orders coming from someone high up?"

"The name's Rusty, please."

"Question's the same," Holland replied acidly as he reached up and disconnected the link between the computer and the autopilot. He pressed the Heading Select button and began banking the 747 imperceptibly to the right.

"Captain, okay. I'll level with you. I am an analyst, formerly FAA, who's been helping with your problem since the incident began. I've uncovered a renegade group within Langley—I found a message they sent to Aqbah in Arabic passing the coordinates to someone ahead of you who now has your ETA and your transponder code. Captain, *please* at least alter course!"

"I am, as a precaution that you might not be insane. Continue."

"Okay." Rusty took a deep breath. "Okay. The renegades are being led by a deputy director of the CIA— the Director's in the hospital in a coma. The man's name is Jon Roth. He's a longtime enemy of terrorist groups."

"Who isn't?" Holland replied.

"Yeah, well, he's built his reputation on squelching them, and now I think he's seized the opportunity to have Aqbah expose themselves to world condemnation by killing you and your passengers."

There was shocked silence on the line before Holland replied. "Why would they do that if they know it will condemn them in public opinion terms?"

That question again! Rusty thought.

"Because, Captain, they're basically insane when it comes to killing Lancaster. Anything's worth that to them. And Roth has handed them that on a platter. Captain, where are you?"

"Calm down, Doctor. I've altered course to the right. The sky's clear ahead. Where was this task force supposed to be?"

"I don't have any idea what you should be looking for, but obviously a flying machine of some sort capable of firing guns or missiles or both. You don't have hostile detection equipment, and the bad guys won't be announcing themselves, so you might not see them in time. You need a drastic course change!"

Dick Robb was entering the cockpit with Rachael right behind. Holland motioned him to the right seat, noticing his alarmed expression.

"If they exist," Holland said, "I'm a former Air Force fighter pilot. I understand the equation."

"Good!" Rusty said.

"Hold on," Holland said.

More silence. In the captain's seat of Flight 66, James Holland thought through the problem quietly, then began shaking his head, his disbelief becoming firmer. It didn't make sense!

He held the mouthpiece of the phone against his thigh and turned to Dick Robb, quickly outlining what Sanders had said. Robb's eyes looked as if they were going to pop out of their sockets, his mouth falling open in disbelief.

"How do we know—" Robb began.

"Exactly!" was the response from the left seat.

James Holland took a deep breath and growled his answer into the phone. "You're nothing more verifiable than an unknown voice on the other end of a telephone, Sanders. I'm not going to fly off in some unplanned direction just because someone's unofficially come up with a conspiracy theory! What if we really are infected? They've got facilities waiting ahead to help us, and get us off this airplane. Our restrooms are overflowing, we're low on food, I have only so much fuel, and I can't circumnavigate the globe."

Rusty tried to control the shaking in his stomach. He had only one chance to convince this man. "Captain, you've got to stay alive and safe for at least another twenty-four hours. If the whole passenger list isn't coming down with this by then, it doesn't exist! You under-

stand what I'm saying? You need to buy time to prove
you're not infected!"

There was no response.

"Captain?"

The voice came back from Quantum 66 low and intense. Holland had arrived at a decision. He pressed the
LNAV button to reconnect the computer to the autopilot,
and the 747 began a shallow bank back to the left to
resume course as he spoke into the phone again.

"I don't believe you, Sanders, or whoever you say you
are. Ever heard of meaconing? Intrusion? Interference?
They're old tricks the Vietcong loved to use on us in
Vietnam. They'd get on our radios and pretend to be
our people and try to lure us into traps. I think that's
what you're up to."

"I don't understand," Rusty said.

"I'm ending this charade right now," Holland said.

"NO! Captain, at least, at least take down my number, or leave the line open, please!"

"Forget it, Charlie. Nice try, no cigar. The sky's clear
ahead. Tell your employer it was a clever plot, but you
pulled it on the wrong GI."

Holland pressed the disconnect button.

ABOARD GULFSTREAM IJSVA

Yuri Steblinko's years of service as a Soviet Air Force
fighter pilot had left him well aware of the dangers of
locking up a target too early with his attack radar. The
enemy pilot would know instantly by the change of
tones in his ear—audible tones generated by his threat
radar and sent to his headset. With advance notice of
even a few seconds, an enemy pilot could run, or get off
the first shot.

But the normal commercial 747 had no such capability, nor did the normal corporate Gulfstream IV.

The prince's Gulfstream, however, had a sophisticated attack radar, and Yuri had locked it on the elec-

tronic profile of Quantum Flight 66 five minutes earlier, knowing there would be no tone to alert the commercial aircrew.

But something wasn't right. First, the 747's transponder had dropped out. The little coded block with "Q66" in glowing alphanumerics he had been tracking, next to the altitude of "F370" for thirty-seven thousand feet, had suddenly evaporated. Then, he'd watched in fascination as the 747 suddenly began turning off course to the right. Yuri prepared to drop out of his high holding pattern to give chase when the jumbo just as suddenly resumed course.

The transponder, however, remained off.

What was that all about? Yuri mused.

The 747 was ten miles out now, coming straight at the preprogrammed position. Yuri double-checked that the Gulfstream's lights were out.

Okay, when he's right under me, I'll start a shallow dive and come in behind him at a range of five miles or so. That should give me a good solution.

His mind went over the unusual procedure. First, he'd extend the missile rack on the left underside of the Gulfstream. Next, he'd arm the two missiles, and prepare to aim the warheads at the 747's left inboard engine. Each missile held a nine-pound warhead, which should be just enough. The warhead should take off the entire engine and engine pod assembly, and with luck, it could collapse the entire wing. If not, he would fire the second one at the right inboard engine.

He adjusted the volume control and began listening to the low growl of the infrared eyes in both missiles as they looked for a heat source ahead.

Two missiles had been enough to bring down Korean Airlines Flight 007, but they had held twenty-five-pound warheads. Two missiles at nine pounds apiece would be enough, provided the shots were right.

Yuri mumbled a small prayer of thanks that the sheik had not demanded the smaller Russian ATOL missiles or the American AIM-9s. Both were too small to kill a 747.

The radar return moved steadily toward the center of the screen. Yuri spotted the 747 visually, the strobes openly pulsing into the night, moonlight reflecting off the silver wings, and the position lights on each wingtip and the tail marking the passage of the aircraft. His left hand curved around the control yoke, his right hand on the throttles, as both thumbs prepared to press the respective disconnect buttons for the autopilot and the autothrottles.

The oncoming 747 had no lights showing from the cockpit as it slid beneath the Gulfstream some six thousand feet below. The jumbo was precisely on his flight-planned position.

And it was time.

Yuri hit the two disconnect buttons and rolled the business jet into a tight right turn as he let the nose down and pushed the throttles up. The 747 was traveling at Mach .80, or eighty percent of the speed of sound. Yuri could accelerate to Mach .87 and slide into position behind him within two minutes, forming a stable platform for the missiles. He heard and felt the speed increase as he descended rapidly out of forty-three thousand feet, remembering many of the combat scenarios he had flown in his career.

This one was hardly a challenge.

In the cockpit of Quantum 66, James Holland had killed most of the cockpit lights to keep his eyes glued to the sky ahead. An attacker would be running without lights, he figured, which would make him difficult to spot, and even though he hadn't believed the ridiculous warning on Rachael's cellular phone, it was wise to be alert.

"I don't see anything out there!" he announced.

Dick Robb was staring wide-eyed as well. Rachael sat on the jump seat behind Holland, holding the Iridium phone in her hand.

It rang again and she looked at Holland, expecting him to signal her not to answer.

Instead, he thought for a second, then held out his hand, and she placed the phone in it.

Holland punched the ON button and put the receiver to his ear, recognizing the same voice.

"Okay, Mr. Sanders," he said, "where's this alleged attacker? We just passed your magic coordinates."

Dick Robb reached down and turned on the weather radar. Suddenly the screen came up full of uncharacteristic interference lines spiraling and spoking across the display.

Holland's eyes were drawn to it instantly, and a frown crossed his face.

"What's all *that* garbage?" Robb asked.

Holland stared at the radar scope, his mouth slightly open. Then, quickly, his left hand moved to the yoke and clicked off the autopilot as he banked the 747 sharply to the left, his eyes scanning out the left side of the aircraft.

"Dick! Kill the position lights and the strobes! Now!" Holland ordered.

Dick Robb hesitated, then complied, alarm showing on his face. "What is it?"

There was no answer as Holland concentrated all his attention out the side window. The huge Boeing was now forty-five degrees off its original heading and turning left with a forty-degree angle of bank. Holland's eyes were still glued out the left window as he spoke.

"Digital radars seldom do that unless someone nearby is blasting radar in your direction."

"You mean someone with weather radar?" Robb asked.

Holland shook his head. "Too strong. That's a tactical radar."

Holland picked up the Iridium phone again with his right hand as his left hand continued to hold the yoke in the turn. Maybe he had been too hasty. Maybe the call was legitimate, and if so . . .

"What was your name again?" he asked Sanders with a renewed urgency.

Rusty told him.

"I want you to hang on the line a minute."

"Are you seeing something, Captain?"

"Just stand by, Doctor."

With a deep sinking feeling in his gut, Holland handed the phone to Rachael and reached up to snap on the seat belt sign and select the PA. Rachael spoke briefly into the phone and then fished a pen from her purse to write down the phone numbers Rusty was giving her.

Holland announced:

"This is the captain. Everyone take your seats and fasten your seat belts, immediately, please. Flight attendants too."

A thousand fleeting thoughts crossed his mind all at once. Memories of tactical procedures and maneuvers, war games, actual combat encounters in Nam. He had helped formulate methods for large transport aircraft to evade fighters under some circumstances, but not a 747 at altitude!

If anyone's out there aiming for us, we're a lumbering bull's-eye. They couldn't miss!

Yuri brought the Gulfstream to redline speed and began to level off at thirty-seven thousand feet. The 747 was five miles ahead, just as he'd planned. He had noticed a slight course change on his last sweep of the attack scope. Now he belatedly realized his target was turning sharply left.

At that moment the position lights and strobes of Quantum 66 winked out.

He knows! Somehow, he knows! Yuri concluded, trying to imagine what was happening on the other flight deck. *Well, turn away, friend, it will do you no good. You can't outrun me in a tub that big!*

Yuri yanked back the throttles and hit the extend switch for the left bank of two missiles. He heard the small hydraulic motors and felt the intrusion in the air-craft's slipstream as the missile rack came out, causing a slight left yaw. He flipped down the transparent target-ing sight on the Heads-Up Display and let his eyes adjust for a few seconds to the lines and numbers swim-ming across the horizon in his field of vision. The attack radar was already engaged, and he nudged the ship left a bit to follow the turning jumbo, tracking the aim point on the HUD to the vicinity of the number two engine, the left inboard power plant on the left wing of the 747. The angle was increasing as the 747 continued to change heading. The growling of the warheads rose in intensity as the spot of intense heat ahead excited their circuitry.

Yuri frowned. He would have to squeeze off a shot within seconds, or maneuver around behind the 747 and follow him, waiting for him to stop turning.

It was a split-second decision, but the instant he made it he knew he was wrong. He felt his finger already in motion and heard the click of the trigger. The missile's warhead tracking unit had been stalking the number two engine, and he had unleashed it. A loud roar staggered the Gulfstream as the missile streaked off its rack, its steady tone still filling his ears. It should have been on target, headed inexorably for the infrared profile of the jumbo's left inboard engine.

But the jumbo was turning too fast, masking the tailpipe with the left wing, and raising the outboard en-gine on the right wing into view instead, its tailpipe puls-ing with infrared light.

Yuri held his breath and waited.

The tiny silicon mind of the missile guidance system had seen only the flare of IR light the pilot had indicated. It had agreed electronically and locked its entire being on flying to that spot and exploding.

But suddenly that spot had faded, and in its place

rose another bright spot of pulsing IR light, much brighter than the first one now was.

Or was that the first one? The confusion was measured in microseconds as the computer chips struggled with the decision to stay locked on a fading image or to conclude that the brighter image was really the correct one and shift the trajectory accordingly.

There was no contest, it concluded. The brightest IR image was the one it was supposed to fly to, and instantly the guide vanes on the tail of the missile were averaged upward a tiny bit, altering the corkscrewing flight path at the turning target, which was getting larger by the millisecond.

James Holland let the nose of his ship drop in the turn, losing several hundred feet of altitude, experience telling him to be unpredictable and keep turning.

"If there's someone out there," Holland said, "I don't see him."

Satisfied that closing rate, flight path, speed, and target lock were all satisfactory, the missile's tiny computer waited for the tip of the warhead to touch the structure of the target. The IR flare grew to enormous proportions in the eye of the tracker, until the signal was received, and the missile did precisely what it was programmed to do: explode.

Holland's voice was drowned out suddenly by something approaching from the left. A thunderous roar of light and sound whooshed over the top of the 747 at incredible speed and in the same instant a shuddering explosion of light and sound and force erupted on the right side of the aircraft.

"WHA!" Robb's indistinct cry of alarm filled the cockpit as his head swiveled in the direction of the sound. There was a small, indistinct cry from Rachael. Holland's heart rate doubled in an instant as a river of

adrenaline entered his bloodstream and the reality of
what had happened sank in.

My God, we're hit!

There really is *someone out there!*

Instantly, Holland and Robb both looked at the forward engine panel. The indications for number four engine all read zero.

All Holland's combat instincts snapped on-line.
Jumbo jet or not, Flight 66 had become a target, and
that status had to be terminated instantly.

Holland yanked the throttles back to idle and increased his left bank to almost ninety degrees as he
jammed his foot on the left rudder to slice the nose
down toward the cloud cover some thirty thousand feet
below. His right hand snaked out and pulled the speed
brake handle at the same time, and the 747 began shuddering under the disrupted airload as it began a high-
speed descent.

"Dick, do we have a fire out there?" The impact had
shoved the 747 to the right.

"No fire!" Robb reached up and snapped on the leading edge lights. He looked back to the right. "It's gone!
There's no engine on number four strut!"

Controls! Do I have flight controls? Holland thought.
He glanced at the hydraulics. System four was dead, but
everything else seemed to be working. His controls were
responding.

The assailant was somewhere on his left. Whoever it
was would undoubtedly lock him up again and shoot a
second time as soon as he could get a good firing solution on the turning jumbo.

Which was exactly what James Holland intended to
prevent. They might survive one hit, but not two, and
there was no way to know how bad the structural damage might be on the right. The whole wing could disintegrate. His only hope was to keep turning into the
attacker and get down, cooling the engines as much as
possible to lower the infrared signature.

The radio! Convince him you're hit!

"Dick, tune up one-twenty-one-point-five in number one radio! Say we're hit and we're going down, right wing's severely damaged, aircraft uncontrollable. Make them think we're dead. I'll do the same on HF!"

"What the hell *WAS* that?" Dick Robb insisted, his voice an octave higher than normal.

"An air-to-air missile."

Robb spun the frequency dial to 121.5 and began yelling into his microphone:

"MAYDAY! MAYDAY! MAYDAY! QUANTUM FLIGHT SIXTY-SIX HAS BEEN HIT BY A MISSILE. RIGHT WING BADLY DAMAGED, AIRCRAFT UNCONTROLLABLE. WE'RE GOING DOWN!"

Robb added the latitude and longitude coordinates as Holland did the same on HF radio.

Holland glanced around at Rachael. He reached down in front of her knee and grabbed the interphone handset.

"Punch one and then three, Rachael, and tell whoever answers downstairs the captain said to kill absolutely every cabin light this instant!"

Robb snapped off the leading edge lights as Rachael nodded, grabbing the handset from Holland's hand as he snapped his head back to the instruments. Their descent rate was frightening and dangerous. If the wing was too damaged, the dive could pull them apart.

But it was a chance Holland had to take.

Yuri Steblinko had watched the missile streak away toward its target, but he could see no fireball. There had been a flash, but far more anemic than expected. That was strange, he thought. The jumbo's left wing had been in his view the entire time. He'd locked up the left engines, but then the jumbo's pilot had been doing a good job of evading the missile with the tight turn.

All at once a nearly hysterical voice was on the emergency frequency declaring "Mayday" and talking about damage to the *right* wing.

The 747 had nosed over in a left bank and begun to dive, consistent behavior for a large airplane that had just lost an engine and perhaps part of a wing on the left side. But the pilot had said the *right* wing had been damaged. Could he have missed a fireball on the far side of the plane? If so, why were they in a *left* bank?

Something didn't make sense, but there was no time to analyze it. The 747 was too close now to follow. Yuri guided the Gulfstream several thousand feet over the diving jumbo and then banked sharply left to follow him down. He pulled out the speed brakes and retarded the throttles to idle, rapidly calculating whether to try another shot. If the 747 was truly in a death spiral, another missile wasn't needed. He should just follow him down and confirm impact.

But if he wasn't hit fatally . . .

Yuri pushed the nose over more steeply, aware of the rising scream of the slipstream past the cockpit.

On the flight deck of Quantum 66 the altimeter was descending through a digital readout of thirty thousand feet as the big jet shook and bucked its way toward redline airspeed. In the cabin below, passengers and crew members clung to their armrests in near total darkness, their stomachs protesting the strange gyrations, their minds rebelling at the thought they might be crashing. The explosion of the missile was an indelible memory of sound and motion.

A food service cart had careened out of control against door 3L, and two of the flight attendants had been forced to dive for their lives. A collective guttural cry of alarm had greeted the explosion; another, the rapid dive.

Holland kept the bank angle at nearly seventy degrees, holding firm back pressure on the yoke to keep the speed under control. The flight controls seemed perfectly normal, as if the outboard right engine had been surgically removed with no wing damage.

At twenty-eight thousand feet, Holland reversed the

turn, entering a tight spiral to the right—as tight as he dared. Whoever was back there would be trying to formulate a new firing solution, he knew. He had to screw it up big-time.

"What are we doing?" Robb almost yelled at him.

"The cloud cover! I'm trying to get us into the undercast. If we can get close to the surface, whoever's after us may not have look-down/shoot-down capability. We may be able to lose him."

"Do you . . . do you think he heard the calls? You think he believes we're hit?" Robb asked, a pleading tone in his voice.

Holland shook his head. There was no way to know.

Yuri cursed in Russian. The 747 wasn't where he expected it to be. He scanned his attack scope and realized the aircraft was off to the right now.

He's reversed the turn!

If the 747 was really uncontrollable, how could that happen?

Yuri calculated the odds. If the other pilot was fighting for control, he might have been able to change the direction of his spiral. But the course reversal could indicate he was still intact and trying to evade.

That had to be the explanation!

He had to get off another shot!

"James, we're overspeeding! We don't know what we've got out there!" Robb's voice was tinged with fear as he watched the airspeed indicator push past the red line and heard the characteristic *clacking* sound that signaled an overspeed.

Holland shallowed the bank a little and pulled more back pressure, arresting the increase as he reversed course again back to the left.

"Dick, call my altitude in thousand-foot increments, please."

"Roger. We're, ah, twenty-one, ah, thousand now, ah, ah, going down over six thousand feet per minute."

"He'll fire again. Just before we hit the clouds, he'll fire again, and even if we make the clouds, if that's an F-15 or a MIG-29, he'll get us from above." Holland was talking to himself. He reversed the spiral back to the right again, expecting an explosion at any second. There would be a bright light and a huge shudder, then a rapid decompression as the cabin structure gave way to the shrapnel of the exploding metal from the warhead.

His controls would go slack, and if a wing had blown off, they'd start to spin, faster and faster, until impact—and he would be unable to do anything but hang on.

Holland shook himself mentally. He wasn't going to give up until there was nothing left, dammit! They still had a fighting chance!

The Iridium phone had been handed back to Rachael many tense seconds before. Rachael realized she was clutching it to her chest. She raised it to her ear now, as if the person on the other end might help somehow.

The line was dead.

Why was someone trying to kill them? She wanted to ask a thousand questions, but she had no voice all of a sudden, just a cold void where her stomach had been. She lowered the phone and held it in a shaking right hand as her left hand grasped the back of James Holland's seat. He was the only hope they had.

With a new firing solution at hand, however briefly, Yuri's index finger massaged the trigger again—the second missile having been locked on the gyrating, diving target below. Without the look-down/shoot-down capability of sophisticated fighters, he had to outdive the 747 and then point the nose of the Gulfstream at the target before launching. The Gulfstream had protested all the way as he risked sliding it through the speed of sound to an uncertain structural fate. But he had to get one last shot.

And now the jumbo was back in his electronic sights. He could hold the dive for only a few seconds more.

The 747 was below fourteen thousand now, with a cloud deck—an undercast—looming below it.

Suddenly the infrared signature of the jumbo began fading, and Yuri knew it was now or never. The computer had been slow to lock on the target. Now it unlocked. Yuri realigned the pipper—the small target circle in the middle of the HUD—and relocked, all in a matter of seconds. The jumbo was entering the clouds, the IR radiation from its engines submerging into the suspended water droplets of the cloud formation.

Now! His mind snapped the command to his finger, then rescinded it just as quickly. This time his finger complied instantly, and the missile remained on its rails.

The target had unlocked again.

Dammit!

Nearly six thousand miles away in Washington, D.C., Rusty Sanders sat on the edge of the hotel bed in a cold sweat and stared at the telephone receiver. The connection had been broken, probably by the wild gyrations of Quantum 66 as it spun out of control.

Sherry Ellis was sitting beside him. Her ear had been pressed to his at an angle, with the receiver in between. She was equally stunned.

Rusty turned to her. "Did . . . did you hear that?"

She exhaled loudly. "I . . . thought I heard someone yelling they'd been hit and were going down. I thought I heard a bang before that."

Rusty nodded slowly and looked back at the receiver, swallowing hard.

"My God, Sherry! They got him! The poor guy wouldn't believe me. He saw something out there—he was starting to believe me—but it was too late," he said, feeling dead inside.

The 747 would still be streaking toward the dark waters of the Atlantic. The horrid image was looming in his mind, like the day he had stood with thousands of others at Cape Canaveral and watched the Challenger blow up, the pieces—including the crew compartment—

falling almost lazily toward the ocean surface. At that moment in Florida he had known the cockpit contained living human beings contemplating their deaths as their craft spun crazily out of control. Now it was happening again, only this time two hundred fifty-five civilians were facing their end.

At this very moment! he thought.

Sherry's voice cut through the horror of the realization. "Try it again, just in case."

Her voice was quiet and low, and Rusty gave her an incredulous look.

"I mean it," she said, more forcefully, "just in case."

He nodded at last and toggled the telephone to get a dial tone for what he knew would be wasted effort. His hand began to shake as the enormity of the preceding events washed over him.

Yuri pulled his finger from the trigger. With the 747 fully enveloped in the cloud cover, it would be a wasted shot. He had been holding just below Mach 1, and with the slipstream screaming in his ears, he now began to nudge the Gulfstream back to a more shallow dive.

I'll go down and look for him! he decided. He would try to confirm impact—or look for a 747 on the run.

With three missiles left, if Flight 66 *was* still in the air, it wouldn't be for long.

The instant the cloud deck swallowed Quantum 66, James Holland reversed the turn to a more shallow bank angle.

"What now, James?" Robb asked, his voice still a strained shadow of its normal tone.

"He'll be behind us. He won't really believe we're down. We have to get low enough to get lost in radar surface clutter and pretend we're dead. We'll run on the surface, in ground effect if necessary, until we're sure he's not back there. That's literally our only chance."

"Six thousand," Robb announced. "You'll need to shallow your descent around three thousand."

Holland nodded. "We'll do it at two."

Robb nodded hesitantly. They were screaming out of the sky in a damaged airplane. If Holland mistimed it, they might not be able to pull out without breaking up or hitting the water.

"Okay, there's two thousand!" Robb announced. "Pull out, James. PULL OUT!"

Holland began pulling the yoke back as the vertical velocity indicator began winding down, but the yoke was resisting. A thundering shudder shook the aircraft as he applied more back pressure, but to release it would mean impacting the water.

There was nothing but blackness outside the windscreen. The level-off would have to be done entirely on instruments, and if he leveled too soon or too high, another missile could streak up an engine tailpipe and blow them apart. Holland knew the assailant was behind them, trying to lock up a final shot. He had to get within two hundred feet of the waves, perhaps closer.

The radio altimeter flashed through one thousand feet. The descent rate was slowing, but the shuddering was making the cathode-ray tube displays hard to read.

"Five hundred feet! Level off, James!" Robb called.

James Holland gave a last, mighty pull on the yoke, feeling the shuddering increase slightly as the radio altimeter unwound through the last three hundred feet.

Yuri Steblinko circled to the right and continued his descent. The target had reappeared on his scope, then faded again. Now it had disappeared entirely. He searched either side, of course, then did a complete three-hundred-sixty-degree turn, spotting nothing but random returns from the waves below. The Gulfstream broke out from beneath the undercast at three thousand feet, but with the jumbo's lights extinguished, there would be no way to spot the aircraft visually over the pitch blackness of the water.

Especially if it had impacted.

Lights suddenly loomed up in the distance on his

right, and Yuri banked in that direction and accelerated. Nothing registered on the radar, but the lights were distinct. As he neared, Yuri could see that they were stationary and low.

It was a ship of some sort.

He broke off and circled back in the direction of the original coordinates, still scanning with the radar and still getting nothing.

Perhaps I was successful after all, he mused. *Perhaps the explosion was simply masked, or perhaps the missile entered the engine tailpipe before blowing up.*

There was a momentary flare of a target to the west. He turned in that direction and tuned the radar. For a few sweeps there was nothing, then a faint return, somewhat west of where it had been before.

Yuri pushed up the thrust levers and gave chase, mentally calculating whether the 747 could have reached that position, some twenty miles away.

The answer was yes.

But the target disappeared, and the scope remained empty of all but surface noise.

He circled twice more, increasing his altitude both times, until at twelve thousand feet and back above the overcast, he decided the deed was done.

Yuri Steblinko sat back exhausted, momentarily adrift. He needed to decide on the next move. He would have to land and disappear until he could reach the appointed rendezvous. He'd already worked out where.

At some point the United States would officially discover what he had done, and a furious search would ensue. No one would be looking for the Gulfstream yet, but later the aircraft's involvement would be terribly easy to establish.

His involvement would not—*unless* he made a major mistake.

Yuri set climb power on the prince's Gulfstream and headed back to cruising altitude and tried to focus on what came next. Fuel was getting low. There were several island archipelagoes within range that had airfields. It would be a simple choice to pick one, land unannounced, leave the aircraft, and slip away. But an isolated island would be more difficult to leave. He had his trusted collection of fake passports in the lining of his briefcase. He could be one of three different men, a Canadian, Jordanian, or Pakistani—the advantage of being a trained Russian agent with a swarthy complexion. The passports were vintage KGB issue, updated just before the collapse.

An image of the impossible throng of people in Cairo imposed itself in his mind. There were a thousand ways out of Cairo and Egypt for a Jordanian with money, and given the Egyptian aviation authorities' normal speed, it would take them a week to figure out that the abandoned Gulfstream at one of their airports was the same one being sought worldwide by an angry Saudi prince.

Then, and only then, would the empty missile rack be found. He could be halfway around the planet by then.

Yuri calculated the distance. Egypt was thousands of miles to the east and well beyond his fuel supply. He grabbed a map and glanced at the circles he had drawn many hours before around possible recovery fields. The Canary Islands were to the west and within range. Another expensive transatlantic business jet dropping into the central airport of Las Palmas would hardly be noticed. He could pay cash for the fuel, refile a flight plan eastbound, and be gone within thirty minutes.

Yuri punched the coordinates of Las Palmas into the navigation computer as conflicting images of Anya and a well-endowed young woman he had known many years before in Cairo played in his mind.

Anya won out, as she always had. As he knew she always would. With the Jordanian passport and a considerable amount of cash, he would evaporate from Cairo like a ghost, only to reappear later at the agreed-upon place and time with Anya—and a Swiss bank account in seven figures.

Yuri's thoughts returned briefly to the 747. Since

there had been no trace of an airplane leaving the area, the only possible conclusion was that the attack had been successful. Somehow, he had blown off enough of the 747's wing without seeing the explosion.

The mission was successful.

But in the back of his mind was a nagging little memory of the 747's course reversals.

TWENTY-THREE

———

SITUATION ROOM, THE WHITE HOUSE, WASHINGTON, D.C.—SATURDAY, DECEMBER 23—5:50 P.M. (2250Z)

The news of the Mayday call from Flight 66 flashed into the Situation Room from several sources almost simultaneously. It had been picked up by other aircraft, an orbiting satellite, and HF radio stations all around the Atlantic.

And there had been no further contact with Flight 66, indicating they were truly down.

Jonathan Roth had been summoned from the adjacent conference room.

"The nearest radar is on the Canary Islands, and that's too far out," one of the staff members told him. "We've got an aircraft carrier, the *Eisenhower,* about two hundred miles west. They're launching a search and rescue effort immediately. The emergency locator satellite is due to pass overhead in another thirty minutes, but so far there are no reports of an ELT, an emergency locator transmitter."

"What conclusions can you draw from that?" Roth asked.

The briefer hesitated. "Well, I'm told it could mean that the impact was too catastrophic even for the emergency beacon, or whoever shot him down hit the tail and destroyed the beacon."

Roth nodded, a grim expression covering his features.

He turned to a young woman at the communications console.

"Get the President on the line for me, please."

She nodded, and within seconds handed him the phone.

In funereal tones, Roth outlined the earlier intelligence of an Iranian-backed threat, and the fact that Flight 66 had reported being hit and going down.

"Mr. President," Roth continued when the news had sunk in, "I know this isn't my area, but the entire world has been watching, and if we get any confirmation of Iranian involvement—this group Aqbah, for instance—I would highly recommend you and your advisors consider a televised statement of condemnation. If enough outrage is created, we may finally get the other intelligence services to help us eradicate these vermin."

ABOARD FLIGHT 66

For just a moment, James Holland had thought they were dead. In the last few seconds of the descent, the radio altimeter seemed to be disproving the idea that the 747 could be leveled before striking the water. But suddenly the trajectory had flattened and the altimeter had stabilized at eighty feet. Holland climbed back to a hundred feet above the surface and held it there for ten agonizing minutes while Robb searched the radar screen, watching for telltale signs that they had been locked up again by the pursuer's attack radar.

But the 747's radarscope was clear of anything but wave clutter.

"How're the controls?" Robb had asked. "Any flight control problems?"

Holland shook his head no. "Only the asymmetric thrust, with one engine missing on the right. I've got a lot of left rudder trim cranked in."

Finally, Holland dared to climb to three hundred feet

and turn the aircraft over to Dick Robb as he reached
for the PA microphone:

"Folks, this is Captain Holland. I . . . there's no
other way to explain what just happened other
than just . . . telling you. So here goes. The explosion you heard was an air-to-air missile aimed
at us. We've been shot at—by whom, I don't know.
Whoever was trying to bring us down succeeded
only in blowing off the outboard engine on the
right side. We can fly just fine with three remaining engines, and we have plenty of fuel, but what
we don't have is an explanation of who would want
to shoot us out of international airspace. What we
also don't have is a safe place to go, since I can't
gamble. Whoever shot us will probably expect us
to fly on to the desert airfield our country's set up
for us. We can't run the risk of encountering that
fighter again, so we're running in a different, unpredictable direction. Now. Remain calm, say a
few prayers if you like, but understand that we're
still safe and flyable and simply going to plan B.
I'll keep you informed. As before, don't lunge at
the cabin crew for more information. They don't
know anything I haven't just told you."

Holland replaced the microphone, with his thoughts
returning to the overriding problem—they were still airborne, but headed where?
Unseen below him wives, husbands, lovers, and
strangers were clinging to each other in shocked silence
as the flight attendants—at Barb Rollins' insistence—
began fanning out through the cabin to reassure any
panicked passengers.
"We're burning fuel at a furious rate, James!" Robb
had cautioned as he frantically searched the map for a
destination.
Jet engines gulped vastly more fuel at low altitude, yet
they couldn't climb again without risking detection. Hol-

land examined the fuel gauges once more. The consumption rate was normal, but the fuel tank gauges told a different story, with one gauge moving rapidly toward empty.

"We've got a fuel leak in number three reserve tank, Dick! I'm going to start feeding everything out of there. Calculate what that does to our range."

Robb buried himself in the appropriate charts for a few seconds, then raised his head and looked over at Holland.

"If we stay on the surface like this, we couldn't even make the Mauritania airfield."

Holland shook his head. "We can't go there anyway. That CIA doctor was right. They'll be waiting for us."

"Where, then, James? We're on three engines, we're losing fuel, if you so much as pulse your wrist downward we're in the water, and we're being hunted. Shouldn't we turn on the radios and call for help?"

Holland shook his head. "What if the fighter back there is listening, or there's a squadron of them looking for us? They think we're down. Let's keep it that way. Make sure all the radios are off. Transmit absolutely nothing." He turned back to focus on the radio altimeter.

Robb nodded and chewed his lip. "Yeah. Yeah, I see that." He seemed in deep thought for a few seconds. Suddenly he sat bolt upright. "Jeez! The passenger satellite phones on the seatbacks! Anybody back there could be using one right now!"

Holland snapped his head around to the right briefly before returning his eyes to the critical radio altitude reading. "You're right. We could be pinpointed with a satellite transmission. Get them off. The circuit breakers are behind you, Dick."

Robb found the breakers and pulled them. He turned toward Holland, who was looking out the window to his left in deep contemplation. Robb glanced at Rachael Sherwood in the jump seat. Her eyes were on Holland, who finally turned back to the right and spoke, resignation and anger tingeing his words.

"Look, we'd better realize something. We're totally alone! We've got no contact with the outside world I can risk, not even the satellite phones, and we're not sure who we can trust until we get this bird safely on the ground somewhere—and maybe not even then."

Rachael was shaking her head, a gesture only Robb saw.

"James, we have at least one friend on the outside. Maybe that CIA fellow can help us. This handheld satellite phone still works, and it's not registered to this aircraft." Rachael held up the receiver slightly.

Holland turned around, spotting the phone in her hand. He thought for a minute, then nodded and reached for it, punching the ON button.

GRAND HYATT, WASHINGTON, D.C.

In the main elevator alcove of the Washington Grand Hyatt, an unremarkable man in a dark business suit scanned the faces spilling from the latest opened elevator door with quiet intensity and cursed to himself. He had memorized the file photo, and the matching face wasn't there. The elevator door closed, and he turned slightly with a studied disinterest that would attract no one's attention. He melted smoothly into a corner and cupped one hand to his face as if in thought, effectively covering both his mouth and the tiny microphone in his palm, which connected him to an equally frustrated partner several floors above. Despite years in the field and a coolheaded determination to carry out orders, the two men were frustrated and running out of ideas. The pursuit was becoming a stakeout, and for that, two were not enough.

Yet there could be only the two of them, devoid of badges or official sanction, and they were expected to surgically remove an operational threat.

On the fourteenth floor another dark-suited man paused near a stairwell, feeling the same frustration as his partner down below. The target's Blazer had been secured and bugged, but the target—a low-level Company analyst named Sanders and his female companion, identity unknown—had effectively been absorbed by the warrens of hotel rooms and corridors. That fact had left both men quietly furious. Office types were not supposed to be able to handle themselves so professionally.

"I'm checking the fifteenth floor now," the man upstairs added. It was the only floor he hadn't cruised. What he could find behind closed doors was probably nothing. But there were no other options, and their orders were clear.

In room 1443 a deep gloom prevailed. Rusty Sanders sat on the edge of the bed repeatedly dialing the number of a satellite telephone he suspected was already on its way to the bottom of the Atlantic.

Sherry Ellis had sat for a few minutes with her arms around him, cradling him briefly as she rested her head on his shoulder. He didn't remember when she had disengaged to turn on the TV to CNN, but the first flash of the Mayday message had cut like a knife through both of them. Even though they had heard the very same words through the Iridium phone, the fact that it was now on the international airwaves made it real.

Flight 66 was down. No one could survive such an impact. Over two hundred fifty people were dead.

The fact that they, too, might have become the hunted was not a consideration.

Hanging up the phone and redialing had become rote for Rusty Sanders. How many times he had done it, he didn't know, but the sudden change on the other end of the telephone almost didn't stop his finger from hanging up once again.

The ringing had stopped, and in its place was a voice.

"Is this Doctor Sanders?" it asked.

"Yes," he said, thoroughly confused. If he had misdialed, how did the speaker know who he was? Or had the bad guys tapped into the line at last?

"This is James Holland, Doctor. We need your help."

Rusty's head was spinning. He stood up unconsciously. "James *Holland?* You're . . . you're alive!"

There was a pause, then Holland's voice. "We're alive, Doctor, but we've got a major, overriding problem."

"What? Tell me. What?"

"You were right. Someone was waiting, and they've blown off one of my engines. Number four. We're still intact otherwise and running on the surface, and I think we've shaken the bastard for the moment. But . . ."

"What can I do to help, Captain? Tell me."

He heard Holland snort softly. "Well, you wanted me to run. So I'm running. But where the hell am I running to?"

James Holland shifted the Iridium phone to his other ear.

"Doctor? Still there?"

"Yes."

"Any ideas? We've got less than two hours of fuel at this rate."

Rusty fought to recover his composure. There was no time for self-indulging in shock. He could be shocked later.

"Captain, anywhere you go is going to spark an immediate demand for you to leave. Remember that the world media have been saying that the virus was confirmed by that autopsy. Even *our* government is acting like they believe it. There's even a chance some military pilot might be sent out with orders to shoot you down before you could touch their soil."

Sanders' voice sounded as frantic as Robb's, Holland thought.

"So what do I do? There are islands nearby, such as the Canaries, but they won't welcome us either."

"Captain, we've got to buy you some time," Sanders said. "At least twenty-four hours more. I don't have any maps here. You say the Canary Islands are close?"

Holland sighed, exasperated. "Didn't you have this thought out before you called me the first time?"

"There wasn't time!" Rusty replied, feeling off-balance. He had saved their lives, or at least tried to. Why was Holland attacking him?

"Captain, I had to move heaven and earth to contact you to begin with." Sanders explained quickly that they were in a purloined hotel room and probably being hunted.

Holland nodded. "Okay, okay. I apologize. I appreciate your help. In fact, you seem to be the last resource we have. I'm just not sure there's anything you can do for us."

Sanders felt a cold fear gripping him. Before, he had been only a bystander trying to send an urgent warning. Now he had somehow gained full responsibility for finding a solution and ensuring the safety of a crippled 747 carrying people who could be infected with a deadly virus—a virus that could spark a devastating worldwide pandemic. He kept the receiver pressed to his ear and closed his eyes, trying to think.

This was a Level Four pathogen he was dealing with. The aircraft could be considered a biological hot zone of the first magnitude, with the possibility of a viral life form aboard that could kill its human hosts within four days of infection. Did he have any ethical right to expose *any* population center to such a threat? He tried to focus on the autopsy results from Iceland. It was possible his gut instinct was right, that no one else aboard was exposed. There was zero evidence of exposure.

But what if he was *wrong?* What if he became ultimately responsible for killing tens of millions?

Nevertheless, he had to help.

Holland had taken over the controls again. Dick Robb had spread out the high-altitude route map over the center console while Holland flew, and Rachael was studying it with him.

Holland told Sanders to stand by as he looked over at Robb. "How about you, Dick? Any ideas? We're running out of time. I've got to head for land."

Robb cocked his head. "The closest ones are the Canary Islands, as you said. There are one, two . . . three, looks like four different airports on as many islands there. The largest is Las Palmas."

Holland shook his head. "Dick, you take over and fly. Keep us at two hundred fifty feet, heading two-seven-zero for now."

Robb nodded and took the controls as Holland raised the phone to his ear again and looked at the map. "Doctor, we went through this in Iceland. We landed and they trapped us there. Anywhere we go, we run the risk of being impounded again. But, come to think of it, isn't that exactly what we want? We stay parked for twenty-four hours, no one's sick, and it's all over, right?"

There was a telling hesitation from Washington. Something Sherry had said was firing through the neurons of Rusty's brain, something about the legendary tenacity of Aqbah. They wouldn't just give up and go home, any sooner than Roth would change his mind. Once they discovered Flight 66 on the ground, the tactics would change, but the overall goal would remain just as lethal.

But *why?* Why would even a cold-blooded terrorist organization purposefully troll for worldwide condemnation by doing such a deed? Was the killing of Lancaster really that important to them? Or was there something more—some darker purpose? Rusty shook his head slightly in frustration. There was a logical answer just beyond reach, but he couldn't seem to grasp it. Yet he knew the Arab mind well enough to know that even in front of a worldwide television audience, Aqbah would find a way to take out Lancaster if they could. Flight 66 would simply become a means to an end.

Sanders relayed the apocalyptic thoughts to Holland, who was skeptical.

"If you're right, it doesn't leave us with many options, does it, Sanders?"

"I'm sorry, no," Rusty said.

"Hold on."

James Holland lowered the phone and turned to Dick Robb and Rachael Sherwood. Holland now felt Rachael to be as much a crew member as Robb, perhaps more. She hadn't said much, but he could feel the warmth of her just inches behind him, radiating support and confidence in him, and it gave him an odd sense of strength.

Holland explained what Sanders had said, and pointed to one of the Canary Islands on the map.

"This one, Dick. I'll plug the coordinates in the computer. Keep us in the air at this altitude—fly the radio altimeter—and head for this one."

Robb looked at Holland carefully. "You . . . think it will be safe to land there?"

Holland cocked his head. "No, I think Sanders is probably right. But we don't have much of a choice. If we can refuel and leave, we will. If not, well . . ." Holland's voice trailed off. He picked up the Iridium phone and explained the decision.

"Doctor, is there any way you could confirm that they have fuel? While you're at it, see if you could arrange catering and lavatory service. Maybe if they don't know who we are—maybe if they think we're a charter diverting in—we could get away with it. It will take us about an hour and twenty minutes to get there."

Sanders nodded on his end. "I'll try! Keep the phone near a window. I'll call as soon as I've got the information."

"Tell them you're calling from Quantum Operations. Tell them anything. It's dark out here, so the small fact that we're missing an engine might not get too much attention. Find out if they've got fuel trucks or hard stands."

"Hard stands?" Rusty asked.

"Places on the airport ramp where the fuel can be pumped from an underground connection."

"Okay." Rusty had pulled a small scratch pad across the end table and was scribbling rapidly. "How much fuel?"

"Full load. Two hundred forty thousand pounds of Jet A or whatever jet fuel they have. And since we're not headed to a rendezvous with the transports they had sent to meet us in the desert, I'm going to need meals for, say, three hundred—anything will do."

There was a pause.

"Wait a minute. We'll have to act like a positioning charter flight with a missing engine, so now we're headed for maintenance somewhere. I guess meals wouldn't make much sense. But getting toilets serviced and potable water refilled would."

"Got it," Sanders said. "But, Captain, if you get all this and get off the ground again, we still have to decide where to go."

We? thought Holland. *Am I letting someone else make the decisions again?*

No. This is my only outside ally! Holland reminded himself. *"We" is right. I need his help.*

Holland exhaled loudly. "What was your first name again?"

"Rusty."

"Okay, Rusty. I'm James, not 'Captain,' okay?"

"Okay."

"I'm thinking we need to go somewhere unpredictable, somewhere very heavily populated. A place where terrorists would dare not attack us. Rio de Janeiro, for instance, or Cape Town, South Africa. That is, if I can stay airborne long enough to get there. Would you research that? Help me figure out where to go if we can get away from the Canaries?"

"I'll do it, James."

"I appreciate that. And I appreciate your help earlier. I'm . . . I'm sorry I didn't listen."

"I understand, believe me."

"Well," said Holland, "I wish I had."

In Washington, Rusty replaced the receiver at the same moment he and Sherry heard the sound of a key turning in the hotel room door.

TWENTY-FOUR

SITUATION ROOM, THE WHITE HOUSE, WASHINGTON, D.C.—SATURDAY, DECEMBER 23—6 P.M. (2300Z)

The security message from Langley had been slipped under Jon Roth's nose with shocking effect, but Roth—his half-glasses resting on the top of his head—leaned back in the overstuffed leather swivel chair and nodded with a practiced air of boredom at the Situation Room staffer who had brought it.

The staffer, painfully familiar with the blasé facades of panicked men in high positions, quickly closed the door behind him, knowing that the deputy director of Central Intelligence would sit forward immediately to scan the message again, his mind racing through the possibilities and complications.

All commercial satellite transmissions from Flight 66 had been monitored—not from Langley but from the Company's new electronic center south of the Beltway. The distress call had come from Flight 66 at 2226Z. They were going down, one of the pilots had said. That meant that within three minutes of the distress call, the 747 should have impacted the water, destroying all ability to access the commercial telephone satellite channels.

Yet, according to the message from Langley, two satellite telephone calls had been made from Flight 66 a full *fourteen minutes* after the Mayday! And the calls had been terminated several minutes later in mid-conversation, simultaneously.

Perhaps, thought Roth, *they kept it in the air as much as fourteen minutes longer, but finally lost control and crashed.*

That was a reasonable possibility, he concluded. After all, the rescue force approaching from the USS *Eisenhower* was tracking nothing on radar in the area, and 747s were hardly stealth aircraft. Any 747 flying away from the presumed crash site should be spotted.

But *fourteen minutes?*

There were two possibilities, Roth decided. The more likely was the delayed-crash scenario.

But the more worrisome—the possibility they had faked a crash and somehow run without detection—demanded immediate action. If they were still alive and flying and had contacted no one, they had to be consciously faking. Otherwise, the captain would have called for help to save him from his attacker. Any unarmed commercial pilot would do exactly that.

Roth exhaled sharply. Everything was at stake. The CIA Director was still in intensive care and unconscious, with little prospect for recovery, but the President hadn't named an acting CIA chief as yet. Roth knew he was the logical choice, but if he whipsawed the President in too many directions, the presidential staff would whisper in their boss's ear and the vacillating occupant of the Oval Office would drop Roth instantly.

Yet, if Flight 66 *was* still in the air, it represented a very real threat to both human civilization *and* his carefully hatched plan to focus the rage of the world on Aqbah.

That's what I have to play on, Roth reminded himself. *The President must be very sensitive to the fact that this is an American aircraft threatening to infect the world!*

Roth got to his feet. The President must not speak out publicly just yet.

Stopping the news conference would be easy.

Convincing the President to unleash the Air Force

with lethal intent against a civilian airliner would be the
hard part.

GRAND HYATT, WASHINGTON, D.C.

Harold and Janie Hollingsworth from Chinook, Mon-
tana, had lingered all afternoon in the National Gallery
of Art. It was the third day of their vacation, and they
were in a great mood by the time they returned to the
hotel. Janie, a striking brunette in her late thirties with a
fondness for micro-miniskirts, was an aspiring mystery
writer and reporter for her local paper. They had dinner
reservations in Georgetown, but first she planned to se-
duce her husband with some new and scandalous lin-
gerie she'd slipped into her suitcase.

She smiled to herself, thankful their sexual appetites
were the same. Harold had fondled her small, well-
rounded rear end all the way up on the elevator and
she'd reached back to reciprocate. Now, heated and
happily impatient, he fumbled with the key to room
1443 before getting it to turn. The door swung open and
Janie shot past him into the room in the process of
unbuttoning her blouse—and came to a sudden halt.

"Who the hell are *you?*" Harold heard her ask.

Harold moved to her side, startled to see a man and
woman in their room, the man holding the telephone
and standing by the bed, the woman pacing.

Both looked caught in the act.

Rusty Sanders replaced the receiver and stood up, his
left hand out in a stop gesture as he fumbled in his back
pocket for his ID.

Harold Hollingsworth saw the strange man's right
hand disappear in a pocket and expected to see it
emerge with a gun. Instinctively he grabbed Janie by the
shoulders and pulled her back toward the open door.

"Wait!" The command came from the woman. It carried enough authority to cause Harold to hesitate, and

in that instant Rusty Sanders found his ID and opened it in front of them, holding it out.

"Please. Close the door," Rusty ordered.

Harold looked closely at the ID.

"Central Intelligence Agency. I'm Dr. Rusty Sanders; this is Agent Sherry Ellis," Rusty said.

Agent Ellis? Sherry thought to herself, amused, but working hard not to react.

Rusty couldn't recall ever having introduced himself like an operative before. It sounded strange, and staged.

"Okay . . ." Harold said cautiously as Janie squirmed out of his grasp.

Rusty pointed back at the nightstand. "You've heard of the police commandeering vehicles? Well, we've sort of commandeered your room to use the phone. We're in the middle of a real, ah, problem, with an ongoing operation, and we had to have a quiet and inconspicuous place. Look . . . I don't have time to explain," Rusty said with authority. "You two please sit down. My partner will fill you in on what's at stake here while I get back to work. With any luck, we'll be out of here in thirty minutes."

"Sherry." Rusty looked at her intently. "Tell them what's happening."

As Sherry nodded, Harold and Janie Hollingsworth looked at each other, their passion suddenly cooled by curiosity. They had heard Washington was a strange town, but to have the *CIA* conducting an operation in their hotel room was worth a decade of storytelling back home—not to mention a new plot for Janie's writing!

Harold held his wife's forearm as they sank together onto the edge of their bed.

ABOARD FLIGHT 66

James Holland called Barb Rollins up to the flight deck for a hurried conference and asked for Ambassador Lancaster as well. Rachael departed to escort her boss back upstairs, and with all of them crowded into the diminutive cockpit, Holland swiveled as far around as he could in his seat to fill them in.

"We've been attacked," he told them, "and we're being hunted." He told them about Sanders and the renegade operation he had uncovered. He outlined the loss of number four engine to an air-to-air missile and how they had tried to dive their way to safety, and succeeded at least temporarily. "We knew everyone in the cabin would be scared beyond words, but there was no time to focus on that or say anything on the PA. We were kinda busy up here."

He described their diminished options and the need to remain low to evade radar.

And he laid out the worst element of all. "This man Sanders tells me we're probably *not* infected, but that this renegade operation has the world—and the President—convinced that we're all dead. They've lied about the autopsy on Professor, ah . . ."

"Helms," Barb said.

"Helms. Sanders says there was no evidence whatsoever of an active viral infection, as he put it. The media is putting out the opposite message, and Sanders says it may be coming from the CIA. Bottom line? No one wants us around, everyone on the planet with a television, radio, or newspaper thinks we're worse than Typhoid Mary, and our own country has written us off. We can't even contact our own *company* now because any outside phone calls could prove we're still flying and attract whichever terrorist group is after us."

He looked around at each of them before continuing. "We're pretending to be dead. We've tried to turn that desperate getaway attempt into a fake crash to buy time. We need to stay alive and apart from the rest of the world for twenty-four hours, or as much of that as possible. When that period of time has passed and if no one aboard has fallen seriously ill, our status will begin to change. In the meantime, we've got the CIA and some fanatic Middle East terrorist group trying to kill us."

Barb Rollins looked down and shook her head, as if to clear away the horrific vision. Her eyes snapped back to James Holland's.

"Let me get this straight, James. There's one other human on the planet who knows we're alive, and to whom you can speak, and this guy is a CIA spook on a cellular phone in some hotel in *Washington?*"

Holland nodded, then shook his head in frustration. "I know it sounds—"

"Why," she interrupted, looking around the cockpit at the various occupants, then back at Holland with an expression of dead seriousness, "why do I keep expecting Allen Funt, or maybe Rod Serling, to walk in?" She was not smiling.

"This is reality, Barb, as strange as it is," Holland said.

"Are you *sure?*" she asked.

Holland pointed out the right window. "There's an empty strut out there where number four engine was. It was blown off the wing by a missile. We all heard it. That's one truth I can fully accept. We weren't in anyone's forbidden airspace. We were over international waters and we were attacked. This whole thing seems nuts, but Sanders makes sense."

Lee Lancaster sighed and spoke up. "Let me add something, James." He looked at Barb Rollins, standing inches from him, then at Rachael, then back at Barb. "At the national and international level, what often appears to us ordinary outside observers to be insane reasoning and bizarre thinking actually starts out as a logical progression of thought in the minds of very ordinary people trapped in positions of extraordinary power. Conclusion A leads to conclusion B, and so forth. The *chain* is logical, but the ultimate conclusion can be illogical, and at times even criminal."

He looked Holland in the eye. "James, you've pinpointed the element that scares me the most. We're now perceived as a major, lethal biological threat to all human life. *We* don't think that's true. The evidence doesn't bear it out, at least not yet. But down there, *out* there among those who make high-speed decisions with low-speed brains, that has obviously become conclusion A."

James Holland studied Lee Lancaster's face. Lancaster's skin was exceptionally black, so much so that his features tended to blend into the darker corners of the cockpit. But the humane warmth in his eyes radiated confidence and calm. Holland suddenly understood how this man could be such a calming influence in a perpetual hurricane of wildly homicidal emotions in the Middle East.

"Ambassador—" Holland began.

"James, my mother named me Lee, not 'Ambassador.' "

"I'm sorry. Lee, you believe Sanders is telling me the truth, then?"

Lee Lancaster cocked his head slightly. "I think you already know the answer to that, James. As you say, we're missing an engine to prove it. The CIA didn't fly whatever craft shot that missile, but it's a good bet they helped set it up. Yes, I think that's possible, and correct. Remember, everything flows from conclusion A. And . . ." He looked down at the floor for a second.

"What?" Holland prompted.

Lancaster looked back up, making eye contact with everyone but Dick Robb, whose eyes remained glued to the radio altimeter.

"Well, James, when different elements of our government—including this renegade group—discover we're still alive, that won't alter conclusion A. It will, however, force some tough decisions *based* on that conclusion."

"Such as?" Barb asked.

"Such as, if we're going to run, could we possibly imperil and infect a population center somewhere? If so, then we'd be threatening the lives of thousands, perhaps millions. Such an act would have to be prevented. If not by reason, then by force."

"Lee, what are you saying?" Holland asked quietly.

The ambassador's eyes returned to his.

"If we go to the Sahara, to Mauritania, whoever tried to get us before will finish the job. That's a logical conclusion. If we go anywhere else, the United States may have to make the decision to kill us themselves so as to prevent us from infecting and killing untold millions of innocent civilians in some foreign nation. What I'm saying is, your plan to disappear for as long as possible is sound reasoning, if there's real hope of pulling it off. Within a few hours the U.S. military may be given search and destroy orders."

"Our own Air Force . . ." Holland's words trailed off in shock.

Lancaster nodded. "Our own Air Force. And our own Navy. Remember conclusion A: We're a flying biological time bomb of historic proportions. We're the Typhoid Mary of the jet age, yet of a magnitude much more deadly."

"What if we just land on the Canary Islands and refuse to move?"

Lancaster smiled. "That may be the best solution, James, but it could be easier said than done. I'm sure you can land. I have no idea how hysterical the reaction will be, but if you stay there long enough, you can be sure the situation will spin out of your control. That's a choice you've got to make as a pilot, as a captain."

Holland inclined his head slightly. "I don't think I understand."

"The choice is between two extremes: One, is it safer to refuel and keep flying while trying to evade the rest of the world, or two, is it wiser to stay uninvited on someone's airport tarmac and let the resulting international incident spin an unbreakable web of control around us? I can't help you with that one. I don't know which is best, but I do fear the latter, even if the media were able to put the glare of worldwide attention on us. Planned mistakes become simple to engineer in the midst of mass confusion and panic, even on live TV."

"Such as?"

"Fire, explosion, frightened trigger-happy security guards, as in Iceland. But then, it may be safer than flying on three engines."

Holland was shaking his head. "This is a tough old Boeing, Lee. It takes more than an engine loss to imperil a ship like this."

"Then," Lancaster said, "you may have already found the solution."

GRAND HYATT, WASHINGTON, D.C.

With the Hollingsworths watching quietly and Sherry using the second line on the bathroom extension, Rusty Sanders negotiated with the airport authorities in charge of fuel for the targeted Canary Islands airport. His telephone credit card bill was approaching meltdown.

"We'd like direct billing," Rusty told him.

There was a long hesitation on the other end. "Eh, I am so sorry, but we will need some credit arrangements to have been filed. We will accept a credit card, however."

Rusty nodded, wondering how to cajole American Express into approving such a purchase on his personal card.

Maybe there's a company card aboard Holland can use, he thought. *Best to get the gas pumped first.*

"Okay, *señor?*" Rusty asked. "The captain will provide the credit card when the fuel is loaded. Okay?"

"What is this airline, again?" the man asked.

Rusty's mind raced through the possible answers. He could see Quantum's logo in his mind's eye: a large, stylized Q flying through a red, white, and blue starfield. It was similar to the famous logo of another airline, and there had even been rumblings of litigation over the similarity.

Of course! he recalled. *United!*

Rusty relayed the name.

"Ah, *sí*. United."

"It's a new division of United, and we're using a leased aircraft," Rusty lied, hoping it wouldn't matter. After all, United could be leasing a Quantum aircraft.

Within forty minutes Sherry and Rusty hung up the phones and compared notes. The fuel and water would be waiting. Latrine service would not. The only latrine service truck big enough to handle a 747 was broken. Those things would have to wait a bit longer.

The issue of dumping potential biologically contaminated waste at an unsuspecting airport also crossed Rusty's mind. Perhaps he should be glad the truck was broken, just in case he was wrong—in case they *were* infected.

He dialed the number of Lancaster's Iridium telephone and relayed the information to James Holland.

"Captain, you should identify yourself as a United flight," Rusty said. "I've told them you're a new division of United."

"*United!*" Holland sounded slightly taken aback. United was a bitter competitor.

"It's all I could think of," Rusty told him. "Your logos are similar. And while you're at it, I'd turn off that light in the back that shines on the tail and the logo."

"That's already been done."

ABOARD FLIGHT 66

Within fifty miles of the targeted island, Holland took over again and dropped the 747 back to less than two hundred feet over the water. There was a Spanish Air Force installation in the islands, but it was unlikely fighters would be scrambled in the middle of the night for some phantom radar return, which was probably appearing and disappearing at random on their scopes.

When the lights of the city rose into view over the curvature of the ocean ahead, Holland began maneuvering to the east, skirting the northern edge of the island until he was lined up with the east–west runway. He turned then and headed straight in at one hundred feet, the shoreline looming ahead of them.

It was a risk, he knew. He had explained it in detail to Rachael Sherwood and Lee Lancaster. They were running without lights, without radar, and with little more than an intelligent guess as to the exact geographical spot at which the low cliffs of the island met the sea.

When he could stand it no longer, Holland pulled the 747 up to five hundred feet and nodded to Dick Robb, who pressed the transmit button.

The radio frequency of the Tenerife control tower had already been dialed into the number one radio.

"Tenerife tower, United Charter Twelve-eleven on final for runway two-seven."

The puzzled, heavily accented voice came back hesitantly.

"Ah, United Charter, where are you, please?"

Holland reached up to the overhead panel and snapped on all the landing and taxi lights the 747 possessed. He knew the tower controller was straining to see something off the east end of his airport, probably with binoculars. The instant sun-storm of light would nearly blind the man, but it would also momentarily confuse him and forestall deeper attempts to wonder about the sudden, unheralded arrival.

There had been no handoff from Approach Control or the oceanic controllers, neither of whom had a flight plan for an inbound jumbo.

"Ah, United Charter Twelve-eleven, cleared to land."

"Roger. Cleared to land."

Holland called for the flaps and landing gear in sequence as they approached the airport. To his relief, everything extended normally. While Robb ran through the items on the engine-out checklist, Holland retarded the throttles and settled the big ship in on a seven-hundred-foot-per-minute rate of descent through the last five hundred feet to the runway. Even with corrective left rudder applied to compensate for the missing engine on the right wing, the touchdown was one of the smoothest in his career.

At the same moment, one hundred forty miles to the southeast at Las Palmas Airport, a ramp serviceman finished plugging his fuel nozzle into the receptacle of a sleek business jet flown by some rich Arab. It was a task the serviceman inwardly despised.

He hated rich Arabs. He had worked under contract for a Saudi company for one year, hoping to make more money for his family. It had been a terrible experience. No one spoke Spanish, and all the rich Arabs whose airplanes he was hired to service treated him like excrement.

He looked up at the turbaned pilot and kept his expression neutral. It would be so satisfying to pull out the other hose and soak the bastard with kerosene, but he would be fired immediately, and good jobs were too hard to get in the Canary Islands.

He watched the pilot as he walked around his aircraft and knelt down to inspect a series of long panels on the Gulfstream's belly. He had never seen panels there on a Gulfstream before and wondered what they were. *Curious,* he thought. There was a streak of black soot, almost like jet exhaust, running from the back of one of the panels along the underside of the aircraft. They would have to get that cleaned off: Soot was acidic, and there would eventually be corrosion damage. *Of course, those rich Arabs don't give a damn,* he reminded himself. *Look at the strutting rooster! He'd let his airplane corrode away, then just go buy another one!*

The refueler pretended to be concerned about one of the grounding wires plugged into the fuselage of the airplane from his truck. He walked over and inspected it, then stood up to get a glimpse inside the open doorway. There would be at least one beautiful woman aboard. There always was. In Riyadh he had nearly been arrested for looking at Saudi women too closely. Saudi men hated that, but they couldn't control his eyes in his own country. He loved to irritate Arabs who passed through his ramp by leering at their women.

But the cabin was empty, and there were no other pilots.

And that was very strange.

He heard a small scraping noise behind him and turned, startled, to see the Arab pilot standing a few feet behind him. The sudden appearance was unnerving, as if his thoughts had been overheard. There was something about the man and his private jet—something vaguely threatening in a way he couldn't define.

TENERIFE AIRPORT, CANARY ISLANDS

With the auxiliary power unit back on-line and powering the aircraft's air-conditioning and electrical systems, James Holland applied the parking brake and brought the engine start levers to cutoff. The sound of the three remaining engines winding down vibrated lightly through the cockpit as a truck-mounted set of stairs suitable for a 747 approached carefully on the left, preparing to dock with the aft left door. Holland had briefed the crew and the passengers thoroughly on the PA. No one was to leave his or her seat, and no one would be allowed aboard. "And," Holland had ordered, "I've got to insist that everyone without exception pull your window shade and under no circumstances raise it. We do *not* want anyone out there to know there are passengers on this aircraft, because we don't want them to know who we are. They believe we're an empty seven-forty-seven getting in position for a charter flight. Our safety depends on your following my instructions to the letter."

According to Barb, there had been no dissent. Everyone was far too scared.

Door 5L was to be opened only a crack, to allow them to confer with the ground crew, if necessary, and Barb

would do the talking. Customs, she would tell them, refused to clear them, so they would be unable to let anyone in or out.

"When they find out who we are, James," Dick Robb
had said, "they're going to be homicidally angry, because they'll think we've just exposed their people and
their island."

Holland had nodded. "Can't be helped. Besides, we
can't expose them to something that, hopefully, we're
not carrying. With luck, we can get back in the air before they figure anything out." Holland looked at Robb
and saw him nod reluctantly.

"I guess. But then where do we go?"

"I think I've got that figured out. We'll discuss it in a
few minutes."

The sound of a cockpit chime rung by one of the
ground crew near the nose gear interrupted them.

Holland selected the appropriate interphone channel
and pushed the transmit button.

"Cockpit."

A frantic voice with a heavy Spanish accent came
back in his ear. *"¡Capitán! ¡Capitán!* You have no engeen at *número* four! An engeen is missing! *¿Capitán,
comprende?"*

Holland shook his head. "Yes, *comprende.* We know.
Please don't worry about it. Just refuel the airplane, but
do not put fuel in the number three reserve tank."

"But, *capitán* . . . you have no engeen! You cannot
fly with one engeen not there, *sí?"*

"It's *OKAY, señor!* Believe me! We are going to ferry
the airplane to a maintenance base."

There was confused silence from below for a few seconds. "We were told this flight is a charter, no? It is a
ferry flight?"

"We're *positioning* for a charter," Holland told him.
"We're ferrying the airplane empty because the engine
fell off."

More silence.

Holland decided to try again. "*¿Señor?* Did you understand about the reserve fuel tank?"

"*Sí, capitán.* We will no fill the number three reserve tank. You have no passengers aboard, then?"

"No passengers," Holland replied.

The man seemed to be thinking it over. His finger was still pressing his transmit button as he conferred in rapid Spanish with someone else on the ramp. His voice finally returned to the interphone.

"Where you go for maintenance?"

"Madrid," Holland snapped. "Iberia's handling it. Okay?"

"Okay, *sí*," the man said, recognizing the name of Spain's national airline.

Within five minutes the fuel quantities began to increase.

In a small airport office facing the lighted terminal ramp, the local Iberia maintenance foreman, Francisco Lizarza, sat behind a heavily scarred wooden desk and drummed his fingers. Why, he wondered, would a competent aircrew ferry an airplane with a missing engine—not to mention dangling cables, burn marks, punctures in the wing, and an active fuel leak—without at least securing the damaged areas? He stared out through dirty blinds at the 747-400, the earlier upset at staying late to deal with a grounded Iberia jet now forgotten.

Iberia Maintenance in Madrid would inherit the problem, the captain had told the ramp service coordinator by interphone. But there was fuel still dripping from the right number three reserve tank, where a series of ugly gashes had perforated the underside of the wing—undoubtedly, he figured, as number four engine had disintegrated and left its pylon.

Lizarza reached for the phone suddenly and dialed the familiar number of Maintenance in Madrid. He asked for the night supervisor and explained the problem. Did they want him to do anything to secure the leak and the dangling cables on engine number four before the crew ferried it to Madrid?

"What airplane are you talking about, Francisco?" the supervisor asked. "We have no such airplane scheduled in here."

The conversation ended, leaving Lizarza even more puzzled. Why would the captain lie? He reached for his copy of the World Aviation Guide to look up United's Maintenance headquarters back in the United States, and considered calling Quantum Airlines to see what *they* wanted done.

But there was something very familiar . . .

¡Madre de Dios! he thought.

Lizarza looked across the small office to where a tiny color television set perched on a workstand. A friend from Radio Maintenance had rigged up a satellite antenna to pull in several channels, including the American CNN. He had been watching it much earlier in the day, but now the TV was off and he lunged across the room to turn it on, impatiently waiting for it to warm up.

Just outside his window the logo lights were out on the Quantum-United 747, but the sodium-vapor terminal lights clearly illuminated the Quantum Airlines logo on the huge tail, and lit the registration number of the aircraft, N47475QA.

The glow of the TV screen flashed on suddenly, the face of the CNN anchor in Atlanta intoning yet another series of headlines. It was the wrenching story he had followed earlier of the American airliner full of people exposed to one of the worst human viruses in history. The virus had been confirmed. The people aboard were almost certainly going to die, and no country in the world had been brave enough to take them in. Not even their own country. Such a virus, if unleashed on a major population, could kill millions. He remembered feeling terrible for those poor people, and frightened of them at the same time. And then had come the news flash that they had crashed, and a rumor that the 747 might have been shot down.

A small box above the anchor's shoulder appeared, containing the picture of the 747 as it had appeared in Iceland that morning. There was a Quantum logo on the tail, and as the cameraman had zoomed in, he brought the registration number fully into view: N47475QA.

Lizarza stepped back in shock. There was an airplane now sitting on his airport ramp with the same registration number and color scheme—*and a missing engine!*

They had survived an attack and landed at his airport without permission! They were alive, after all!

But . . . *were* they? This was the death ship, a flying scourge the media had said was extremely dangerous to human life. They were imperiling everyone! His wife and kids lived a few miles away. So did his neighbors, and thousands more!

In complete confusion, Lizarza moved to his desk and grabbed the phone. The number of the police was in red under the glass top, and he dialed it with a shaking hand, not knowing whom else to call.

Dick Robb and James Holland had taken turns leaving the cockpit to visit the restroom and walk around for a few minutes while the fuel quantities increased. Suddenly Robb's voice was on the PA:

"Captain to the cockpit immediately, please!"

Holland looked at Rachael, with whom he'd been sitting in the upper deck compartment, and sighed.

"What now?"

"May I . . . come up there with you?" she asked.

The shadow of a smile crossed his features. "I'd feel abandoned if you didn't."

Together they walked the few steps to the flight deck. Dick Robb swiveled his head around as they entered. "They've figured out who we are, James! The fueling's stopped. We have less than half a load. Several cars have pulled up under our nose, other trucks have backed off, and a nearly hysterical voice on the interphone asked if we were Quantum Sixty-six."

"What'd you say?" Holland asked.

Robb shrugged. "I told him I couldn't understand what he was asking."

Two cars with rotating red beacons on top came racing onto the ramp now and screeched to a halt a hundred feet in front of the nose. Several armed guards could be seen holding weapons and standing near the arriving officials, and within a minute a more measured voice returned to the interphone, speaking a lightly accented English.

Holland turned on the overhead speaker so Rachael could hear as well.

"Captain, are you there?"

"Yes," Holland replied.

The man gave his name and identified himself as the airport manager.

"You did not have permission to enter our country! You are carrying a dangerous illness. You must not open any doors, do you understand?"

"I understand," Holland said, "and if you'll simply finish fueling us, we'll get out of here."

"I am asking my government what to do, Captain. I do not have the authority to release your airplane. We have asked for instructions. Our customs and immigration chiefs are also on the way here, and they, too, are very upset by your actions."

"We have a damaged airplane and we were losing fuel. I had no choice. This is an exercise of emergency authority by the captain of a vessel or aircraft in international airspace. I'm entitled to land."

"Captain, you are endangering everyone on this island. We must decide what to do, and I cannot make that decision alone."

"That decision has already been made. We want to

leave as quickly as you do, if not more so. Please continue the fueling."

Lee Lancaster's words were whirling in his mind. The
situation would spin out of his control now, with governments and military elements getting involved.

"Captain, my government certainly knows about your
disease. My government will talk to your government,
and who knows? I'm just a little manager. All I can do is
call Madrid, and I have done that."

"And you won't continue the fueling?"

"No, Captain. I have no authority."

James Holland stared out the windscreen, imagining
the face of the man some forty feet below on the ramp.
They were trapped again unless he moved fast. A plan
had already formed in his mind in case this happened. It
was almost a daydream, a bizarre twist of roles that had
seemed mildly amusing at the time.

Now it seemed the only way out.

Holland thought through the idea. Every commercial
pilot knew about hijackings. They read about them, they
studied them, they and their carriers and the FAA had
formulated methods of dealing with them. In fact, Holland thought, commercial flight training in the United
States could serve as a virtual school of hijacking: how
to plan it, how to do it, how to survive it.

But James Holland would never think of engaging in
such conduct, James Holland reminded himself. He was
the beaten-down and often victimized company man
trying to stay invisible.

"*I don't trust you,*" the elderly woman downstairs had
said. "*I don't trust you because you're not thinking for
yourself.*"

Holland shook his head at the thought. She had been
right at the time, but now the situation had changed. *He*
had changed!

And he was tired of being the victim.

"Dick, flip on all the exterior lights, including landing
lights," Holland ordered.

Dick Robb looked over at him, puzzled, and hesitated.

"Now, please!"

"Okay. Okay. Could I ask why?"

"Watch," Holland said as he adjusted his headset and keyed the interphone.

"Señor Ignacio, are you still there?"

"Yes, Captain, I'm here."

"Now listen carefully to me," Holland began. "As you have figured out, we're not a United flight, we are Quantum Sixty-six, and you're right, we're all infected with a virus which, if let loose here on Tenerife, would kill the entire population within four days. We ourselves will begin falling ill with this in less than twenty-four hours. We'll all be dead within two days. Do you understand this?"

There was a long hesitation from below, and finally the sound of the transmit button being pushed was followed by the suddenly cautious voice of the airport manager.

"Sí, señor, I understand this. It is a great tragedy. I am so sorry for—"

"Cut the crap, Ignacio. I don't care whether you're sorry or not. The fact is, we're a major threat to you, do you agree?"

"Yes, Captain, I agree."

"You would not want us to expose your airport workers or the islanders, is that correct?"

"That is correct, Captain."

"Okay, then understand this quite clearly. At this very moment I have stationed my flight attendants at every one of our ten exit doors. Each exit has an emergency escape slide. If I give the word—and make no mistake about it, I *will* give the word if I have to, because this is no bluff—if I give the word, they will immediately open all ten exits, deploy the slides, and push all two hundred forty-three infected, contagious passengers onto the ramp into the damp air of your island. The virus will go everywhere with each breath from each mouth. You don't have enough fire power to kill us fast enough to prevent this, and even if you did, the first contaminated person out that door will infect your island. Do you clearly understand what I'm going to do if you don't comply with my demands?"

"Yes, Captain, but that would be a murderous act! Why would you kill more people? Why—"

"Shut up and listen! The why is not important. This is all you need to know: Unless the refueling begins immediately and continues until my tanks are full, except for the number three reserve tank, I will give the order and Tenerife in four days will become a depopulated rock with nothing but skeletons. We'll all die together. You got that?"

"Captain, Captain . . . please! You must understand—"

Holland cut him off.

"I don't have to understand anything. I'm in charge here. Your life, and that of everyone on this island, will be exchanged for full fuel tanks and a full water tank, and for following my orders to the letter. If you comply, we'll simply fly away. If you don't, you die. And get those damn cars away from my airplane! When I'm ready to fire off these engines and taxi, there will be no attempt to stop me, understood?"

"I don't have the authority to make such decisions . . ."

"Then you'll *be* the authority who assassinated the entire population of Tenerife by failing to act. Have a backbone, man. What I'm demanding is simple. My flight attendants are standing by. What's your answer? I don't see my fuel gauges increasing yet, and you have precisely thirty seconds to restart the fueling."

The button was pressed on the microphone below, but Holland could hear only frantic exchanges in Spanish. Then Ignacio returned.

"We are doing as you ask, Captain, but we must reconnect the hose, and . . ."

The predictable delay tactic. He knew it, expected it, and anticipated it.

But it wasn't going to work.

"Okay, doors one left, one right, two left, and two right, prepare to open and deploy slides and passengers," Holland said.

"No, no, no!" Ignacio yelled. "We are complying, Captain, we are reconnecting the hose!"

"Flight attendants, in thirty seconds if you don't hear from me, open the doors and deploy. If you hear any gunshots, do the same thing."

Ignacio, convinced the message was being heard by a cadre of waiting crew members with their hands on the door levers, fairly screamed into the microphone. "WE ARE REFUELING, CAPTAIN! WE ARE DOING AS YOU ASK!"

Holland purposely let fifteen seconds of silence fill the interphone before replying. As he punched the transmit button, the fuel gauges began winding upward again.

"Okay, Ignacio, I see the fuel starting," he said. "Understand this clearly. If there is a single gunshot at this airplane, especially this cockpit, everyone will leave the airplane. Any attempt to impede us in any way will result in the same thing."

"Captain, I do not understand the word 'impede'!"

" 'Impede' means to try to stop us or get in our way. ¿Comprende?"

"Yes, sir! We will not impede you!"

"Start moving those cars away from my airplane. NOW!"

"Yes, sir!"

Holland felt a gentle hand on his right shoulder and turned to see Rachael Sherwood smiling at him.

"You should have been on the stage!" she said. "You had *me* convinced. I was wondering when you'd talked to the flight attendants."

"I hadn't," he said.

Holland glanced at Robb, who looked stunned.

Holland sighed. "The fuel trucks are on the right side. As soon as we're within five thousand pounds of full, we'll start engines one and two. They'll panic, but that's exactly what I want."

Robb had begun shaking his head. "Jesus Christ, James! I'm *never,* and I mean *never,* playing poker with you!"

The sound of motors firing up and cars being hastily withdrawn from the vicinity of the 747 could be heard through the skin and the windows of the cockpit. There were sixty thousand pounds of additional fuel to be loaded. It would be a race, Holland knew, between the fuel pumps and the closing net of officialdom. If they could beat the inevitable orders from Madrid to call his bluff, they might make it.

TWENTY-FIVE

When the tanks of the Gulfstream were full, a car appeared from nowhere carrying two men intent on talking to the fueler. They stood apart from the man's truck and exchanged animated bursts of Spanish too fast for Yuri Steblinko to follow. Yuri felt himself tense as he saw the fueler turn suddenly and point at the Gulfstream. Earlier he had watched the fueler trying to peek inside. The Spaniard's curiosity had been too great for comfort, and now something new had happened.

But the two men jumped back in their car and sped away as fast as they'd come, leaving the fueler alone with Yuri with no offer of an explanation.

The fueler scribbled figures on a handwritten invoice and passed it over to the pilot he presumed was a Saudi. Yuri paid in American dollars and included a two-hundred-dollar tip, knowing what the reaction would be. He could tell what the fueler thought of Arabs. The man would be inwardly contemptuous of the tip—but he would take it.

The fueler counted the money and pocketed the tip with a small thank-you. He began to turn away, but Yuri caught his shoulder and turned him back.

"¡Señor! ¿Qué es la problema con sus amigos?"

The man looked trapped.

"¿Qué?"

"Sus amigos, en el automóvil. ¿Que dicenos ellos a usted?"

The man shook his head, puzzled.

"Can you speak English?" Yuri asked.

The man nodded. "A little, yes."

"Okay, let's try English. Your friends were excited about something. What was it?"

"My . . . friends?"

"Amigos, in the car."

"Ah, *sí!"* The expression brightened slightly. "There is a . . . a . . . strange happening at Tenerife. My friends are telling me this."

Yuri cocked his head. "What's happening at Tenerife?"

The man nodded again. "A large airplane landed there with illness aboard. They land without warning and want fuel. It is a *siete* . . . uh, a seven-four-seven. *¿Comprende?"*

"Sí," Yuri replied. "I understand what a seven-four-seven is."

"A seven-four-seven is a four-engine airplane, but this one has only three. One has fallen from the airplane."

The words hit Yuri like a lightning bolt. He struggled to maintain composure, but his head was reeling. A 747 with an engine missing and full of sick people. The only possible explanation was Flight 66! Somehow, they had escaped, and all his missile had done was remove an engine.

The fueler was still talking. "They are calling threats to the airport manager if fuel is not loaded."

"Threats?"

"Sí. If the airport doesn't give fuel, they will unload their sick passengers and infect everyone."

Yuri grabbed the man by the shoulders. "Is the airplane still there?"

The man looked startled. "I . . . do not understand, *señor."*

"The seven-forty-seven. Is it still on the ground at Tenerife?"

The fueler raised his hands slowly, palms up. "I do not know."

"Do you have a radio? Do you have contact with your superior—your *jefe?*"

"*Sí.*"

"Call him!" Yuri thrust two hundred-dollar bills in the man's hand and watched him look at it with raised eyebrows. "Call him and ask him to find out whether the airplane has taken off yet from Tenerife. *¿Sí?*"

The man smiled slightly.

"*¡Sí, señor!*"

The urge to return to the Gulfstream and start the engines and get airborne immediately was nearly overwhelming. He had seen Tenerife on the map. It wasn't far. He remembered the name from the terrible collision in 1986 of two 747s on the ground. He could be there inside of thirty minutes, though he'd still have to figure out what to do on arrival.

His whole future—his and Anya's—depended on his destroying that aircraft!

The fueler pulled a large walkie-talkie from his truck cab and spoke rapidly to his dispatcher. There was a long silence from the other end, then an answer. The fueler turned to Yuri.

"He is telling me he has heard radio reports. The airplane is there now, but he is ready to leave and has started his engines."

"*¡Muchisimas gracias, señor!*" Yuri said as he turned toward the open door of the Gulfstream and broke into a sprint.

The fueler watched with growing curiosity as the man with the turban dashed off toward his Gulfstream. The Arab's English sounded more like that of an American. And it was strange, he thought, that the news of the 747 would cause such a reaction. What was his hurry? The man scratched his head in puzzlement.

SITUATION ROOM, THE WHITE HOUSE, WASHINGTON, D.C.—7:10 P.M. (0010Z)

The President of the United States leaned on the communications console with folded arms and tried to focus on the fact that the American airliner supposedly attacked by terrorists and downed in the Atlantic was in fact now reported on an airport ramp in the Canary Islands, and missing an engine. The presence of an American-registered biological nightmare on Spanish soil had not gone unnoticed. A rapidly accelerating diplomatic earthquake was lashing out with shock waves from the epicenter in Madrid, and a collection of State Department officials were milling around in the Situation Room along with an Air Force three-star general and CIA Deputy Director Jon Roth, who had filled him in on the latest.

"Mr. President," Roth began, "there's a C-17 leaving the Mauritanian airfield at this moment for Tenerife. They've got some of the medical team on board with the biologically safe space suits. As General Lawson here can elaborate, one of the C-17 pilots is a reservist who's also an airline pilot in civilian life and seven-forty-seven-qualified. If worse comes to worst, he can fly the damned airplane to the desert himself."

The President raised his hand to stop Roth. "Are you telling me the captain of Flight Sixty-six refuses to fly any farther?"

Roth shook his head. "We don't know, sir. The crew has turned off all their satellite radios and refuse to talk with anyone but the airport authorities. They're demanding fuel, and threatening to release their infected passengers if they don't get it. The Spanish government is scared to death."

"Did you fellows consider that maybe that captain is trying to get fuel to fly on to the desert?" the President asked.

"Sir," Roth continued, "we don't know what he's planning, but one possibility is that he's planning to fly back west to the U.S. The problem is, we've already been through the mill with the question of where it's safe to send him, and the only answer was Mauritania or a similar Saharan site. If he heads anywhere else, he's a major threat to civilization. You remember the details from earlier."

"I remember clearly," the President said, "but what I haven't heard are the results of the autopsy on the professor."

Roth looked startled. "I . . . I'm sorry, sir, I thought you'd seen the note I sent up earlier."

"Just brief me, Jon."

Roth nodded. "There was an unauthorized leak from Keflavík that the autopsy proved the professor was infected. That didn't come from our team up there. What they found was inconclusive. There was no evidence that clearly tied the virus into the apparent heart attack, but their findings were unable to prove that the professor wasn't infected, and we just don't have any way of knowing that he wasn't infectious."

"So where does that leave us?"

Roth pursed his lips and looked the President in the eye. "With the presumed presence of a Level Four pathogen that we can neither prove nor disprove. Helms was definitely exposed. No question. Even if he didn't have an active case, he could have exposed everyone else on the aircraft. If we assume otherwise, we're risking a world epidemic of historic proportions on a mere gamble. To tell otherwise, at least three more days would have to go by, and we'd need electron microscope results for the samples taken in Bavaria and Iceland."

The President studied Roth's face for several seconds. "What, precisely, are you suggesting, then, Jon?"

"Well, we've asked the Spanish not to let him leave, of course . . ."

"Of course. But if he *does* take off and heads somewhere else, what are our options as the CIA sees them? I'm giving you the lead advisory role on this because of the agency's expertise with the international aspects of

this virus. I'm told our Army Research Center at Fort
Detrick is deferring to you because they have no idea
what bug this is."

Jon Roth looked down at his shoes briefly, then
looked up and glanced over at the Air Force general
with whom he'd discussed the options, then back at the
President.

"Sir, if the captain of Flight Sixty-six refuses to cooperate and heads for any place but Mauritania, I don't
know any other way we can deal with him but force."

The President unfolded his arms and stood away from
the console, his mouth open.

"You mean, threaten to *shoot him down ourselves,* if
he doesn't obey? Some damn terrorist has already tried
that, and the whole world is hearing the details on CNN
right now. You're telling me we may have to threaten
our own people with the same thing, and we're not even
sure they're infected?"

Roth nodded, then began shaking his head. "Not just
threaten, Mr. President. Given the very real biological
threat they probably pose, and depending on where they
try to go, we may actually have to do it."

GRAND HYATT, WASHINGTON, D.C.—7:12 P.M. (0012Z)

With confirmation that Flight 66 was on the ground at
Tenerife, Rusty Sanders decided to make an essentially
dangerous call to an old friend in the Defense Intelligence Agency. The call was brief and over unsecured
lines, and the fellow analyst was guarded and uncomfortable hearing from a CIA employee on the run from
an alleged renegade group within the Company. Nevertheless, he took the number of Sherry's handheld cellular phone and promised to monitor developments from
the DIA's point of view.

Rusty carefully omitted any reference to his continuous contacts with the captain of Flight 66.

"I wouldn't do this even for you, Rusty," the DIA man said, "if I wasn't convinced your concern was legitimate. I know you've been working the problem since last night."

"I appreciate it more than you know, Stan."

"Well, only someone on the inside of that operation could know that you guys skunked us last night. It's fascinating now to speculate why Jon Roth was so determined to beat us."

"Just interdepartment rivalry at that point, I'll bet."

"I'll be in touch."

There was one more call to be made to Flight 66, but Rusty could see it was time to leave the Hollingsworths' room. They had already heard far too much. He and Sherry thanked the couple and slipped into the hallway, noticing the housekeeper's cart to their right. They turned left, hurriedly entering the fire stairwell at the end of the hall.

Instinctively Sherry put a finger to her lips and moved back to the small rectangular window to scan the hallway. There was no one in sight.

"What now?" Sherry asked.

"Did you turn on your portable phone?"

She nodded. "Where do we go? They're still at Tenerife, right? Are they waiting for us to feed them any information?"

Rusty shook his head and glanced toward the hallway.

"No. Holland hadn't decided where to go, though, or even whether to leave. I need to call again and find out what their plan is, in case we can help. We're the only ones he can safely talk to for the next twenty hours!"

Sherry fell silent and scanned the hallway again, spotting a man in a dark suit leaving the elevator. He turned down the hall in the opposite direction from their stairwell, but she continued to watch as he passed the service cart of the housekeeper and knocked on a door near the far end, where he stood waiting. The man carefully looked in both directions before producing a key and unlocking the door. In a second he had disappeared inside.

Rusty had sensed her increasing nervousness.

"You thinking we're targets?" he asked.

She nodded, still looking through the small window.

"So do I. I've had a gut feeling, Sherry, a very bad feeling that Roth is going to try to clean up this little problem by getting rid of us, or am I sounding like a raving paranoid?"

Sherry Ellis looked at him without expression for a few seconds, then cocked her head. "We suspect Jon Roth helped Aqbah target Flight Sixty-six, and we now know someone shot at them and managed to knock off an engine. We don't know who it was, but you told Roth it was going to happen. If he really *is* responsible, you—and probably I as well—are loose ends. The Company doesn't really assassinate people anymore, according to the official version of the rules, but if Jon's done what we think, he's not playing by the rules."

"Which means?" Rusty prompted.

"Which means, no, you're not paranoid. Anything can happen. Don't forget the goons in your condo."

They began moving down the stairwell without looking through the window again. Unseen, behind them, the man in the dark suit emerged from the room he had entered and walked the short distance to the housekeeper's service cart. She was inside the adjacent room, and he reached up to knock on the open door to gain her attention. If someone was hiding on the fourteenth floor and refusing her services, she would know.

There would be a service elevator, Sherry assured Rusty, and they found it within a few steps of the stairwell as they exited on the fifth floor.

She was sure the elevator would open up on a basement service area, and she was right. They exited the service elevator and moved through the employee break room without challenge and up a back stairwell to the rear of the restaurant area.

"There'll be a back entrance to the kitchen for sup-

plies," Sherry whispered. "We can slip out to the street
from there."

The job of watching the lobby and six different possible
exit points at once had taken its toll on the leader of the
two-man cleanup team dispatched to deal with Rusty
Sanders. The leader spoke into his palmed microphone
as he entered the service areas of the hotel to check the
back exits once again. He was turning back when Sanders himself moved through the kitchen and right past
him, headed toward the rear exit, a woman in tow.

There was no time to alert his partner.

The majority of the kitchen staff were busy elsewhere.
Sanders and the woman were in a back hallway with no
one else around. The timing was ideal.

He stepped forward. "Excuse me! Sir! Ma'am! Could
you wait a moment?"

Rusty heard the voice but decided to press on as if it
weren't meant for him. The second shout caused him to
stop and turn. A man in his mid-forties approached with
a broad smile on his face. Rusty was vaguely aware of
the fact that Sherry had also stopped and turned and
was now walking back to his side.

The man was smiling broadly, disarmingly. Probably
hotel security, unhappy about their intrusion, Rusty concluded.

"Yes?" Rusty said.

"Could I ask for some identification, please?" the
man said, expecting both of them to fumble for their
cards. As Rusty reached for his wallet, the man reached
into his coat and produced a silenced revolver.

"Rusty! Look out!" Sherry's cry of alarm caused
Rusty to look up, but too late. The barrel was aimed
squarely at his chest, and Sherry froze as well, waiting
for the inevitable sound of a muffled shot.

Instead, the man smiled again. Keeping the gun leveled at Rusty, he said, "Dr. Sanders, we've been waiting
for you."

"Who's 'we'? And put that thing down," Rusty said.

The man shook his head. "You've had us quite frustrated trying to find you. You were supposed to call in."

Roth's team! Rusty concluded. Roth had told him to find a hotel and call in.

"Why the gun? If you're Company, why the gun?"

The man raised his other hand and spoke into the palmed microphone, arranging for his partner to bring their car to the back door. That completed, he eyed Sherry while keeping the gun on Rusty.

"We'll explain everything in due course." He gestured to Sherry with the gun. "Who's this?"

Rusty stayed silent. Sherry hesitated, then stepped forward.

"Jon Roth's personal assistant. Who the hell are you?"

The man wavered. It was an insignificant, momentary waver, but for the brief period of a few seconds the entire mission was in doubt. Roth's name had been spoken with authority. Roth had an assistant. What would she be doing here? If he took the wrong person . . .

As the questions ricocheted in his head, Sherry saw his fingers change their grip on the gun. The barrel dropped an inch or so. She began a broad, curious smile and raised her arms above her head to thoroughly distract his eyes at the moment her right leg gathered years of muscular training behind the singular goal of instantly emasculating the gunman before her.

She kicked him in the groin with all her might.

The man's trigger finger had been momentarily removed from the trigger. Now it closed helplessly around the gunstock as a pain beyond anything he'd ever felt shot through his middle and instantly convulsed his abdominal muscles. The man pitched forward with eyes bulging, not even hearing his own yelp of agony as Sherry slapped the gun away, catapulting it to one side.

"Get the gun!" she ordered, and Rusty shook off his shock and scrambled to comply. He leveled it at the man, who wasn't interested in fighting. She reached inside his coat pocket and ripped out the transceiver, checked for additional weapons, and then yelled at a kitchen worker.

"Call the police! This man's accomplice will be at the back door in a few seconds with another gun. Lock him out!"

The confused worker looked frightened to death as Sherry placed the gun in his hand. "Cover the bastard! He's an assassin."

She grabbed Rusty's hand and led him toward the front of the kitchen past other gathering workers and through the double doors, knocking down a waiter who had picked that moment to enter. They ran to the front entrance. There was a cab in the driveway and Sherry yanked the door open and jumped in. Rusty tumbled in after her.

"Drive!" she commanded.

"Where?" the cabby asked.

"Anywhere but here! Go west! Go toward Richmond."

The elderly black man shifted to drive and tromped on the gas pedal as he wheeled the car into traffic.

Rusty caught his breath long enough to look at his companion.

"You . . . you probably ruined that guy, you know?"

"You didn't understand the situation, did you, Doctor?"

"He was going to take us somewhere . . ."

"Yeah, to talk or to die. Remember I said we could expect anything? He could have had orders to dispose of us. Two shots to the head. No heart shot needed. The Covert Ops people are always talking about such techniques, usually to scare everyone else. But hell, show me the wrong end of a gun and I'm not willing to gamble."

"You're *serious,* aren't you?"

She nodded. "Could be there was already a disposal point planned for the bodies. You and I, mister, would simply cease to exist. The Company would make all sorts of worried inquiries to preserve the public record while they quietly rewrote the private one."

Rusty just stared at her.

She shook her head. "We're in deep trouble, Rusty. Until we, can expose Jon Roth, we're targeted. Even if all that goon wanted to do was talk."

The cabby was enjoying the challenge. He took a second corner at breakneck speed and Rusty leaned forward.

"Not *that* fast! We don't want to be stopped."

The cabby nodded, smiling to himself. The fare wanted a fast ride, the fare would get a fast ride.

There was a chirping from Sherry's purse and she removed her cellular phone, handing it to Rusty.

"For you, I'll bet."

It was Rusty's contact from DIA. Something had happened, he said, that disturbed him greatly. The Air Force and Navy were being tasked with a search and destroy mission. He was greatly afraid that the target was Flight 66.

"Search and destroy? What are you talking about? They're on the ground in Tenerife. It was on CNN."

"They were, Rusty. They flew away about twenty minutes ago without a trace. There's a flight plan filed for Iceland, but no one believes it. They think he's headed west. Maybe back to the States."

"Jesus!" Rusty said. "Who's giving the order to shoot him?"

"The White House, Rusty. I shouldn't, of course, be giving you this heads up, but someone over there's lost their mind! Can you imagine the fallout over this? I've got to go. See what you can do on that end."

Rusty thanked him, punched the OFF button, and relayed the word to Sherry, who was massaging a bruised right hand, which was still hurting from slapping the gun away from the goon at the Hyatt.

"Try calling him," she said. "We're a moving target, and they obviously didn't know who I was before. They won't be tracking this phone yet."

ABOARD FLIGHT 66

James Holland and Dick Robb had plotted the departure course before the last gallons were pumped into Flight 66's tanks. They had also carefully calculated the ability of the aircraft to lift itself with nearly a full load of fuel on three engines. It would be marginal, but it was possible.

With the remaining three engines started, Holland encountered no resistance taxiing to the end of the runway for an east departure. He turned immediately and set takeoff power on engines two and three to begin the takeoff roll with symmetrical thrust, bringing in engine number one as the airspeed moved above eighty knots. Slowly, steadily, the 747 accelerated, reaching rotation speed just as the red lights at the end of the runway threatened to disappear under the nose.

Holland leveled at a thousand feet and turned north in accordance with the flight plan, keeping the transponder off and talking to no one. Fifty miles north of the island, Holland descended to one hundred fifty feet and began a long, slow, arcing turn back to the west. It was part of the plan. Pretend to be heading back to Iceland while in fact heading west.

Before takeoff, Rachael Sherwood had leaned over his shoulder and asked, "Where have you decided to go?"

"Provided no one gets sick in the next ten hours, I'm going to take us to either Barbados or the Virgin Islands," he told her.

Rachael looked shocked. "The West Indies? Why?"

"Close enough to Miami for the media. Within hours we'll have dozens of TV cameras watching us. No one would dare hurt us with that kind of scrutiny, and as soon as it becomes apparent that no one aboard is sick or infected, it'll all be over."

"Can we just fly in and land?"

Holland nodded. "I thought about just popping up and landing in Miami, or maybe Charleston, or even

Washington, D.C. But we still have coastal radar, and we'd be intercepted far enough out so if someone panicked, they could start shooting. Barbados or the Virgins should be wide open for an airplane running essentially on the surface. We'll drop down four hundred miles out. It should work as simply as Tenerife did."

The Iridium telephone had been placed by the window to Holland's left. When it rang, he transferred control to the copilot and punched it on.

"Captain Holland? James? This is Rusty."

The voice was garbled electronically, but Holland could make it out.

"This is James Holland. I'm having trouble hearing you."

A wave of weird electronically generated noises pulsed over the line, followed by Rusty Sanders' voice. ". . . are you?"

"Where are we?"

"Yes."

The line seemed to clear suddenly. Holland filled him in on their position, and their plan.

"You can't, James! The Air Force and Navy are ginning up a search and destroy operation. I have information that they may try to shoot you down, and if you come anywhere close to the mainland of the U.S., they probably will!"

James Holland glanced back at Rachael. She was wearing an expression of grave concern. There was no time to explain to her what Sanders had said. There was an intermittent beeping now in the earpiece she could hear even a few feet away.

"Oh Lord, that's the battery! The battery's dying!" she said.

Holland turned back to the phone. "Rusty? Are you sure? Are you certain they've launched the military after us?"

"You're considered an unprecedented biological threat to humanity, James. There are people making decisions here that are out of control. Can you head somewhere else? If you can get on the ground somewhere remote and sit tight for twenty more hours with no illness, we're home free!"

"Where the hell? I have limited range with three engines, the airplane's beginning to stink, we're almost out of food, and the only thing we've got in abundance is water."

The beeping of the battery warning was becoming more insistent.

"What's your range, James?"

"I figure four thousand miles safely, that's a little more than ten hours in flight. Hold on. We're looking at the maps."

Rachael helped him spread the aeronautical chart of the Atlantic on the center console as he put the phone in his lap. A four-thousand-mile range could get them to Iceland, Canada, the mainland of the U.S., South America, the West Indies, and a scattering of islands in the South Atlantic, plus most of Africa and Europe.

"Remote. We need a remote spot. We need a place without U.S. military hardware."

A small dot representing a tiny island—the tip of a mostly submerged mountain peak that rose from the Mid-Atlantic Ridge thousands of miles from nowhere— caught his eye. James Holland measured the distance roughly, then leaned over and entered the latitude and longitude coordinates in the FMC computer as a fix. The island was about thirty-four hundred miles distant.

They were within range.

And no one on Earth would be expecting them to show up there.

"Dick, I'm entering these coordinates. Plug up the LNAV and head for it."

Dick Robb nodded.

James Holland lifted the Iridium phone.

"Rusty? I'm going to divert south to Ascension Island. I'm going to need to know what facilities they have . . ."

There was no sound from the earpiece.

Holland looked around at Rachael. "Do you have a spare battery?"

She was already shaking her head. "In our luggage. We can't, I guess, reach the baggage compartment from in here?"

He shook his head dispiritedly and handed her the phone.

"That was our last friend." He relayed to both of them the chilling news that the U.S. military had been turned loose to find them.

"Would they really do that, James?" Dick Robb asked, wide-eyed. "Would our own government really try to kill us?"

James Holland snorted and looked out at the darkness of the nighttime sky for a few seconds before meeting Robb's gaze again and nodding.

"For at least the next twenty hours, Dick, we have no friends. We're the mouse, and God only knows how many cats are out there hunting for us."

TWENTY-SIX

The 14th Street Bridge was a blur in the windows of the cab as Rusty Sanders lowered Sherry's cellular phone to his lap and sighed. "I don't believe it! The *battery* died! Before he could tell me where he's going, the damned battery died!"

"But he's away and he's safe," Sherry reminded him. "That's the most important thing."

Rusty nodded, the image of the damaged 747 hanging in his mind. He glanced at Sherry as they shot off the west end of the bridge. The Pentagon was visible on the right, but the cabbie was holding his course to the west, toward Richmond.

Sherry Ellis reached out and held Rusty's hand, and he looked up at her in response.

"Rusty, it's out of our control now. You've done everything possible. We've got to worry about our own asses for a while."

Rusty shook his head. "I just can't get rid of the image of that poor guy flying off in the middle of the night, alone, out of contact, no support, and targeted by his own country. Can you imagine, Sherry? Can you imagine what he must be going through? Right this minute out there somewhere?"

She nodded slowly as Rusty continued, his hands in midair in a gesture of helplessness. "He's got over two hundred and fifty people depending on him—people who a few hours ago were told they were doomed by illness. Now they may be doomed by circumstance."

Rusty turned to her. "What if Aqbah finds them?"

"Rusty, *we* don't even know where he's going. How could Aqbah?" she asked.

Rusty sighed again and shifted his gaze out the window. "I don't know. But I have the terrible feeling they haven't given up yet."

"Where are *we* going?"

Rusty looked at her blankly. "What?"

"We're rocketing westbound in a taxi at warp two. Where are we *going?* What's our plan?"

He shook his head.

"I . . . guess I hadn't been thinking about us. My head's been out there over the Atlantic somewhere."

She nodded. "Okay, but our *bodies* are here, and I'm kinda fond of mine."

"I suppose they could trace this cab . . ." he began. She nodded.

"And," Rusty continued, "I guess we need to assume Roth's given orders to eliminate us both, though he probably doesn't know you're involved."

"He will if the guy in the kitchen can still talk."

"Sherry, you were in the field, in Cairo, right?"

She nodded. "A short stint in Covert Ops, yes."

"So you're trained in these things. I'm not."

"You want a suggestion?" she asked.

He nodded.

"Okay. Let's turn around and head for National Airport. The more people around us the better. They could be looking for this cab by now. You have any cash? Please say yes, several hundred."

"In fact, I do," Rusty replied, looking puzzled. "Three hundred or so."

"Yes!"

"Why?"

"Shuttle tickets to New York. We can disappear more easily up there."

"How?"

"Find a hotel under an assumed name, bolt the door, and try to figure it out from there."

Rusty's eyes were staring deeply into hers. His expression, and the way he'd suddenly shifted himself sideways in the seat as if he were looking at her as a partner and a companion for the first time, made her feel a disturbing bond between them that made clever comments at once unnecessary and trivial.

They were in mortal trouble.

But they were in trouble *together*.

Sherry felt herself blush as Rusty ordered the cabby to reverse course, never taking his eyes from hers.

NORTHWEST OF LAS PALMAS, CANARY ISLANDS

Roaring into the night from Las Palmas Airport, Yuri Steblinko pushed the Gulfstream IV to redline airspeed trying to get to Tenerife before the radar trace of Flight 66 disappeared to the north.

It was too late. His radar showed nothing where Flight 66 should have been.

Air traffic control had confirmed the 747's flight plan led to Iceland, but Yuri knew his quarry was no fool. The captain of Flight 66 would expect the unknown assailant to be lurking somewhere close by. He would file a false flight plan and then head somewhere else—somewhere at least ninety degrees away from the northbound course that led back to Keflavík.

"The seven-forty-seven departed eighteen minutes ago," the Tenerife tower confirmed. With a climb speed averaging between two hundred fifty and three hundred knots, the jumbo should have gained a seventy-five- to hundred-mile lead, Yuri calculated. The attack radar was sweeping a two-hundred-mile area ahead, but there were still no returns, and Yuri could feel his apprehension rising.

He leveled the Gulfstream at fifteen thousand feet,

adjusted the throttles, and held a northerly course as his mind worked frantically on the problem.

Where would I go? What would I do in his shoes?

If the 747 were already flying south, the two aircraft would be moving apart at a combined speed of a thousand miles per hour! The 747 was out there somewhere and in range, he knew, but he couldn't search the entire area around the Canary Islands fast enough. If he guessed at the wrong direction, Flight 66 would be out of range before he could try another. The only real chance of catching him was to follow the same path of logic the 747 captain was using. If he could do that, he could figure out where Flight 66 was headed.

He wouldn't go back to the east because he'd expect me to be waiting there. He would figure that any attempt to fly east toward the Sahara would bring another attack, because coastal radars would see him and they might just be helping me.

East wasn't the answer.

Okay, how about north? I concluded he wouldn't go north. Am I missing anything?

Again the answer was no.

That left west and south, and Yuri banked the Gulfstream to the west as he struggled to work out which was more likely.

The radar scope still showed no targets ahead. He flipped the range to three hundred miles, then back to one hundred fifty, but nothing flared on the screen.

If he runs west, he'll be headed back to the United States. If he runs south, there are only a few islands, South America's east coast, and more of Africa.

The 747's fuel tanks had been filled, he had been told by the departure controller. But the jumbo had only three engines, and that meant more drag and less range. He could probably fly four thousand miles maximum. Enough to reach Miami. Enough to reach Recife, Brazil, and maybe even Rio de Janeiro.

A target suddenly flared ahead at the ninety-mile range, held for two sweeps of the radar beam as it appeared to move due south, then disappeared again. When it failed to reappear, Yuri decided it was nothing.

Yuri had monitored as many commercial broadcasts as he could find in the previous hours, and the latest ones had confirmed that the passengers and crew of Flight 66 had in fact been exposed to the deadly virus released in Germany. For a while, the aircraft was said to have crashed at sea, then it was reported at Tenerife, holding the airport hostage. Now, as Yuri monitored a Voice of America broadcast, an announcer echoed the worldwide worry that Flight 66 had become a renegade flown by an out-of-control aircrew that was refusing to go to the desert and die quietly.

Yuri felt a flash of kinship for the American captain of Flight 66. He was a fellow pilot, and even as he chased him in order to kill him, Yuri could feel empathy for the man.

And moreover, he felt he could understand his thinking. Any pilot who could do such a masterful job of evading an attacker had been trained as a military pilot, possibly in fighters. He would know he was still being hunted, and he would do something no one was expecting.

He would head for home. He would fly west.

Yuri keyed in the coordinates of several westbound way points in the flight management computer and executed the changes. He would climb to thirty-two thousand—an altitude commercial jets seldom used—and race westward. His closing rate on Flight 66 should be at least sixty knots, which would mean an intercept within two hours. They would be more than a thousand miles out over the trackless Atlantic when that moment occurred, but with his remaining three missiles, he could finish off what he'd started.

SITUATION ROOM, THE WHITE HOUSE, WASHINGTON, D.C.—SATURDAY EVENING, DECEMBER 23—8:20 P.M. (0120Z)

At 8 P.M. a running telephone conference that had begun several hours earlier at the Center for Disease Control in Atlanta, Georgia, and ranged from Washington, D.C., through Bonn, Germany, to the former Soviet Union culminated in the arrival of a United States Army colonel at the White House with word of an urgent conclusion.

Colonel Jerrett Webster, second in command of the Army's Medical Research Institute of Infectious Diseases at Fort Detrick, suppressed the butterflies in his stomach as a cadre of presidential advisors ushered him into the small conference area of the Situation Room. Jon Roth joined the group as Webster sat down uneasily, opened his battered leather briefcase, and pulled out several sheets of paper containing enlarged images taken by an electron microscope and faxed in on secure military communications channels from Germany. The President, he was told, would join them in a few minutes.

"Gentlemen," Webster began, "although there is some remaining controversy among us, the overall feeling among the epidemiologists working on this is that we're dealing with a serum-transfer virus. Bottom line? It's a Level Four pathogen, all right, but it can't spread by air."

The President's foreign policy advisor sat forward and pulled two of the pictures toward him. "Is this it?"

Colonel Webster nodded. "Those are images of the virus isolated from both the laboratory victims in Regensburg, Bavaria. By themselves, they only suggest similarity to a known class of viral pathogen that we do know is highly communicable and without a known vaccine or cure. But this type transfers only through a bodily fluid medium, and then most effectively when blood from an infected victim enters a cut or a mucous membrane of another. We have no reason to believe that a victim can exhale these particles in quantities sufficient to infect."

"Translate that to English, please, Colonel," Roth asked.

Webster looked at Roth and nodded. "Okay. In plain terms, there is almost no chance this Professor Helms could have infected anyone aboard that aircraft who didn't come into direct contact with him, and even then, without a blood transfer, it's highly unlikely."

"But several people gave him CPR," the foreign policy advisor said. "Would that be enough?"

Webster nodded slowly. "Perhaps. But even then, it's unlikely. I'd certainly want quarantine of everyone for at least four days, but I'd really be far more concerned about separating those who touched him from those who hadn't. Those who haven't touched him are at almost zero risk."

Roth looked stunned. "How can you be so sure?"

Webster shook his head. "We can't be absolutely certain, sir. But the autopsy team at Keflavík has now examined Professor Helms's lungs, and the virus isn't present in any discernible quantity in the alveolus tissue. Without that, there's no way for the man to have been exhaling viral particles into the air."

Webster looked around the room at the various faces. They were all waiting for him.

"So," Webster continued, "if I understand it correctly, our forces have been given a shoot-to-kill order regarding this aircraft. In the most direct terms, that's not justified by the medical evidence. I'm here to recommend to you—and the President—that the order be rescinded immediately. Wherever those poor people come down, all we need to do is keep them isolated for the requisite number of days. Everything else is quite containable."

• • •

Within minutes the President had been informed and word was flashed to the Pentagon to cancel the contingency rules of engagement regarding Flight 66.

"Have we told the captain?" the President asked when he reappeared in the Situation Room.

All the highly paid, presidentially appointed heads around him began moving slowly from side to side. One of the Situation Room aides looked at Jonathan Roth, who had been so quick to speak in every instance before. Strangely, Roth was silent this time. The deputy director of Central Intelligence seemed to be in shock as an Air Force general spoke up.

"Sir, I believe attempts are being made, but when he departed Tenerife, he went into radio silence. No one has been able to raise him, including his company."

The President looked over at Jon Roth, who was studying the top of the communications console.

"Jon, what's the chance he might be listening but not responding?"

Roth cleared his throat, a hundred conflicting thoughts competing for attention in his mind as he tried to work through the contingencies. He had never expected this! He had been so certain . . .

"Jon?" the President prompted.

Jonathan Roth looked up at the President and tried to smile.

"I, ah, think we might have a chance to reach him if we saturate world broadcasts with the word. Someone aboard is probably monitoring Voice of America, and maybe we can broadcast out there on the emergency frequency for airplanes. He might still be listening to that."

"Okay, let's do it!" the President ordered. "Get that poor bastard safely on the ground somewhere before something else occurs!" The President turned to the Air Force general. "Bill, you and Admiral Tomasson marshal everything you can to find him and escort him safely back to the Canary Islands or somewhere, and if there's any hint of who shot at him earlier, I want to

know about it instantly. And, General, make sure
there's no record of, and no leak regarding, those contingent rules of engagement."

The general nodded. "Yes, sir."

Jonathan Roth had already drifted toward a corner of
the room as the President left. There was an extremely
urgent message that had to be sent almost instantly.

Roth caught one of the aides by the sleeve.

"I need a secure line to Langley. Is the one in the
conference room okay?"

"Yes, sir," the man replied, "the far one on the table."

Roth hurried into the adjacent room, lifted the handset, and punched in the appropriate number to Langley.
Mark Hastings' voice answered, and the light indicating
a scrambled connection and a secure connection
blinked on.

Roth spoke in a low voice, watching the doorway. He
explained what had happened.

"Send our man a flash message on the satellite to
knock it off, disappear, and show up at the appointed
place and time as arranged. But do it fast, and have him
confirm by return flash. He's done his job."

Aqbah had attacked the 747. The fact that they had
failed to bring it down was immaterial. That alleged attack would be enough to focus the world's indignation
on the terrorist organization.

"How about our local mop-up?" Mark asked. "Sanders was with Sherry, as I told you. She took out one of
our two people downtown, hurt him badly, and took off.
We're searching for them now."

Roth's hand was massaging his temple. How in hell
could this have become so damned complicated so fast?
It had been the perfect opportunity. It still was, as long
as they could control the story.

"Okay, that continues," Roth said. "Bring them in."

"Sir, they have nothing hard. You've got the disk and
everything here's sanitized. Maybe we should just jetti-
son the both of them."

Roth shook his head in an unseen gesture of frustration. He should have known better than to allow an outsider analyst into the inner circle. An outsider, he reminded himself, running around with a story that could end his career if anyone believed it. And with Sherry, to boot. He had always considered her loyal.

"Take care of it however you think best, but we can't leave them out there with what they think they've found. Remember the old adage, Mark. Plug it *before* it leaks."

THREE HUNDRED TWENTY MILES WEST OF THE CANÁRY ISLANDS

Yuri Steblinko checked his watch and realized he'd made the wrong choice.

Flight 66 had *not* gone west.

He rechecked a sheet of calculations. The 747 would have had a head start of sixty miles when Yuri turned west. With the Gulfstream's airspeed, he should have been closing on the jumbo at more than sixty knots, and he'd flown for forty-five minutes. If he was really following the big Boeing, the 747 should be no more than ten miles ahead.

The radar, however, showed nothing, and the 747 would have had to climb to a higher altitude by now, Yuri knew. Turbojets burned far too much fuel at low altitude. Only in the thirty-thousand-foot range or higher could the 747 traverse an entire ocean.

Even if Flight 66 was angled off as much as thirty degrees to the north or south of his westbound course, the Gulfstream's radar would have found it within a hundred-and-fifty-mile cone.

Yuri worked the dials of the radar one last time, finding nothing. He disconnected the flight computer then and turned the Gulfstream to the southeast before pulling out a pencil to work out which angle of intercept to use.

If Flight 66 was southbound—and he had to assume

the 747 was heading south, down the middle of the Atlantic—the plane would be more than four hundred fifty miles away by now. But flying directly at his current position would place the Gulfstream even farther behind. He'd have to angle his intercept path toward the position the jumbo would occupy in five hours, the time it would take to catch up. But where was Flight 66 headed?

He pulled the map closer and ran a pencil point south. On a due-south heading, Flight 66 would pass very close to the Cape Verde Islands off the coast of Senegal. In fact, Yuri figured, the captain of Flight 66 would probably steer a course significantly to the west of the islands to avoid radar detection.

He erased the line and redrew it to pass three hundred miles west.

So what's beyond?

There was open ocean for a thousand miles before the tiny Brazilian archipelago called St. Paul's Rocks, a pair of tiny islands—two peaks of a submerged mountain range known as the Mid-Atlantic Ridge—neither of which held an airfield.

But beyond that . . .

Yuri's finger had traced south, but there was another outcropping to the southeast with a name he remembered. It was a terribly remote, tropical, and sparsely populated British possession, but it had an airport. The runway ran between two mountains, but it was long enough to be an alternate landing site for the American Space Shuttle on each and every launch.

Ascension Island!

Beyond that, Flight 66's fuel supply would be dangerously low. That had to be it!

Yuri traced the line to Ascension Island and calculated the appropriate speeds and angles. He wrote down a pair of way points and punched them into the flight management computer, then checked his work before engaging the autopilot.

The die was cast. In a little more than four hours,

either he would find himself closing in on the radar return of Flight 66, or the sky would be empty and he'd be forced to land at Ascension by himself to try to buy a tank of fuel—while hoping that no one had been alerted to look for the stolen business jet.

There was no other choice. If he had guessed wrong —if the 747 was headed east or north—his mission was all over anyway.

Yuri thought back to the message he had sent over the satellite system to his client as he raced westbound from the Canaries: "Target headed west from Canary Islands. Am in pursuit."

There had been no reply, nor had he expected any. Now, of course, he would need to revise it.

Yuri checked the autopilot and climbed out of the seat to raid the galley once again, his mind preoccupied by the possibility that Flight 66 wasn't headed to Ascension Island and had gotten away.

He brewed a fresh pot of coffee, then punched in the revised satellite message and pressed the send button as he was taking the coffee forward with a basket of bread, unaware that his shirt had caught the edge of the cover for the communications console, dislodging it slightly.

The pleasant sound of creaking leather filled his ears as he settled into the captain's seat again, a sound that drowned out both the brief chime announcing an incoming message and the small report of the satellite receiver lid as it closed once more, accidentally turning off the power switch in the process.

Yuri settled back and sipped the prince's coffee, planning the next few hours. He would set a tiny alarm on his watch and get an hour of sleep.

There were continuous shortwave radio broadcasts available, and the prince's aircraft came equipped with a powerful worldband radio. But he had listened to endless hours of shortwave newscasts and was growing weary of them.

Suppose something changes? he asked himself. Perhaps he needed to know what the media were saying.

Yuri thought for a few seconds and shook his head. He already knew all he needed to know. If anything changed, the client could reach him by satellite. And if the jumbo was reported to be somewhere else, he wouldn't believe the report anyway.

There was no reason to listen to commercial radio, and no reason to listen to the normal oceanic aviation frequencies. He was, after all, an airborne ghost.

Yuri reached over and turned off the commercial worldband radio.

TWENTY-SEVEN

**NATIONAL AIRPORT, WASHINGTON, D.C.—
SATURDAY EVENING, DECEMBER 23—
8:20 P.M. (0120Z)

Rusty Sanders was profoundly frightened. The sea of faces flowing steadily through the hallways of Washington National Airport seemed harmless enough, but he knew that one of them might belong to a CIA employee assigned to end his life.

Sherry Ellis had briefed him as they raced toward the airport in early evening traffic.

"If Jon's goons show up, there will be at least two of them, each carrying silenced weapons. They'll be under orders to find both you *and* the woman seen with you at the hotel. The object will be to force us into some undistinguished car waiting at the curb."

"To take us where?" he asked, already guessing the answer.

"On a one-way trip, Rusty. Remember what I said before?"

He nodded, hoping she hadn't heard his loud attempt to swallow.

"The main entrances could be watched," she warned, "so we'll enter the terminal one floor below where the rental car shuttle dumps people off. There's an elevator around the corner that opens into a back hallway."

Rusty was to go to the concourse bookstore and lose himself in the back shelves while watching for her to reappear. That was the plan.

"So, what happens if *you* get caught?" he asked.

Sherry smiled. "If it's another normal vulnerable male, I'll consider the same technique." She grimaced. "Although my toe still hurts."

"I don't doubt it!" Rusty replied. "My crotch still hurts just thinking about it! You neutered that guy without a doubt."

"It was him or us," she said.

Within seconds of reaching the main terminal floor, Sherry disappeared in the direction of the ticket counter while Rusty tried to look invisible as he let the sparse crowd carry him along the hallway. There was a small bar on his left with a television tuned to CNN. With most of the passengers already on their way to evening departures, the bar was half-deserted. As Rusty passed, the news anchor in Atlanta was coming on under the banner of a special report, and suddenly the logo of Quantum Airlines and the image of a 747 appeared on the screen. Rusty came to a dead stop and eased into the open front of the bar, out of the stream of passengers. The sound was barely loud enough to hear:

"In a late-breaking development, CNN has learned that disease-control experts have concluded that the passengers and crew of Quantum Flight Sixty-six are unlikely to contract the dread virus which killed an American professor aboard the plane."

Rusty found himself leaning heavily against the wall in shock. The report continued through a brief background of the odyssey, and promised more within the hour.

They've changed their minds? How? Why?

The logo of the Central Intelligence Agency appeared over the anchor's shoulder. At first it didn't register in Rusty's peripheral vision, but suddenly he focused on the screen as the name of the hospitalized CIA chief echoed in his ears:

". . . who had been Director of the CIA since 1995, had been in a coma for the past two months after suffering a massive cerebral hemorrhage. His death this afternoon came as no surprise to the administration, which had refused to name an Acting Director out of deference to the family. But now, sources close to the President say he will undoubtedly appoint the CIA Deputy Director Jonathan Roth to the post. An announcement is expected from the White House sometime early next week."

Rusty's mind raced through the possibilities. Holland was out of contact. Was there any way he could know that no one would get sick? Or was the broadcast part of a worldwide ploy to get Holland to reveal himself?

But why could anyone feel sure that Holland would be monitoring worldband radio broadcasts? The poor guy was racing for his life.

But maybe, Rusty thought, *just maybe, he might be listening. Or someone aboard might.*

But, more likely, after what he'd been through, James Holland wouldn't trust such a report. Too much had happened. He'd still find a place to land and let the full twenty-four hours go by.

There was a sudden lull in the number of passengers streaming past his vantage point, and Rusty turned to examine the remaining faces, knowing that doing so made him even more visible.

Did this mean they were still targets, or not? Roth was going to be nominated Director. Would he call off the hits now, or continue and take the chance he could cover up their murders? Could Roth even reach his goons if he wanted to call them back?

Rusty walked to the bookstore trying to suppress the panic gnawing away at his stomach. He entered and moved quietly to the back, where he pulled a book off a shelf at random and began scanning the customers while pretending to read.

Roth was terribly vulnerable whatever he did.

Or was he?

Rusty remembered handing the computer disk over. He still had the hard copy printout, but that could have been forged, they would say. He had no real evidence that Roth had done anything wrong. The men in his condo, the one at the Hyatt—none of them could be readily identified as Jon Roth's men.

So what do I have on him? Rusty thought. The answer was painfully obvious. Other than his and Sherry's shared suspicions, there was no evidence. Roth could act innocent and get away with it. Roth had already hoodwinked the President, apparently, though Rusty reminded himself that the announcement of Roth's appointment hadn't been formally made.

But why kill us, then? Why take the chance? Why not let us tell our tale, brand us idiots, and be done with it?

Rusty realized he was shaking his head slightly. There was no reason to kill them now, but Sherry had seemed so convinced and the gun they had been staring at less than an hour before had been all too real. It was far too confusing to be certain.

A small memory suddenly appeared in a corner of his mind, rapidly diverting his attention. He thought of an insignificant computer program he had written a year before: a final backup to protect against accidental erasures. It was unorthodox and essentially undetectable—and it would have automatically captured and saved both the original version of the Cairo message and the Arabic message from his computer. And anything the program stored would be saved under an off-the-wall file name on the CIA's own mainframe computer!

In other words, he *did* have the evidence!

Rusty realized he hadn't been paying attention to who had entered the store. He looked back toward the front counter, his eyes scanning the customers.

There were four people browsing. One man too old to be dangerous lounged against a shelf to Rusty's right, slowly studying the selection. To his left, Rusty could see a young girl in a slinky, skintight dress that showed off her body. There was also a businessman in his mid-thirties who was apparently upset with the clerk for not having a certain book in stock, as well as a silver-haired older woman in a tailored suit who was wearing glasses and perusing the shelves to his left. The woman was slightly chunky and looked just like an irritable librarian he'd once encountered.

That left the upset young man at the counter. Rusty wondered if his exchange with the clerk could be a cover. He was about the same age as the agent Sherry had mauled back at the hotel.

The man suddenly looked up in Rusty's direction, his eyes landing squarely on Rusty's. A cold chill began at the base of Rusty's spine and shot upward as the young man looked away again and resumed berating the clerk in a low growl.

Rusty had made no sounds. There had been no reason for the man to glance back in his direction, *unless* . . .

The man turned suddenly and left the store. Rusty watched him head toward the north end of the terminal and stride away. Was he going for his partner?

I'm panicking again.

Rusty closed his eyes momentarily to purge his fear. When he opened them, the young man had not returned and no one else had rushed into the store.

Rusty shook his head slightly and snorted to himself. *False alarm.*

The thought brought with it a small feeling of relief—punctuated by a sudden, powerful stinging sensation in his left side.

Startled, Rusty looked down and tried to knock away whatever was stinging him.

Someone's arm was there close by his side. Something sharp and pointed brushed past his fingers as the arm withdrew. He turned to his left, confused when he saw the woman he had typed as a librarian. He looked down again, incredulous. There was a syringe in her hand—an empty syringe she was dropping in her purse! She met his gaze, her right arm shooting out to grab his left elbow.

"What . . . *what the hell?*" he stammered.

Rusty could feel the presence of powerful arm muscles as she turned him back toward the front of the shop and pulled him close to her, growling in his ear at a volume only he could hear.

"Dr. Sanders, listen carefully, and do not look back at me or resist." Her voice was low and almost guttural, yet it was a woman's voice.

"I—" he began.

"Shut up and listen! You've just been injected with eighty cc's of a very effective neurologic agent. In twenty-five minutes your nervous system will collapse and kill you. Even if you yell for help, within fifteen minutes—while paramedics are rushing you into an ambulance—they'll notice that you're conscious, but for some reason paralyzed and unable to speak. The chemical will begin to shut down your autonomic functions, including your heart. You'll be dead on arrival, regardless of where they take you, or what they give you."

Rusty tried to look around and felt the woman's grip tighten on his arm to the point of pain.

"Don't look at me again!" she commanded.

"What . . ." Rusty swallowed hard. His throat was bone-dry. The names of several neurotoxins crossed his mind. All were significantly different. Antidotes took hours to figure out.

"What do you want?"

Again the voice in his ear. Quiet, steady, threatening, and in control.

"You will follow me out of this shop without hesitation. I'm going out the front entrance to the curb, where another agent is waiting. We'll inject you with an antidote there. If you're not right behind me when I open the car door, we'll leave immediately—*with* the antidote. You will die on the sidewalk with your eyes open, helpless and pathetic. You understand?"

He nodded. "If I don't come quietly, I'm dead."

"That's right," she said.

"And if I do come, I'm dead. You're going to kill me anyway, aren't you?" Rusty heard himself say the words. He wondered how he'd gotten them out, his worst fears verbalized. He was shaking inside and imagining the progress of the neurotoxin through his body. It seemed unreal. He didn't have a fighting chance!

His side still hurt. There was no question she'd injected him.

"We're not here to kill you. We just want to talk with you."

The woman nodded in the direction of the door and Rusty began to walk, fighting for control of his shaking legs. It was one thing to face a gun, but he had been chemically raped. He was already dead if they didn't produce the right antitoxin.

What if they're lying about the antidote? What if they just want me to get quietly into the car so they can dispose of my body more easily?

The woman was pulling ahead of him now, no longer grabbing his elbow. She seemed wholly disinterested in whether he followed or not.

But he had no choice.

She turned left out of the store and began walking briskly as Rusty tried to keep up. He thought he could feel the tips of his toes going numb. He wondered which muscle group was next. Could he even make it to her car?

Where in God's name is Sherry? Do they have her too?

His captor was passing through the terminal's main entrance with an energetic stride. She hadn't even bothered to look back. She knew he'd follow. To do anything else was suicide.

Sherry Ellis had stuffed the two one-way tickets to New York in her handbag and was hurrying toward the bookstore. She stopped short when she spotted Rusty walking toward the main entrance. Something about his demeanor kept her from calling out to him.

Sherry looked carefully around and behind him. There was no one close to him, and no one seemed to be forcing him toward the street.

What the hell are you doing, Sanders? she thought.

Rusty was clearing the outside door as Sherry started after him, trying not to be too obtrusive. Several people glanced at her as she hurried toward the same portal, calculating how long it would take to intercept him.

A skycap with a loaded baggage cart got in the way and Sherry had to wait for him to get by. She saw Rusty close to the curb, still moving at a rapid pace. She could see numerous cars waiting, but a black sedan in the second lane caught her attention. Its right rear door was being opened by a chunky woman with silver hair who turned around suddenly and looked in Rusty's direction.

Sherry broke into a run and caught him before he stepped into the first lane. She swung him around to face her, aware that the silver-haired woman had turned to watch.

"What the hell do you think you're doing?" Sherry asked.

He was panicked. She could read the terror in his eyes.

"Rusty? What is it?"

He pulled away, trying to break her grip. "Get out of here, Sherry! They've got me."

"Who? Who's got you?" she asked, yanking him back around as he leaned in close to her right ear.

"That woman over there by the car. She injected me with a neurotoxin. She's got the antidote in the car. Without it I'm dead meat in twenty minutes. I have to go with her."

Rusty straightened up and looked at Sherry. He was breathing hard, and she saw his eyes glistening.

"Let me go, Sherry! Run—get out of here!"

They could both hear the sharp voice of the silver-haired agent over the traffic noise. "Last chance, Sanders!"

Instead of letting go, Sherry solidified her grip on his sleeve and almost yanked him off his feet toward the bright lights of the terminal as she snarled at him over her shoulder.

"Run! Now! FOLLOW me!"

She pulled him with surprising strength, and he followed reluctantly, then accelerated to keep up as she hauled him back into the terminal—aware that the other woman was standing and watching in disbelief by the curb.

They moved rapidly past the ticket counters and turned down a hallway. The elevator alcove they had used before loomed on the right, and Sherry pulled him into the hallway and through an open door into one of the airline offices where she flashed her badge at a secretary. "Got an office I can use for a few minutes?"

The woman looked startled.

"CIA. I don't have time to explain."

The woman nodded. "You can use this one. I'll step out."

"Don't tell anyone we're here, understand?"

The woman looked frightened. She nodded and left, closing the door behind her.

Sherry spun Rusty around to face her. He had been following in numb obedience, certain he was dead.

"Rusty, listen to me! You're not going to die!"

"I don't know what toxin that was, Sherry, but she said . . ."

"There isn't any toxin! Did she use a syringe?"

He nodded.

"A sudden jab in the side or butt?"

"In my side."

She was nodding. "I thought so." She gripped his shoulders harder and shook him.

"Rusty, it's an old trick, and a good one when you're dealing with an amateur. That was water. Nothing but water! Glucose at worst. You're not going to die!"

Rusty stared at her wide-eyed, not believing the reprieve.

"A . . . a . . . *trick?*" he stammered. "How can you be certain?"

"I was trained to do the same thing. That way she doesn't have to march you out at gunpoint in front of everyone. Either you follow like a whipped puppy, or you die. The needle convinces you instantly. Clever as hell."

He was nodding. *A good sign,* she thought.

"It sure fooled me!" he began. "That needle hurt. I thought I could feel the toxin beginning to work."

"You're a doctor. *You* understand psychosomatic symptomatology, right?"

"Yeah. Yeah, I do."

"Okay. That's what you felt. You all right with this?"

"I suppose. It was such a shock!"

"I know it was! I had it pulled on me once, as a damn joke by another couple of agents. I believed them too! It was put out or no antidote."

"They raped you?"

"Terrorized me. It was a stupid initiation game into the fraternal order of CIA spies."

"You passed?"

"No. Women weren't admitted. They just wanted me to think I was. You've heard of the glass ceiling."

He nodded. "Yeah. Yeah, I have."

"So?" she asked, reaching up to hold his chin in the palm of her hand and looking closely at one eye, then the other. "We okay?"

"Yeah," he said, "we're okay. I'm not gonna die."

She smiled. "At least not from that injection, you're not." She loosened her grip and looked around at the employee bulletin boards and other back-room paraphernalia, then back at him. "But if we don't get out of here fast, they'll be hunting us down with less sophisticated methods. I'll bet grandma out there has already called for reinforcements. We're in desperate trouble, Rusty, I won't kid you. I'm not sure whether they're trying to kill us or bring us in first, but either way, if they succeed, Jon will get away with mass murder."

He filled her in on the CNN reports. She didn't seem surprised.

"I suspected Roth would be named Director," Sherry said, "but I didn't figure on a clean bill of health for

Flight Sixty-six. It could be a ploy to get Holland to surface."

"I know. I thought of that. But even if it's true, I'm sure Holland doesn't know about it yet, either." He looked at the floor and sighed, the image of the Quantum 747 unshakably in his mind's eye.

"We might lose them still, you know," Rusty said. "He's out there, short one engine and still a target."

Sherry Ellis had backed up against a desk, staring at the door as Rusty fell silent for a few seconds.

"We've got to expose Roth," Rusty said at last. "He set that shoot-down attempt in motion, unless I'm missing something."

"You're not missing anything, Rusty," she said, "you're dead right." She glanced at him and grimaced. "Sorry. Poor choice of words."

Rusty began again. "That woman out there, the one with the needle, said they only wanted to talk to me. I'm sure she's speaking for Roth. Is there any way that could be true?"

Sherry was still staring at the door. She looked up at him, finally. "It's possible. But are you willing to gamble our lives?"

"We are a huge threat to him, aren't we?"

"I wish we were," Sherry said, "but you gave the only evidence we had against Roth to Jon himself. The disk."

Rusty smiled suddenly and turned to face her.

"Wrong."

Sherry met his gaze with a puzzled expression. "Wrong? Why? You have something I don't know about?"

He told her about the hidden backup program and she stood away from the desk and grabbed his arm. "Really? It's still there? You're *sure?*"

"I can't be absolutely sure until I can get into the computer, and I'm certain our access codes are locked out for now. But there's no way they would suspect it was there. It's in the personal files section, but not under my normal access code. I made up a new one to keep it secure."

"But it *is* likely to still be there?"

He nodded.

"Okay!" She turned away, rubbing her chin. "Rusty, there's one guy Roth doesn't own. Jon's always trying to manipulate him, but he's nobody's fool and he rides herd on the Company."

"Who? Not the President?"

She sneered and turned around to look at him. "You kidding? That creampuff? Putty in Roth's hands. No, I'm talking about Senator Moon. Jake Moon of Arkansas. Chairman of the Senate Select Committee on Intelligence."

"Moon's a legend. You *know* him? Well enough to *call* him?"

She nodded. "I think I even know how to get his home number."

Rusty hesitated, trying to focus on the date. "Wait a minute! The Senate is still in session. It's that pre-Christmas filibuster. They're trying to get finished for Christmas, but the loyal opposition won't give up."

"Which means?" she asked.

"Which means that Moon's probably on the Senate floor, or in his office!"

There was a sudden burst of conversation outside the door to the hallway. Rusty instantly recognized the agent's voice. With his finger to his lips, he grabbed Sherry by the elbow and propelled her through a door on the other side of the office just as the door behind them opened with a bang.

They were in a service hallway on the second floor of the terminal. There was a stairway to their right. They ran to it and took the stairs two at a time, finally emerging in a dingy hallway between airline operations offices. Sherry moved in front and yanked open the door to one of them, moving past two startled pilots gathering their paperwork. There was a cipher-locked doorway to the ramp beyond that had just been opened by an incoming

agent. Sherry flipped her identification at him as they
elbowed past. The startled man yelped but stood aside
as they moved into a baggage staging area where several
baggage tugs sat idling, each hooked to a train of baggage carts. Sherry jumped on the nearest one and motioned Rusty onto the seat beside her. She snapped on
the headlights and jammed the machine into gear,
lurching out of the garage with six baggage carts in tow
and several startled baggage handlers yelling and chasing their runaway tram.

"Where are we going?" Rusty yelled.

"Delta's ramp! Fastest way out."

She pressed the gas pedal hard, ignoring the sounds
of spilling luggage and yelled epithets behind her.

"How the hell do you know so much about this
place?" Rusty yelled.

"Summer job with TWA, three years running in college. I was a ramper. You learn every nook and cranny!"

At the windows of the terminal above, two Company
agents spotted the purloined baggage train speeding
away from the terminal just as two more of their number emerged on the ramp below. The agents above saw
their comrades hesitate, then head for the first idling
vehicle they could see—a set of mobile airstairs set on a
modified pickup truck body. The two jumped into the
airstairs truck and roared off in chase.

A Boeing 757 with its bright taxi lights on loomed
ahead of them and Sherry tried to steer the shortest
course between the east side of the concourse and the
north–south taxiway. Hanging on tightly, Rusty looked
around and spotted the mobile stairs truck coming after
them. Its headlights were on too, but he could make out
the vehicle in the bright lights of the nighttime ramp.
Sherry sped between the right main landing gear of the
757 and a fuel truck hooked up to the right wing of the
aircraft, running over the refueler's grounding wires in
the process. The refueler jumped from his ladder in
shock as the tug roared by, spilling baggage everywhere.
The agent driving the mobile stairs truck had been clos-

ing on them, but he realized at the last second that his vehicle was too tall to go under the wing. He braked hard and lurched to his right, losing time as he maneuvered around the 757's right wing and the fuel truck. Within seconds, however, the airstairs truck was back on a steady course after them and accelerating once again. Rusty could see the occupant of the right seat holding something out the window, something that had to be a gun.

Sherry steered close to the edge of the terminal arm and shot just behind a push-back crew shoving an MD-80 back from the gate. The tug driver looked thunderstruck as they passed, and Rusty could hear several ground handlers yelling at them.

The mobile stairs hadn't appeared around the corner yet, but it would be just seconds before they did. The Delta Shuttle facility was just ahead, and Sherry jogged to the right suddenly, throwing Rusty into her lap as she tried to get around another moving baggage tug, whose driver hadn't seen them. The other driver spotted her suddenly and slammed on his brakes while swerving to get out of Sherry's way. His four carts tumbled over, scattering their baggage.

The control tower had belatedly spotted the errant baggage tug as it left the 757 and ordered all aircraft to hold their positions. Two more push-back crews and a taxiing 727 braked to a halt as a result. Rusty looked over his shoulder again and saw the mobile stairs emerge into the clear after passing around the MD-80. The driver had it floorboarded, and the unstable vehicle was rocking left and right dangerously.

Rusty heard the ping of a bullet striking metal, and the whirr of a ricochet past their ears, a hollow sound like some incredibly large hornet passing at high speed.

He turned to Sherry.

"They're shooting at us!"

"Keep down!" she yelled, jerking the wheel left to use the baggage carts as a shield.

Another bullet whirred past their heads just as one of

the instruments on the small panel of the tug exploded. The bullet, Rusty realized, had passed right between them.

A Delta 727 had braked to a halt short of its terminal in obedience to the ground controller's orders. Sherry steered to the right suddenly as the three-engine jetliner loomed ahead. The baggage carts followed behind them, moving into position between the tug and the mobile stairs, now less than fifty yards behind.

"Hold on to something!" she yelled at Rusty.

"I *am* holding!" he yelled back at her.

More bullets hit the carts behind them. The shooting would have to stop as they neared the aircraft. Even for a team of renegade Company agents, there would be no salvation if they ignited an airliner full of passengers with a runaway bullet.

Sherry was aiming at a spot beneath the empennage of the 727 right under the tail skid, her foot to the floorboard of the tug. The pinging of bullets had stopped, but the sound of the truck engine propelling the mobile stairs behind them could be heard now above the loud whine of the tug's engine.

The 727 was just ahead of them. Sherry held a steady course until the aft end of the fuselage flashed over their heads, then she threw the steering wheel to the left, almost overturning the tug.

As she had intended, the baggage carts behind her shuddered and lurched and spewed baggage to their right as they tried to follow the errant tug, and the rearmost cart turned on its side as Sherry accelerated again and aimed halfway between the right main landing gear and the right wingtip. The aircraft's flaps were up and she had calculated how tall the baggage carts were. The driver of the mobile stairs truck wouldn't be able to follow without going around, buying them precious seconds.

Rusty was looking back as the baggage carts moved far enough to one side to give him a clear view of the truck behind them. The driver had been concentrating on his quarry, so the looming mass of the 727's right wing didn't register until the stairway riding on the modified pickup truck fairly exploded into the wing's rear section. With a moderate amount of fuel remaining in the plane's tank, the resulting explosion of flame and fire engulfed the truck below in a sudden fireball. The truck, stripped of its stairs and on fire, skidded to a halt, the two occupants spilling out of their respective doors, one of them with flames licking at his back. As the fireball engulfed the entire right wing, the emergency exit slides began appearing on the left side of the aircraft and the passengers began spilling out. The tower ground controller hit his crash alarm and picked up a handset to direct fire trucks to the scene.

Rusty, stunned, turned back toward the front of the tug as Sherry drove it headlong into the baggage area of the terminal and slammed on the brakes. Rusty followed when Sherry jumped off the tug and ran toward the moving conveyer belt ahead. She rolled onto the belt and pulled him with her, letting the machine carry them through the portal onto the baggage carousel beyond.

With the sound of sirens in their ears and the attention of most of the crowd focused on the burning 727 on the ramp beyond, Sherry and Rusty jumped off the carousel, ignoring the stares of startled passengers, and raced toward the front entrance. There was a line of passengers waiting for cabs. She headed for the nearest taxi and yanked open the door, propelling Rusty inside as she turned to the dispatcher, who had turned angrily in her direction.

"U.S. government emergency!" she yelled at him, knowing the words would confuse the man just long enough.

"Go, go, go, go, go!" she said to the driver, holding out her CIA badge as he nodded and pulled away from the curb.

They accelerated into traffic and headed for the 14th Street Bridge. Rusty could see black smoke from the

burning airplane rising over the park behind them and
the flashing lights of a score of emergency vehicles that
had converged on the scene.

Sherry pulled the phone out of her purse and dialed
information. She secured the number of Senator
Moon's office and punched it in as they emerged from
the eastern side of the bridge.

"Where should he go?" Rusty asked. "Which building?"

"The Hart Building!" she replied.

As they passed L'Enfant Plaza, Sherry snapped the
phone shut and turned to Rusty.

"The Senator's on the Senate floor right now. They're
going to get him back to the office. You heard what I
told his Administrative Assistant. We're to go straight to
his office."

For ten minutes they rode in silence, looking behind,
fearful that they were still being chased, until the cab
pulled up on the south side of the Hart Building. Rusty
hurriedly paid the driver and followed Sherry into the
building, past security, and up the elevator to the second
floor.

They were about to round the corner of the last corridor when Rusty grabbed her shoulder and held her
back.

Sherry turned and looked at him in alarm. "What?"

Rusty shook his head. "I don't know. It's a feeling,
like it's too easy. Half the government should be looking
for us by now."

"This is a safe haven, though," Sherry urged. "Security would have nabbed us if that were the plan. If they
knew we were here."

"What if Moon's assistant called Roth?" Rusty asked.

"Why would she do that?"

Rusty thought a second and nodded. "Okay. Okay,
but wait a second." He moved to the corner of the corridor and carefully peered around it. Sherry joined him.
The offices of Senator Moon were halfway down on the
left, in clear view. The door was open, and there were

apparently no other individuals waiting in the broad corridor, though people he assumed were staff members were walking briskly in either direction.

Sherry nodded to Rusty and they both moved into the corridor toward the office.

Rusty's stomach was in a knot. If the senator was on the Senate floor when they called, had there been enough time to call him back? Probably not. Less than fifteen minutes had elapsed. There was nothing illogical about having them come to his office, but Rusty had a nagging feeling that something was wrong.

Through the open door of the office less than twenty yards ahead, Rusty could see several people standing in the waiting room. One of them leaned out slightly to check the corridor, spotting the two approaching CIA employees. The man moved back inside the doorway, and Rusty could sense sudden movement within. Sherry stopped as a second man sauntered past the doorway, looking squarely at them, and pausing when he realized they weren't moving. There was a moment of indecision, and the man suddenly moved into the corridor.

"Dr. Sanders? Is that you?"

Whether it was the voice or the use of his name, Rusty couldn't explain. But the closing trap was all too obvious. He grabbed Sherry's arm and propelled them both back the way they had come, well aware of several men cascading out of the senator's office after them.

He knew the Hart Building well. There was a stairway just ahead that would take them down to the tram tunnel that led to the Capitol Building. There was no way even a renegade agent would risk firing a weapon in a tunnel full of senators.

They took the stairs two at a time, cognizant of the footsteps gaining behind them, and ran down the ramp toward the shuttle at full speed. A shuttle was just leaving and they pushed past one of the guards and into the last seat just before it moved forward.

Three men appeared on the landing, one of them hurriedly speaking into a radio as another spoke to the guard. Rusty looked forward. There were at least three senators aboard he recognized, and the Secretary of Commerce. They wouldn't stop the shuttle, but Rusty was sure there would be a reception committee at the other end.

"What do we do now?" Sherry whispered to him.

"Get your ID ready. We'll have to talk fast. The people at the other end will be the Capitol Police."

Rusty turned for a last look behind them. Two of the uniformed guards were arguing with one of the agents. A second agent was trying to restrain the first, who was obviously angry. As Rusty watched, the angry agent shoved the guard and in an instant a flurry of guns were drawn and aimed at the three CIA employees. The shuttle rounded a bend and obscured the view as Rusty dared to hope the action would stay on the Hart end of the tunnel.

The shuttle moved underneath the Capitol and came to a halt. There were guards there as well, but no one seemed to be paying any attention to the two of them as Rusty guided Sherry up the ramp and into the elevator. Two other guards burst from around a corner, running toward the shuttle. As they passed, they spotted the elevator door closing and skidded to a halt, one of them trying to lunge for the door in time to stop it. Rusty saw the guard's hands thrust forward just as the doors slid shut.

The elevator began to move upward. Several people were inside, all of them wondering what was going on. Radio calls to the floor above would be in progress. The guards would have only a partial description, and there were three other women aboard.

"Separate!" Rusty whispered in Sherry's ear. "Follow me separately to the cloakroom."

The doors opened to reveal a collection of six policemen, all scrutinizing the exiting passengers without interfering, all of them looking for a man and a woman together. Following another man, Rusty was one of the first off the elevator. Sherry had moved back as far as she could. She exited with another woman, talking to her as if they were together.

A couple toward the back of the elevator walked together through the door and were surrounded instantly.

Rusty moved down the familiar corridors to the guarded section leading to the Senate cloakroom. He presented his ID to the guard and asked if Senator Moon was ready.

"For what?" the man asked.

"I'm here to escort him to a briefing. Is he on the floor?"

Rusty was aware of Sherry's entering the room behind him. He gave no sign of recognition as the guard scratched his head, satisfied the ID was real.

"If you'll wait here, Doctor, I'll check."

The guard turned his back on Rusty and began to walk toward the cloakroom. Rusty motioned in a small, sharp gesture to Sherry who moved to his side, and they followed the man through the stanchions. The guard had entered the cloakroom itself before something told him he was being followed. He turned around, instantly angered to see Rusty behind him. At the same moment, Sherry spotted the senator several yards away.

"Hold on! Right there!" the guard ordered. The presence of Sherry confused him. "Who are you, ma'am?" he asked.

She ignored him and tried to slip past into the alcove.

"Senator Moon?" she called. Heads turned in the cloakroom.

The guard had Sherry by the arm and was blocking Rusty. There were footsteps running down the corridor from which they'd come, and a voice shouting, "Hold them!"

"GET DOWN, EVERYONE! HE'S ARMED!" one of the shouting figures yelled. A gun cleared his coat. Rusty could see a silencer on the end of it. His mind shifted into high speed as the images before him slowed to a crawl.

The gunman slid to his knees in a shooter's stance, his

muzzle aimed in the general direction of Rusty's head. The hammer clicked into position with an unmistakable sound. There would be no time to duck. The inevitability of being shot washed over him just as a tall man brushed past from behind and moved between Rusty and the gunman.

"Hold it!" the man's deep baritone voice commanded.

The gunman instantly uncocked his weapon and got to his feet.

"It's okay, Martin," the tall man said to the gunman. "I'll take care of it from here."

Rusty heard a single "Yessir." He heard Sherry gasp.

The unmistakable voice of Senator Moon came from just behind them.

"What the hell's going on out here?"

The senator moved beside them as Rusty focused in disbelief on the face of the tall man who had saved his life.

Jonathan Roth!

Roth looked at Rusty Sanders.

"Been spinning some conspiracy theories, have we, Doctor?"

Senator Moon's voice interceded again. "Sherry Ellis! What are you doing here?" He turned to Roth. "Are these the two you mentioned, Jon?"

"Yes, Senator."

Rusty turned to the senator. "Sir, I've got evidence . . ."

Moon held up his hand to stop him. "You talk to your boss here, and then you and Sherry and Deputy Director Roth are invited to meet me in my office in thirty minutes."

Senator Moon turned and walked back toward the Senate floor as Jon Roth's right hand came down gently on Rusty's shoulder. Rusty turned to look at the deputy director, who was alternately looking at Sherry and him.

"You've got this wrong, you know," Roth said. "Both of you do."

"I don't think so, Director," Rusty said.

"Things aren't always as they appear. You've misread clues, Rusty, jumped to conclusions, and apparently thought we were trying to get rid of you. We need to talk. Immediately. Thanks to your two-person demolition act, I've got two people in the hospital, a burning airplane at National, and the chairman of our oversight committee madder than hell at being disturbed with a cockamamie claim that the deputy director is out trying to hire terrorists to shoot down that seven-forty-seven."

Roth began steering them back toward the corridor.

Rusty refused to move, and Roth turned to look at him with a sigh.

"What, Doctor?"

"I gave you evidence of an internal renegade operation. You said you'd take care of it."

"You did, and I acted immediately. You never called in, did you, Sanders? I told you to dig in and report back to me. I never had the chance to tell you that what you'd found was not what it seemed. You uncovered a plot, all right, but it wasn't hatched by the CIA, and it wasn't hatched by me. Okay?"

Rusty glanced at Sherry, then back at Roth.

"Can we go now?" Roth said, the familiar irritation in his voice replacing the feigned friendliness he'd used in front of the senator.

"Where?" Sherry asked.

Roth sighed. "To the senator's office, of course."

TWENTY-EIGHT

"*There!*"

Yuri Steblinko's index finger tapped the glass of the
tactical radar display, which was set to the hundred-fifty-
mile range. A minute before, a bright, steady blip had
crawled onto the scope dead ahead of the Gulfstream.
For seven sweeps of the antenna he had waited to see if
it would disappear, but it remained—precisely when and
where he had expected.

Yuri checked his watch. He would reach firing position less than a hundred miles north of the island.

ABOARD FLIGHT 66

It was time.

On the flight deck James Holland reached up and
nudged a small, vertical plastic wheel toward the nose-
down position, beginning a gentle autopilot descent. Ascension was a hundred fifty miles ahead and showing
now on the radar. He wanted to be at five hundred feet
above the water by fifty miles out.

Dick Robb was climbing back in the right seat, deep
circles under his eyes, his collar open, his airline regulation tie long since discarded.

• • •

Rachael, too, had returned to the cockpit after a few hours of sleep. She found James Holland alone, and felt relieved. There was no reason to dislike the copilot, but she felt out of place in his presence.

For thirty minutes Rachael sat in silence beside Holland in the observer's chair. James finally turned and smiled at her—and reached for her hand. She found the combined rush of warmth and need that engulfed her immensely startling, but she smiled back and squeezed his large hand in return. His presence brought a feeling of security that defied the logic of their predicament.

And when time came to wake the copilot, Rachael felt a small wave of resentment.

"How're we doin' on fuel?" Robb asked as he settled back into the right seat.

"About where we figured. We've got about twenty-three thousand remaining," Holland replied, giving him a long, appraising look. "How're you doing, Dick? Get any real rest?"

Robb nodded, rubbing his eyes. "A bit. Enough. When the hubbub settles down after we land, I'll need more."

Holland nodded. "So will I. So will all of us."

There was a pause as Robb glanced at Rachael and smiled a friendly smile, which she returned. He looked back toward the captain.

"James, I was lying back there thinking. Maybe we should check the shortwave broadcasts again, just in case something's changed, or just in case someone's organized an armed reception for us at Ascension."

"If they are, they are. We don't have enough fuel to go anywhere else," Holland said.

Robb nodded and thought it over.

"I guess you're right," he said at last.

Holland glanced at him. "Actually, Dick, I did try myself a while ago with a small worldband shortwave one of the passengers has on board. I couldn't pick up anything. The signal strength down here below the equator is too low with all the electronic interference we're generating inside this cockpit. All I get is static and loud squeals."

There was another return on the radar now, dead ahead about sixty miles north of the island, and Robb pointed to it.

"Looks like we've got a weather cell out there. I see red in the middle."

"Isolated thunderstorm." Holland nodded. "That's a little surprising for the predawn hours. It's probably the remnant of a real monster from yesterday."

"You going to steer around it?" Robb asked.

Holland nodded. "But not until we're a bit closer."

A moonless starfield hung before them on the other side of the windscreen against an ink-black sky. The sun wouldn't begin painting the horizon for another half hour. In the meantime, there was nothing below but blackness passing at seventy-two percent of the speed of sound. Holland began dimming the cockpit and instrument lights to adjust their night vision. A hint of fuzzy light on the horizon announced the presence of Ascension Island. The small thunderstorm cell was twenty miles ahead now and Holland eased the autopilot to the west so that the plane would clear it by ten miles as it moved east. There were occasional lightning flashes from within the cloud, and a steady red blob on the radar indicated it was a tightly packed little storm with quite a bit of power. But elsewhere the picture was clear, and the mass of Ascension was crawling steadily across the radar screen toward them.

"Not enough of a cut," Holland said as he changed course to head forty-five degrees to the right.

Holland peered into the night as Dick Robb watched the radar screen. Robb began staring at it intently, puzzled by lines that suddenly appeared on the screen, then disappeared.

He felt a chill up his back. He had seen such lines before—as they had approached the African coast many hours ago.

"Uh, James . . ." he began.

Holland looked at him and followed his gaze to the screen, which just as quickly cleared of everything but the echoes of the island and the storm.

Holland looked at the radar screen, then back at Robb, sensing his discomfort.

"What was it, Dick? Were you seeing something?"

Robb remained still for a moment as his eyes tracked the screen, then shook his head in the negative.

No need to sound paranoid. Fatigue is making me jumpy.

"Just some lines on the scope, sort of like before. But no fighter could have followed us across three thousand miles of ocean."

Yuri Steblinko switched his attack scope to the fifty-mile range and checked the Heads-Up Display. The 747 was dead ahead now, less than ten miles and closing—though much closer to the island than he had planned.

No matter. The Boeing's wreckage would still fall in deep water.

The 747 was running dark, without position lights or beacons, which made it invisible against the dark starfield. But Yuri's attack display clearly showed the Boeing as a phosphorescent target.

The jumbo had been descending for some time. Yuri estimated the altitude now at five thousand. Obviously the captain had learned how to run on the surface to avoid radar.

Yuri smiled to himself and shook his head. *So that's how he slipped away before!*

He maneuvered the Gulfstream slightly to the right. The plan was simple: lock a missile on to the heat signature of the 747's right inboard engine and blow it off the wing. The 747's captain would suddenly be faced with a worst-case flight control problem: two engines gone on one side.

And, with any luck, Yuri thought, the explosion would

take the wing off at the same time. If not, there were two more missiles.

This time, he doesn't suspect I'm here.

Yuri triggered the switch to lower the left missile rack into the slipstream and felt the plane respond to the drag. As soon as it stabilized, he walked the pipper onto the target and began moving it to the right, searching for a clear definition of the infrared signature from the remaining right engine.

A few more miles!

The Gulfstream's closing speed on the Boeing was in excess of a hundred knots. Yuri calculated he was close enough and pulled back the throttles, letting the business jet slow to match the jumbo's velocity exactly.

The number three engine—the inboard right one—flared brightly now on the attack screen, and he pressed the appropriate button to lock the missile's warhead on target. They were down to fifteen hundred feet, the descent shallowing, the 747 still clipping along at more than two hundred fifty knots.

Yuri decided to wait until he leveled out, regardless of how low the 747 went. An explosion just above the water would give the pilot no recovery room. Even if they were still flyable, a panicked maneuver could drive the 747 into the waves and finish it.

Sure enough, Flight 66 descended through a thousand feet, slowly stabilizing at five hundred.

Yuri checked his navigation display. They were fifty-two miles north of Ascension.

That was close enough! It was time.

He brought the Gulfstream two miles aft of the 747 and rechecked the lock-on, which was set to drive the warhead right up the tail pipe of number three engine. The infrared tracker was growling at high pitch and warbling in his ear with excitement. He caressed the trigger and reviewed everything once again. The captain had been immensely crafty, he thought. It was a shame the man had come so close to making it to Ascension before being blown out of the sky. It would have been prefera-

ble to finish him off many hours ago, before hope had
had a chance to grow again for those poor people.

Yet there could be no hope, Yuri reminded himself.
Whether the wreckage sank near the Canary Islands or
in the middle of the trackless South Atlantic was immaterial.

*Remember, they're all about to sicken and die anyway.
Some may already be dead.*

Yuri pressed the trigger.

Immediately, the sound of a rocket motor igniting
and propelling the missile off the rails toward the jumbo
ahead filled the cockpit. The glow of the rocket exhaust
seemed to corkscrew in front of him only a fraction of a
second before reaching the target. Then the sudden, almost painful flare of the explosion loomed amazingly
large where the 747 had been.

There was a huge explosion to the right of Quantum
66's cockpit. The soul-jarring impact illuminated the
whole side of the aircraft in a bright orange phosphorescent flare, accompanied by a massive shudder as the
number three engine exploded off its pylon and pieces
of disintegrating turbine and fragmented engine parts
clanked and crashed into the wing and fuselage, as if the
pilots had just flown through an airborne junkyard.

"WHAT THE HELL?" came from Robb and Holland almost simultaneously.

In the cabin below, a collective gasp could clearly be
heard above the roar of the explosion as sleeping passengers came awake with a jolt of adrenaline and the
reflection of fire in their peripheral vision. They gripped
armrests with hearts in their throats, momentarily convinced they were crashing. They looked toward the
right, spotting the dying flames and sparks from the
number three engine, then realized they were still flying.

On the flight deck James Holland grabbed the control
yoke and clicked off the autopilot in one fluid motion as
he looked hard toward the engine instruments. Dick

Robb's face had snapped to the right, the light partially erasing his night vision.

"Number three is down!" Holland said.

Robb looked back to the quadrant, fighting to see around the bright spot hovering in his visual field.

"How the hell could that explode?" Holland asked.

Robb's eyes were still affected, but his mind's eye was not. He thought of the momentary spokes on the radar minutes before.

"Another missile, James! Our assailant is back. We're being chased!"

"Couldn't be the same bastard!"

"Airspeed!" Robb called.

Holland nodded. He'd already boosted the two engines on the left wing, and pressed the rudder hard to compensate for the aircraft's tendency to roll to the right.

"How far out are we?" Holland asked.

"Forty-five miles," Robb answered.

"Sonofabitch!" Holland swore as he looked left. He rolled the airplane in the same direction, into the good engines, pulling the nose up to climb at the same time.

"What're you doing, James?"

"Whoever's back there is waiting to see what happens. We have to give him—or them, if it's a them—a show. We can't bore straight ahead or he'll shoot again."

The 747 was in a forty-five-degree left bank and climbing through eight hundred feet as Holland struggled to see anything behind them. The attacker would be able to turn with them, but . . .

Holland turned to the right. "Gear down! Flaps one!"

Robb looked momentarily shocked, but his hands were already complying.

"Gear down, flaps one," Robb repeated, watching the gauges for any asymmetrical movement of the leading edge devices or the trailing edge flaps. "So far they're coming out okay."

Holland pulled the power back to idle and leveled the

wings. He pushed the nose over and let the 747 drop back down to a hundred feet before bringing the power back in and turning gently with a shallow bank to the right, holding the turn until he was moving to the southwest and in the general direction of the island.

Time seemed to go by with agonizing slowness. He expected another explosion at any second.

"If . . ." he began, struggling to talk while concentrating on the flying, "I . . . can keep him confused . . . we might get close enough."

"James, we're at a hundred feet. Don't dig a wingtip in the water or we're dead!"

"Watch me like a hawk, Dick! Watch the radio altimeter! We're gonna make it!"

Yuri pulled up immediately after the explosion of the 747's engine, worried about flying through the debris. He banked right and moved laterally a half mile to the west before resuming course and straining to see the jumbo out to the left.

The radar return was still there and getting stronger as it . . . *turned left!*

Another maneuver, eh? he thought. *This time you've nowhere to run.*

Yuri banked the Gulfstream to the left, wondering whether the captain would fly a complete circle or settle down in some other direction. Or did he even have a plan? The explosion had not blown off the wing or taken their flight controls, as he had wished.

Yuri leveled at one thousand on an eastbound heading as he watched the scope. The return appeared to be breaking up.

Aha! Descending to wave level again, are we?

Yuri dropped his altitude as well, turning to the left slightly to bring his radar squarely onto the point where the return from the jumbo had disappeared.

He settled into three hundred feet, picking up nothing but wave clutter from up ahead. A brief target flared farther to the north, but he refused to believe it. A second target flared to the right, then broke up again.

He looked at his infrared scope, but could make out nothing ahead.

Maybe he went in? Yuri thought, then immediately remembered that the same mistaken conclusion had cost him dearly before.

No, he's still out there, and he's too low on gas to go anywhere but Ascension. This time I know where to find him.

The scope was still clear ahead. Yuri banked left to sweep the ocean surface in that direction, then back to the right. At the range he was searching, there was nothing but waves.

Very clever, but I'll get you on the approach to Ascension!

Yuri began climbing back in the direction of the island. He would race to the south of the approach path to the east–west runway, and then loiter there, flying a loose holding pattern as he shot his radar back toward the airport. When the 747 showed up, he would see it without question.

There were two missiles left.

ABOARD FLIGHT 66

In the crew rest facility at the rear of the aircraft, Gary Strauss awoke in pain and panic as the force of the explosion amplified itself at the aft end of the 747 with a pronounced lurch to the left.

Stefani awoke at the same moment and gripped his arm. The soft warmth of her presence had lulled him to sleep and the flight attendants had turned off the lights. Now the two of them held on to each other in pitch darkness, wondering what was coming.

"Stefani?"

"I'm here. What was that?"

He shook his head before remembering the darkness. "I don't know!"

"Can you move over?"

"Why?" he asked.

"Because I want you to hold me. I'm very frightened."

He felt himself swallow hard as the jumbo lurched and Stefani rolled into the bed and molded her body to his.

In the first class cabin, Lee Lancaster saw the orange flash of the explosion and guessed what had happened. He looked to his right at the ashen faces of Garson Wilson and his secretary—and the wide eyes of the older couple Rachael had pointed out before. He smiled at them, and they tried to smile back as the huge aircraft began a violent roll to the left—and seemed to start climbing!

By door 2L, Barb Rollins froze a regulation smile in place and tried to dig her fingers into the cover of the jump seat without anyone's noticing. She should be numb by now, she thought, but she was more frightened than ever. The thought of calling James flashed through her mind, but whatever had happened now was going to be keeping him very busy. She could wait. Pray and wait.

There was nothing but blackness beyond the windscreen. Holland struggled to hold the 747 a mere hundred feet above the water, fully aware that one mistake would kill them all. The jet was bucking and only marginally cooperative. Holland and Robb both suspected extensive metal damage under the right wing, but the big Boeing was responding to all control inputs, and they still had two hydraulic systems.

Holland knew that whoever was trying to kill them would have time to find them again, but if he could keep the plane low enough to the water, he might be able to evade the fighter's attack radar. It was a pure gamble, but it was all he had left.

Bringing the heading back left until the heading selector needle was sitting squarely on the island, Holland saw the distance remaining click down to forty-two miles. He pushed the remaining two engines up as far as he could and held the nose of the Boeing down as the airspeed increased to two hundred eighty knots.

"You gonna leave the gear down?" Robb asked.

Holland nodded. "We've got it out and locked. Let's not fool with it."

"Roger," Robb replied.

There was no sign of the assailant, but they knew he was still out there. Maybe there was more than one. And why? Why were they being attacked? That was something they didn't have time to think about. The attacker had been like a ghost in the blackness.

"How about sounding a Mayday?" Robb asked.

Holland shook his head. "Won't do any good. Any fighters on Ascension would be looking to join him in downing us."

"Who *is* he?" Rachael asked. Her voice was thick, her throat obviously dry. She had been gripping the center console and watching with wide eyes.

James Holland shook his head. "I can't believe it's the same guy who attacked us before, but if it is, he's like some sort of demon who won't leave us alone. We don't have a clue what kind of airplane that is. Fighters can't fly three thousand miles without refueling."

"Twenty-five miles, James. We're closing on it."

Dick Robb was watching the numbers click downward slowly as they raced toward Ascension at four and a half miles per minute.

"There's a rise to the runway," Robb continued, glancing at the map. "The threshold sits a hundred feet off the water."

Holland nodded. "We'll pop up at three miles out."

He glanced at the outline of the runway Dick Robb

had built on the flight management computer screen. It
ran about forty degrees to the left of their heading.

"Build me an aim point on the screen three miles to
the west on the approach, Dick. I'll use that as the pop-
up point."

Robb's fingers typed a rapid series of keystrokes into
the box and a tiny diamond-shaped point appeared at
the appointed spot.

"We're eight miles from it," Robb announced.

"Make a PA, Dick. Get them ready."

The Gulfstream passed abeam the Ascension airport at
a range of eight miles and an altitude of a thousand feet,
its radar return thoroughly puzzling thé island's American contract air traffic controllers, who had been watching a strange progression of high- and then low-altitude
returns from the north, all coming toward them without
transponders, without clearance, and without radio contact.

"If this were back in the Falkland war with Argen-
tina," one of the controllers said to his supervisor, "I'd
think we were under attack."

The blip that had moved to the southwest of the airport now seemed to be turning back to the north. As
they watched, it ran two miles north and then reversed
course to the south, picking up speed and then turning
and slowing to the north again, as if waiting for something.

A streak of light was beginning to paint the eastern
sky as the sunrise sequence began, but there was nothing but inky blackness in the direction of the radar returns to the west. The tower controllers strained to see
something with their binoculars, but there was nothing
visible.

"A UFO, d'ya suppose?" the controller asked.

Yuri had just turned north on his second circuit when
the blip generated by the radar echo from Flight 66

flared on his attack scope. The 747 was headed almost straight for the runway, as expected.

"Got you!" Yuri said aloud.

He mentally plotted a course to fly past and turn quickly. The jumbo was getting too close to shallow waters and the island.

I can't let him reach the shoreline.

Yuri flew within a quarter mile of the 747 before reversing course with a sixty-degree bank to the right. He could barely make out the hulking shape of the machine in the beginning glimmer of dawn. He steadied in behind the jumbo and dropped to a hundred feet above the water as he walked his pipper to the inboard left engine.

Damn! The missile rack!

He'd forgotten to extend it. Yuri reached over and toggled the right-side missile rack to the extend position.

Nothing happened.

He hit the switch again, and a second and third time.

Oh no!

There were rows of circuit breakers behind the empty copilot's seat as well as his. He struggled to remember which ones had been added to control the extend/retract feature of the armaments. It was behind the copilot, he thought, about eight rows down.

But to reach for that at a hundred feet above the water was suicidal. Yuri shoved the power up and started a climb to a thousand feet, knowing he would pop back up on the island's radar. He snapped on the autopilot and turned on the circuit breaker panel lights as he leaned to the right, fumbling to see the breaker.

It eluded him. He strained to see around the back of the seat, trying to read the nomenclature.

It was indecipherable.

Yuri looked back at the remaining distance. He was within nine miles. It was now or never.

He strained again, his body almost horizontal across

the center pedestal as the Gulfstream's autopilot flew mindlessly toward the southeast.

The word RACK loomed in his vision in an almost inaccessible alcove.

There!

The breaker was indeed out!

He reached to touch it, but it was too far away. He strained harder, and finally, slowly, felt his fingertip move over the top of the breaker far enough to let him force it down and in with a satisfying pop.

Yuri sat up. The sound of the breaker popping back out met his ears.

"Nyet!"

He was less than five miles from the end of the runway now. Flight 66 was at three, ahead and below. He was going to lose the shot.

Yuri leaned over again and strained to reach the breaker. He shoved it in, and this time—with pain shooting through his back and side and finger—he held it in while his left hand reached for the toggle switch to extend the rack. At last his finger closed around the switch and moved it. The sound of the missile rack coming out beneath him reached his ears.

Yuri sat up as quickly as he could and retightened his seat belt. The 747 had popped up to several hundred feet now, but it was considerably below and less than a quarter mile ahead of him. There was no way he could drop into position and fire now before the jumbo reached the runway.

With a sinking feeling, he realized that the element of anonymity was lost. If they made it to the runway alive, he would be unable to land in the same place without being captured. There wasn't enough fuel to go anywhere else. So he'd have to ditch at sea—and die in the process. A fleeting thought of Anya crossed his mind and was quickly suppressed.

Yuri's eyes flared with a sudden thought. There was a chance—a slim one, but a chance nevertheless. If he destroyed the 747 on the runway, then ditched the Gulfstream by the shoreline, maybe he'd be able to swim in and tell some contrived cover story in the tiny outpost. It was a wildly slim chance, and probably futile, but he had to try.

Yuri banked hard to the right. He would do a three-hundred-sixty-degree turn and lock on to the 747's tail as he rolled out. With any luck, they would start their auxiliary power unit, presenting a brand-new target to the heat-seeking missile, which would then reprogram itself to fly right up the Auxiliary Power Unit's tailpipe. Not even a 747 could survive that.

There's a fuel tank in the tail too! he remembered.

James Holland called for the last flap setting he dared use with only two engines running. He let the 747 settle down to a seven-hundred-foot-per-minute rate of descent for the last half mile. There seemed to be no activity ahead of them. No flashing lights, and no red warning flares from the control tower, wherever it was. Ascension couldn't be aware of their presence.

The runway lights were steady and the runway itself barely visible now in the early glow on the eastern horizon.

"Jeez! We've got a flap asymmetry, James!" Robb almost yelled.

Holland was already rolling the control yoke hard left.

"Which . . . *where?*"

"Left side flaps are out farther than the right ones. They've stopped in position. We've got about ten degrees of flaps on the left, seven on the right."

"I can feel it! She's trying really hard to roll right, and I'm almost out of control authority! Try the alternate flaps! I can't hold it!"

Holland's left foot was pressing the left rudder pedal as hard as he dared while his hand pushed in a slight increase of power on the left two engines. With power only under the left wing, coupled with an out-of-symmetry flap condition trying to roll them to the right, the 747 staggered the final half mile toward the runway, threatening to roll over on its side.

Robb had already reached for the alternate flap switch. He snapped it on now and toggled the flaps back toward the up position, a click at a time, feeling the 747 respond as the undamaged left flaps moved back toward the seven-degree position and the controls brought them back to wing level.

"That's good! Stop it there!" Holland commanded as Robb let go of the switch.

The threshold was disappearing beneath the cockpit.

"Fifty feet, forty, thirty . . ." Robb called out the radio altimeter readings as Holland retarded the thrust levers and worked the rudders to straighten the aircraft, flaring slightly, letting the 747 settle onto the hard surface before pulling the spoilers and stepping on the brakes. He could see a huge hill looming just to the right of the runway, another to the left, but there seemed to be a turnaround taxiway leading in a loop off to the left and back on the runway at the far end. Holland let the speed drop to twenty knots and began turning left on the turnaround.

"Thank God!" Robb said.

"Amen," Holland echoed. "Whoever it is won't have much of a target with us on the ground. The engines will cool fast. There won't be an infrared target. Let's run the After Landing Checklist."

Dick Robb ran through the after-landing flow, repositioning switches according to normal procedure. In passing along the forward panel, his hand routinely placed the APU switch to the run position, and hundreds of feet to the rear in the tail cone of the 747, an electric motor began winding up the small jet engine that provided electrical power and pressurized bleed air on the ground. When it reached a certain minimum number of revolutions per minute, the engine control computer ordered the fuel valve to open and the ignitor plugs to fire, igniting the fuel—which rapidly accelerated the APU as it spewed hot gasses out its tailpipe with temperatures exceeding six hundred degrees centigrade.

Yuri completed his turn and accelerated before looking at the infrared signature of the 747 rolling out ahead of him. There was a sudden flare from the middle of the tail section just as expected.

He's starting the APU!

He brought the Gulfstream into a steady, shallow dive and locked the pipper on the APU exhaust as he pulled the throttles back to cross the runway threshold at less than two hundred knots.

The bright IR flare jogged to the right suddenly, surprising Yuri. Then it began fading. His finger felt the trigger. The 747 was turning off the runway. If he didn't get the missile off in time, the target and the hot engine exhaust pipes for the engines on the left wing would be masked.

Yuri jammed his finger back on the trigger and felt the missile roar off the rail as he passed over the end of the runway. He could see the 747 turning rapidly to the left. He saw the missile exhaust disappear straight down the runway—and realized almost too late the height of the hill on his right.

Yuri pulled up sharply, barely clearing the top of the hill, and banked left to watch.

There was a tremendous explosion almost beneath him as the missile impacted the 747's tail section. Flames and debris erupted in all directions, and in the glare of the light, he saw the entire tail of the jumbo twist and fall to the concrete—*as the 747 continued to taxi!*

"God, what now?" Robb yelled.

The explosion had shaken the entire aircraft and thrown the three people in the cockpit back and forth with a frightening vengeance.

Holland moved quickly, checking instruments and calling out to Robb.

"Dick, call the back! See if we've got a fire."

Dick Robb grabbed the telephone handset and pushed the all-call button. Barb Rollins and several other flight attendants answered almost instantly.

"What's our status back there?" Robb asked.

"There was a terrible explosion! There's a hole in the back of the cabin. I'm not sure it didn't get the crew rest loft! I see debris hanging down at the back. One of the number five doors is open, or gone. Do you want us to evacuate?"

"Tell her no, Dick! This is a bad spot. Unless the cabin starts filling with smoke, give me enough time to get us to that ramp!"

"Not yet!" Dick Robb said. "Any smoke in the cabin?"

"No," Barb replied, "but I think I can see some flickers out the back area, maybe out the side windows. I don't know. There's no smoke, though."

"Stand by, Barb. We'll call you. But you call us instantly if there's smoke!"

"Okay." Her voice was frightened, but steady.

Holland pushed up the throttles for engines one and two to hurry the process of taxiing back to the runway.

"Do we still have hydraulics, Dick?"

Robb looked at the gauges. "One and two are still steady. The APU's zeroed. I think he . . . they . . . someone hit our tail area, or the APU exploded."

"It feels like we're standing on our nose. We're very nose-heavy," Holland said almost to himself.

Yuri couldn't believe the 747 was still moving on the runway. In spite of his mission, his respect for the 747's structural toughness had increased tenfold with each failed attempt to destroy it. He couldn't help admiring it —and the skill of its indefatigable captain.

What a magnificent airplane!

He could see fire where the tail section had exploded and literally fallen off, but the rest of the airplane was still intact.

One more chance!

Yuri pulled up and began a whifferdill, a sudden course reversal to get back to the runway—an aerobatic maneuver business jets were not supposed to use.

Yuri had a split-second decision to make. There wasn't enough room to land in front of the intersection where the taxiway reentered the runway surface, nor was there time to steady out the Gulfstream and fire from behind. The 747 was trying to reach the intersection ahead of him.

But there *was* enough room to land, roll by the jumbo, then turn and shoot the last missile.

How he would get away after that was unimportant now. All his instincts from years as an operative pushed everything else from his mind. He had zeroed in on the goal, and nothing else mattered.

Yuri snapped the gear down as he ran the flaps out and slowed. The 747 was moving at probably fifteen knots back toward the runway. He should pass the jumbo's nose just as the 747's nosewheel entered the runway. It was going to be close!

Yuri armed the last missile on the right rack. There was no time for a checklist. The gear and flaps were down and the Gulfstream settled into a glide through the last few hundred feet. He kept the landing lights off, though at the last second he thought better of it and reached for the switches.

In the cockpit of Quantum 66, James Holland had made the decision to retake the runway and dash to a broad open ramp on the south side before ordering an evacuation. The runway was just ahead. The 747 felt very strange, as if half of it were gone.

Suddenly to his left a set of halogen landing lights blazed into view from an aircraft on short final approach.

"Someone's landing, James!" Robb called out.

Holland pressed on the brakes and pulled the throttles back, then just as quickly released the brakes and shoved the throttles up.

"What are you doing?" Robb yelled.

"That's the son of a bitch! He wants the runway! But he's not going to get it!"

The 747 continued moving forward, its speed cut to ten knots. Holland reached up and snapped on every landing light he had.

Yuri saw the lights of Flight 66 come on suddenly and realized the jumbo was still moving toward the runway boundary. He understood instantly.

The Gulfstream settled through the last fifty feet and Yuri kept it flying, milking the landing and stretching the glide to pass the 747's entry point as fast as possible.

The jumbo's nosewheel rolled across the runway boundary just ahead. The 747's captain was accelerating, trying to block the Gulfstream's path. Yuri let the main landing gear touch and used the rudder to steer left. He was within two hundred yards of the 747 now, moving at a hundred twenty knots. The jumbo was a quarter of the way across the runway and showing no signs of turning or slowing.

Yuri edged farther to the left, the remaining tarmac becoming more and more constrained as the tailless 747 passed the midway point and continued toward the left boundary.

The big Boeing was in his windscreen now, just to the right, moving in on him. He had miscalculated the speed. Yuri dared not touch the brakes, but he'd have to brake hard on the other side if he made it. The Gulfstream was still traveling at more than one hundred thirty miles per hour.

The nose of the 747 was a blaze of moving lights to his right as Yuri moved the last few feet to the left on the runway, the left main gear tracking almost off the edge. There was a flash of light and motion, and for a split second he expected an impact and a spinning crash as the right wing impacted the 747's nose gear.

But in the same instant he passed.

He jammed on the brakes then, his heart pounding as the aircraft began to slow down.

James Holland had his teeth gritted hard enough to break a tooth. He prayed for the sound of an impacting wing below as the assailant flashed past from left to right. In the same instant he realized they had missed, he had to slam on the brakes and jam the nose steering tiller to the right to keep from sailing off the left side of the runway.

A business jet!

Could it be that *wasn't* the assailant? Holland fought for control as he steadied the 747 back in the middle of the runway and let it accelerate toward the decelerating biz jet.

"What the hell?" he said out loud.

Dick Robb was pointing over the glareshield.

"James! For God's sake, he's got a missile rack on that mother! On the right side!"

"A *Gulfstream?* Impossible!"

"He does!"

"Call the tower, Dick. Do they know who he is?"

"They don't know who *we* are!"

"I know, but do it."

Robb had preselected the tower frequency hours before with no intention of using it. He turned up the volume now and transmitted.

"Ascension tower, this is the 747. Do you have an identification of the other aircraft on the runway?"

The response was shrill and instantaneous.

"Good Lord, man, he's the bastard who just shot your tail off! We don't know who he is. You're on fire, if you didn't know it!"

"Thanks!" Robb said.

The Gulfstream was braking hard ahead in the distance. Holland saw the entrance to the ramp area coming up on his left. That was the plan, to go left. But the Gulfstream . . .

"Dick, did he have any missiles left on that rack?"

"I . . . I think so. I'm guessing."

"He's going to fire again. He may have guns!"

Holland's right hand shoved the remaining two throttles up almost to the firewall as an alarmed Dick Robb stared at him.

"What are you going to do?" Robb asked.

"Deny him the pleasure!" Holland said.

"James . . . we need to evacuate! James?" Robb's eyes went forward. The Gulfstream was halfway around now, some two thousand feet distant and less than a thousand feet from the end of the runway, which terminated in a small cliff.

The digital readout in front of Holland registered twenty-eight knots and accelerating fast. He was having to steer hard left to keep the asymmetric thrust from driving them off the right side of the runway, but the ship continued accelerating, the lights bracketing the business jet, which had passed a thousand feet beyond the far entrance to the ramp area. There were no other taxiways or exits from the runway. He knew he was tunneled in now, but he couldn't think about that. The Gulfstream was not going to escape.

Yuri fingered the trigger as he wheeled the Gulfstream around in a one-hundred-eighty-degree turn on the runway. The infrared signature from the front of the engines should be enough to attract the remaining missile, he thought, and in the resulting confusion, maybe he could slip away.

The lights were confusing. He expected the 747 to still be halfway down the runway, but when he completed the turn, he realized it was looming toward him in what appeared to be a takeoff roll.

What the hell is he doing? He doesn't have a tail! He can't fly that thing!

The answer came in a chilling revelation. The last exit from the runway was too far ahead to reach. He couldn't take off over the 747, and he couldn't get out of its way.

And his victim—the sitting-duck jumbo jet he couldn't miss—was moving at high speed and accelerating, the sixteen huge tires of the four main landing gear assemblies tracking straight down the runway toward the prince's multi-million-dollar jet.

Yuri centered the pipper, locked the radar, and pulled the trigger in one continuous sequence.

Nothing.

He glanced in confusion to the right, wondering about circuit breakers.

No, the rack was out. The other missile had fired.

He squeezed again.

Nothing!

The fighter pilot's instinct to go to guns ran through him, but there were no guns on the prince's jet.

Again he squeezed the trigger, and again nothing happened below.

The lights ahead were closing. The speed of the 747 had to be over eighty knots now, bearing down on him inexorably. There was nowhere he could maneuver the Gulfstream to let the jumbo pass without being run over by the landing gear on one side or the other, but if he taxied off the runway surface, the Gulfstream would be junk—unflyable.

Once again he squeezed, knowing it was too late now even if the missile fired and found its mark. The warhead below was armed. If the jumbo hit him . . .

The circuit diagram! Suddenly he remembered the air/ground sensor switch. It was wired to the missile firing mechanism. The airplane had to believe it was in the air to enable the pilot to fire a missile!

He reached over calmly and disarmed the missile. It was hopeless.

James Holland reached eighty knots and pulled the power back. There was too little room to decelerate on the other side if he damaged the landing gear with what he was about to do. The sleek Gulfstream was caught like a deer in his landing lights. He could see the pilot trying to push up the power. Holland knew the only choice left to the Gulfstream's pilot was to dash for one side or the other.

Holland's left hand gripped the steering tiller, waiting for an indication of which side it would be.

"Come on, bastard!" he muttered. "Make your move!"

Yuri had fire-walled the throttles, but this wasn't a sports car with instant accelerator response. It seemed to take forever to begin moving as the huge apparition ahead of him closed in. Suddenly the engines boosted him forward and he cranked the steering tiller to the left, noting at the same moment that the 747 began swerving in the same direction.

He forced the tiller back to the right, deciding on a forty-five-degree angle off the runway. The engines had reached maxiumum thrust. The 747 was moving left in his windscreen, and he prayed the pilot had been too slow to react to the changed direction.

"Gotcha!" Holland muttered as he reversed the tiller to the left and aimed the wing gear as close as he dared to the edge.

"James!" Robb yelled. They could hear the roar of the biz jet's engines from two stories below their feet as the nose of Quantum 66 passed over the Gulfstream and snagged the T-tail.

Yuri was spun to the right by the impact of his tail section with the underside of the 747's nose. Suddenly he was accelerating not toward the runway edge but toward the rolling thunder of the main landing gear heading straight for him. He cranked the tiller frantically to the right and felt the Gulfstream claw for traction.

But it was hopeless. He was aimed right down the throat of the number two engine.

The five-hundred-thousand-pound aircraft engulfed him, the main gear rolling over and obliterating his left wing and part of the right fuselage, the number two engine nacelle taking out the rest of his airplane.

Yuri felt himself spun around amid horrible noises of ripping metal as the structure disintegrated around him and the image of his patient lover suddenly filled his mind. He gave a last cry.

"Anya!"

Holland instantly began the process of stopping the giant behemoth, jamming the brake pedals to the limit and moving the only remaining engine, number one, into reverse. The end of the runway loomed ahead, but the brakes were responding. The impact had been shattering and there had been an explosion somewhere below, but getting stopped was now the number one priority.

Slowly, agonizingly, the inexorable movement toward the red lights at the end slowed, but the brakes seemed to have given out. They were rolling at less than five knots, but they were still moving toward the cliff. The brake pedals were pushed to the floor, the emergency brake system obviously depleted. Holland pulled on the number one engine reverser even harder, feeling the entire ship shake and pivot as its compressor stalled repeatedly.

The red lights moved in slow motion under the nose and out of sight. The nose gear crept slowly, slowly to within yards of the edge, finally coming to a reluctant halt, stopping the huge ship's forward motion at last.

Holland brought the number one thrust reverser to idle. The 747 stayed in place.

Instantly the interphone buzzed with Barb on the other end.

"We've got flames at the rear licking into the cabin. We hit something down below!"

"Evacuate, Barb. Evacuate now to the right side only, and the forward four doors."

"Roger!" she said. Her voice could be heard almost instantly on the PA as Holland ordered the emergency evacuation checklist, and he and Robb began methodically running down the items.

From the viewpoint of the tower, the duel between the 747 and the Gulfstream had been somewhere beyond incredible. They had recognized the Quantum logo immediately. The word that the U.S. military simply wanted the aircraft impounded when found had already reached them.

Not through official channels, but over CNN.

One of the tower controllers had picked up the receiver to their satellite line as the sequence began. He replaced the phone now and spoke rapidly in a shrill voice propelled by adrenaline. "They say it's okay to talk to them and help them, but not to touch anyone without wearing gloves. They'll be sending Air Force transports with the proper gear. London's been notified. I've told the fire units."

The evacuation slides had come out on the right side of the aircraft and people were already rocketing down them to the runway surface. The blazing remains of the Gulfstream were fifteen hundred feet east of the 747. Quantum 66 sat pointed westward less than five hundred feet from the end of the runway surface.

The fire trucks were already rolling toward the scene. The smoke pouring out of the truncated tail section of the 747 was intensifying, and one of the tower operators had already directed the firemen to forget the Gulfstream and concentrate on the Boeing.

"Be careful! There're people everywhere down there coming out the right side!"

James Holland made certain Rachael had gone down the slide right after Lee Lancaster, before making a quick survey of the remaining people aboard. One by one he forced his crew out, including Robb, whom he'd ordered to organize things on the ground.

He could hear the fire trucks throwing foam on the tail section, but the smoke was beginning to enter the cabin. He moved back as far as the last coach section and tried to get up to the crew rest facility, but a blast of smoke boiled down the stairs as he approached and he could feel the searing heat of the flames even around the corner of the small passageway.

If anyone was still up there, he realized, it was too late.

James Holland went down the nearest slide, got to his feet, and turned around to look in horror at the twisted metal at the aft end of the fuselage where the tail section of the 747-400 had been. There was debris trailing from all the main landing gear assemblies, including the body gear under the middle of the belly, and a sizable chunk of the Gulfstream's mangled forward fuselage had been dragged along with the cockpit area, had split open, and was partially crushed.

Holland resisted the impulse to go look for the pilot. No one could have lived through that. It would be a gory scene at best. Whoever he was, he'd paid for the assault with his life.

Several people had been injured coming down the slides in the evacuation. Three of them were being carried away from the right side of the 747 to the edge of the runway. There was a man in a torn and bloody suit who seemed to have been badly banged up, and two people with leg injuries lay nearby.

Holland knelt down and examined the passenger in the business suit. He was unconscious, but breathing normally. He had lacerations on his forehead and chest, but none looked life-threatening. Nothing about the man looked familiar, and that startled him, though it was stupid to think he could memorize all two hundred fifty faces. He'd undoubtedly been one of the sea of faces in the coach cabin.

A familiar figure passed to his left, and he turned and yelled at his lead flight attendant.

"Barb!"

"James!"

He held open his arms and she came to him with a bear hug.

"You okay?" he asked.

She looked up and smiled and nodded.

"Those people in the back, Barb. You told me someone was in the upper loft . . ." His voice trailed off as Barb Rollins pointed to the edge of the crowd of milling passengers where a young woman was sitting with someone else on the ground.

"They're okay! They came tumbling out of that loft just in time when the explosion hit!"

"Thank goodness!" Holland muttered, catching sight of Rachael several yards in the distance.

Dick Robb found the captain. The airport fire chief was right behind him. Holland stood and faced the man, wondering why he would approach the group at all. Hadn't he heard who they were?

"That was one helluva show, Captain!" the chief said.

Holland shrugged. "We . . . did what we had to. Whoever that bastard was, he attacked us on the descent." Holland turned to look at the wreckage of the Gulfstream again, remembering the range of such an airplane. It hadn't been a fighter chasing them. It had been an armed business jet all along.

He turned back to the fire chief and wiped his forehead. "And, I guess, this is the same one who attacked us last night near the Canary Islands."

Was it the Canaries? Or was it Africa? It was all beginning to blend together.

"Captain?" the fire chief said.

"Yes?"

"I'm told these are probably the worst injuries." He gestured to the three laid out before him on the ramp. "Of course, whoever was in that other machine"—he gestured to the Gulfstream—"is undoubtedly dead."

Holland nodded.

"We've got an ambulance on the way," the fire chief continued. "This isn't much more than an outpost, but we'll make do. The British commander is on his way to talk to you about—"

"Look"—Holland had raised his hand, palm out, to stop the chief, then looked down and took a deep breath before meeting the man's gaze again—"You're a brave fellow to come out here and help us like this, but perhaps we should keep everyone else away for at least the next twelve hours."

The chief smiled and shook his head in puzzlement. "Whatever for, Captain?"

"Do you know who we are? Have you been following the news?"

"Certainly!" the man replied. "The whole planet has been pulling for you."

"Well, until sometime later today we're still a potential threat to anyone. We could still be carrying the virus they uncorked in Germany."

The fire chief was shaking his head. "Captain, during the night the news broke that whatever you've been exposed to can't be transferred by air. You hadn't heard, then?"

Holland shook his head. "We couldn't risk using the radios, and we were too far out for the commercial broadcasts."

"I see. Well, except for those who actually had physical contact with the infected passenger, the way I understand it is, no one on board your aircraft really has much of a chance of infection. By the way, your Air Force is already on the way with medical help and supplies. We just got the word," he added.

James Holland looked around at the mauled remains of the almost new 747-400, and at the smoking wreckage of the Gulfstream—the comparatively tiny machine that had tried so hard to kill them through the night. None of it seemed real.

"Captain?"

A passenger with a blanket around her shoulders had moved away from the main group and found him. Holland looked around and recognized her instantly. Her words and her disapproving glare had echoed in his head more than once during the past thirty hours.

"Hello, ma'am. You okay?" he asked.

She stood her ground for a few seconds as if studying him, then smiled slightly and nodded.

"Well, we made it," he added, feeling awkward.

In a sudden gesture, she extended her right hand, and he took it, feeling a firm grip despite her years.

"Captain, you remember what I told you so many hours ago?"

He nodded and smiled as he covered her right hand with his left one as well.

"You didn't trust me because I wasn't thinking for myself."

She nodded. "I was wrong."

Holland looked down at the runway surface for a few seconds and took a deep breath, then met her eyes once more.

"No ma'am. You were right. At that moment in time, you were all too right."

EPILOGUE

Rusty Sanders handed the small stack of newspaper articles back to Sherry Ellis, shaking his head in amazement. The same photograph of the crippled 747 on the runway at Ascension Island stared out at them from a half-dozen clippings.

"If Roth *wasn't* responsible, Sherry, maybe he should have been. Every civilized nation on the planet has declared war on Aqbah. Even Iran is promising to help. However this happened, Aqbah's finished, and the Saudis have been leading the charge. That sheik who lost his jet was ready to start a holy war!"

Sherry had been staring out the window, her mind elsewhere.

"So what's your vote?" he prompted. "Guilty or not guilty?"

She turned slightly, looking at him over her shoulder. "Us, or Roth?"

"Roth, of course. What do you mean, 'Us'?"

She smiled and turned back to the window.

"I honestly don't know, Rusty. Could be innocent. Could be guilty. Jon moves in mysterious ways."

"I thought that was God. *God* moves in mysterious ways."

She nodded. "Given *our* delicate position, I'd say they were effectively one and the same." She turned and looked at him. "After Jon's amazing performance in

Senator Moon's office, I was so confused I almost decided we'd been hallucinating."

"I know. Me too. He never seemed ruffled, all the evidence had disappeared without a trace, and he had an explanation for everything we saw. But if *he* wasn't the renegade, who was? *Somebody* helped Aqbah commit suicide. *Somebody* was trying to kill us!"

"Maybe," she said.

"Maybe? They were shooting at us at National Airport! They destroyed a jet chasing us!"

Sherry raised an index finger toward the ceiling and shifted to an artificially low voice. " 'But, Dr. Sanders,' said Jon Roth, 'they were only trying to hit the tires of the baggage tug you stole. If they'd wanted to kill you, they would have done so. They were trying to bring you in. That's all!' "

Rusty shook his head, then said quietly, "I know what I saw."

Sherry looked at him for several moments before replying.

"Do you? I've got to admit, Rusty, I can't absolutely say he's lying, and the intelligence fraternity will forever be convinced that spymaster Jonathan Roth pulled it off, whether he did or not."

Rusty shook his head. "I wonder if we did the right thing?"

"We had a choice?" Sherry asked, just as quickly.

"Well . . ."

She turned and put a hand on his shoulder.

"It was a Hobson's choice, remember? Just like the old English stablekeeper in, what, the sixteen hundreds? You can have any horse you want, Hobson used to tell his customers, as long as it's the one closest to the door!"

He nodded.

She moved her hand to his chin and brought his face around until their eyes were locked.

"You remember Jon's deal, Rusty? 'Shut up, forget your delusional accusations, and you two can keep your positions. *Or,* you can take your wild, unsupported story on the road and face the consequences.' In forty-eight hours we would have been branded insane and dangerous, we would have been unemployed, and Jon would have let the aggrieved parties at National Airport know where to send the subpoenas for all the damage we caused. The horse closest to the door was the only choice, bubba!"

"I know, I know."

She removed her hand. "Okay. Just remember what we promised each other. We can watch him better from the inside. What's done is done."

"I suppose. At least everyone on the jumbo got home, with three days of quarantine, no illnesses, apologies from everywhere, and first class passage. Only the insurers of the wrecked Boeing and the squashed Arab in the business jet were casualties—unless you count Aqbah, of course."

"You're forgetting Professor Helms and that young mother in Iceland," she said.

He grimaced and nodded. "You're right. I'm sorry. But the point is, Sherry, by sheer happenstance Roth looks like the sage advisor whose steady hand carried the President through a difficult crisis, rather than the Machiavellian liar who almost triggered a holocaust. He tried to play God and almost slaughtered more than two hundred and fifty lives by helping Aqbah, and we don't even know how. He's broken more laws than I can count by launching a major covert operation without a presidential finding, probably lied to the President a dozen times, lied to a senator, manipulated everyone, tried to kill us, wrecked my apartment, shattered my nerves, and . . . and . . ."

"And currently enjoys the full confidence of the executive branch and the Senate, which will rubber-stamp his confirmation as CIA Director, because not even we are sure those accusations are true," Sherry added.

He nodded. "And the only two people who really sus-

pect he's a snake remain under his direct control!"
Rusty thumped his chest with his hand. "Us."

Sherry smiled at him and cocked her head. "If you're
gonna live in a jungle, you gotta expect snakes. We do
work for the CIA. We *still* work for the CIA. There are
worse fates."

Rusty nodded and stood.

"Someday, though," he began, "some horrible virus
like that one *will* hitch a ride on a commercial jet, and
we'll lose control in a matter of hours."

The sliding glass door was unlatched and Rusty
opened it slightly, letting the thundering roar of the
waves fill the plushly decorated beachfront room. The
moon had risen over the Atlantic ocean, full and huge,
on an unusually balmy winter's evening. Below them, on
the boardwalk, a couple strolled past, obviously enjoying
each other's company as others celebrated New Year's
Eve in the distance. Even with the parties and the fire-
works, the resort community had an off-season, deserted feeling.

And Washington, D.C., lay safely in the distance, a
hundred miles to the west.

"Rusty, I'm glad you called me. I was hoping you'd
call."

Rusty turned to find her standing beside him, her hair
almost iridescent in the moonlight. He felt a bit off-
balance.

"I . . . wasn't sure, you know . . ."

"Yes, you were," she said with a smile and a toss of
her head.

"Well, how I felt, *yes,* but I mean whether you . . ."

"You knew that too!" She put a finger to his lips to
block his response, then gently put her hand on his arm
and turned him to face her.

"How long do we have here?" she asked.

"I . . . made reservations for three days."

"For only this room?" Sherry glanced over her shoulder, affecting a puzzled expression. "But . . . there's
just one bed. Where are *you* going to sleep?"

There was momentary confusion on Rusty's face as he stammered a reply.

"Well, I thought . . . I thought . . ."

"You did, huh?" Sherry asked, a grin spreading across her face as her hands began unbuttoning his shirt. Rusty smiled back at her.

"You thought right," she said. "The lady *is* willing. So! Come take me to bed, double-oh-nothing."

OVAL OFFICE, THE WHITE HOUSE, WASHINGTON, D.C.—TUESDAY MORNING, JANUARY 16

Jonathan Roth had forced the meeting, and the presidential chief of staff had made room on the calendar with undisguised reluctance. The President's schedule was impossibly hectic, but Roth had insisted he would want to hear the final report immediately.

Roth entered the room precisely on schedule at ten A.M. with an Army brigadier general, the commander of the Army infectious disease unit at Fort Detrick. The President, noting the grim expressions, motioned the two men to the couches opposite his desk.

Roth was holding a thick folder, but he did not hand it over. Instead, he cleared his throat and gestured to the general sitting nervously next to him.

"As you know, while our medical response teams were holding the crew and passengers at Ascension, we . . . I . . . recommended a longer quarantine."

"I remember clearly, Jon," the President said. "I took the responsibility for letting them come back home in three days. No one was sick. What's your point?"

"But they were, Mr. President, and we didn't know it."

"Explain that, please."

Roth already had his hand up.

"Sir, as you know, it takes exhaustive electron microscope examination of blood samples or tissue samples, done by researchers in bioisolation suits in a Level Four environment, to try to determine what a dangerous virus looks like. By the time the 747 arrived at Ascension, we had the initial pictures of the virus that killed the two researchers in Bavaria. They're calling it the Hauptmann Strain for obvious reasons. Almost at the same time, we received pictures of the virus infecting Professor Helms's blood."

Roth turned to the general, who picked up the narrative.

"Helms was definitely infected, sir, but the infection had nothing to do with his heart attack. There was a significant viral presence in his blood, and it seemed to match the Hauptmann Strain almost exactly. It even fluoresced, which is a process that helps us verify if a virus is the same as one we're comparing it to. We then drew blood from each of the passengers and crew on Flight Sixty-six while in quarantine, and it's taken us this long to confirm the results."

"You're drawing out the suspense, gentlemen. Get to the point," the President said as he leaned forward with his elbows on his knees.

"The point, sir," Roth said, "is that despite our conclusion that the virus could only infect through a fluid medium, we were wrong. Eighty-two percent of the humans aboard that flight were infected."

The President straightened up with a startled expression.

"Wait a minute! No one was *sick!* No one has become sick, and we're weeks down the road!"

"Actually, they were, Mr. President," the Army general said. "The virus mutated. The deadly Level Four pathogen that killed those two men in Bavaria mutated in Professor Helms as it infected him. Something, perhaps only one protein, changed. We have no idea what, but the viral program that began running riot in Helms's bloodstream suddenly lost the ability to sicken and kill humans, and its incubation period changed. Helms infected almost everyone aboard that seven-forty-seven, but not with the Hauptmann Strain—it was a mutated version, which takes several days longer to fully incubate. We're calling *it* the Helms Bavaria virus. Most of the passengers reached full infection status at home here in the U.S., but because there were no overt symptoms, we didn't know it, and neither did they."

"This . . . this virus . . . this Helms Bavaria is not dangerous?"

The general shook his head. "We can't assume that. It could mutate again and return to a lethal status, but now, you see, we've utterly lost control. It's out there in the population, quietly infecting without causing illness. But if it mutates again . . ."

"It could show up anywhere, at any time, as a Level Four epidemic," Roth added.

The President sat back hard on the couch, his mind racing.

"My God! That aircraft really could have been a vessel of doom. You remember we went back and forth on that." The President sat in thought for a few seconds before addressing Roth again. "Okay. How long does it take for the virus to disappear? Do you build an immunity?"

Roth looked the President in the eye as he answered.

"If we had kept them quarantined at Ascension for a month, the virus would have been totally gone. As it was, this symptomless infection was raging as they came back to their families on the twenty-seventh, and probably peaked several days after that. Each person probably infected a dozen others, and so on. The general here tells me there may be an immunity to the Helms Bavaria built up eventually in our population, but not necessarily an immunity to any future mutated version."

The general nodded. "It's like dealing with some clever alien in a science fiction story. We don't know what it's capable of, but we do know it's out there now, and beyond our control."

"In a nutshell, sir," Roth continued, "we screwed this up. We got the diagnosis wrong about airborne transfer and the incubation period, and we released those people far too soon."

"What's . . . the bottom line on this, Jon?" the President asked.

Roth looked down and studied his shoes for a few seconds before looking back up at the chief executive and replying.

"We should make some tough decisions right now on what to do if anything like Flight Sixty-six ever happens again. Sir, the facts are, if the Hauptmann Strain hadn't mutated, we could have lost up to ninety percent of the population of North America. There would have been no way to stop this once it got started."

ESTES PARK, COLORADO—TUESDAY, MAY 14

As a little girl, Rachael Sherwood had always loved the Rocky Mountains, but only as an idea. The thought of waking up among them had never been a considered possibility. One didn't live in the Rockies. One merely visited there on high-speed vacations in the family car.

She smiled at the memory now and stirred her coffee as her eyes traveled across the magnificent view of snow-capped granite peaks and deep blue skies. She was still having trouble jogging in the rarefied air of seven thousand feet above sea level, but her endurance was improving and the altitude headaches had stopped.

A billowing column of cumulus clouds was clawing its way skyward over Longs Peak some thirty miles to the south, diverting her attention in that direction. She had decided to climb Longs next year. It was a firm goal.

There were still letters to write. She preferred letters to phone calls for the more profound partings from longtime friends on the East Coast. Phone calls were too immediate, and she wanted to feel the distance in space and time. Besides, there was no way that the beauty before her now could be adequately described in a phone call. The vista outside the glassed-in living room, the new house on Devil's Gulch Road, and her new life all demanded a careful telling in her own hand, preferably accompanied by snapshots. Yes, only letters would do.

A plume of dust announced the presence of a car on the dirt road a half mile distant, toward the town of Estes Park. She glanced back over her shoulder toward Devil's Gulch Road as it crested a small ridge leading toward the tiny village of Glenhaven. A determined flight of buzzards had been circling ominously over the ridge all morning, and her curiosity was growing.

She looked back toward the town in anticipation. The car was a quarter mile away, and she could make it out now.

He was right on time.

The whirlwind of activity and publicity following the trauma of the Christmas flight, and the intense media attention on Lee Lancaster's role, had almost engulfed her through early January. Lee had been hailed as one of the heroes of the drama, and she'd been proud to be his assistant—and prouder still of the self-effacing way he'd met those accolades.

But the real hero was the quiet man in the left seat of the 747, and he had all but disappeared trying to avoid the spotlight. There were book and movie offers in seven figures, she had been told, as well as television shows clamoring to get him on and a thundering herd of media people aiming their lenses and their pens at James Holland.

But James Holland was nowhere to be seen.

She had assumed he was back in Dallas—until the doorbell to her small apartment near Georgetown rang on the cold, rainy night of January 15 and he had been there, dripping wet, embarrassed, unsure what to say, but determined to find out whether she would be willing to go out with him.

"Why didn't you call?" she remembered asking, not unkindly.

"I . . . frankly wasn't sure how to, ah, what to . . ."

"What to say?"

He nodded.

She smiled and said, "Well, you could start with, 'Hi, Rachael, will you go out with me?'"

He looked down self-consciously, but she could see a smile on his face before he looked up again.

"So it really would have been that simple, huh?"

She nodded, suddenly aware of her slightly accelerated heartbeat.

"So here I am," she said at last, shifting her weight to her other foot, "if you want to give it a try."

"Okay," he said with a broadening smile, "let's see if I can get this right." He cleared his throat as she cocked her head and regarded him with a feigned skeptical look.

"Rachael?"

"Yes?" she said.

He stepped forward without warning and enveloped her in his arms, kissing her hungrily as her hands wavered for a second, then closed around his back, pulling him closer.

Just as suddenly he pulled away and reached up, cupping her chin with his large right hand and raising her eyes to his.

"Rachael," he'd said then, "will you marry me?"

The car was approaching the front drive now, and as expected, it was the small gray Blazer. She moved to the front door and waited for James to get out. They had been married for three months, but every day—and every night—was a honeymoon, and they kept surprising each other with the depth and variety of their lovemaking. The shared experience of the new house, the mountains, and the eternity they had spent together aboard Flight 66 bridged the occasional silences, but he was working hard on that, and she understood.

He had moved from Dallas gleefully, she from Washington reluctantly, but the idea of leaving Estes even for a day now seemed assaultive. Living in these mountains

had been James's lifelong dream, and now her enthusiasm was as intense as his. She'd already grown accus-
tomed to his commuting to Dallas to pick up his flights
for Quantum.

She'd persuaded him to accept the joint invitation
from the FAA and the Air Line Pilots Association to
come back to Washington, D.C., to be honored. It was
far more than presenting a medal and plaque, they had
explained to her when James turned his back on the
idea. He represented what was good and solid and de-
pendable about airline pilots. He was an example. The
nation needed a positive example.

James finally, reluctantly, agreed to do it, and they
were to leave for Washington in the morning.

Rachael had lounged in her bathrobe all morning,
wearing nothing else, waiting for his return from Dallas.
Now she loosened the sash around the robe and let it
fall open as James came through the door.

A broad smile painted his features. He hurriedly
closed the door behind him and came to her.

NATIONAL AIR AND SPACE MUSEUM,
WASHINGTON, D.C.—THURSDAY, MAY 16

The formalities were impressive, but James Holland's
discomfort at taking center stage as the honoree was
obvious. Halfway through the reception that followed,
however, Rachael finally saw him relax.

She turned away for the first time, intent on finding
the ladies' room, as a dark-haired man of medium build
moved quietly to the captain's side.

James Holland sensed the man's presence, turned,
and took his outstretched hand.

"Captain," the man said, "permit me to add my con-
gratulations. What you did with that aircraft was magnificent airmanship."

"Thank you. And you are?"

"An admirer, and a fellow pilot."

There was a hint of an accent in the man's voice, but his face seemed familiar, an image from somewhere in the past, a face he knew instinctively he'd have great trouble placing.

James cocked his head slightly. "You . . . weren't aboard my aircraft, were you?"

There was a slow smile in response—a rather sad smile, James noted. The man's gaze had wandered to the far end of the hall. He turned back now and spoke.

"There were many with you that day who were not physically present," he said.

"That's very poetic," James replied, turning the phrase over in his mind.

The man looked at James and met his gaze, his smile brightening as he brushed away the subject with his right hand. "Anyway, I just wanted to meet you in person and tell you that all this"—he gestured toward the reception—"is richly deserved."

James smiled. He had been listening to similar embarrassing accolades all day. His response was becoming familiar, and rote.

"You're very gracious to say that, but it was a crew effort. What it came down to was teamwork. I was just the visible element as captain."

The man was shaking his head slowly and knowingly. For several long moments he didn't speak.

"No, Captain," he began at last, "what it came down to was an impossible duel between unequal adversaries. Sometimes when the hunted refuses to die, the overconfident hunter loses his life. Reversing the pretended death spiral when you lost your first engine was brilliant, as was your final move at Ascension."

James Holland studied the man's eyes. There was a hard kindness there, he decided, and a glow of true respect. James extended his hand again and the man took it and pumped it gently.

"You . . . must have studied the details of the accident report very thoroughly," James said.

The man nodded as he withdrew his hand.

"More closely than you can imagine."

He nodded and turned before James could say more.

There were others competing for the captain's attention on his left, and James watched the man stride quietly toward the door before turning back to a line of smiling faces that included the Secretary of Transportation.

James Holland nodded and began speaking appropriate words to the secretary, but stopped himself in mid-sentence to turn back toward the door. A faint memory of an injured male passenger lying on the concrete at Ascension Island had suddenly floated across his mind. James looked in the man's direction just as he stopped at the door and looked back as well.

No, James concluded. *He said he wasn't aboard my aircraft.*

The man smiled suddenly and gave the captain a smart, military salute. James returned it in abbreviated form—puzzled—his mind turning over the man's words again and again.

Yuri Steblinko pushed through the front doors of the National Air and Space Museum and hurried down the steps as he glanced up Independence Avenue to where his American-made car was parked, a fantastic new Buick registered, along with the comfortable house in the Virginia countryside, to a new American named Yuri Raskolnikov, an employee of the Central Intelligence Agency at Langley.

The choice of a last name had been his—a small Russian joke of his own, with a wink of respect to Dostoyevsky.

Yuri glanced at his watch and quickened his pace.

It was four o'clock, and Anya would be waiting.

Here's an excerpt from *MEDUSA'S CHILD*, John Nance's next blockbuster bestseller:

WASHINGTON APPROACH CONTROL FACILITY —4:20 P.M. EDT

Pete Cooke said nothing to the controller as he listened to the new Flitephone conversation between ScotAir 50 and the FBI. He slid into an extra chair as quietly as possible and stayed out of the way behind the controller's console as he began scribbling notes. The fact that FBI headquarters and an assistant deputy director were involved raised the stakes even more.

But why did they want him to go to Pax River? The explanation had left Pete stunned.

My God, plutonium! No wonder the FBI is working the case.

Pete wrote down the names of those aboard as they were being passed to the FBI. The name of Dr. Linda McCoy seemed familiar, but from where, he wasn't sure. He made a mental note to ask his research assistant at the *Wall Street Journal* to check her out on the computer. For a few seconds, he was so absorbed in trying to place her that the captain's words about "something strange" nearly passed unnoticed.

The captain was describing a pallet of cargo he had aboard—a metal container and a screen displaying a message the captain slowly repeated word for word.

WHAT?

Pete pressed the earpiece deeper into his ear, straining to hear every word as the pilot described the warning on the screen.

He re-read his hastily-scribbled notes, wishing his handwriting had not deteriorated so much in previous years.

"WARNING! The fact that this device is now
located within the physical confines of the Penta-
gon has been detected and locked in memory.
ANY ATTEMPT TO MOVE THIS DEVICE
FROM ITS PRESENT LOCATION—OR ANY
ATTEMPT TO DEACTIVATE—WILL RE-
SULT IN INSTANT DETONATION!"

Detonation! My God, what does that mean?
Pete stood up and moved silently behind the controller, mentally comparing the position of ScotAir 50 on
the screen with the approximate position of the Pentagon.
They were significantly different! The aircraft might
have passed over the Pentagon, but it was holding between eight and eighteen miles away now, and the thing
in the cargo compartment of ScotAir 50 didn't seem to
know it.
Pete sat back down, his mind racing. Suspected plutonium . . . a message threatening detonation . . . the
FBI is involved . . . a large metal container on a cargo
aircraft . . .
*My God in Heaven, they've got a live nuke flying around
over DC!*

IN FLIGHT, SCOTAIR 50—4:25 P.M. EDT

The wail of a new electronic warning horn from the
cargo compartment reached the cockpit just as the revised clearance to Pax River Naval Air Station was coming through. Doc remained at the controls with Jerry
backing him up in the engineer's seat as Linda led the
way to the back·with Scott and Vivian following. This
time the noise was many decibels higher in volume, and
different in tone.
Linda swung around the rear of the container and
pressed forward to read the screen as Scott approached

on her heels, almost losing his balance as the 727
bounced through the turbulent air.

She touched the screen and the horn stopped instantly.

"The screen is changing," she said.

Scott pressed in beside her to read the message.

WARNING: This weapon is now fully armed.
All anti-disarming safeguards are activated. One
person—Mrs. Vivian Henry—possesses the ability to disarm this weapon, provided she does so
in person within the next fifteen minutes. If not
deactivated within fifteen minutes, final countdown sequence will begin.

The symbols "15:00:00" appeared and began counting
backwards.

Scott motioned Vivian over and she, too, pressed forward to read the words—which changed once again.

The presence of Vivian Henry has been detected.

She jumped back. "How? How does it know I'm here?"
Her voice was alarmed and almost indignant. Linda Mc-
Coy moved to her side and took her arm to calm her
down. "He could . . . *it* could . . . be guessing."

A deep male voice boomed through the cargo cabin
without warning, causing Vivian to feel trapped and
doomed.

"Vivian, as the screen says, I can detect your
presence. Are you curious as to how?"

Vivian gasped audibly as her left hand flew to her
mouth, her eyes wide with fear.

Linda glanced at Scott, who looked at the container.

"There's a large speaker down there, I guess," he said. "That's either a tape or a computerized voice."

Linda turned to Vivian. "Is that your husband's voice?"

She nodded, breathing hard, as the voice began again, full of sarcastic expression and oily self-confidence. If it's a computer synthesizer, Linda concluded, it's very advanced.

"Step forward, Vivian, my dear, up to the screen. If the people gathered here want you to disarm this weapon, and I'm sure they do, all you have to do is enter some numbers. It's a simple task. Even a brainless idiot like you can do it."

Vivian remained rooted to the spot.

The computerized voice resumed with an angrier tone.

"STEP FORWARD, VIVIAN! I know that's you. The pacemaker your doctor implanted in 1991 was modified by me. It contains a special transponder so I could always locate you electronically. I know you're here, and I'll know if you try to leave, and if you try to leave, I'll detonate this device instantly."

"It's a digitalized voice, Vivian!" Scott said.

Vivian seemed transfixed, her hand over her mouth.

"It's not him, Vivian," Linda added. "It's a thing your husband programmed."

Vivian pulled away from Linda and squared her shoulders, then moved slowly back toward the screen. When she was within a foot, the voice resumed.

"Vivian Henry, you are the last chance every computer, database, telephone and communications switching center, and every other electronic circuit within two thousand miles, has of remaining functional. If you screw this up, you'll doom Washington, D.C., the Pentagon, National Airport, Arlington, and the economy of the U.S. to ruin. But to disarm this device, simply reach in, put your hand on the keypad beneath the screen, and key in our old five-digit PIN number from our joint banking account."

Vivian slowly inserted her hand, the familiar PIN numbers running through her mind over and over. Her stomach was twisted up in fear, and her hands were shaking, but she forced herself to push each number deliberately.

Linda McCoy stood a few feet away wondering what Rogers Henry had been trying to accomplish. If the threat was real, and if he was going to permit it to be disarmed, why the game? Why force his ex-wife to remember an old PIN number with the penalty for mistake being a nuclear detonation?

Why, indeed, unless he was toying with her.

"VIVIAN!" Linda yelled, starting toward her. "STOP!"

"What?" The final number had already been keyed as she turned toward Linda.

"He's setting you up to get it wrong!"

An ear-splitting blast of electronic sound filled the compartment, followed by a new, small beeping sound and the sarcastic digitalized voice of Rogers Henry once again.

"You entered the wrong PIN number, Vivian, so the countdown to detonation will now begin. This whole thing is your fault, Vivian!"

Vivian turned back toward the device with an overwhelming feeling of rage. He had done it to her again! Even from the grave, he had set her up to take the

blame for everything that went wrong, no matter how
obvious the ploy. She felt a guttural scream begin in the
back of her throat as she flung herself at the thing and
pounded it with her fists.

"NO! NO, NO, NO, NO, NO!"

Linda McCoy moved toward her. "Vivian!"

"One-six-five-five-two! I got it right! I punched it in
right, you son of a bitch!"

"If you hadn't left me, Vivian, there would have
been better ways to introduce this weapon, and
better ways to punish the fools in the federal
government who tried to prevent the building of
this weapon. Oh, by the way, say hello to Medusa. This sample, proof-of-concept version is a
twenty-megaton-yield nuclear device, specially
built by me. Just in case anyone has any question about what's happening, let me make it
clear: The U.S. military canceled my project.
Now, thanks to my stupid ex-wife, I'm going to
cancel the rotten core of the U.S. military, and
the nation can start over. The generals have precisely three hours and thirty minutes from this
moment to evacuate Washington and the twenty-
five-mile radius this weapon will destroy. If
there's immediate compliance, up to one million
lives can be saved, although I fully expect Medusa to kill at least a million others—most of
them, no doubt, useless bureaucrats. And, of
course, there will be no way to protect against
the Medusa Wave this will create, nor prevent at
least a million more deaths from radiation
poisoning in the next few months. Perhaps future
generations will thank you, Vivian, for stupidly
triggering Medusa. After all, the Pentagon and
all of Washington D.C. has outlived its useful-
ness. Think of this as a very effective way to
reduce the size of the federal government."

Scott and Linda moved in on either side of Vivian, taking her arms and moving her back, away from the embodiment of Rogers Henry, as the voice began again.

"I detect you have moved a short distance away, Vivian. If you move more than fifteen feet away, detonation will occur instantly, and you will take a million more innocent people with you who might otherwise be saved. You will remain here and die in less than three hours and thirty minutes, or you can die trying to walk away and murder more. Your choice, Vivian."

"Let me sit here. I'll stay here." Vivian told them as she sank to the metal floor of the 727.

Scott looked at her in confusion. "You said it was a dummy! A mock-up! That's probably still the case, right?"

Vivian shook her head as Linda knelt beside her, feeling the chill of the cold floor. "I'll find some blankets, Vivian, if you want to stay here."

"I have no choice," she said. "He's thought of everything. He's won again. He always said I'd never get away from him. He said he'd kill me. Now he will."

"Is that true, Vivian, about the pacemaker?" Linda asked.

She nodded. "I have one. The date's right. A transmitter inside would explain a lot of strange things."

Scott knelt beside her as well. "Vivian, he's already made a mistake. He said it would explode if it left the Pentagon. We're more than eight miles away from the Pentagon and moving constantly. It probably *is* just a mock-up."

She was staring blankly at the device, but shaking her head in a slow, resolute manner.

"That was wishful thinking, I'm afraid. I gave you false hope."

Linda and Scott looked at each other.

"What do you mean?" Scott managed.

438 JOHN J. NANCE

She looked up at the young captain.

"I was married to Rogers Henry for twenty-three years. In all that time, I never once knew him to bluff."

MEDUSA'S CHILD — The electrifying thriller by John J. Nance, now available from St. Martin's Paperbacks!